NIGHT OF TERROR

It seemed strange that there was no light on in the cottage. Grandpop had probably fallen asleep.

Bobbie ran up the porch steps and headed for the old man's bedroom.

But the thing came at him before he got there. Making guttural noises and with a knife that came slashing down at his neck.

He screamed and fell back against the wall. "Grandpop!" he screamed. "Grandpop, it's me—Bobbie."

He threw up a hand as the knife cut another arc upward and grabbed hold of the arm, but the strength there stunned him. This wasn't a frail old man; the muscles felt taut and powerful.

"Gonna get rid of him, Gladys," Grandpop rasped, and even in the gloom Bobbie saw the glint of hate in his eyes. "Never needed no new young cock in the barnyard. Too much trouble to have around." He threw off Bobbie's hand and the knife slashed down. This time it caught and carried away a bite of Bobbie's shoulder. "Gonna slit his gizzard, fry 'im up for supper. Just you and me'll eat 'im."

This wasn't his grandfather. This was a crazed *thing*. . . .

TERRIFYING HORROR FROM ZEBRA

HOME SWEET HOME (1571, $3.50)
by Ruby Jean Jensen
Timmy's parents said it would be fun — two weeks vacation in the mountains with nice Mr. Walker. But the other children stared at him and awoke screaming in the night. Then Timmy peeked through the keyhole of the forbidden locked door — and he knew there was no escape from the deadly welcome of . . . HOME SWEET HOME.

THE STALKER (1434, $3.50)
Lewis expected a normal summer helping his father in the seed business. But soon he finds that unspeakable horrors lurk in the dark warehouse where he is to spend summer's sun-filled days. Horrors that will call him back to face THE STALKER.

ROCKABYE BABY (1470, $3.50)
by Stephen Gresham
Mr. Macready — such a nice old man — knew all about the children of Granite Heights — their names, houses, even the nights their parents were away. And when he put on his white nurse's uniform and smeared his lips with blood-red lipstick, they were happy to let him through the door — though they always stared a bit at his clear plastic gloves!

THE TRIDENT (1552, $3.50)
by Joel Hammil
Olivia was a lovely little girl with just one slight blemish marring her beauty: a tiny, three-tined stain on her smooth upper thigh. But the mark had the power to twist her cherubic smile into a demonic leer, and round her childish body into seductive curves, for it was the kiss of Satan . . . THE TRIDENT.

SWEET DREAMS (1553, $3.50)
by William W. Johnstone
Innocent ten-year-old Heather sensed the chill of darkness in her schoolmates' vacant stares, the evil festering in their hearts. But no one listened to her terrified screams or believed the nightmare was true. And now it was Heather's turn to feed the hungry spirit — with her very soul.

Available wherever paperbacks are sold, or order direct from the Publisher. Send cover price plus 50¢ per copy for mailing and handling to Zebra Books, Dept. 1656, 475 Park Avenue South, New York, N.Y. 10016. DO NOT SEND CASH.

SOUL-EATER
BY DANA BROOKINS

ZEBRA BOOKS
KENSINGTON PUBLISHING CORP.

ZEBRA BOOKS

are published by

Kensington Publishing Corp.
475 Park Avenue South
New York, NY 10016

Copyright © 1985 by Dana Brookins

All rights reserved. No part of this book may be reproduced in any form or by any means without the prior written consent of the Publisher, excepting brief quotes used in reviews.

First printing: September 1985

Printed in the United States of America

Dedication:
FOR VICTORIA BROOKINS
Her own book

Chapter One

"HOUSE."

Charlie Groves was the first one to arrive at the office of *The Daily Way* (long ago gone weekly due to poor circulation—in a town the size of Edgar Falls the ladies' hotline knew everything before you could get the type set; so who needed the press?) with the latest copy in his hands.

"What the hell is this anyway, Lobe?" he demanded. "I thought twenty bucks guaranteed me the headline today."

Lobe Peters, owner, editor, reporter, printer, and ad gatherer for *The Daily Way* had known this was coming. But he'd been too excited all week to remember Charlie. Now he pulled off his Ben Franklin glasses, worn not from need but because they gave him an image of himself he liked, wiped them with his shirttail, put them back on and leaned confidentially across the counter to peer over them at Charlie. "Two hundred bucks, Charlie," he said. "Came by mail. Cashier's check payable on the spot. Had a typewritten note with it. No heading."

"I don't give a fart about that," Charlie said hotly. "We made a deal. Headlines was to announce my new alarm system so's that punk broke into my store last month'll know I'm ready. I want my money back."

"Come on now, Charlie," Lobe wheedled. "I gave you the lead article spot. That's always been worth twenty bucks before—the headline forty."

"You give me the break friend to friend," Charlie said unhappily. "Now I find you sold me out to the highest bidder."

"But two hundred bucks, Charlie. Somebody came into your hardware place and offered you two bills for a twenty dollar rebuilt mower, you going to turn him down?"

"If I promised that mower to a friend," Charlie said, saying the word as if Lobe had just soiled it.

Both of them knew he was lying, but it didn't matter to Lobe with the excitement still on him. "Don't you want to see the note, Charlie?" he asked. Charlie turned and stomped back out the glass door, slapping his feet down like an angry kid. Lobe stared after him, fascinated by the way the morning sun shot a beam of light off the other man's bald head, thinking there was a poem somewhere in that sight. Then he shrugged. He'd smooth it over with Charlie, maybe give him next week's headline free. He could afford to do that right now.

Well, if Charlie Groves didn't want to see the note, Lobe Peters did. He'd had it out of his pocket so often this past week there was hardly anything left of it. Nothing this mysterious had ever happened to Lobe before. His instincts sensed there was more story than just the note, the money, and the one-word headline, upper case, the money paid for.

He pressed the paper out on his counter and read it carefully, lovingly. "This cashier's check, cashable at any bank, is by way of payment for the headline in your next issue of *The Daily Way*. The headline is to read simply HOUSE." That was all the note said.

No signature. No heading. Nothing. It was good, bond paper with a common watermark. Lobe pulled the envelope out of the drawer built into his work side of the counter. Now here was the biggest mystery of all. The envelope was postmarked St. Louis. Who in St. Louis knew anything about how *The Daily Way* operated? Damn Charlie anyway for not wanting to see. All week Lobe had had to keep his mouth shut because he wanted the strange headline to surprise everybody. Now he wanted to talk about it.

"HOUSE."

That was the headline. And what it might mean was driving Lobe wild.

The door opened. Lobe looked up. Smiled. Ah. Action at last. Enter Miss Penny DuJong, the fastest mouth in Edgar Falls. She was seething, he could tell that from the way her overpainted mouth had pursed itself into a little bow of disapproval. "Naughty, naughty, Lobe," she said.

Lobe made a pistol out of his thumb and forefinger and pointed at her. "Gotcha, Miss Penny," he said. He knew she was here to see how much information she could pump from him to hit the hotline with. So Lobe stuck his letter in his pocket and slipped the envelope into its drawer. Let her suffer. For years she had been getting the scoop on him. She knew when Gary Purdy ran off before he did, knew before he did that Mrs. Letkins out on Averton Road had given birth to triplets (two of them born dead). Miss Penny probably got the message on when he had to take a crap before he did.

The door opened again. Lobe straightened and ran a hand through his thick shock of graying hair to make sure he'd combed it this morning. Tressa Allen, on her way to The Brewery to help Bruzz Logan make up the day's chili and stew pots, had stopped in. The sun did marvelous things with her red hair that made Lobe wonder something he'd wondered often: whether the rest of her body hair was red. He stirred uncomfortably and even managed to forget his mystery a moment.

"What's that mean, Lobe?" she said in her husky voice. "What kinda headline is 'House'?"

Lobe jerked himself out of his revery and shook his head. "I dunno," he said. "It's as big a mystery to me as it is to you."

Tressa's question was one that Lobe, to his delight, would be asked dozens of times in the next few days. Never mind that he couldn't answer; he had faith the mystery would be revealed to him. Some higher power knew that he'd had all his talents stuck in Edgar Falls for years because the big city papers were so closed in on themselves they'd never recognized his genius. Someone had looked down last week and finally taken notice of Lobarth Peters and presented him with a real story. He only had to wait.

Meantime he enjoyed the attention, and when nothing new came in the mail that week (that was a disappointment, but his staying power was merely being tested) he ran a three-column story front page the second week of June issue, printing the mysterious note itself and making some guesses as to what the headline meant. Someone was either going to come to town looking for a particular house or build one. Or maybe somebody named House was going to move to Edgar Falls; these speculations were in the article. He asked, with an eye to maybe publishing them in his third week of June issue, the townspeople to write letters about what they thought the headline meant.

Bobbie Topin, a twelve-year-old and sixth grader come fall, wrote a great letter. He suggested the word "house" might be code, that maybe outer space aliens were trying to contact Americans, and what they were up to would be revealed soon. Bobbie had brought the letter to Lobe in person.

"I'll bet you really made it up yourself, Mr. Peters," he said, his dark eyes glinting conspiratorially. "Just to get everybody talking. You're the only editor in the whole world who lets people buy headlines. Who'd know that outside Edgar Falls?"

Lobe reached across the counter to rumple his hair, surprised he didn't have to lean over — kid was taking after his grandfather's height. "Did I make up a two hundred dollar cashier's check?" he came back. Bobbie grinned. "Well, it's a good mystery anyway," he said. "Everybody's talking about it."

Lobe preened at that. It was true. He'd had to run four hundred extra copies last week. Folks were reading *The Daily Way* who hadn't read it in years.

Still — this couldn't keep up forever. Something else had to happen soon, else people would lose interest. You couldn't trust the public. It had the attention span of a fruit fly.

The day the letters came out in print, Bobbie Topin couldn't believe it. But there it was, even at the head of all the rest. And here was his name. *Bobbie Topin. By Bobbie Topin.*

He hadn't expected Lobe Peters to publish the letter; it had been a sort of joke. No aliens were coming to Edgar Falls. Bobbie smiled at that, carrying the paper home from Amway's Pharmacy where he'd gone to buy Grandpop some zinc tablets. Well, an alien *might* come to Edgar Falls, but he wouldn't stay long. The town wasn't very pretty, and the people didn't like strangers, even human ones. Bobbie's smile broadened. He didn't know if he believed in aliens.

The letter had just been a way to exercise an imagination he didn't let loose in public too often. Mrs. Prinmans, his teacher last year, hadn't gone in much for imagination, and Bobbie had early on stopped writing English themes about anything except his chores around the house. Even then, when he'd wandered off and embellished a little, Mrs. Prinmans had dryly suggested he "stick to the facts."

He gave a little hop, heading back for home. *By* Bobbie Topin. Boy. He should have signed the letter Robert Louis Topin maybe. "Won't that be something?" Mom had once said when they talked about his future. "My son wants to be a writer. I'm glad I gave him a writer's name. And won't I be *proud*?" Bobbie could hear her voice now, humming by on the wings of a bee that came in close to his head and then veered off at a sharp right angle. Mom had liked bees. She had liked all the little creatures of nature. It was what had kept her going after they moved to Edgar Falls.

"Here it is, Mom," Bobbie said to the summer air. "It says *by* Bobbie Topin." He had to share with somebody — even if just a memory. Grandpop was in one of his moods today. That's why Bobbie had walked the long, hot road into town. He'd read in a library magazine that old people going what the article called "senile" sometimes lacked zinc. The tablets had cost all the meager allowance Grandpop had finally remembered to give him this month, and they'd have to be dissolved in cocoa or something.

Bobbie folded *The Daily Way* up and tucked it under his shirt. Next to his heart. Where he could feel the word "by" beating. And he went on home, content. Well, as content as he ever felt in Edgar Falls since his mother had died.

Not long after the first letters came out in print, Lobe looked up from an ad layout to find Bobbie Topin at his counter again. The boy had a shy smile spread all over his kid face. "You printed my letter," he said.

Lobe didn't need an interruption; he was busy trying to figure out how to pare down some ads to fit a couple more on a page so no one would notice they'd been shorted. But he was always ready to set aside anything to talk about the mystery headline. "Sure did," he responded. "Best of the bunch."

"I don't really believe in aliens."

"Didn't figure you did."

"I just wanted to say thank you." A few people around town who never spoke to Bobbie had spoken this week.

"Think nothing of it. Made good copy."

Bobbie looked all around the room with a kind of bashful interest.

"You interested in the newspaper business?" Lobe asked.

"I'm interested in anything connected with writing."

"Well, why don't I show you around then? But just for a minute. I'm busy."

When Bobbie Topin left *The Daily Way*, he headed home, reflecting on how nice it had been of Lobe Peters to show him around. The man hadn't really wanted to be interrupted.

Funny. When he thought of the headline just now, a chill had suddenly crossed his shoulder blades; that hadn't happened when he first read it.

"Cat just walked over somebody's grave," he said. That had been one of Mom's favorite remarks whenever one of them felt an unexplained chill.

Couldn't be a cat, though. There weren't many pets in Edgar Falls. Probably because they had to be looked after and money spent on them.

Which brought up something he'd considered once or twice: getting a dog. Something live and warm to hug sometimes and have for companionship. But he'd have to leave it home with Grandpop come school, and it would worry Bobbie too much that the frail old man might trip over it and break a hip or something. For just a second, though, thinking about a dog gave Bobbie a warm glow.

Then he shrugged. Hey. He had another bit of a warm glow anyway: Lobe Peter's kindness today. He smiled again and then sobered. He hoped that chill hadn't meant he was catching a summer cold he might give to Grandpop.

Back at *The Daily Way*, Lobe made a face. That had been an ordeal, having the kid around. Oh, Bobbie Topin was okay as kids went. But Lobe didn't hold much truck with kids; he'd never wanted any of his own. And there was a kind of intensity about the one who'd just left. As if he had some kind of need Lobe Peters certainly couldn't meet — wouldn't even try to. Probably came from being an orphan and an outsider in town to boot.

What the hell was this anyway? He didn't have time or inclination to bother himself about some kid. He went back to figuring out how to cheat his customers without being noticed.

The next mystery letter came the first day of July. Lobe had planned to run a headline reminding people about the chamber of commerce picnic on the Fourth out at Amy Semple MacPherson Pond. He had the article all written up, including a bit of local history about the pond's being named that because when the trains ran through, the famous evangelist had once stopped here and offered a few uplifting words from the platform car. This week Miss Penny DuJong had graciously lent Lobe the faded photograph of her as a girl standing on tiptoe to present a bouquet to Sister Amy. He had the front page made up early, along with mention that the picnic was being held to raise money for an operation for little Cindy Newman, who'd had her foot crushed by a stampeding cow.

But now, on the first, came the letter. Ed Kroger, postmaster and Lobe's fellow member of the town council along with Thaddeus Amway and Rev. Leonard Botts, didn't even put it in Lobe's box. He was too excited and held it back to hand Lobe personally. When Lobe went into the one-room post office attached to Blainey's Meat Market that morning, he knew it had happened again. Ed's pale face was all lit up.

"St. Louis," he said, handing the letter reverently to Lobe. "Looks the same."

Lobe had to hold still a moment so his hand wouldn't shake when he opened it. His heart pounded like he'd just won the national lottery, and he had to fight to keep from breaking into a silly grin. Play it cool—every inch the close-mouthed reporter.

"Sorry I can't read this in front of you, Ed." He took the letter, and it tingled his fingers.

"I understand," Ed said. "If it's headline stuff, you want to spring it on us. It was a pleasure just to hand it over. Wonder who she is."

Lobe was so intent on the letter, it took a second for that to sink in; then he raised his head sharply. "She?"

"Smell it," Ed said.

Annoyed that Ed had discovered something before he did, Lobe nevertheless raised the envelope. "Lilies of the valley," Ed said. "The mystery deepens."

All over the town of Edgar Falls, people were buzzing about the latest *Daily Way* headline. Folks who had laughed at little Bobbie Topin's solution to the puzzle of the first headline now reconsidered it. Oh, not that anyone believed in flying saucers. The only one they'd ever heard firsthand news of had been seen by Sheriff Hille over in Gloaming, and everybody knew the sheriff saw stranger things than flying saucers when he was in his cups — which was often. But Bobbie had said the house message could be code. It had to be.

In his hardware store, Charlie Groves hadn't unlocked his front doors yet. He had to have his morning coffee to get him ready for a public that was getting more and more uppity about wanting too much for their money when they bought a saw or can of carpet tacks. The fact Lobe had run Charlie's headline the week after the house one had saved him from canceling his subscription to *The Daily Way*, and he sat with it on his counter now, staring at the new mystery. What the heck did it all mean anyway?

"CHANGE THE APPLE-SHOOTER TO P AND ADD A CUT OF PORK."

It had taken Lobe two lines to get it all in. Charlie sipped his too-hot coffee and stared at that, puzzling on it, till his eyes gave out and started shooting little black p's around.

All across town, frustrated people studied the headline. Tressa Allen was late getting into The Brewery, and Bruzz would have yelled at her except he'd lost track of time himself. He was leaning on the bar studying the headline. "Beats all," Tressa said. "What's that cut of pork bit anyway?"

"Dunno," Bruzz said. "Butt maybe?" He came to at that, smirked at his own humor, pinched Tressa on the part in question and suggested she get it to work. "Payday at the factory," he told her. "Double the beans and half the hamburger in the chili." Lobe would be in at noon as usual, and he'd ask him about the headline then.

Probably the only person in town who did not read the headline was Bitsy McCall. Bitsy McCall was practically the only thing the town had left it could call white trash. Now that the tracks had long ago been pulled up, there really wasn't any territory you could call the wrong side anymore. A couple of decent houses had been built down south in the past years, and since one of them was owned by Carl Bergins the banker, who was also the mayor, the old town lines didn't hold anymore. Turned out now white trash was all an attitude. Bitsy McCall would be white trash if she lived in a palace. It had to do with her physical self, which was fat and untidy, the fact she'd been known as a "retard" in school, although she was a whole lot brighter than the Rainey boy who'd been born one hair below dull and sometimes forgot he was potty trained.

Bitsy was the youngest of nine kids deserted by their old man. The rest of the family had dwindled out of town the moment they were old enough to raise a thumb. The old lady was buried now on the edge of the Edgar Falls cemetery in the potter's field part. Only Bitsy had stayed on in town. It was as if she wouldn't know what to do if she moved anywhere else and got treated nice.

A few years back she'd wandered over to Gloaming and made contact with one of the town messes there and married him. She had five kids, and at twenty-three, she looked forty-seven. Her name was actually supposed to be Mrs. Gary Purdy now, but everybody still thought of her as Bitsy McCall and referred to her passel of snotty-nosed, filthy kids as the McCall Clan. Not long ago Gary Purdy had blown town, leaving Bitsy and crew the only welfare recipients in a town that prided itself on upholding the American work ethic.

It was all right. If people gave it any thought, they wouldn't know what to do without the McCall Clan. Success was a relative thing, and you needed someone to look down on to keep your perspective. There were actually people who missed the tracks and wished Banker Bergins had built somewhere else—just to keep the lines drawn. They missed having the other white trash around: the Muncks, who'd lit out for California some said; the Gehaffey's, the Porters.

This morning Bitsy was too busy punching kids around her two-room shack to bother with the newspaper Lobe Peters magnanimously had a boy pitch into her yard free every week. The only time she read it anyway was when she couldn't snitch a confession magazine down at Amway's Pharmacy and had nothing else to do. She wished Gary had thieved the pharmacy instead of the Groves Hardware Store a few weeks back. That way he could have gotten her some pills to stop this ugly feeling she often had lately that she was going crazy. And he could have gotten her some magazines.

She wondered where he was. No good son-of-a-turd. Upping and disappearing just like her daddy. And Gary the cause of all their trouble because of that hard thing he was always planting in her. Wasn't that just like a man to make a bunch of babies and then take off and leave a woman to suffer? Maybe if she had the strength today she'd pick a wild daisy bouquet and take it out to Mama's grave. She hadn't appreciated her mother when she was a kid, but sometimes she did now. She wondered if she'd die young, too.

"CHANGE THE APPLE-SHOOTER TO P AND ADD A CUT OF PORK."

Everybody in town knew that Lobe Peters had received three hundred dollars for those words. It was practically the only subject discussed at the chamber of commerce picnic. One person was relieved about the whole thing because it got her out of the spotlight somewhat. Cindy Newman had dreaded the picnic. Her mother had insisted she dress in a frilly dress. "Let them all see that foot. Make them shell out a little harder."

Cindy wanted the operation. After all, it wasn't any fun to have to hobble around on the deformed thing at the end of her left leg. She couldn't run so good in the clumpy special shoe. The operation she could get in the city didn't guarantee she wouldn't have a limp still, but the specialist said he could fix all the teeny crushed bones Doc Jennessey couldn't handle when she got hurt so's she could at least run around better. What she didn't like was the way they were getting the operation.

People had been donating money for months now. There had been bake sales in her honor and a St. Patrick's Day dance. The town had taken to regarding her as its own personal possession, the local cripple. On the street she had to curtsy to everyone like Mama had taught her, the bad foot going out behind her. You never knew when the mere, pitiful sight of her might cause someone to stop in Mr. Bergins's bank and leave a donation in one of the Buy Cindy a New Foot jars.

On the Fourth of July, she arrived at the picnic with her parents (both of them waving to the crowd as if they were celebrities) looking like a caricature of old

Shirley Temple movies. Mama had curled her long, dishwater blond hair into ringlets (refraining from dying it a golden blond only by a hysterical fit on Cindy's part). She wore a little gold heart around her neck and a little gold bracelet and a little gold ring, all suitable for an M.R. four-year-old. The stage had a big red, white, and blue banner across it that said Help Our Cindy. It made Cindy want to throw up. Look at her parents going through the crowd, her dad shaking hands, Mama casting her eyes downward in that poor us, the Lord sure shouldered us with a burden look.

Later on Cindy would have to get up on that truck platform stage and give the speech Mama had written: *Thank you all you dear, sweet neighbors. I know that Jesus must be smiling on you.* As if Jesus had time to think about her foot!

Two things saved the day from total humiliation. One—everybody was buzzing about the new headline in *The Daily Way*. And two, Bobbie Topin said to her parents in his sweetest manner, "May Cindy walk with me?"

Bobbie looked so dear to Mrs. Newman with his hair all slicked down and his face so earnest, she said, "Go ahead, children. But don't stray far. Isn't it sweet the way the children haven't ignored her?" Mrs. Newman said to Miss Penny at her side. She had to change the word "ostracized" to "ignored" in a hurry. In the old days Alicia Newman lorded it over these people she had grown up around with the two years of college she'd gone off to get. But one had to keep her place these days. Keeping her place meant being eternally grateful. That way the foot would get paid for, and she and Clyde would never have to let on they'd been stashing money in a Gloaming bank for years. The money was designated for old-age travel, and for a while it had looked as though it might have to go to the foot. Until Lobe Peters took it on himself to start a charity drive.

Bobbie took Cindy's hand and walked her away. "Hi, crip," he whispered.

Cindy rared back and whammed him alongside the head. He grinned, and she grinned back. What a relief to feel normal.

"Hey, you want to sneak into the woods and climb a tree?" he demanded.

Cindy looked wistfully off at the rim of trees that signaled the woods that surrounded them on three sides in the distance. "All I need's to tear this dress. Mama'd kill me. Especially if she found out sweet little old Bobbie Newman is taking me into the woods. She'd make more than tree climbing out of that."

Bobbie's grin widened. "Maybe when we find out what it is we're not supposed to do, someday we can try it," he said teasingly.

Cindy smiled fondly at him and wondered if girls were always smarter than boys. But then she'd had someone to tell her things and Bobbie didn't. He only had his grandfather, who was too old to remember what it was they shouldn't do in the woods. Bitsy knew. Bitsy was an expert. She had, as she put it, raised her skirt over her head for a lot more guys than Gary Purdy. It was fun, she'd told Cindy. But don't do it, because babies came out of it. That had settled it for Cindy. She didn't plan to have any babies, even though she adored them. She planned to be an investigative reporter, not a mother.

Cindy spotted Bitsy off on the edge of Amy Semple MacPherson Pond with her horde of straggly kids around her. Bitsy lay on a torn blanket, a newspaper over her face. Her huge stomach was a mountain the babies were trying to climb.

Cindy longed to go over and play with them. She

wished she could have gone down to the shack to clean them up for today. That was how Cindy had gotten to know Bitsy—through the babies. One day Bitsy had been roaming through town and one of them (they were always around her, like a dirty little cloud) got into the street. Cindy had to hobble fast to snatch her up before a car hit her, then helped Bitsy get them home. She knew better than to tell her mother she'd been in conversation with the local "tramp," but she rather liked Bitsy. The older girl seemed more her own age and talked frankly about things no one else would talk to Cindy about. So sometimes she sneaked down to the south side.

She kept her distance today. She didn't want the babies greeting her like a long-lost relative. But she felt bad because she knew they would be eating bologna sandwiches while everyone else ate chicken and apple pie.

"When you going to get the new foot?" Bobbie asked as they roamed over to the pond.

"We need another two thousand dollars." Cindy kicked at a twig, studying the ugly special shoe.

"Phew."

Cindy turned weary eyes on him. "I hope it works. The doctors don't give us any big guarantee."

"Better work," Bobbie said ominously. "Or the town'll kick you out."

He was still grinning at her, and she punched him in the side. Bobbie was good for her. The other kids had come to stand a little in awe of the fuss being made over her, all the while plainly wearing looks that said they literally wouldn't want to be in *her* shoes.

"Want to know a secret?" The grin had left Bobbie's face, but his eyes danced. They had reached the edge of the pond where a small afternoon breeze made ripples coil against the bank. He sat down and waited for Cindy to settle beside him.

"I bet I know the answer to the headline," he said.

Cindy pulled in a little gasp. "Really? Tell me."

But Bobbie did everything in his own good time.

Cindy knew he wanted to be a fiction writer someday, and he had a writer's ability to pause for the dramatic effect. So Cindy, playing his game, looked off toward the distant woods where steam from the bog spots was already beginning to rise.

"Pellam Woods," Bobbie said finally.

"I know that's Pellam Woods." She stared at him in exasperation.

"No, no. That's the answer to the puzzle."

Cindy snorted and tossed the Shirley Temple curls. But he only smiled in a superior manner and said, "Change the apple-shooter to p. Think a minute. Who was the apple-shooter?"

Cindy stared at him hard, as if she could pull the answer from his dark eyes. "I don't know."

"William *Tell*," he said. "Change the t to p and you get Pell."

"So okay," she said, her interest quickening. "But how about the cut of pork part?"

"Has to be ham. Get it? Put them together, you get Pellham."

"Ham for 'am?" She snorted. "That's pretty farfetched."

"Would be a little if I didn't remember something you don't. What was Edgar Falls's last name?"

"Pellam," she said. "Everybody knows the town founder was Edgar Falls Pellam and that he was named Falls because he was born near one in a mountain town in Colorado."

"Don't you remember how that schoolbook Miss Penny wrote, the one with the awful grammar, spelled Pellam? It was about the only word she did spell right

23

in the whole dumb book. It used to be Edgar Falls Pelham, but over the years everyone got to spelling it wrong because the 'h' was too hard to remember."

Light dawned all over Cindy's face. "Pell ham," she said and gasped. "That's it. That's what the puzzle says." She smiled at him in wonder. "You're the smartest kid in town," she said.

"Kid?" he demanded. "No adult's figured it out. Look at them."

Cindy glanced back toward the crowd. Picnic baskets were starting to come out and be opened. People were spreading blankets and laying out utensils. Everywhere there were copies of *The Daily Way* in evidence. While women shook out cloths, men huddled together holding onto a community-shared paper with one hand, a beer in the other. Lobe Peters strutted around as if his five-foot-six frame had suddenly grown to sixten. Everywhere people pressed cold beer on him and tried to get him to reveal his secret.

Cindy and Bobbie watched him. "He doesn't know," Bobbie said.

"But what does the headline mean?" Cindy demanded suddenly. "Is it a message of some kind?"

"I think so," Bobbie said. "I'm not sure. But something about a house is going to happen in Pellam Woods soon. Nothing else is named Pellam around here anymore."

"I bet you figure the rest out before anybody."

Bobbie nodded appreciatively. But his mind had strayed. He was wondering about something he'd felt lately. Why had all this business about the headlines started making him uneasy? He hadn't thought much about the first headline; just had that little chill which couldn't have anything to do with it, he'd thought then. But the second had made him strangely wary. It was a feeling he'd had before, and he didn't like it. Mostly it came on before an electrical storm. Bobbie always knew a storm was coming before anyone did, but he kept his mouth shut. A few other times, though, he had had the feeling, one terrible day in particular, and it hadn't been weather brewing.

All that day he had sat in school feeling uncomfortable and somehow scared. Just a vague, floating feeling as though his grip on reality had slipped a little.

In the middle of the night they had taken his mother, crying and holding her head, off to the city to the hospital. "Massive brain hemorrhage," Bobbie and his grandfather had been told later. "Nothing we could do. It was an aneurism she was born with. Could have got her at sixteen, but it waited till she was forty-two."

Afterward, Bobbie hadn't been able to tell anybody about the bad feeling. In Edgar Falls, the slightest difference and people could turn on you overnight, like they had Cindy until the town decided to take her on as a project. Even now the kids talked about her behind her back and imitated her limp. Bobbie didn't want to be any more different than he already was.

But he couldn't help his feelings. He felt the same way now he had the time right after Mom died. Something bad seemed about to happen, and it was all tied up with those crazy headlines.

Along toward late evening someone else did finally come up with Bobbie's answer: a free-beer-drunk Lobe Peters. He made the announcement from the exact microphone where little Cindy Newman had given such a beautiful thank you earlier. Five hundred dollars had been cleared today from the sale of beer—sold by the men—and other delicacies thought up by the ladies' auxiliary of the chamber of commerce. Edgar Falls was one of those few places left where things were still done the American way. Ladies were permitted an auxiliary—and it was a good thing, they all said, because the men certainly never accomplished anything without them—but the club itself remained solidly male and safe from contamination. Not even Gloriana Reege, who'd moved into town last year and opened up a realty business, was permitted in.

Gloriana had not come to the picnic today, though she had privately mailed the Newmans a check for one hundred dollars which they would find in their mailbox soon. Gloriana wasn't sulking over the chamber of commerce blackballing; she had her own secret in Edgar Falls.

Anyway, Lobe figured out the answer to the new riddle. Well, he didn't figure it out exactly. It just popped into his head with such clarity it gave him a blinding pain. Then he went lurching and giggling up to the stage, where he had to shout to get attention because people thought he was just drunk, but pretty soon someone heard him yelling, "P for Pell," and they started listening. He didn't get the woods part. It was Bobbie Topin who shouted that up to Lobe. It was okay to look as if he'd figured something out on the tail of Lobe's discovery because that way people wouldn't know what a brain he was; in Edgar Falls, being a brain made you different. Someone knuckled his head in admiration, and Bobbie slipped back into the crowd.

So now they had something resembling an answer. Somebody with a whole lot of money was going to do something connected with a house in Pellam Woods. But what? There weren't any houses out there now—trees too thick in some places and some of the ground mushy.

After Bobbie finished helping Lobe out, everyone's eyes went to the extensive woods surrounding Edgar Falls on three sides. The sun was getting ready to drop over the west part, and it covered the mists rising from the bog spots a dull, smoky orange. For a moment everyone became aware of the odor. Hardly anyone ever noticed it. Only the rare newcomers, out-of-town company mostly, went around the first few days of their visits screwing up their noses. The whole town carried the smell of spoiled salad.

Why would anyone build a house in Pellam Woods?

And who *could* in the first place? Most of the woods was government land except for some acreage on the west side bought up years ago by a developing company that had never developed anything.

Well, answers had a way of coming to you if you held patience. Someone passed Lobe up a fresh beer, and the local fire department got ready to send up the annual fireworks. The fireworks were a gift to the town from the chamber of commerce every year, and never mind that this year's batch would have finished off enough money to get Cindy her new foot. People expected the extravaganza of bright stars shooting out over Amy Semple MacPherson Pond, and Cindy would get her foot sooner or later anyway. Probably by Christmas.

Folks oohed appreciatively at their bursting sky and squealed when a couple of duds crashed into Pellam Woods. All in all, it had been a good day, and they went home satisfied with their Fourth. By ten-thirty everyone was indoors and getting ready for bed.

Except for Bitsy McCall, who was throwing up in her black-ringed toilet. It was the baloney, she told herself. It had to be the baloney. Never mind that the kids hadn't gotten sick too; they hadn't inherited her weak stomach. She sat on the worn, cracked linoleum, not even caring that her hair was getting wet from the vile and burning stuff her insides were rejecting.

* * *

Cindy was glad she'd come down to the south side to Bitsy's today. She'd come along a back road so she didn't have to go limping by any of the "dear, sweet neighbors" who didn't see her as a person anymore, if they ever had, but only as the Town Foot. No one ever said, "How're you doing, Cindy?" It was always, "We're going to get us that operation, Cindy." Who was *us* supposed to be?

Cindy stirred guiltily. They were just being kind in their own way. And they *were* going to help her look at least close to normal again. But she liked to forget the foot *sometimes*. And she didn't like always being reminded that she was going to have to be put to sleep and have a lot of pain—the doctor hadn't tried to cover that up—and stay all by herself in a strange hospital. "Jakie," she said quickly before she got off on that. "You be Papa this time."

It was the day after the picnic, and they were in Bitsy's front yard, if you could call this mess of trash a yard. Every wind that ever came into Edgar Falls seemed to regard Bitsy's as *the* place to dump trash it blew past the town limits.

Bitsy had been in the ramshackle little house, taking a nap. She'd looked happy to see Cindy show up—as happy as Bitsy was capable of looking. "You can play with the kids all you want," she'd said. "I don't feel too hot. That farthole Blainey sold me some rotten bologney for the picnic yesterday, and I can still taste it."

"Allie, you be the mama," Cindy said. "And I'll be the grandma." She liked to be the grandma when they were playing house; she didn't have any grandparents of her own. "Pammy will be the baby." She smiled at her own nonsense and at the towheaded baby crawling by. What else could Pammy be at nine months, an aunt?

"Okay now," she said. "Jakie, tell me where we're living."

"In the thity," he lisped.

Right. In the city. Somewhere far away from Edgar Falls.

And what kind of job do you have?"

"I'm a carpen . . . carpen . . ."

"Carpenter," she said fondly. She was teaching them to grow up and get out of this town where they would always be thought of as trash.

But there wasn't any point in being silly about it. Bitsy's kids weren't ever going to be teachers or doctors. She wanted them to have real goals. Maybe if she played with them often enough, she would rub some of her ambitions for them off on them. Although she couldn't get down here as much as she liked.

Down here she wasn't just a foot. The babies were too young to realize she was crippled.

"Here comes the grandma to visit," she cried. "She's coming up the walk right now. She's wearing a chapeau." Cindy was also trying to improve their vocabulary. "Here she comes. She's at the door now. Knock knock."

Allie threw open the imaginary door. "Well my my," she exclaimed. "Look who's here."

"Grandma!" they screeched with joy, getting full into the game, and jumped on her. She lost her balance and they went down in a heap on the hot summer earth. The babies had their own idea of what a grandmother was for, and they wrestled with her, even baby Pammy crawling over to join in the fray.

"Can you stay for dinner, Grandma?" Allie cried, bouncing onto Cindy's stomach.

Cindy screeched with laughter. She had fallen on a milk carton or something that lumped against her back. But she stayed where she was and let the babies pummel her, laughing in a way she never did anymore since the foot.

People stopped on the street to gape at the car as it cruised slowly along White Oak Avenue, the main street through Edgar Falls. "What is it?" they asked.

Lobe got a call as soon as it swung off the highway east of town. He came out on the street to watch it go by. All up and down the block, people stood open-mouthed.

"It's a Rolls," he said in an awestruck voice.

Charlie Groves had wandered down from his store to stand beside him. "Who in this town knows anybody with a get-up like that?" he demanded. "Is that a chauffeur?" Charlie, at fifty-seven, had never seen a bona fide chauffeur, only movie ones. And they were always black. This one was white. He squinted his eyes. The figure in the Rolls sat in shadow, but he could tell it was female by the long blond hair. "Anybody around here know a movie star?" he asked Lobe. "Maybe there's a story in this, Lobe."

Lobe shook his head. "Don't think so," he said. He was pretty sure the woman in the back of that limo was black, long blond hair notwithstanding. And if she was, there could only be one reason for her to be in Edgar Falls: hunger. Her driver had probably spotted The Brewery sign on the highway, along with the notation that it was the last food stop in thirty miles. Nobody in Edgar Falls knew any black people.

Lobe smirked to himself. Bruzz would feed them all right; a customer was a customer to him. But all Miss Fancy Pants was going to get was a glob of greasy chili or stew. "Imagine they're headed for Bruzz's," he told Charlie.

"Maybe I'll wander on down there," Charlie said.

"Maybe it's somebody we'd recognize off TV. You want to go, Lobe? I can leave Pulie in charge. With a little luck he won't destroy the place in a half hour." His nephew's real name was Augustine, which fit him, but behind his back Charlie called him Pulie, which fit better. He couldn't stand his sister's weakly kid, but he employed him parttime because it kept her off Charlie's back.

"Let me lock up," Lobe said. He really shouldn't leave. Something more on the mystery was bound to come through, maybe by phone since he hadn't gotten any mail in over three weeks. But he didn't want to miss the look on Charlie's face when he discovered his "celebrity" was black.

The limo was only a block ahead of them when they started walking. As if the woman in the back wanted to get a close and leisurely look at a picturesque little American town. Charlie probably had her pegged. She was a big rock star or something. Probably took dope. Lobe hoped she had some with her; she was going to need it after The Brewery.

The noon sun stood straight overhead. Not the prettiest time of day to take a look at Edgar Falls. Edgar Falls was a town that needed shadows, otherwise you got too close a look at the peeling paint on houses, the rutted shutters, the patchy-grassed lawns. Most of the town income came from the plumbing factory out on the east side. Ace Sanitary Plumbing was a glorified name for a place that made custom bathroom fixtures. In recent years, business had fallen off. The big city factories made inferior stuff, but it sold cheaper. Nobody cared about quality now.

Ace used to be union and wages good. But a new group that operated absentee had taken over four years ago, and the company had managed to break the union's back. Men now worked for half the old-time wages, and it showed in the town.

Lobe liked to think of it all as genteel weathering. But the truth was, the rare stranger just had a tendency to think of everything as decaying. The odor from the bog spots didn't help.

"Maybe I can get her autograph," Charlie said. "I hope she's got big tits."

"Why? You think she signs autographs with them?" Lobe grinned. Charlie punched him on the arm. "Say, maybe it's Dolly Parton," Charlie persisted. He quickened his steps, and Lobe's shorter legs had to give a leap forward to keep him up.

"Whoa now," Lobe said suddenly.

Both men stopped. The car had slowed and was barely inching along. By now, something like a crowd had gathered to watch its progress.

"They're not headed for The Brewery," Charlie said. "They look like they're looking for an address."

"And found it," Lobe declared as the car curved like a stretching cat against the curb in front of the New Horizon Realty Company.

Charlie and Lobe had to push through the people gathered to watch the chauffeur, a tall, sleekly handsome young man with longish hair, get out and come around to open his passenger's door. When she got out, an audible gasp went through the crowd, led by Charlie. Not only was she good and black, not your beige or tan, but in the spiked wicker-woven heels she was wearing, she stood six feet tall. That plus the gold hair, which could only be a wig Lobe surmised, made her such a spectacular sight, the crowd just stood there like one gaping mouth.

The chauffeur tipped his hat to her and then preceded her to the door of the New Horizon Realty Company. Gloriana Reege came out, casting a look of maliced pleasure at the crowd. "Ms. Benedictine," she said in a loud voice. They shook hands, the chauffeur held the door, and they all disappeared inside. People pressing forward to a window saw the two women go into a back room and the chauffeur take a seat and pick up a magazine.

"Now what the hell is that all about?" Charlie demanded. The woman had been so startling, he'd forgotten all about Dolly Parton.

"Dunno," Lobe said. But he suspected he did. All of a sudden he suspected that this whole thing had something to do with the mystery he had heretofore regarded as totally his own. He had gotten a decided whiff of lilies of the valley as the woman passed by, and even though he kept his face blank, he was seething inside. Because he had the awful feeling that right this moment Gloriana Reege was getting the jump on the next part of the mystery.

Not in years had this kind of excitement hit Edgar Falls. It was a quiet town with only the usual share of noteworthy incidents. Some weeks Miss Penny DuJong had to resort to enlarging minor happenings. Her latest rumor circulating was that Bitsy McCall might be pregnant again, this observation having been made at the chamber of commerce picnic where the swelling of that mountainous stomach had seemed to Miss Penny just a little more than usual. Not that a pregnancy in Bitsy was news. It was much juicier to find out something about your more conventional neighbors.

But now something new tremored through the town and brought people down to White Oak Avenue in bunches. Unmarked trucks trundled through, carrying all kinds of equipment and men. Things were happening on the west side of town. Lobe's prediction was coming true. A house was to be built out there, nobody knew whose.

Well, that wasn't entirely true. Gloriana Reege must know, and she was keeping it all to herself. "In good time," she told Lobe that first week the trucks started coming.

"It's connected with the big black woman, isn't it?" he asked. But Gloriana only smoothed back her auburn hair bun and smiled Mona Lisaish. "I'm sworn to secrecy, Lobe," she said. "All I will say is I was sales agent between the developer and the party who owns the property now."

Once Lobe took a good look at her when he'd wandered down to her office to see if he could make her reveal something more. Gloriana Reege, at maybe thirty-nine, was a rather nice-looking woman. He'd never noticed before, not being one for strong-minded women who ran businesses.

Now Lobe noted that Gloriana had large eyes of clear blue behind her squared-off glasses. Not a bad mouth either, and Lobe regretted he hadn't taken a closer look sooner. Maybe they could have got something going, and if they had, she'd be willing to impart the information his gut yearned for now.

Gloriana wasn't talking, however, which reduced Lobe to standing on the street watching the trucks go by, same as everyone else.

Lobe drove across town in his pickup that first morning, hoping to get some information from the men. They were big, swarthy specimens wearing t-shirts with the sleeves cut out, hard hats, and muscles bulging. Usually the humidity from the bog spots this time of year made hard labor a real chore, but these guys went at it like they were playing with tinker toys.

None of them paid any attention to Lobe, and he roamed around a while. They appeared to be getting ready to pull down trees. "Morning," Lobe said amiably to one of the men finally. "Like to send out a round of beer for you guys. Sort of a welcome to Edgar Falls."

"Thanks," the man, a big black, said. "We don't drink on the job."

"Going to be some building going on, huh?" Lobe said, only a little insulted that his offer hadn't been accepted. Beers for a crew this size he didn't really want to pop for.

"Looks like it," the man said. "Excuse me. No time to talk."

That was the way it had gone every day for a week now. Lobe wandered out to the activity site, along with curious townspeople who regarded the proceedings from a healthy distance. Except for Pulie Gordon, who very nearly got squashed by a falling tree. Later, Charlie had privately told Lobe it would have been a boon to the family if the kid'd got scrunched.

"Hey, what's happening, Lobe?" People always greeted him. They only had two sources in town to look to for information, and even though both Miss Penny and Lobe came to the site every day, neither one of them seemed to know anything. The town didn't like the feeling. Someone ought to know something about what all these strangers were doing.

Then, at the end of the first week of August, when the men had been working out there a week, felling trees with the verve of a crew of a hundred, trimming off branches so fast their hands seemed to blur and then having the trunks lifted onto semi beds by a giant crane, a new event occurred. Lobe, being shrewd, had made the connection between the black woman and the current activity. But he never dreamed the limo would come purring through town and cuddle up to his own curb. It happened.

Same scene. A crowd gathered. The chauffeur let *her*

out and then opened the door to the newspaper office. She moved like something Lobe had never seen before: slow and with style, like her car. She came straight for where he sat behind his desk. He was too taken aback for a moment to rise. She wore a dress of pale, tawny silk and was even taller than he remembered—six-two maybe. He half expected her to speak in a foreign accent and was a little surprised when her voice came out soft and slightly southern.

"Mr. Peters, I believe," she said. She stuck out her hand, and he remembered to get to his feet, although he hated to; she towered over him. She shook his hand with the strength and confidence of a male. "I have some business to conduct with you," she said.

Five minutes later, the big car was gone, *The Daily Way* office had filled with curious people, and Lobe Peters was staring dumbfoundedly at a cashier's check for five hundred dollars.

"What was that all about?" Charlie Groves demanded excitedly. "What'd she want this time?"

"To buy another headline," Lobe said dazedly. "She's the one who's been doing it, only this time she came in person." Five hundred dollars? He had barely cleared that in a month since he'd taken over the paper twenty-five years ago.

Miss Penny came pushing to the fore. She had been shopping in Loman's Department Store and regretted having missed the limousine for the second time. She had to make up for lost time or her reputation for getting the best news the fastest was in jeopardy. "What's it going to say, Lobe?" she asked.

"Now I can't tell you that, Miss Penny," he said. "Otherwise nobody'd read the paper this week."

Miss Penny had the neck of a bull and she craned it now, trying to see over the counter. "You're welcome to look at the check," Lobe said, turning it for all eyes to see. "It doesn't have any name on it. Only mine. Doesn't have to have." Personally, he was a little disappointed in what the headline had to say. What he was really excited about and trying to keep to himself (though if anyone had looked closely, a little jumping nerve in his throat might have been observed) was something else the woman had said to him when he tried to pump her: "One thing I *will* tell you now, and that is that I am only a representative for the party building the house—a go-between if you will—and my employer wishes to remain anonymous," she had said. "All will be revealed soon, Mr. Peters. And I assure you, outside of our contact here in Edgar Falls, you will be the first to know so that you can carry the story. Suffice it to say, something wonderful is about to happen to this town."

Lobe knew who that contact was, but he'd given up hope of getting any information there. "Patience," the woman had said to him as she turned to leave his office. And something stranger than anything else: "Glory to the deserving." It was a remark Lobe would ponder for days, sitting in the ugly quiet of his room over *The Daily Way* office.

All the next week the plain, unmarked trucks bearing license plates for several states rumbled through town, and a portion of the woods got eaten away right before their eyes. A few people grumbled over the fact that out-of-town labor had been brought in when there were plenty of able-bodied men in town who could do it and needed the money. But curiosity overcame all else. This week the headline in *The Daily Way* read, "WHOSE HOUSE IS IT?" It was the same question everybody had been asking all along. But seeing it in a headline paid for by a five hundred dollar cashier's check brought the curiosity to a fevered pitch.

* * *

In his own opinion, Lobe Peters was a helluva better reporter than people might figure. Just because a lot of them had known him since he was a tad, him being born in Edgar Falls and never going away except to do his patriotic duty in the service, folks didn't think of him as having big city writing skills. But he had them; they just lay dormant.

For years, Lobe's one dream had been to get a story into a city paper. He had submitted some stuff to the *St. Louis Post Dispatch* and the *New York Times*, always getting back, "Thanks, but our staff has already . . ." Lobe knew goddamn well that the staff hadn't already anything; they were plagiarizing the hell out of him.

Well, he'd stopped feeding them material long ago and shifted his dream to writing a fiction book about something nobody could filch: a book with a poetic bent.

He thought maybe the elements of his plot had come along with the house, and that made him bounce around with a spring to his feet he hadn't felt since he was a snotty-nosed showoff who knew he was going to take over his daddy's newspaper and was therefore special in this life.

Lobe did some investigating, sitting up in his room over the paper. When he wasn't thinking about Lucy, that is. Lobe and Lucy Peters had made their own news a couple of years ago when they broke up and she moved back to San Antonio where he'd met her during his army days. It still rankled.

But he did manage to run down some information. Sheriff Hille owed Lobe a couple of favors, like for the time Lobe had gone driving out on MacLean Road in Gloaming, trying to figure what had hit Lucy, and had come upon the sheriff balling the hell out of Tippy Bocaccio, fifteen-year-old daughter of Gloaming's mayor. Lobe had spotted the sheriff's car under some trees and got out to investigate, scared someone had waylaid the sheriff. The only thing getting laid was Tippy, and from the way she clutched onto the fifty-year-old lawman when Lobe flashed a light on them, it was evident she wasn't being molested. Lobe had promised to keep his mouth shut, not out of any regard for the sheriff or that slut of a kid, but because a mouth shut at the right time might call out a favor some day.

He'd been right. Sheriff Hille traced the limo and came up with an address and phone.

The only problem was the lady named Benedictine didn't own the car; a guy named Podenski did. Lobe called him in St. Louis. He had a swishy voice, which turned Lobe off right away. Podenski was proud of his car and more than willing to talk about it. "Went to England to get it myself," he said. "Only cost me thirty thousand. I make good money renting it out to people who like class."

The price of the phone call clicked in back of Lobe's mind, but he didn't want to annoy the guy, so he let him talk a second about how he drove the car himself, dressed up in a uniform.

"Wait a minute," Lobe said. "I've seen you in Edgar Falls."

"Edgar Falls?" the guy said. "Oh, yeah, that dumpy little burg that smells funny."

Lobe rankled but held his tongue. "I've seen you," he said. "You brought a woman here I'm interested in. Her name is Ms. Benedictine. She's black."

"Ah, Ms. Benedictine." The other guy's voice brightened with respect. "I'm afraid I can't tell you anything about her."

"I have to know where I can reach her."

"Sorry."

"Look, I'll pay for the information."

The voice at the other end of the line became curt. "Mister," it said, "even if information about my clients wasn't private, which it is, I couldn't tell you a thing. She just calls ahead and shows up the next day, and I take her where she wants to go, no questions asked. She pays in cash, buddy, and doubles my fee."

Lobe found himself suddenly with a dead phone in his hand. It took him a second to get control of the urge to throw it across the room. Damn swish. Talking to him in that superior tone of voice.

Lobe thought a while, came up with another possibility. He was now hotly sniffing a bigger mystery than ever and was determined to print some information in *The Daily Way* before the big black woman magnanimously offered it to him.

He got on the ball and called a guy he'd met in San Antonio in service who'd become a private eye in St. Louis after the army. Lucy had gone to school with A.O. Battersea's wife and kept up on them through correspondence.

It took Battersea a moment to remember Lobe. "Oh, yeah," he said finally. "Little guy."

And you were greasy and a letch, Lobe wanted to say. But didn't.

Sure Battersea would stake out the limo place. Be glad to stand around and wait for the black woman to show up. For a price.

"A hundred dollars a *what*?" Lobe gasped. "Jesus H. Christ."

"What'd you think I'd do it for?" Battersea huffed. "A few bars of 'Auld Lang Syne'?"

So much for that. Lobe would have to find another angle.

Lobe hadn't given up trying to get his own newsbreak on the house—jump the folks moving in, so to speak. For a while he had run up against a brick wall.

A check of county records back after he'd called the swish chauffeur had turned up only the fact that the property in Pellam Woods was in the name of Jewelline Benedictine, which meant she was fronting all the way for the person she worked for. Not for a moment had he doubted her sincerity when she announced herself a go-between. Colored never had the kind of money required to build the house.

After a time, Lobe thought of something else and made a run over to Sheriff Hille's office to talk to the lawman again.

He found the paunchy sheriff in an obstinate mood. "Done you one favor," he said. "Don't feel called on to do another. Not as if you was after a crook or something. Looks to me like you're just plain ready to shit your pants because something's going on you don't know about."

"Isn't next year an election year?" Lobe asked archly.

The sheriff narrowed his eyes so that they were slits under his puffy lids. "This wouldn't be by way of a blackmail threat, would it, boy?" he asked softly. Neither one of them had ever mentioned the incident on MacLean Road. Lobe decided not to mention it now.

The next day he swallowed his I've been had feelings and called A. O. Battersea. "What's all this horseshit anyway?" Battersea wanted to know. "I got bigger money things working than chasing down a bunch of license plates for you."

"All I want is a telephone number," Lobe said. "I'll send you whatever you want." "Forty bucks," barked Battersea. Lobe hung up reminding himself Battersea had always been an oily son-of-a-bitch, even as a green rookie.

Forty bucks got him four St. Louis phone numbers. "There *isn't* one number for all of them," Battersea said over the phone. "They don't come from one company like you thought. These guys are all independents. Whoever's building that house hired truckers who own their own rigs and do construction, too. Free-lancers. They operate out of their homes."

When Lobe recovered from the shock of paying Battersea's cut rate for four numbers, a hundred and twenty bucks, he got to work calling. The first two numbers in the city didn't answer. But then the third one brought him the gruff and suspicious voice of one Carlos Mendoza, which turned out to be too bad. Lobe had hoped to make contact with a wife to pump, figuring all the men were out working in Pellam Woods. But a man with a heavy cold answered. "What you trying to find all this out for, buddy? The person hired us wants this a secret, that's their business. For the money being paid me I wouldn't blab an atomic bomb was coming to my mother. Hey. You wouldn't be the little prick with the funny glasses always asking questions, would you?"

Lobe hung up. He didn't try the other two numbers again, or the fourth. He just sat in his place over *The Daily Way* seething with impotence. Who the hell was this anyway who could pay out money for all that silent muscle meat, and who in the name of Jesus H. Christ was this bozo who talked to him like a bug crossing his path?

"Well, what can you expect from a spic?" he asked himself.

Chapter Two

The atmosphere out by Pellam Woods had taken on the air of a carnival. Every day now a large crowd gathered, mostly women and children, although several men, including Bobbie Topin's senile old grandfather, Arnold Wetterley, wandered out sometimes. It was a pretty good walk for the old man, so someone often wound up taking him home — usually Mrs. Botts, the Baptist preacher's wife. She had a special interest in old people and had a lot of them gathered up into a club that met on some afternoons. She took them places like the show in Gloaming and once recently on a tour of a rose garden in another town. She used the church bus to do that, driving them herself, and came home looking wild-eyed with a crew of giggling old people. Someone — she never found out who — had smuggled a bottle of wine on board.

"Twenty-one people drunk on one bottle of wine," Mrs. Botts said, disgusted. "I didn't know what was wrong until Mrs. Lowington ate one of the prize blooms." To punish them, Elizabeth Botts had not held a meeting in four weeks.

But, in her good heart, she tried to remain charitable. She never let herself think that she might be kind to old people because she had sent her own mother to a convalescent hospital three years ago. She couldn't help it, after all, if her mother had turned her face to the wall and never gotten out of bed again.

Sometime soon, when she felt the old folks properly chastized, she would start up their club again; it was the only social life some of them had.

She took Mr. Wetterley home from the house site for two reasons. One, the hot weather, and, two, Mr. Wetterley doggedly refused to get involved in her club or any other church activities. It was a crime to be a heathen at his age. She seized the trips to the house to impress upon him how near the end might be and how necessary it was to be saved. "Get him for Christ," became her motto.

Sometimes Mr. Wetterley knew what was going on at the house and sometimes he didn't. Once he got it through his head the men were building a missile site and went ranting through the crowd that they would get cancer from the fuel fumes. Nobody paid him much mind. He was harmless. And there wasn't any concern over the boy's living with him. Bobbie seemed a good, sensible kid (if you gave him any thought at all). The old man had a pension, and that seemed to get them by.

Mr. Wetterley had moved here a few years ago with a wife, who promptly died. His one child, Bobbie's mother, was married by then, and when the husband left her eventually (a fact wormed from her by Miss Penny), she worked at odd jobs in the city a few years and then came to live with her father, bringing her young son. Then *she* died. *Cremated.* Some folks still shuddered over that.

The old man didn't seem to fathom the responsibility Bobbie represented, and anyone watching Bobbie cater to the old geezer would have wondered who was in charge of whom. But outsiders didn't trouble the minds of Edgar Falls for long.

Out by Pellam Woods, the people brought sandwiches to sit on the grass and watch the men work. Fascinating things went on daily.

Probably a hundred trees had been pulled down, clearing an acre of ground.

Then some strange contraptions got hauled in, and men began pumping the bog holes. The people rankled a bit there. Those bog holes, despite the odor and humidity they produced at times, engendered a kind of personal pride in the townspeople.

Archeologists had come out once to study them to see if any prehistoric animals had blundered into them and left any bones behind. (They hadn't.) The holes were about as old as time, the professors told Lobe Peters in the last decent story he'd had. An underground river fed them, only by the time the water pushed up toward the ground surface there wasn't much left, and it turned everything to mud instead of producing clear springs.

So how could they be drained now? The people sat back and smirked at the out-of-town workmen, particularly three days later when they gave up on their draining. Any fool knew you couldn't siphon off an underground river. Maybe now the whole project would fall apart, and a certain mood of disappointment edged the crowd's triumph.

But the men consulted. A little later, more trees came down, south of those already removed. There were only a couple of bog spots here, and whoever was moving to Edgar Falls didn't mind having them in his back yard.

The digging began. And the crowd grew daily. Nobody could believe the size of that hole.

"What the hell they building there?" Bruzz Logan,

dragged away from The Brewery by all the wildly flying rumors, had come down to take a look himself. "That cellar's big as Meramac Caverns."

"A restaurant probably," Charlie Groves said. "Somebody's taking pity on the town and driving you out of business, Bruzz."

Alarm shot over the big face. "You know it's going to be a house," Bruzz said.

"Then what'd you ask for?" Charlie muttered wryly.

It was Saturday and uniformed girl scouts went through the crowd selling homemade fudge for Cindy Newman's foot.

"Wonder what those boys make for Saturdays," Clyde Newman, who was a bench-caster at Ace Sanitary Plumbing, wondered aloud. More for a day than he made for a week, he bet, and him with a crippled kid. The town was taking care of the foot, he reminded himself.

Yeah, but she'd still need special shoes. Who would pay for those?

Sometimes he got really pissed. If the kid was going to get run over by a stampeding cow on the north side of town where some farming still went on, why couldn't it have been a cow that belonged to someone? As it was, old lady Jenkins had died. It happened in town, her stroke, and nobody thought to see to her cow, which went without feeding several days. The cow took matters into her own hands and went crazy and busted through a fence at the exact moment Cindy wandered out that way. Clyde watched the workmen with malevolence in his heart.

Consensus finally had it that some millionaire had decided to build a retirement home in Edgar Falls. Why not? It was a pretty little town, wasn't it? The people exceptional. High moral values.

The retirement home idea both flattered and

annoyed them. It was nice someone who had probably passed through once had fallen in love with Edgar Falls. But nobody wanted a bunch of rich bitches lording it over them. They'd better be just plain folk made good, or the town would cold shoulder them in a hurry.

Outside of the black woman, only Gloriana Reege must know the builders, and she wasn't talking, which didn't add anything to her status. Gloriana was an outsider who'd come along one day and opened up her realty company—nobody knew why; property rarely turned over in Edgar Falls. Only the fact she was a widow woman and childless and had to make her own living (information wrested from her by Miss Penny) made folks talk to her at all.

The third week in August, fresh excitement gripped the town. This time trucks came rolling in with truly fascinating things to see. Great piles of huge rocks cemented together. Stacks of lumber with white paint peeling off them, bound together with chains. Three tall pillars came through on separate truck beds. Giant bags of cement and crates marked "roof" on the sides. The house was underway.

Hardly anything else got talked about anymore. Cindy Newman was the chief beneficiary of all this new interest. Heretofore her foot had been the main topic of conversation.

Cindy was free to sit on the edge of the watching crowd with Bobbie Topin. She couldn't figure out why Bobbie had gone so quiet lately, but the other kids played wild games she couldn't join, so she appreciated the reflectiveness that kept him sitting out here by the woods. She had companionship, albeit silent.

One afternoon they watched as a giant crane settled the first big hunk of stones cemented together into the ground. An involuntary cheer went up from the crowd, and Cindy, caught in the mood of jubilance, joined in. Only Bobbie sat there glumly.

"That isn't a new house," he said when the cheer died down. "It's an old one they're rebuilding. I don't like it."

Cindy turned quizzical eyes on him. Around her, people buzzed about the same thing he'd just remarked on. It had been a topic for several days now — that someone was moving a house here, not just building one. "Probably an old family manor," they speculated. "And Edgar Falls is just a nicer place to live than where it was before."

When Bobbie didn't say anything more, Cindy demanded, "Didn't like what?"

He turned his head slowly and stared for a long moment — not really at her. More like through her.

"I don't know," he said. "A feeling." Then his eyes seemed to snap to; he seemed to hear himself, to catch himself as if he'd said too much. His mouth clamped shut, and he turned back to watch the next batch of stone lowered into place. When he didn't say anything for a long time, Cindy, bored, got up and went to find her mother and ask if she could have a quarter for one of the popsicles being hawked through the crowd.

The zinc wasn't working. Bobbie stared out the kitchen window at the tall, thin form gazing at the ground. Grandpop could stand by the hour regarding something like a gopher hole, as if with intense interest. But if you got a look at his face, you would see there wasn't anything there.

Bobbie sighed. He was feeling the need for companionship today. In town this morning, where he'd gone to study the vitamin counter in Amway's, his classmate, Craig Jorgenson, came in. Bubbling with excitement. "Got to have some sunburn oil, Mr. Amway,"

Jorgenson had exclaimed, maybe extra loud for Bobbie's benefit. "My pop and me going fishin' over to Hanberry Lake in Slopetown."

"Say now," the little druggist said. He wiped his brow and glared up a moment at a ceiling fan stirring nothing up but a couple of drugged-looking flies. "Probably be cooler out there."

"Gonna get us a mess of catfish," Jorgenson chattered on. He threw Bobbie some kind of significant glance, grinning. "Gimme some oil good for red hair."

"That where you gonna wear it?" Mr. Amway said laconically. Bobbie smiled a little. Craig Jorgenson wasn't noted for grammar or any other kind of scholarship. He'd been held back in fourth grade, in fact, and was older than the other guys going into sixth. But there wasn't any point feeling superior over *that*; Jorgenson had something he didn't have. Bobbie saw a sudden picture of Jorgenson and his father, a short, stocky man with hair the color of his son's, lazing around together on the shore of Lake Hanberry.

Bobbie had seen a lake once. He and Mom had taken a city bus to the outskirts and rented a little boat. She let him row. It wasn't much of a lake really, more a pond. But they'd pretended to be pirates looking for a frigate to plunder. They'd stayed out on that boat all afternoon. The setting sun had turned the water around them to gold and then when it went down, everything turned silver. "Magic," Mom had said. "Just like magic, Bobbie."

"Pop says it'll be just the two of us," Jorgenson declared. "Like old times."

Bobbie had left Amway's on that. He didn't have any old times with a father; he barely remembered his and hadn't really thought of him in years. It was his mother whose "old times" he missed.

In the kitchen, he pushed the picture of Craig's eager

face out of his head and opened the back door. "You want some iced tea, Grandpop?" he called.

The old man didn't stir. He was looking off toward the house site now. Bobbie went out back.

"Maybe you'd like me to take you over there, Grandpop?" Bobbie hadn't said anything—it wouldn't do him any good—but he worried the times Grandpop headed there alone. Those weird bog holes could be treacherous. An old man who sometimes only saw what was in his head might blunder in. Bobbie was grateful to Mrs. Botts for taking Grandpop under her wing, even though he understood her motive and didn't figure she was going to get anyplace with a person who, as far as Bobbie knew, hadn't believed in God when he was whole-minded.

He took Grandpop's hand. But he didn't tug. The ancient fingers hung slack, and he didn't think the old man even realized he was there. Well, maybe he'd wander on over himself later. Look for Cindy.

The late afternoon sun glinted off sweat-shiny backs. The men who had looked small from Grandpop's back yard were, up close, a mass of rippling, easy muscle. Bobbie watched them, ignoring the fact of the house itself, and filed their picture away for someday when he might write them into a story. Cindy wasn't out here with the rest of the usual crowd, maybe because she had been yesterday.

But someone else was.

Bobbie stared at him, surprised. What had happened to the big fishing trip?

Jorgenson didn't look at Bobbie as he went on by, kicking somewhat savagely at rubble the workmen had tossed aside. But in a second, he turned and snapped, "If you're wondering, *she* went and got a stupid headache. She *always* gets headaches if Pop and me plan anything."

She must be Jorgenson's stepmother. Bobbie didn't know much about his classmate's family except that Craig had a stepmother, and he only knew that because Jorgenson had had to read a story he'd written out loud to their fifth grade room last year, and it had been a wild, rambling, grammarless thing about stepmothers. There was a king in the story, and the king banished all the stepmothers from the kingdom. Jorgenson had read it in a singsong fury.

"I'm sorry," Bobbie said. He didn't know what else to say.

"Yeah," Jorgenson said. And kicked a rock so hard it went rolling back to stop at a workman's feet. "Watch it, kid," the man warned.

"Watch it your own self," Jorgenson snapped. "You guys are makin' a big mess."

He went on walking. Bobbie shifted where he sat and heard the jingle of a couple of coins in his pocket, two gleaming half dollars he was saving to give Grandpop on his birthday.

But all of a sudden, another use for the coins struck him. Grandpop wouldn't know the difference. If he was in a mood, he wouldn't even realize when his birthday came.

Hey, Craig, he wanted to call out. *Come on. I'll buy you a cone at The Sweet Lady's.*

But he stared at the back of Jorgenson's head, eyed the angry set to the other's boy's shoulders. And for all he knew, what was bottling up inside Jorgenson might come spewing out at him. Bobbie was okay for playing with at school — he was a good athlete, though not as good as Jorgenson; nobody was. But the rest of the time, he might as well not be around.

He watched Jorgenson roam up a knoll, kicking at grass clots as he went, half hoping the boy might read his mind and turn around and call, *Hey, sure, Topin, I could use a cone about now.*

Bobbie had to grin at himself for that; Craig Jorgenson was the last kid in town to have telepathy. He sensed his own grin. "Hey. Do you have such a bad life?" he asked himself.

The answer was no. It had been a lonesome day. But the sun was going down, and sometimes Grandpop perked up when the heat lessened. Maybe Bobbie would pop some corn and they could listen to some music on the little walkman Mom had given him a couple of years ago. And if Grandpop spaced out? Well, Bobbie could take the music out on the front porch and read a while. Maybe he'd even take a late-night walk in the woods; he hadn't done that much lately.

A pale, near September moon rode the sky above Pellam Woods. The steamy bog mists had faded to a few whiffs of white substance that drifted in wraithlike batches among the trees. It had been an unusually hot day even for this time of year. People said it probably heralded bad winter, one extreme often contrasting with another. Now, near the midnight hour, no breath stirred in the woods to bring relief.

Bobbie Topin sat on a small boulder left behind by some ancient flood. It rested near the house, giving him a good vantage point.

The woods were Bobbie's special place. His mother, in a trait rare in motherhood, had trusted him from the time he was very young to take care of himself. She knew in Edgar Falls that he often got up in the middle of the night and went prowling about—sometimes in the house, sometimes the neighborhood, on occasion in the woods. Nothing much had ever happened in Edgar Falls. Nobody had ever molested children. There had been only one murder, and that many years ago when two men had gotten into a skirmish over the girl they both loved. Bobbie had heard the story of how one young man shot the other. How the girl was fated not to get him either because three weeks later the young man escaped from the Gloaming jail and into Pellam Woods, never to be seen again.

Some said he jumped into one of the bog spots and committed suicide. But Bobbie had his doubts about that. Things had a tendency to float on top of the bog spots instead of sinking. But some said his ghost walked the woods some nights.

The idea had always amused Bobbie, even though it would be easy enough to believe in ghosts on a night like this. That thin stream of mist over there beyond those trees—it had the shape of a woman. And the cry of a nightbird would be enough to convince some people an otherworldly being stalked the woods tonight.

But Bobbie did not believe in ghosts despite the fact he loved to read about them. He was a very practical boy. At five he had been old enough to face the reality of his father's leaving. Five has, already, a concept of death and a knowledge it will die someday. Bobbie, when he reflected, thought that was perhaps the hardest thing he would ever have to accept. He had been inconsolable the night he first realized it, coming screaming out a dream in which he had died and crossed a long, dark river to find a man standing on the other side. "Not yet, Jesus," Bobbie had waked up screaming. And though his mother had held him for a long time, her arms had not comforted him. No one could comfort him when she died either. Some things all the arms in the world couldn't help, and you were alone. At twelve, Bobbie Topin understood this.

Maybe for this reason, the woods never frightened him. Cindy had said that most Edgar Falls kids didn't even like the woods by day. But if you knew that you only had to fear death and that death could not come to anyone careful in the woods, what could you be afraid of?

That was why the feelings he experienced now were so strange.

He had slipped away from the cottage a while ago, leaving Grandpop snoring in a chair. The old man fell asleep there night after night.

Bobbie always just left him. Sometimes he found the old man still there in the morning, awake, his eyes on the tree outside their cottage, staring with that vacant intensity.

Thinking what in his head?

Bobbie certainly hadn't started out for this place. He had selected the south woods to walk in, where there always seemed to be more night life. Birds twittered in whatever after-dark conversations birds carried on, sometimes growing so raucous you could hardly think. More rabbits lived on that side, and if you sat very still they romped almost to your feet. Sometimes, on a particularly lucky night, he got to see a fox nosing along with bright beady eyes.

Bobbie felt good in the woods. Natural. Like part of things, a feeling he seldom had anyplace else. Orphans were different in a town like Edgar Falls. Maybe every place for all he knew. That was why no one had anything to do with him outside school. Sometimes he saw just that little catch in an eye that said, "You're not quite like us."

Little wonder that he never expressed to anyone how this house going up made him feel. Only that once to

Cindy, and he had caught his tongue then. Cindy was an outsider, too, though she probably wouldn't be when she got her foot fixed, and he wanted to hold onto the special thing they had without her thinking him strange.

"What is it?" he said to the house. What had drawn him over here tonight of all places? For weeks now, he had avoided this part of the woods after dark.

Bobbie sat on the rock a long time, his knees drawn up to his chest.

Impressions. A sigh someplace in the rafter beams? They had the first floor done now. The moon glanced off bits of white paint made shiny by the mist moisture, leaving gaping crevices of darkness where there was no paint.

A creaking sound in the stone foundation and cellar sunk deep into the ground?

Bobbie glanced around, uneasy. Then back at the house.

Fourteen rooms—and large—on the ground floor. It would be the biggest house ever built in Edgar Falls. No one knew how many rooms would be on the next floor, or if there would be a third. The workmen joked and called out insults to each other, but they clammed up when the townspeople asked them questions.

"Someone is sure making this all a big mystery," Bobbie said, needing to hear his own voice. It rooted him. Otherwise his head seemed to want to take off on a wild flight. It ached a little from his having to hold it down.

The great oblong place seemed to want to get inside his senses. As if it had something to tell him, something he didn't want to hear.

He wanted to leave, but he couldn't. He hadn't wanted to come here in the first place. But maybe it was like he had to challenge himself—prove the imagination that kept returning to this house was overworking.

"Stay." Was that a breeze coming up, whispering through the vacant, glassless windows? But nothing stirred except the sweat that broke out suddenly on Bobbie's forehead. He stared at the house. Did something get up in the shadows inside there—shake itself, awakening from a long, torpid sleep? Did it stretch languourously and look about—and see the glassless windows—and know that someone sat out there on a rock, too paralyzed to move?

In Bobbie's mind, a shadow moved toward a window. And it came to the openings one by one, searching.

Did something chuckle low at the sight of a boy sitting there in the pale moonlight? If it did, its amusement was short-lived. For Bobbie Topin found his feet and ran. Away from the woods that had never threatened him before.

Across fields he pounded, gasping for breath, his side hurting, grateful for the natural sound of a dog barking somewhere in the distance. "It was only imagination," he said panting, rushing up the walk and into the house, wanting to throw himself against the welcome body of his grandfather sleeping still in the chair by the window, but rushing on to his own room where he drew the shade, despite the hot and humid night.

Maybe it was only his imagination. But he knew he would never go into that part of the woods again at night.

It was mid-September now, and a fall sun shone down on the nearly finished house. A small crew of vigilants sat around on fading grass watching a workman nailing the last of the shingles in place. Every one had been hand lain; they hadn't used those phony strips you saw so often these days. One man stood on a high ladder, painting the last of some trim beneath one of three dormers. The sun had moved into the afternoon sky and lay on the back of the house, so that the dormer windows, when Bobbie came along, had a dark opaqueness to them, like Amy Semple MacPherson Pond before a storm.

This was the first day of school. Bobbie had entered the sixth grade. He liked his teacher, Miss Larimer, okay, and the day had passed uneventfully. Except for those moments when his mind trailed off on the house and Miss Larimer caught it. "Bobbie's got the first day back blahs," she told the class. The house, ever since that night in the woods, was more and more with him, getting into his dreams and squatting on the back of his waking thoughts like some warped gnome.

He didn't know why. He didn't want to know why.

Bobbie had been true to his own word. He hadn't gone into the woods at night again. But the house drew him by day, as it drew a lot of other people. Some came and went, stopping by every week. But a certain little group showed nearly every day.

Miss Penny DuJong, who owned the candy and ice cream shop called The Sweet Lady's down on White Oak Avenue, had hired a young mother, Mary Haffey, to come in every day. Miss Penny let her bring Kevin along, so Mary came down to the shop for an hour at noon with her little boy and returned in the afternoon from four to five. Those were the hours Miss Penny came out to the house. Long ago she had gone beyond the urge to come because something noteworthy to report might happen.

She sat today on a grassy knoll, surrounded by her friends but oblivious to them. The house held her. "Isn't it the whitest?" she said to herself. "Pure white. So white it hurt your eyes. All her life she had wanted to live in a house like that. Three stories high if you counted the attic up there behind the dormer windows. Twenty-four rooms. Nothing even remotely resembling it had ever existed in Edgar Falls before. Even the few people with money didn't aspire to anything like this. Banker Bergins now, he had twelve rooms. And his house was built of brick. But it didn't have the expansiveness or charm of the mystery house, as people had taken to calling it.

Look at that porch and those tall pillars. Miss Penny's heart ached. She deserved a house like that. Life had not treated her well. Spinsterhood had not been her idea, but only one man had had meaning in her life. Miss Penny always thought of Albert and her sister Rose when she looked at the house, thought of them with the thin hate that went trickling through her veins even after all these years.

If she had married Albert, they could have stayed in Edgar Falls and worked together and saved, and they could have had a house like this. By now anyway. Then today they could sit on that porch together in highbacked wicker chairs (that porch cried out for highbacked wicker chairs) and watch the setting sun dapple the other two sides of the woods and turn the leaves to sparkling bits of autumn gold.

An old line in Dickens came to Miss Penny. From *Hard Times*. Mrs. Gradgrind was ill and she lay upon a couch and said something to the effect, "There is a pain floating in this room, and I sadly fear I have got it." Miss Penny couldn't remember the exact words anymore; it was the only line she remembered from the Dickens books her eighth grade teacher had foisted on her class. (Miss Penny preferred Barbara Cartland these days.)

But there was a pain somewhere here right now. And she sadly feared she had got it. Miss Penny sat in the darkness of her might-have-beens and stared, mesmerized, at the house. In her heart, someone grabbed up a butcher knife and hacked her sister Rose somewhere in Europe into a million pieces, and then an ageless man and woman came out on the porch of that house, hand-in-hand, and sat down in the high-backed wicker chairs.

Augustine Gordon, called Pulie by his uncle and some of the kids in the high school in Gloaming, rode his bike around the woods from Gloaming and home. He hadn't intended to go by the house necessarily. But something drew him.

He didn't like looking at the mystery house. It reminded him of other things he didn't like. Like Christmas trees shining in windows of other houses. Why did they always look so homey and friendly? Pulie knew that all the people behind those glowing windows lived happy, joyous lives. While the artificial tree in his house always seemed to be on the verge of decay, like his mother.

Their house reeked of her medicines, and measures of her mortality permeated everywhere. They only had one bathroom in the tiny cottage where they had lived alone since his father died. In that bathroom hung the paraphernalia designed to keep his mother alive. The douche bag, ever dangling from the shower rod, and one of two nozzles on it at all times. One was the big black spigot shaped like a man's thing that was for keeping her withered female organs clean. The other was a tinier nozzle for enemas, which his mother took with regularity since she had long ago given up expecting her body to perform its necessaries.

Pulie had years ago pinpointed the times she was most prone to indulge herself in these cleansing processes — could it be accident that one coincided with his coming in from school?

Stopping by the house got him over the afternoon school time today. If he delayed long enough, he would not have to hear the sighs and groans emanating from the bathroom, the sounds that made him hate himself because they brought a reaction in the most detested part of his body.

"Nasty, nasty." He could hear his mother's voice now going back to his early childhood when he had discovered the appurtenance hanging from his body. "That's for wee-weeing with," she had told him countless times, the smack of her hands growing sharper as the years went by. "Augustine, what are you doing in there under the covers?" He had never been able to take a few moments alone for himself without her hated question. Even now she asked it.

Pulie sat on the seat of his bike, his long legs reaching to the ground, and stared at the house, his mind like everyone else's, suddenly centered on the thought of possessing it. Twenty-four rooms! The dislike for it dissolved as he realized what that house could mean to him. Seven baths. Seven! He would never have to see those things hanging in a bathroom. She could have her own, and he his, and they would never have to even pass in the halls. He could lie under covers and do whatever he felt compelled to do. It would drive her mad because if she roamed through those halls seeking him out, it would all be over before she even found him. Pulie smiled. And started wanting that house.

Cindy Newman spotted Bobbie standing apart from the rest of the crowd and limped over to join him. "What do you think of Miss Larimer?" she asked. It hadn't been a good day for her. Miss Larimer seemed to think her foot was something in her imagination that she could overcome. Consequently, she had insisted on Cindy's playing ninesquare. Cindy slowed the game, and the kids had spent the afternoon in class throwing her baleful looks. On top of that, her foot had ached all day. She had deliberately come by the house today, knowing Bobbie would probably be here. She hadn't seen much of him lately; she spent every minute she could steal from home with the babies. Bitsy had never really felt well since the picnic, and when Bitsy felt bad, she took it out on her kids. Cindy's presence curbed a lot of that, and she had taken to regarding herself as protector of the babies.

"Miss Larimer's okay," Bobbie said. "But she shouldn't've made you play games unless you wanted to."

"I didn't want," Cindy said, grateful he understood.

A sudden gasp went up from the crowd. Bobbie turned back to the house. The ladder had swayed suddenly, and the man on top had to flail out and grope for the edge of the roof. He got the thing righted okay and went back to his painting. The crowd quieted.

"Who do you suppose is going to live in it?" Cindy asked. The house was as big a puzzle as ever. "And how come they didn't just build a new one? How much do you think it cost to bring it from wherever it came?"

"A lot of money," Bobbie said absently. His mind stayed on that workman who had nearly fallen.

"It's beautiful, isn't it?" Cindy asked. "It looks like it belongs in a fairy tale. I love that iron fence they're putting up around the roof."

The fence stood three feet high, made of black wrought iron, with occasional spiked rails. A small section where the workman painted remained to be put up.

Bobbie kept silent. He didn't like looking at the fence. It didn't sit quite right. It angled a little downward on the left, just enough off kilter to make him feel slightly dizzy. A lot of the house struck him that way. He stared at the dormer windows. That one on the right—it couldn't be more than a quarter inch off in its angle. But it *was* that quarter inch off. Bobbie had a feel for symmetry, and these tiny, out-of-line quirks about the house bothered him in a way he couldn't put into words.

If you stared at it long enough, the whole house seemed to be a mass of weird tip-tiltings. It reminded him of a crazy quilt, nothing quite right but all fitting together into a whole. Unless he was mistaken, the left pillar of the three stood just a hair shorter than the others, the upstairs porch roof attached to them slanting downward just a hair more than it should.

Couldn't the builders tell? Something popped into his mind suddenly: a description in *Haunting of Hill House*, Mom's favorite book. The house had formed itself, the writer had said—something about flying together into its own pattern. Like the builders could only do what *it* wanted.

"Why didn't they just make a new house?" Vaguely, Bobbie became aware that Cindy had repeated her question, that she was determined to draw him into conversation when he wanted to study the house. Did all the strange little miscalculations in design make him think about it so much? "Someone's probably attached to it," he said. "Maybe they didn't like living where they were anymore and wanted to move to a woods. I don't know. We'll find out soon, I guess, since it's almost finished."

"It'd be nice to love a house that much," Cindy said. "And nice to have the money to be able to move it on trucks, don't you think?"

Bobbie wanted to tell her to shut up. But Cindy had had a rough day with the kids mad at her. He sighed and turned to her, seeing something desperate in her face. "Come on," he said. "I've got enough money for a candy bar. Let's go down to The Sweet Lady's and I'll split it with you."

"Okay," she said. "Miss Penny's over there watching the house." Cindy seldom went to The Sweet Lady's much as she loved candy, because she couldn't stand the way Miss Penny simpered over her, calling her "poor little thing." The free treat she always forced on Cindy somehow tasted sour. But the beehive hairdo was plainly notable in the crowd. Mary would be at the shop, and Cindy could play a moment with little Kevin. She might not be able to get out much to Bitsy's now, what with school, and the days getting shorter.

Bobbie took Cindy's hand, and the two of them had walked across a grassy area the length of a half block when they suddenly heard a cry of horror go up behind them. Both of them spun at once and went tearing back to where the man who had been painting lay still on the ground.

"Get a doctor," one of the men shouted to Pulie. Pulie hesitated a moment. He didn't want to ride madly through town making a spectacle of himself. But the man, a huge black, straightened up from where he had been leaning over his companion, and he was so big and so terrifying, Pulie sprang into immediate action. Five minutes later, he threw his bike down on the ground and went tearing into Doc Jannessey's office where he panted out what had happened and then went racing off on his bike for home. The sight of all that threatening power in the man's muscles had affected

Pulie strangely, and much as he wanted to know if the other one was dead, he didn't have the strength to pedal over there again.

Doc Jannessey, wearing a white suit marred with permanent spots, hopped out of his car where the road ended and went bouncing along toward the house with his black bag smacking at his thighs, grateful for a little excitement. Nothing much ever happened in Edgar Falls, and he had been listening to old man Holmstead's never-ending lists of complaints when Augustine Gordon had burst into his office.

The crowd had risen to its feet, and while maintaining a respectful distance, craned its collective neck to see the man on the ground. Miss Penny swiftly totaled up in her head the absentees from the crowd so she could get home and hit the phone and report the news. She saw, with a registering of appreciation, that Lobe Peters wasn't there. *Scoop again*, she thought.

Doc Jannessey, much too heavy for a man of sixty, reached the fallen workman, huffing. Kneeling and gasping for breath, he lay his ear against his chest. "Wasn't any need to rush me," he said disappointedly— he had had visions of appearing a hero to the crowd as he fought valiantly to save the man's life the way they did on television. "Any fool can see he's dead. Probably knocked his brains haywire."

Bobbie, fascinated when he didn't want to be fascinated, had drawn nearer than anyone to the man on the ground. He could see the white streak of paint the man's brush had left down his face as the ladder went out from under him. Bobbie hovered close enough to hear the other workmen groan. The two had been working on the roof got down and came around the side of the house. Two more had emerged from inside, still carrying paint brushes. Shell pink, Miss Penny saw. Her heart squeezed. Shell pink was her favorite color; she had it on the walls of her shop.

The men began to swiftly and silently gather up their things. Brushes disappeared into cans that reeked of turpentine and were sloshed around and wiped clean. The six of them began to load everything onto the smaller trucks they had been using since the heavy work ended. It all happened with such incredible speed. Cindy, who had crept up close to Bobbie, stood with her mouth open.

"I'll put in a call to Sheriff Hille, and he can get the county coroner over here," Doc Jannessey said. But no one paid any attention to him. "Hey," he cried as the black man and another started to pick up their fallen comrade. They set him upright on the passenger side of one truck and strapped him into the seat belt. His head fell forward. The crowd gasped.

"Now wait a minute," Doc shouted. "Violent death is a coroner's case."

Men mounted the trucks. Four motors flared into life. In a moment they were bouncing across the open meadow to where the road began. They hit the road in a line, kicking up a small cloud of dust. The crowd stood in a body watching the procession speed out of town toward the highway.

"Goddamnit anyway," Doc Jannessey exploded. "Don't they have any sense of a man's jurisdiction? I got to call Sheriff Hille." No one knew what for. There was rather a sense of relief in the crowd that they hadn't gotten stuck with the body of a stranger in town tonight.

The sun had begun to drop fairly rapidly. Shadows stretched out from the woods. The townspeople began to move by twos and threes back toward their homes. Doc Jannessey went off by himself, still complaining, wondering who was going to pay him for his time.

Only Bobbie and Cindy remained.

Bobbie stood a moment, staring at the spot where the man's body had been moments before. Then suddenly he realized that the shadows of the house had fallen across him and Cindy. He grabbed her hand and yanked her backward with such force she stumbled and nearly fell and hollered, "Hey, cut that out!"

Standing in what was left of the sun, Bobbie stared back at the house, looking up at the section the man had finished painting just before the ladder went.

"That was a terrible accident," Cindy said shakily.

"Yeah," Bobbie said and couldn't erase the thought. *I'm surprised there hasn't been more than one.*

He didn't say it out loud to Cindy. She wouldn't have understood. He wasn't sure he did either. But he had a feeling the house did.

Chapter Three

The day after the accident, a double crew of workmen swarmed through, over, and around the house. The daily crowd sat watching a scene not unlike one in a Mack Sennett comedy. Brushes seemed to fly, hammers pounded with staccato taps so close together they could hardly be distinguished. Within three days the house stood gleaming white all over and could not have been told from a new one. Workmen swept their trash out the doors, bundling it up and putting it on their trucks, and one knew without seeing that the inside sparkled, too.

That first day after the accident, new events stirred the people up. The coroner in St. Louis who took possession of the body when it was presented to a mortuary there sent an investigator out to see Doc Jannessey. He was pissed, to put it mildly. "How the hell'd you manage to let a body get away from you?" he said fuming.

Doc had been all over it the night before with Sheriff Hille, likewise pissed. "Judas Priest," Doc exploded both times. "What'd you want me to do, sit on him? Those guys are giants."

Hille hadn't been able to trace the trucks on the

highway. "Must've taken a lot of side roads," he'd declared. The coroner's investigator got it worked out, of course, because after all, there hadn't been any foul play. But he left Doc Jannessey grumbling about how it was all caused by outsiders anyway.

Then the black woman, universally known as Ms. Benedictine, arrived at noon in town. Same scene as before. The chauffeur getting out and respectfully tipping his hat, the woman sweeping inside the building — this time Doc Jannessey's. The workmen had merely been looking after their own, she said.

To say nothing of protecting the identity of their employer, Lobe thought to himself later. Lobe missed it, damnit, on business in Gloaming. He'd like to have thumbed his nose at that fag chauffeur. Miss Penny arrived hot on the heels of the woman's leaving to stare in awe at the two hundred dollar cashier's check doc held. "Tried to tell her I didn't do nothing," he said. "I mean, a twenty would've done." The two bills went a long way toward soothing his ego.

Most intriguing of all was that the dead workman had had a name. Carlos Mendoza. "From St. Louis," Doc said. And Miss Penny went hurrying off with her tidbits to spread them on eager ears. When Lobe heard, he smirked to himself. There was some kind of poetic justice in this somewhere.

By the third week in September, the yard was finished, too. A truck had arrived carrying boxes of sod, and a large area around the house now boasted a fine, green lawn. Not that it would last long. The grass the crowd sat on was turning yellow.

The day the trucks left for good the people sat silently watching the men pull away. Like a crew of ghosts, people said. Now you see them, now you don't. They left behind a place of such splendor everyone just sat and stared. For a while, people felt a sense of loss that the work had ended. After all, watching the house had gotten a lot of them through the last part of a dull summer.

But in a little while, a ripple of excitement ran through the group. Now they could watch to see who would move in. Speculation opened up again as to whether it might be colored, despite Lobe's insistence it couldn't be. Gloriana Reege would have a lot to answer for if she'd sold to colored. But they couldn't do anything except wait and see.

The dust on the road had long since died down when Miss Penny took the bull by the horns and decided to satisfy her nagging curiosity. Others watched while she boldly walked up the new flagstone path to the porch, mounted the steps, and peered through a window beside the front door.

She stayed there so long, people began to call, "What do you see, Miss Penny?" But she was speechless, staring through lacy curtains into what they all knew to be the largest of the rooms, big enough to be a ballroom. Tressa Allen, here on her lunch hour after the rush at The Brewery, was the first to finally follow Miss Penny up. They stood together, carefully shielding their eyes in such a way as to not printing up the window. "God," Tressa breathed. "It's like a fairy palace."

Miss Penny turned on her in the midst of a violent rage of possession. She didn't want anyone else looking into this window of this house that had come to fill all her fantasies. But Tressa remained oblivious to the fire in Miss Penny's eyes. "Those floors," she said. "Did you ever see anything gleam like that?"

Others took up the challenge and came creeping timidly up the porch. "Oooh," they said. "Ahhh." Every soul of them longed to get inside that house and feel part of it.

All but Bobbie Topin. He came by the house late that evening. He had gone to the store to get some noodles and rerouted himself to look at the house. Only one person stood out here this evening. Lobe Peters.

"Mystery should be solved soon," Lobe said to Bobbie.

Bobbie nodded, his eyes on the house. All the white paint and the new grass didn't fool him. Something was wrong with this place.

That night he stood in his bedroom window looking out across the meadows. He could see the house from here, white against the night sky and the woods, and his unease grew. He wondered if his grandfather would change rooms with him if he thought up a good enough reason—the old man seldom slept in his anyway. But his grandfather didn't like change, and Bobbie knew from experience that the old man could be stubborn. Still, he thought he might try. It disturbed him having the house in sight. He wished they didn't live on the outskirts of town, or that there were other buildings between him and the house. Looking out on it had become a kind of ritual he performed every night before going to bed. The necessity bothered him; why should he feel he needed to keep an eye on it?

Tonight a moon shone brightly down, and Bobbie could make out the dirt road that led nearly to the house. It was very late, but suddenly he saw a figure moving near the road. A strange fear quivered near his heart. *Don't go near the house*, he wanted to shout. As if the person could hear him!

Who was it? Bobbie strained his eyes, but he couldn't see more than a moving shadow. Miss Penny maybe. Of all the others, she seemed the most fascinated with the house. Bobbie had seen something nearly maniacal in her eyes when she looked at it. Well,

Miss Penny was a grown woman, and he wasn't about to romp over there tonight or any other night. What would he say anyway? "Something's wrong with this place, stay away from it"? He would get laughed at, and his warning would go unheeded. Who paid attention to the instincts of a child?

It was Bitsy McCall on the road to the house, taking her time walking the mile and a half. She hadn't been feeling well enough lately to come down and take a look at it. But Cindy had stopped in after school today to play with the kids and told her it was finished. And tonight you just better bet she had to get out of her shack for a while or go bugsies. The kids had all fallen asleep finally, two of them on the twin mattreses scrounged from the town dump on the east side of town.

She didn't know what she'd do if it weren't for George Neeley who ran the dump. George kept an eye out for things she might need and had even delivered some of the stuff like the ratty old stove in the middle of the night. She knew what was coming, of course. George was old and wrinkled and had a wife and a dozen grandkids. His wife was a dried-up old thing, and lately George had mentioned once or twice how he liked his women fleshy. About the next time he found her a useful item, she would have to pay. Oh well. If she kept her blouse over her head and pictured some of the goings-on in her love magazines, she could get through it.

Bitsy needed something for her limited imagination tonight. The woods scared her, but she didn't have to go into them to see the house. She never did much walking, day or otherwise. But tonight she felt crampy and the walking would help. Bring this damn period she'd been skipping on. Show her she'd just had the flu on and off the past few weeks.

Since she'd first seen the house, she'd thought a lot about it, about how if things had turned out different in life it might be hers. Was it her fault she'd been born a McCall with a drifty father? How come some people got borned into palaces, and she got the pits?

And that crap they fed little kids in fairy tales. All about Prince Charmings coming along to rescue the cinder-covered princesses. It didn't happen that way. The princes had peckers—they hadn't put *that* in the fairy tales. Or how the princesses would get all hot and worked up so that nothing would help them out of their misery but that selfsame pecker. It made her sick right now to think how much she needed Gary's. And him off shoving it into Lord knew how many women, leaving her to get on welfare.

Well, anyway, his hadn't trapped her this time. She felt sure the cramps meant a period, and a good walk would help bring that on. Mama had taught her that.

The house had seemed a natural destination. This way she wouldn't have to run into Miss Penny, who, she knew, hung out at the house. Miss Penny couldn't face her with the question she loved so much—that being, "When are you going to get yourself fixed?"

The road Bitsy took curved, so that she had to round a small bend and was nearly on the house before she could really see it. Then she stopped still, struck with awe.

It looked twice as big at night. And twice as white. In a place like that Rapzel—Rapunnel?—had let down her hair. It was the closest thing Bitsy had ever seen to a castle.

Enchanted, she found a rise of grassy ground and sat down. Never mind that the woods behind the house would frighten her if she gave them a chance. Or that some bog mist still hovered around the bushes in there. The house held her full attention.

"Hello," she said.

In his bedroom, Bobbie Topin tried very hard to fall asleep. But the fact that someone walked out there on the road near the house disturbed him. A memory of the sensed shadow in the house kept drifting through his mind. He struggled for the better part of a half hour. "I won't go out there again," he whispered through clenched lips. He kept his eyes tightly closed, willing himself to sleep. But the shadow stirred on.

"It's just a house. There's nothing wrong with it. You're just like Grandpop. You don't like change. A bunch of kids will probably move into a house that size and they'll be stuck up and look down on everybody, and nothing will be the same in town again."

Good talking. Keep it up.

On the other hand, maybe they would be good people. Maybe they'd look out around for charities and see Cindy's foot and pay to get it fixed so that this town would stop treating her like somebody who owed it constant thanks. If Cindy lived to be a hundred, she'd never get them paid up for their big favor.

Soon the mystery would be over, and he could stop thinking about the house. Once it got people in it, Bobbie knew he wouldn't feel the same about it. Silly, to think a house could be bad.

Now where the heck did that thought come from? We're supposed to be talking ourself to sleep. Don't think about the house.

Houses couldn't be evil. Only people could be evil. Yeah? Then what about the house in *The Haunting of Hill House*? Hadn't it eaten up that crazy lady?

That was fiction.

How about the hotel in that book *The Shining* you got for a quarter at the thrift store last year?

Fiction, fiction, fiction, stupid. You're going to have to quit reading that stuff.

"It's only entertainment," he said to himself.

Bobbie got up and looked out the window.

Bitsy McCall's mood had changed. "I hate them! I hate them all!" She rose from her grassy knoll and stared from the depths of her blackness at the house. God stank. What kind of God would let her get born into a family of no-goods? No-goods all of them. Did they ever come around to see was she okay? Fuck no. They'd all headed out for other parts years ago leaving her stuck with Mama. And then Mama died, copping out on the whole thing. And what was *she* supposed to do? Ignore the need that warm arms filled for her? She knew people talked about her. She knew people called her a tramp. If she ever got hold of Gary again, she'd hack that thing right off his body. Five kids. *Five*. And her never wanting any.

Oh, she knew about the pill. She'd tried to take it. But it made her boobs twice as big as they already were, made them huge, sore weights to carry around. Besides, she never could remember to take the pills. She'd tried other things, too, that the county lady over to Gloaming had given her. Silly little things. Got your hands all messy trying to get them inside right, and Gary shouting all the time, "Hurry up, hurry up for crap sake. I'm losing it."

Five kids. Five years and under. All snotty-nosed, whining. Sick all the time. Winter was coming on. She had a heater in the shack, but it wouldn't do much good when the snow and the winds came. There wouldn't be enough to eat; there never was, not even with the food stamps Mr. Pender, the grocer, took with a sneer on his face. She ought to just start walking tonight. Keep on walking.

And leave them all here? All the snotty-nosed little McCall kids, stretching out the line forever? Sure, leave them behind. They had to grow up and have more McCall kids so the town would always have somebody to snivel at.

Bitsy stared at the house. She glared and blinked once or twice. Now, why did she seem to have a funny memory of her hand turning a doorknob, of a door opening easily? She'd wandered off in her head daydreaming a while ago was all. All the soft, enticing pinkness of walls was in her mind. If she had a torch, she'd burn the house down. Who did they think they were, coming in here and building a thing that size? It was bad enough before. Now there'd be a whole passel of new people to look down on the McCalls.

McCall. Filthy, ugly name. Did the McCalls ever own anything like this? Shit no. The McCalls lived in a shack with newspaper stuffed in the cracks and no hot water heater. The McCalls had grown up on the wrong side of the tracks, and kids made fun of them while they were growing up. Soon the oldest of her own crew would be in school. It would be the same thing all over again that she'd had to face. People snubbing you because your shoes had holes. Nobody ever inviting you to a birthday party, and what difference did it make: You wouldn't have a quarter for a present anyway. Oh, yeah, there was one thing different. There had still been other poor people on the south side back then. At least you had someone to play with, even if the rest of the town thought you were a pile of dog crap. Worse. Dog crap they could clean up; the south side folks they couldn't get rid of. Oh, they tried. They tried with nasty looks and tipped up noses, and the teachers tried, acting like you were too dumb to be in school. And eventually it worked.

Everybody else got out. Even all the McCalls. Only Bitsy remained. And her crew, of course. Her bunch of chains around her neck.

Wonder if she got free of them. Wonder if they had never happened. She could be in some other town, now that Mama was dead. No, not town. City. Big City. Where nobody knew who she was. She could find a job as a waitress and go to beauty school and open her own place and meet a man who kept his pecker clean. Wouldn't that be something. Wonder could it happen.

Why not? Why not just keep walking.

She turned away from the house that had got her started on this kind of thinking. It was because it made her see everything she wasn't, everything she could never be. Because she'd been borned a McCall.

Well, we'd see about that. Keep on walking.

Bobbie managed to doze off at last. But he didn't sleep easy. Someone kept laughing in his sleep, and he didn't like the tone.

Bitsy skirted the town on the dirt road, unmindful of the woods or the night sounds inside them. But then suddenly her feet seemed to take on a will of their own. "This isn't the way out of town," she told them. But she kept on walking. In time, so totally caught up in her black thoughts she didn't realize where she had been heading, she stopped and looked around.

Outside the cemetery bushes? Jesus Holy God. She didn't want to be in the cemetery tonight. Maybe she had come to say good-bye to Mama? She stood under a tree and lit one of the cigarettes she had ripped off from an introductory case Mr. Amway had on the counter in his pharmacy. She had gone there to spend good money on some Rolaids to help her nausea and had had a pretty good foraging trip. She wasn't as good as Gary, but she'd done okay. Managed to get a new confession up under her skirt and two packs of cigarettes. She didn't like them—lowest in tar, they said. But they'd been the best she could do.

She stared at the cigarette and thought about the Rolaids. They hadn't done her stomach any good. It wasn't an ache anyway. It was the kind of heartburn she always got when she was pregnant, the kind that often brought hot, burning puke into her throat so that she went around with a bad taste in her mouth.

The bath hadn't done her any good either. Or the walk. She realized that, staring at the glowing tip of her cigarette. What the walk had done was get rid of the crampy feeling. She didn't feel anything warm and welcome oozing down her legs.

That's because you're p.g. and you know it. It was blow up the balloon time, here comes that tramp Bitsy McCall again, putting another mouth on welfare; time for the "something ought to be dones." "Someone ought to get a court order and stermalize—steerlize?—her." She knew what they said. Miss Penny always kept her mouth going loud enough for Bitsy to hear.

Fuck Miss Penny. No, that was a laugh. Probably no one ever had, had ever wanted to.

"Hello, Mama," Bitsy said on the cool night air. "You started it all." She didn't realize she had moved inside the cemetery. She came out of a funny daze kneeling on her mother's grave, slashing at it with a sharp rock she didn't remember picking up.

"Fuck you, Mama," she sobbed, and began tearing at the loosened dirt with her hands, throwing it everywhere, getting it all over herself. Grave dirt? You didn't want grave dirt on you! She stood up, swiping wildly at herself, trying to get the grave dirt off.

Well, what was wrong with grave dirt, she asked herself? There was going to be a whole lot more of it being dug real soon.

She started walking again. Passed the last glowing remains of a cigarette she couldn't recall throwing away. The night came and went in her head.

Somebody had to stop it someplace. Pull the rug out from the town. Maybe it couldn't survive without the McCall Clan to kick around. Maybe she'd found a way to destroy the whole town. People couldn't get by without somebody to look down on.

If the McCalls were gone, there would only be the house and the new people there looking down on *them*. Bitsy smiled at her own logic.

Keep on walking, something hissed in the back of her mind.

I will, I will. There's something I have to do first.
No, you don't want to do that. You want to keep on walking.
I said I will, damnit.
But Bitsy.
But Bitsy.
But Bitsy.

She stood outside the shack a long time. Maybe she should go in and look at them. But no, then she might talk herself out of her plan. Get a look at the littlest's curly blond hair. That got her sometimes, in spite of everything. She mustn't look at her, at any of them.

This was for the best. In time, when she had her own beauty parlor and a house like the one in Pellam Woods, all this would be behind her. She would always know she had done the right thing.

Sure wasn't right to let the poor little passel of babies

come up in this town. And as long as she had them, they were all trapped here. On her own, she could make it.

They would understand. Sometime, someday when they were all together in Heaven, the babies, as Cindy called them, would all gather 'round their mama with their little angel wings blowing, and they would say, "Thank you, Mama, it's been so much better here." She was really doing them a favor, you see.

It wasn't hard to get the thing started. A torch made of some of the newspapers stuffing the cracks served very well. Then she just went around lighting the other newspapers long ago ground into the sides of the walls. Fray them a little, they flared right up.

The ancient wood caught almost immediately. And the whole place took.

Good-bye, babies. Good-bye, McCalls.

Start walking. Keep on walking.

It would have been all right if one of them hadn't waked up and started screaming. She hadn't counted on that. They were supposed to just go off in their sleep.

Bitsy stood uncertainly in the glow of the flames. Which one was it? She'd better go see.

At the last minute, she realized what she had really wanted to do: burn down the house in Pellam Woods.

Oh, well, couldn't think about that now. Tomorrow was another day.

The heavy pounding on their front door woke Cindy from a sound sleep. Experience had taught her to come down carefully on the bad foot even when startled, so that she got out of bed gingerly, grabbed her bathrobe and hopped for the door. Her parents were just stirring themselves in their bedroom, mumbling a series of sleepy, "Whuzzits?" Cindy opened the door.

Mr. Kroger from the post office stood there in his volunteer fire outfit. "Tell your dad we need him," he shouted. "The McCall place is on fire."

Her father had stumbled into the living room and heard that. "Be right with you," he called.

"Bring your own car, Clyde," Ed Kroger said. "Got to get on down there."

The McCall place? Bitsy McCall's place? The place *where the babies lived*?

Frantically, Cindy ran for the bedroom, forgetting to favor the foot, and was dressed before her father. "What are you doing in your clothes?" her mother demanded when she raced back for the living room. Her mother hung onto her bedroom doorjamb, half asleep.

"I've got to go down there, too, Mama," Cindy cried.

"Down where?" Her mother yawned widely, laying her forehead against the woodwork.

"To the McCall house. With Daddy."

"Don't be ghoulish," her mother said. "You can see the flames from here if you want to. But only sick people chase fires for the kick." She threw a pointed look at her husband rushing through the living room in his slicker and hat.

"But you don't understand," Cindy cried. She ran after her father. "Take me, too!" she cried. "Somebody might be hurt."

"Since when," her mother slurred, "were you going to grow up and be a nurse? Get back to bed, Cindy, and stop being silly." She turned back into her room.

"Daddy?" Cindy chased him out to the driveway. But his frown said she'd better get back inside. She stood helplessly on the sidewalk a moment. "Cindy!" Her mother's bedroom was on the front side of the house.

"I'm coming."

She stood for a moment on the sidewalk, staring off toward the glow on the south side of town. Terror for the babies choked her. What if they were in there? "Cindy!"

She went inside the house. It wouldn't do any good to tell her mother she had been visiting Bitsy' sometimes. And it wasn't her mother's anger that upset her. It simply wouldn't do any good. Nobody was going to let her go down there.

"It will mean a spanking," she told herself.

So okay. It had almost been a pleasure when her parents finally got over treating her like a case of high explosives and her mother took to smacking her again now and then.

"Leave the bathroom light on for your father," her mother said sleepily.

"I will."

Cindy turned off the other lights her father had flipped on, making a show of stomping noisily through the house. Then she shut her bedroom door loudly as she went inside. And in another moment she was out the window, crawling on her hands and knees under her parents' room, and on her way down the street.

Tears burned in her throat and eyes. "Please don't let anything hurt the babies," she found herself saying over and over. What had happened? Had Bitsy fallen asleep with a cigarette? Maybe she'd lit that ugly old heating stove. But it wasn't that cold tonight, and Bitsy was scared of that heater; she only used it when she had to.

She hadn't gone more than a block when her foot started paining. And she had a long way to go. It would all be over when she got there, and who would save the babies if the babies needed saving? She had the awful feeling the town wouldn't strain itself.

"You going to the fire, too?"

Cindy turned her head sideways. Augustine Gordon was sliding along the curb on his bike. Cindy let out a "yes" on a sob.

"It's exciting, isn't it? Fire?" Augustine said. He went on by.

"Wait!" Cindy cried. "Can you give me a ride?"

He braked, let one foot slide along the curb. A car sped by them on the way to the fire. "I don't know," he said. "I've never carried anybody before."

"Please," she moaned. "I've got to see if the babies are okay."

"I guess you could ride on the back rack," he said. "You're pretty big. If I put you up front, I won't be able to see."

Good grief, did he have to figure it out scientifically? "Okay, get on," he said after a careful testing of the rack. "But hold on tight. I get going pretty fast sometimes."

It felt strange to have the little girl riding on the back of his bike, her arms around his waist. Sort of a heady feeling, it gave him. Of power. He could feel part of her pressing against his behind, and that made him feel stranger yet. Uncomfortable. But pleasant in a way. Pulie pedaled for all he was worth, faster than he had ever pedaled before. Till they were like their own wind.

Cindy, terrified at their speed, could hear the panting of his breath, could feel his stomach muscles heaving as he drove his legs up and down. She closed her eyes. If they crashed, they were both done for.

Don't think about it. Don't think about the babies.

The babies would be all right. God wouldn't wipe out a whole family of babies.

Two blocks from the fire, Pulie finally began to slow. Cindy opened her eyes and saw that the flames had died. Huge cinders floated in the air, drifting to the street beside them. But they weren't glowing. The smell of burnt wet wood hung on the night.

Bitsy's shack was the only one left in the next block. All the others that used to dot the south side had long ago been torn down. Good thing, people said later. Or they might have had a major fire catastrophe on their hands.

They got as close as they could to the smouldering pile that had been Bitsy's place. Cars and the old secondhand fire engine the town had bought from Gloaming lined the streets. The volunteer firemen still raced about. Cindy saw Doc Jannessey's car out of the corner of her eye. Good. If any of the babies had gotten burned, he was there to help them.

Pulie braked the bike so abruptly the two of them nearly catapulted off. Cindy got herself righted and climbed down. Her legs felt stiff and sore, and her chest hurt from holding her breath against the expected crash. But she ignored all that and raced toward the ruins.

She could have at least thanked me, Pulie thought. That was hard work. He watched her run, her gait unsteady; he was mesmerized by the way the body that had been pressing against his only moments before moved. Cindy Newman would be a woman soon. When she got her new foot, she'd be a good-looking one, too. In time. Pulie turned his attention to what was left of the McCall place. What a shame he hadn't heard all the commotion sooner. He did like fire, but he hardly ever got a chance to watch one in Edgar Falls; only the occasional summer brush ones. Now and then he toyed with the idea of starting one himself, but he didn't have the guts.

"Where are they?" Cindy shouted to no one in particular. "Where are the babies?"

"Stay back, kid," one of the men ordered. Then he took a look at her. "Cindy Newman, what are you doing down here? You'll get your hide tanned." It was Mr. Pender, the grocer. He had his fire helmet in one hand and was running the other across his bald head, smearing it with black soot.

"Where are the babies?" Cindy yelled.

"You mean the McCall kids?"

Cindy wanted to haul off and kick him with the heavy special shoe for his denseness.

"They're bringing them out now."

What? What!

"Doc sent for an amblians over to Gloaming. But it won't do any good. They've all had it. Nothin' could survive that. Bitsy's alive but won't be long."

Cindy stood still a long moment. All her insides had stopped functioning. Only her ears worked, and they were filling up with a scream. It was some time before she realized it was her own, or that Mr. Pender, uncomprehending, had nevertheless caught her in a bear grip and wouldn't let her go.

"They're not dead," she shrieked. "Not the babies."

But they were bringing them out, like he'd said. One by one the volunteer firemen came picking their way out of the smoking ruin. One by one they laid a small burden down on the ground. Lined them up.

Doc Jannessey hurried over there. It was like a movie going on in front of her eyes. She didn't believe any of it.

One, two, three, four, five, she counted, all the time unaware she fought and scratched and kicked at Mr. Pender. He was no match for her animal fury, and he let her go suddenly, so that she pitched forward and fell on the ground and then scrambled the rest of the way on her hands and knees.

One, two, three, four, five.

"Cindy!" That was her father's voice, full of anger. "You get the hell over to my car, young lady," he shouted. "What do you think you're doing down here?"

Cindy raised her eyes. Her father stared at the soot-covered face, at the wild, crazed look in it, and actually backed off a step. "I liked to come and play with them," she said in a flat voice. "Nobody knew. Mamma wouldn't let me. This is Gary Junior, and Allie and Jakie and Carmen, and that little one's Pammy." All lined up in a row they were. Cindy got to her feet.

Funny little black babies. My, it was going to take some scrubbing to get them clean. About the only baths they ever got were the ones she gave them. They hated cold water, and Bitsy never cared whether they were clean or not. Cindy certainly had her work cut out for her. It would take an hour to get Pammy's gold hair clean alone.

"Cin?" her father said in a voice gone suddenly soft. "Come away, honey."

Cindy looked around. She couldn't see the bathtub in the pile of black rubble. What should she use? Maybe she should get a bar of soap and take them all down to Amy Semple MacPherson Pond. She had to go and find Bitsy and ask where the soap was. She hoped she had some. Bitsy stole a lot of things but never anything useful.

Her father tried to take her hand, but she pulled it away from him. "Where's Bitsy?" she demanded.

"Cin—"

"I have to see her. I have to ask her something," she screamed.

Clyde Newman pointed.

Doc Jannessey had gone back to where Bitsy lay on the ground. In the distance, a siren wailed. "Ambulance coming," someone said.

Cindy walked sedately to where the mound of flesh lay. "What do you think happened?" someone was saying.

"Heater maybe," came the answer. "Electrical fire?"

"Hello, Bitsy," Cindy said. "The babies are awfully dirty tonight. I thought maybe I'd take them down to . . ." Her voice faltered. She stared at the girl with the gouged, black flesh. Underneath, pink oozy splotches showed. Bitsy didn't seem to have any clothes on. For goodness sake. Bitsy maybe didn't have much of what the town called morals — she'd told Cindy that often. But she was modest; she didn't just go around any old place naked. "Cover her up," she ordered her father, who had followed her and stood helplessly above her. He looked at Doc Jannessey. Doc shrugged. Clyde Newman took off his fire coat and laid it across the girl. It would mean buying a new one. He'd never wear *that* again. Maybe she should be buried in it.

Cindy leaned over Bitsy. "I need some soap," she said. And then turned her head and looked bewilderedly back toward the babies. One, two, three, four, five.

Something was wrong here. Panic started to rise. "Soap," she said again, unsteadily.

"Cindy."

The voice coming out of Bitsy McCall belonged to some alien being, not a human. "Cindy, the house."

Cindy looked at her father and blinked. "Please," he pleaded. "Cin, come *on*. Come away."

Cindy looked back at Bitsy. Funny. Bitsy didn't seem to have any eyes. It was hard to talk to someone without any eyes.

"The house," Bitsy said. "The house, the house, the house . . ."

This time Cindy took her father's hand. He led her away from there. But not before Cindy Newman had asked Doc Jannessey to stop by his place on his way home and give Cindy a sedative.

That person was screaming again. Cindy wished she would shut up. The sound hurt her ears, threatened to burst her head. "Tell her to shut up," she told her father. "There isn't anything she can do. They're all dead."

Chapter Four

Something awful lurched down White Oak Avenue. Behind it snaked a length of dirty winding cloth, and the stench of the thing's tomb-centuries fouled the air. "Look out, look out," someone cried. "It's coming."

At the main entrance to the town of Edgar Falls suddenly rose a black-robed figure, arms outstretched, clawed fingers convulsing. A high, winged collar embraced a face the color of bleached bone. The eyes were piercing, blacker than the night and shiny and darting as those on a rat scavenging in a pile of dump garbage. A hissing sound poured from its throat, passing through a mouth the color of blood, and slowly the slick lips parted and exposed the dripping fangs that carried eternal damnation. "Go back, go back," someone cried. "In the name of the Father, the Son, and the Holy Ghost, get out of Edgar Falls."

In the woods on the south side of town, something prowled through the bushes, snuffling and growling. And the one voice that knew it cried out, "Oh, please. Leave us in peace."

While out of a bog spot, a creature hideous as all the others rose slowly, shaking its massive head, and stood there oozing mud. The bolt that held the massive head in place gleamed in a ray of moonlight. It looked about puzzledly, wondering in the dim piece of criminal brain who had summoned it from sleep. And finding no answer here, it began to move toward the town. While the voice of the one person awake in all this place began to mew and whimper with terror.

The thing on White Oak Avenue, hearing the others coming, stopped and turned to wait for them. Now they were all in the town itself. They met in the center and stared upon each other with recognition and respect. Then, one by one they smiled and began to advance on the houses. While the knowing voice whimpered on and on.

But wait! There was still another. Something white stood on the edge of town. It was only a house at first, built of odd angles and minute twistings. But then a gigantic mouth gaped open where its door should be. The teeth were like those you could buy in a trick store, and they chattered and giggled insanely as the house stood on massive legs and began to lumber into the town.

The others heard it coming and paused at the doorways they had reached. Excitement tremored through them. Because the greatest of them all was coming to join the night's frolic. "Soul-Eater," they whispered with joy. Soul-Eater was coming. What a night this would be. All of them together! All of them no human had ever been able to destroy. They were untouchable. Eternal. And if they were conquered for a while, they had only to hide and then rise again. Again and again.

The owner of the one small voice saw Soul-Eater coming, and he screamed and screamed, until the chords in his throat ruptured, and blood poured out of his lips. And still he screamed, only no one heard. The town slept on beneath the pale full moon and, staring out on it, the owner of the voice knew with abject simplicity what he had to do.

He alone held knowledge. He alone must stand against them. And in that truth he saw his doom.

But the one with knowledge always had to go. So he went to another room in his house and drew out a small item from a jewel-clasped box. He went to his front door, opened it, and stood there sobbing a long moment before he moved into the night.

Bobbie Topin came awake with a moan. Swiftly, he flicked on his bedlamp and then lay there blinking rapidly, his heart beating with such swiftness it felt as though it would burst from his chest. "Oh, jeez," he whispered. "It was only a dream." From the living room came the sound of his grandfather's comforting snore.

But he couldn't shake its effects. He lay there, drenched in sweat, trying to calm his trembling body enough to let him get up and go into the kitchen to make some hot cocoa.

When he could finally manage, he got out of bed and set feet that felt like jelly on the floor. The first thing he did was pull his shade. And then he went tottering into the kitchen, where he pulled those shades, too, and then made himself the cocoa.

For the first time in his life, he regretted the one great love he'd always had in reading. He'd gotten it from his mother who always said horror movies were the best kind of escape you could have. "It's good to scare yourself with unreal things," she had said. She'd called it something, a—a catharsis. She'd explained that that meant a draining off of other fears more real, like fear of war or fear of starving or fear of dying.

They used to read the books together sometimes, curled up before the fire, her voice sometimes silly as she tried to imitate whatever monster they shared that night. And they saw every horror movie that came their way. It was maybe the single thing Bobbie missed about her most. He could see her eyes now, widened as she read of a vampire advancing on its victim. When he was very little, she used to turn out all the lights when a good one came on TV. And then she would cuddle him next to her, and the two of them would shiver together with delight.

Bobbie, sitting at the table with his cocoa mug in his hands, summoned that image now. It comforted him. "Wow," he said to himself after a while. "All of them at once. And a new one I made up." That was pretty wild dreaming. He'd really thrown himself into it; his throat hurt. With the warm liquid in his stomach, he could even smile at himself. Mom would have loved that dream. She'd be jealous.

Something scraped against the kitchen door, and in spite of his humor, Bobbie started. But then his grandfather lurched sleepily into the room. "What's going on, boy?" he grunted. "You woke me up."

"I'm going back to bed now, Grandpop," Bobbie said and stood. He bumped against the table, and when he heard a muffled little clunk, he absently stuck his hand in his pajama pants' pocket, wondering what he had put in there.

Puzzled, he drew out the tiny gold cross on a chain, one of several his mother had owned that her mother had given her.

How had it gotten in his pocket? Some weekend mornings he cleaned house in his pajamas. He must have come across it sometime. He tried hard to remember. Maybe it had fallen to the floor one of those times he pulled out Mom's old jewel box to fondle her little prizes. He would replace it before he went back to bed. Or, on second thought, maybe he'd start carrying it around. So he wouldn't forget Mom, he told himself.

In vain, Lobarth Peters waited for further news on the house. More and more he took to driving out that way, telling himself he had supplies to buy in Gloaming. The house stood near the old road that had been hacked out of the southwest woods years ago as a shortcut to that other town. In truth, the supplies could be found at Loman's Department Store, but Lobe told himself things were cheaper in Gloaming; thus he had a legitimate reason to pass by the house.

Keeping a proprietary eye on it, too, he told himself, since he'd been the first, in effect, to know about it.

Now and then someone else sat out there in one of the meadows now turned entirely to gold. Those days Lobe just waved and kept on driving. But there were times he had the view all to himself. And he would brake his old pickup and sit in a state bordering melancholy as he looked at it.

The house had brought some excitement into Lobe's life for a while. Made everybody sit up and take notice of him and his paper. Now, even though people were still curious, time had taken some of the excitement out of it. Folks had problems, more lately than usual. There was talk of shutting down Ace altogether.

Oh, he'd had other stories lately. The fire had filled space. But when he'd tried to get town reaction, nobody had much to say. People felt bad, they admitted, about those children dying. But Bitsy McCall shouldn't have had them all in the first place. She should have pulled herself up by the bootstraps years ago and risen out of the muck being a McCall represented.

Nobody had managed to contact any of her relatives. Any addresses she might have had had burned up in the house. So the county paid to bury the family out by

Bitsy's mother. A few people like Miss Penny DuJong showed up at the short graveside service where Reverend Botts of the Great Day Baptist Church said a few words about the will of God sometimes being an enigma to man.

Lobe went. And gathered another little tidbit. Helman Schwartz, who took care of the cemetery, stood by to fill in the huge grave (three of the children resting in one adult-sized casket, the two larger ones in another, and Bitsy in her own). He drew Lobe aside when the handful of people started to leave.

"Don't know if it's related to Bitsy or not," he said. "But something weird went on out here the other night. I've smoothed it all over now, but somebody made a mess out of Bitsy's mother's grave. Had a hole hacked half across it. Now who'd do a thing like that? A grave robber would've picked on somebody maybe wearin' something valuable. Whoever it was smoked Carltons, that's all I know."

The story had been worth a couple of inches in *The Daily Way*, that was all.

The only other thing that happened in connection with the fire was that the day after he printed the story, Cindy Newman rushed into *The Daily Way*.

Lobe was standing at his counter, looking over an ad layout, when Cindy burst through the door. "Why don't you watch your print better?" she shouted at him. "You got the 'e' and the 'l' mixed up in baby Pammy's name. And Bitsy had a real name—Pauline!"

For a second Lobe had stared into a pair of eyes that glistened with madness. Then the girl was gone, leaving Lobe to wonder what the hell brought that on.

The fire story died. Nothing else came along. Lobe's thoughts always returned to the house, but he had run out of ideas to keep it alive. Something else needed to happen. A month had gone by and not a sign of the owners. It was like reading a book you were fascinated with, only to find when you got near the end that somebody had ripped out the last few pages. Lobe had an unsettled feeling about it all.

Sometimes he pondered the house's importance to him. The mystery book he'd tried to start never got off the ground. He simply wasn't a fiction writer. He'd toyed with the idea of writing up the house story, submitting it maybe to the *Post Dispatch* since the workman was from St. Louis. But when he got to thinking about it, it didn't even make good enough copy outside Edgar Falls to steal. No one else would see what a great advent this had been in Lobe's quiet town.

Lobe thought about that a lot these days, about how quiet — even dull — Edgar Falls was. The old restlessness had come back; the feeling that had made him sign into the service years ago to get a taste of the world. But the world hadn't seemed much different from this place, and he'd come home. He'd brought a wife and lost her now, gone off to find out who she really was. "A city woman," Lucy called herself. He missed her sometimes, but she hadn't really filled his needs.

Lobe really had only one need in his life, and all his dreams fed it. To be somebody. To have people say admiringly as he passed by, "There goes a man with power."

Hadn't happened. Would it ever now?

He sat out by the house one mid-October afternoon and practically prayed to it. He hadn't lost the odd feeling that there was more story here, and if it would just reveal itself to him he'd feel better about himself.

A kind of panic got hold of him. "I'll be forty-eight next month," he said. The thought brought a rush of unreality to his head. "Forty-eight, and where have you gotten?" Nowhere.

On the downhill run. No, not run. Stumble. Life was a good three-quarters over. And the years ahead full of bleakness and failure.

Lobe looked at the house and smiled grimly at himself. Lord, this was what it was all about, was it? What all his dreams had been for? Not wars or exposing Watergate or going underground with the mafia? It had all led pitifully to sitting on an old road waiting for something to happen with a *house*? Jesus H. Christ.

The house stood unconcerned beneath a pile of storm-threatening clouds. Lobe drove back to *The Daily Way*, too defeated to even continue on his business to Gloaming; he could not, in fact, remember what he'd started out to do.

The storm came rolling and crashing into Edgar Falls, signaling the official end of summer. When it was over, Halloween was only a few days away, and the weather had turned nippy.

Bobbie Topin faced Halloween with a faltering heart.

"Man, you must have been crazy," he ranted at himself all the way home that day after he'd agreed to spend it with some guys at school.

But it wasn't craziness; he knew he only wanted to be friends.

He stopped at Blainey's Meat Market to get some chopped steak for him and Grandpop — it was practically the only kind of meat the old man could chew anymore — and carried on a running dialogue in his head while he waited for his turn.

"You said you'd never go out to the house at night

again."

"I know. But they *asked*."

"They asked in the swoop of victory. Because you won the spelling bee today for the boys' side of the room."

"I don't care *why* they asked. It's the first time anybody's asked me to go anywhere. Maybe they're starting to like me."

"So go on out there, stupid. Go visit old Soul-Eater. Maybe it'll gobble your dumb head up."

Standing in the normal activity of the meat store while a couple of women vied to get the last of some lamb chops on sale, Bobbie told himself this whole conversation was pretty silly. "You've known all along you'd have to go back sooner or later," he said. "Just to prove to yourself it's all dumb." Better to go when you had companionship. Joey Hetherington, Mike Bottoms, and Craig Jorgenson were the ones who'd asked him. They planned to sneak out about eleven-thirty, after the trick-or-treating was over, and meet at Amy Semple MacPherson Pond. Then hike on over to the house.

"Why the house?" Bobbie had asked when they'd invited him to go along.

"Because you got to play some kind of trick on Halloween. Nobody's ever been in the house before. Nobody'll know but us, but it'll be fun. Everybody in town's been dyin' to see the inside, so it'll be a good trick to play on them we're in there first."

Bobbie didn't really see much point to it.

"Besides, it's spooky. Ain't you noticed? Look out your window some night, you'll see." That had been Craig Jorgenson doing all the talking.

Bobbie had perked up at that. And he'd felt a small touch of relief. So he wasn't the only one who reacted to the house that way.

But after a few more moments of conversation he realized that the other guys didn't mean much of what they were saying. They were just trying to whip themselves up to some Halloween enthusiasm. After all, in a year or two they'd be too old to celebrate their favorite holiday. They had to build this house thing into something big.

He wondered what they'd think if he added his two cents about the house. Well, he had no intention of letting them know. Somehow he would get his feet inside there for a couple of minutes. He had somebody to spend Halloween with, and he was willing to pay a high price for that.

As if being asked to trick-or-treat weren't great enough, Grandpop was in one of his alert spells when Bobbie got in from school. Actually puttering with a broken kitchen cabinet drawer Bobbie hadn't gotten around to fixing. "What say, boy?" he muttered.

"I say I got me some guys to trick-or-treat with," Bobbie came back with a touch of his eagerness poking at the corners of his mouth.

His grandfather took shaky aim at a nail with a small hammer. Hit it. "Hey! You did it, Grandpop," Bobbie exclaimed happily.

" 'Course I did it." The old man turned around with a question in watery blue eyes.

"Of course you did," Bobbie said. Grandpop didn't realize he had moods. He just came and went in them with hardly a blink. It had been better lately; Bobbie thought maybe it was the cooler weather. Or maybe that darn zinc was just slow working; he hadn't give up there. Whatever — Bobbie grinned at him. "I brought some chopped steak for supper," he said. "I'll fry it up early."

Grandpop nodded and turned back to his drawer to run fingers over it. "Got to sand this down and varnish it someday," he remarked. "Chipped a hole."

Bobbie went to stand beside him. "Hardly any."

The old man looked down at him. "Trick-or-treating you say?" he asked. "You'll be out late?"

"Well, listen," Bobbie said quickly. "I don't have to go." Maybe Grandpop liked Halloween as much as Mom had. The guys would understand, wouldn't they? Ask him somewhere else?

"Halloween is for addleheads," Grandpop said. And then one of his rare smiles flitted across the long-boned face. "But I wouldn't," he said "pass up one of them penny Hersheys if you brung one home."

Bobbie didn't tell him there was no such thing as penny candy anymore. "Maybe I'll get you a big one," he said with his happiness now spreading from ear to ear. He was going out after all. Man. He had buddies to trick-or-treat with. And Grandpop was in the best spirits he'd seen since spring. Maybe the good mood would last this time.

At six o'clock, Bobbie left his house carrying a gunnysack and Grandpop's little can of shoeblack. He turned on the TV first to a comedy show and left the old man dozing in his chair. No need to worry about handing out treats; no one would come out this far tonight except the little Letkins kids from up the road, and he'd gone over there before dinner and left off a small bag of his lunch potato chips for each of them. Looking at the two-year-old, he remembered that she'd been born the only one alive of triplets. He wondered if that would affect her someday.

The night was clear as Bobbie set off. He didn't look over toward the house. Time enough for that later. For now, he just let himself churn with excitement. At long last he must have proved himself enough; the kids wanted more of his company. And on Halloween.

The couple of Halloweens before last year here in Edgar Falls, he'd spent with Mom, reading ghost stories to each other and eating popcorn. Maybe he hadn't had anyone to go out in the night with, but his mother was great company. Last year, with her gone, he hadn't done anything. Now he had three buddies to trick-or-treat with, and he'd thought himself too old for this kind of eagerness.

"So you're Bobbie Topin," Mr. Bottoms said when Bobbie stopped by there first. "Enjoyed your letter last summer."

Bobbie roared with laughter when he went to Mike's room, and they climbed into their costumes. They were wearing exactly the same things: gunnysacks. And they blacked each other's faces. Mike looked great with his blond hair sticking up over his smeared face, and the two of them went off to meet the others, punching each other with glee, half expecting Craig and Joey to be wearing the same thing.

But Craig was in an old coat of his father's that dragged along the ground—and a monster mask. They all fell apart at Joey's. His mother had him dressed in one of her dresses. He had an old fox fur draped around his neck with the little fox mouth biting onto the tail, and beady eyes and dangling feet. She had teased a gold wig down around his face and painted huge lips on him.

"How do you like my new daughter?" Mrs. Hetherington asked. But they were laughing too hard to answer. Man, what a night it was going to be.

And what a night it was. Bobbie wasn't particularly

fond of sweets, but Grandpop liked them. By nine o'clock, he had enough in his sack to keep the old man supplied until Christmas. Wonder of wonders, there was actually a Hershey he'd traded Craig a Baby Ruth for.

They had a lot of good laughs, the four of them, charging up to porches ahead of gangs of little kids, shouting, "Trick-or-treat!" Joey kept falling over his dress, and they were forever hauling him off the ground, till finally he took it off and looked twice as silly charging up to doors in his own clothes with the fox fur and the wig and the lipstick still on.

Now and then the good time they were having overwhelmed them, and the four of them would get into a wrestling match on somebody's lawn and roll around and punch each other, making the most of each other and the night.

Bobbie got in some good jokes, and on the rare occasion when a homeowner insisted they do some kind of act before they got their treats, Bobbie took the starring role, doing a Charlie Chaplin pantomime. "Hey, you're good!" Mike exclaimed each time it happened. And he was. A couple of people gave them extra bags saved for special trick-or-treaters.

That night for the first time Bobbie Topin felt he belonged in Edgar Falls. So he wasn't even concerned about the house as he finally headed for home. "See you at the pond," he said to each of his buddies as they parted company.

It wasn't any kind of trepidation that kept Bobbie from looking at the house as he trooped on home alone. He simply wasn't thinking about it. He'd filled up with the joy of the night, and there was more yet to come. He didn't think beyond the fact he would be meeting the guys later.

He passed the Letkins's home and went on into his

own. Grandpop was awake, still alert, looking at some kind of Olympic documentary on their old black-and-white TV.

Bobbie called him into the kitchen and dumped his loot on the table. Some of the stuff was chewy, and Grandpop wouldn't be able to eat it. But he opened the Hershey and started on it immediately, then selected himself out some candy kisses and took the other candy bars Bobbie pressed on him.

"You have a good time, boy?"

"The best," Bobbie said. And Grandpop rubbed his grandson's head with his hard knuckles and went back to the TV.

Bobbie sat for a long time staring at the empty doorway leading into the rest of the house. His head smarted from the knuckle rub but he didn't mind. Grandpop was in rare good spirits tonight. Often, whole days passed with the old man saying little of anything to his grandson, even when the going-away-in-his-head mood wasn't on him. Those times made Bobbie wonder if Grandpop was thinking what a bum deal life had given him, slipping him a kid in his old age. No welcome had ever been issued, but Bobbie told himself that didn't hurt. It was enough Grandpop had let him stay when he could have set him to an orphanage. If there was never anything much outside the far-apart smiles that resembled affection, Bobbie could live with that.

Still—his stinging head felt good. He smiled to himself and looked at the stove clock.

A wind had risen so that the normally placid pond rippled with waves. Bobbie arrived first at their agreed-on place and stood on the bank looking back at the town. Only a few lights still burned; Edgar Falls was an early-to-bed place. The piece of moon illuminated the tops of bending trees, and except for the hum of wind and the gentle slapping of the pond, all was peaceful.

Bobbie's insides weren't quite as peaceful as everything else. The last hour, after the excitement of the trick-or-treating and the pleasure over Grandpop's condition had subsided a little, his mind had insisted on reminding him that he didn't like the house. The thought came back to him now.

"Don't have to like it," he said. "Just have to survive it."

Fidgeting from one foot to the other, he waited for the rest of them. Twenty minutes went by. What if they weren't coming? Or what if they'd gone without him? They wouldn't do that, would they? Tonight had been really good. It wasn't going to get spoiled now, was it?

But in another moment, he saw three shadows approaching. The shadows jumped and tore around in a little clump, and Bobbie could hear their laughter now that they were out of hearing range of the town. A momentary pang of loneliness hit him. These guys had grown up together, were inseparable. Could he ever really be part of them?

Craig had spotted him. He came rushing up to deliver a mock punch to Bobbie's midsection, the moon coloring his hair to cooked carrots. In a moment, they were all pummeling Bobbie, and the loneliness faded. They went off together, giggling and punching and falling down in the meadow grass as they cut toward the house. Long ago there had been a lot of farms out this way. But then the factory had come to town and you could make better money there. Some of the old-time farmers still owned the land, but they were retired and had let it go back to nature. The autumn grass felt good as you crunched along in it, and it smelled sweet when it clung to your clothes.

Craig carried a small back pack full of tools hanging from a strap down his back. "Somethin' in this little old sack'll get us in," he said. He grinned conspiratorially at Bobbie. Excitement ran high, and if there was a certain slight nervousness in their silly laugher, nobody mentioned it to another.

They reached the dirt road that led to the house. They could see the gables now, and Bobbie ordered himself to cut out the silliness when his heart skipped a couple of beats. "Just a house, just a house," he told himself. He looked around at his buddies and grinned suddenly. Their eyes had begun to cast uneasy glances at the woods that now skirted the road. Off inside, something cried out—just bird sound. But Bobbie saw the others stiffen and realized the woods at night unsettled them.

"We could save a few yards cutting through here," he said, digging it to them a little—maybe for the couple of years they hadn't seen his sterling qualities as a buddy.

A small silence. "Shit, we don't wanna do that," Mike said finally. "We'd come up on the side, and we want a good view of the house." Good thinking, Bobbie applauded him.

In a moment they rounded the bend, and all stopped as if on signal. The house waited a few hundred yards from them.

Serene beneath the moon.

For a moment no one spoke. Then Joey said, "How old do you think it is?"

"Hundred years maybe?" Mike speculated.

Bobbie hadn't thought about that too hard before. Now he stared at the stone foundation. Why did he suddenly get the feeling the house was a whole lot older than Mike had suggested? As if it had stood like this for as long as there had been a moon to glisten under.

"You think anybody's ever going to move in?" That from Joey again. "My mom says if somebody doesn't soon, Miss Penny's going to go berserk and break down the door. Says Miss Penny wants to get into that house so bad she just about pees in her pants."

"What makes you think Miss Penny wears pants?" Craig said. They all giggled. And went silent again.

"Be a good joke on Miss Penny if we got in there first," Mike mumbled at last.

"Good joke." They all repeated the words and let them die out.

The wind whistled around through the trees beyond the house for a while. "Well," someone said eventually.

Well.

Craig pulled his bag around to the front of his body and held it against his stomach a minute. "Let's get it over with," he said.

The order brought an explosion of laughter.

"Not so loud," Craig said giggling. "Don't let the house know we're comin'." Bobbie glanced at him sharply, but it was just meant for cleverness.

They moved a few steps nearer. Stopped to contemplate it again. "What's that iron fence for I've always wondered?" Craig demanded. "Rich people keep dogs on their roofs, do you think?"

This brought another round of laughter. "Just for show probably," Bobbie said. They had come close enough now that the house seemed to tower above them. Looking it over, Bobbie felt the old uneasiness moving through him. Had something heard them coming? Was it stirring inside there now?

All of a sudden something stark moved through him. He couldn't go in there. He couldn't. *Damn*. His insides had begun to shake. It was all up. They would see his trembling in a second and know he was a coward, and goody-bye buddies.

He thought fast, sucked in a deep breath. "Listen, you guys go in," he said.

"Without you?" They all turned on him suddenly, making him uncomfortable with their questioning eyes.

"I got something to do first," he said, his brain racing wildly and groping for something. Anything. "I've got some rabbit traps set in the woods, and I want to check them out. Only take me a few minutes. Hey, you guys could come with me, and then we could all go in the house together?"

That was a stroke of brilliance. Joey visibly backed off a step, and Bobbie breathed an inward sigh of relief. There had been the small chance they would call his bluff—he didn't have any rabbit traps. If he had, they wouldn't be near *here*. But his pell-melling brain had counted on the other boys being more afraid of the woods than the house.

"What do you have to check your dumb traps tonight for for crap sakes?" Craid demanded.

"Grandpop's been sick, and I haven't been able to get over to this part of the woods lately." The lie made his mouth taste bad, but it was meant to save his future. "If I got any rabbits, I don't want them rotting in the woods."

They were all staring at him. "You knew we were coming out here," Mike said. "How come you didn't just check your traps earlier and meet us here?"

He didn't like what he heard in Bottoms's voice. They all waited. He understood what their silence was telling him.

Damn. A stupid old house. He saw it all clearly—the years ahead—facing the looks in their eyes. It would be worse than before when they had merely ignored him a lot of the time. He thought of the trick-or-treating, saw them rolling and giggling and having a ball.

"We'll wait for you," Joey said. "Right here."

They were giving him a chance. But he heard himself say with a sinking voice, "No, you go on in. I'll check my traps and find you inside."

"Sure you will," Bottoms murmured.

Bobbie went sick in the pit of his stomach. He thought he saw them rib each other. "Forget it," Joey said. And then he hollered, "Charge!"

The three of them took off running for the porch. Bobbie stood in misery while Craig opened his bag, pulled something out, and tinkered with the door a second. *Wait a minute, I'm coming,* he wanted to shout. But couldn't; he didn't have any voice.

"Hey," Craig gasped. "It wasn't even locked!"

Bobbie's heart nearly stopped. He saw the black cavern yawn behind them. *Come on back,* he wanted to holler.

But he knew it would bring all their unspoken disgust pouring down on him. The massive door shut. Bobbie stood there, starting to shake hard, listening for sounds of them. But it was as if the house had swallowed them up.

He didn't know how long he stood there, still fighting with himself, his trembling fingers running absently along the handle of the flashlight hanging at his side. He had lost it *all* because he was a whining sissy. How come he couldn't just walk right up that porch and push open the door? But they'd be in distant parts of the house now; he'd have to go through it alone.

Or maybe they stood in a window staring out at him, jeering? "Man, we sure had old Topin figured wrong. Imagine him being scared of a silly old house. Look at him out there ready to piss."

Tears of fury clogged his throat. Yet he knew that

even if he mounted that porch, at the front door his feet would balk. He hated himself at that moment, really hated himself. But it didn't do any good.

Very slowly, he turned. The thought of the house looming behind him crawled up his spine. He thought he heard the house give a slight hum as he started walking, like a chorus tuning up for a song. The wind whistled around its corners, chilling him.

He kept on walking, trying to shake the thought that it was watching him. *Keep on going. Don't look back.* The shadow waited.

A sudden, piercing shriek nearly made him faint.

Involuntarily, Bobbie spun. It was Craig Jorgenson screaming. The boy had climbed over the iron railing of the roof fence that had intrigued him so much a few minutes ago. He was holding onto one of the spearlike rails, backpack drooping off his shoulders, swaying out over the lawn, a puppet dangling with the house for a backdrop.

"Craig!" Bobbie shouted through panic. "Get down from there."

"Hey, look at me," Craig hollered. "I'm a bird. Wheee!"

Bobbie stared in horror as Craig swung close to the roof and kicked out again; the wind whipped the carrot hair around his face.

Bobbie ran forward again, his eyes riveted. The moon showed the expression Jorgenson wore. Bobbie studied that expression a long second before he shook his head and began to shout again: "Get down! Get back on the roof. That thing may cave in." If Craig had picked on a section of roof over the porch, the porch might break his fall, but he hung out in space three stories up with nothing between him and the ground.

Oh, Jesus. Bobbie hovered there, uncertain, the terror out to grip him twice as hard. But something was wrong with Jorgenson up there, something the moon had shown.

Bobbie ran for the porch. Mounted it. Heard his footsteps like a crashing announcement that he was coming. He shoved hard at the door, holding a breath, expelled it on a frantic, "Joey! Mike! Get up to the roof. Jorgenson's gone crazy." No one answered him. Above him to his left, Craig whooped and hollered.

Bobbie stared into the black pit. "Hey, I'll bet I could fly home from here," Craig shouted gleefully. And Bobbie, because it was beyond him now, stepped swiftly through the door.

The house. He was alone in the house.

He thought he heard that hum again. Welcoming. He grabbed at the flashlight strapped at his waist. Did the hum increase?

Don't think! If he thought, he'd panic all the way and it would be screaming time for Robert Louis Topin. He had to get up to the roof. If he didn't, he had the awful feeling there would be one less kid in Edgar Falls. Shouting the names of the others, he managed to fight the flashlight loose with shaking fingers. The beam looked pitifully inadequate as it came on, and he took off running for the staircase he knew so well from weeks of construction watching, one which cut up through the middle of the house.

Wind sound—moving down the fireplaces. That's all the hum could be, right? Bobbie made the stairs on one breath and tore upward.

Wait a second. He spun back. Oh, jeez. Was that a shadow that slipped around that doorway back down there? He flashed the light on the stairs behind him. Something made a noise. "Joey?" His voice came out of a cavern.

"Mike?"

Nobody down there. Nothing.

The sound again. Like a snicker. From under the staircase. One of the guys—not knowing what was happening on the roof—trying to scare him? Well, he was succeeding.

"Cut it out," Bobbie cried.

Maybe he didn't have to go up. Maybe Jorgenson had already fallen, was lying bloody on the ground, and the other two boys would find him.

Would anyone ever find Bobbie Topin?

A million times in his life he'd told himself only one thing could really terrify you: the prospect of dying. Knowing it had happened to Mom had nearly driven him crazy for a while.

Now he thought there might be something worse. Maybe you could disappear and never be part of the things you had known. Maybe something that snickered obscenely in the dark could get you and put you someplace unspeakable, and you would be like those fun things he'd always read about—that couldn't die.

He had two choices. Go on and save Craig if he was still on the roof. Or retreat.

Bobbie turned again, let the light filter up ahead. A black pit waited at the head of the stairs. He shouldn't have stopped. He felt hung in space, trapped. Get moving. *Keep* moving.

He made the decision and began to cry, but he didn't know it, and started up again.

It hadn't gone away. He felt it on the stairs behind him, felt it like some slimy creature low to the ground that slipped and slithered up behind him, smirking to itself. Twice he whirled and splashed the darkness behind with light. There was nothing there. But he knew any second something slimy was going to close around his ankle.

Somehow he made it. Made it to a landing. Leaned against a wall, then jumped away.

Think. Christ, Topin, think.

Which way? Which way was the side of the house where Craig played his grim game? A new thought struck him. What if Craig wasn't up there at all—that the house had played a trick to get him in?

Don't stand here. Don't give it a chance to get hold of you. "A rolling stone gathers no slime," he mumbled softly to himself and heard a horrible, hysterical giggle; it was a moment before he realized it was his own.

The light flashed around. It was beginning to dim badly. Damn. Grandpop must have been using it to poke around the shed or something. Hurry, hurry. What would happen if it failed completely?

I said *don't think. It wants you to think.*

He turned to his left. Cast his failing beam up the next set of stairs. It made grotesque shadows out of the nothingness.

"Hey, boy, look at the whirlybird!"

Craig's voice coming down into the pit was a lifeline. Bobbie grabbed hold.

And he was running again. Up the stairs. Up another shorter flight. He heard Craig's voice going on and on: "Look at me, look at me!" He turned into a small room. Moonlight came through the open dormer window at the other side.

A kind of insane glee filled him. "You didn't get me," he shouted. "I've found him."

He ran for the dormer window.

The outside wall went down four feet below. Bobbie slid down it, keeping his eyes on the carrot hair. The boy still hung onto the railing, laughing and shouting. Bobbie reached the fence, saw out of the corner of his eye that the fence was heavily bolted into the small, porchlike ledge around the roof. Otherwise, Jorgenson would have been a goner from the beginning.

Bobbie looked down on his buddy. "Craig," he called. "Come on now. Game's over. Let me help you."

He half feared Craig wouldn't hear him. But as he peered down through the grating, the other boy stared up at him. "You want me to let go and fly?" he demanded. The blue eyes wore a crazed, impish look, the same look that had sent Bobbie into the house — was it only minutes ago?

"I know you could fly if you wanted to," Bobbie said. "So you don't have to prove it. Come on up. Let's get back to the other guys." All the time his voice came tumbling frantically out, he kept looking back over his shoulder. Any second he expected something to come at him.

"I could really do it," Craig said. Bobbie cast a swift look at the ground; the act made him dizzy.

"Some other time," he pleaded. "Look, I'm hungry, aren't you? Let's go back to my house and make some cocoa and eat some of that good Halloween candy."

"We had a great time tonight, didn't we?" Jorgenson's voice sounded like he'd been on a heavy binge down at the Brewery.

"Sure did," Bobbie said. "And we didn't get a chance to talk about it much either. Come on up. You can climb around the edge of the fence the same way you got down." The bolts on this part of the roof were creaking ominously. If Craig hung out there much longer, the whole thing would be out of Bobbie's hands to help. He wasn't even sure if the fence would hold when Craig began to try to climb back over it. He thought of inching his way out, but the double weight would send the thing crashing to the ground for sure. He had to get a grip on whatever sense Jorgenson had left.

"What if I can't fly?" Craig said suddenly.

Bobbie latched onto that. "Maybe you can't," he said. *Oh, Jesus, Craig, cut it out. Get up here so we can get away.* Shadows were moving in the house; he could feel them.

"Then I'd splat all over everything, wouldn't I?"

Bobbie stared at the ground again. It looked a hundred miles down.

"They'd be sorry, wouldn't they?" Craig said.

"The guys?" Bobbie said desperately.

"Pop and Bessie. Give them something else to think about instead of bitchin' at each other all the time."

"What are you talking about?" Bobbie demanded. "Come on up, Craig. You can tell me up here."

"All the time, all the time," Craig moaned. "Bitchin' and yellin' for crap sakes so you can't even sleep at night. It goes on and on and on. You get in bed with it and you get up with it. Mostly Bessie. If she hated his fucking guts, what'd they get married for?"

"Craig, please."

"If I splatted on down there, wouldn't have to listen to them anymore. Be the first chance I got to sleep in a long time."

Bobbie was close to tears again. "Please," he said.

Memory of the first ghost story his Mom had ever told him sneaked around on the edges of his mind. A little boy lay in an upstairs bedroom, and something was on the stairs.

"They wouldn't miss me."

"But I would. I like you. I've never had a buddy since I came to Edgar Falls."

"Then I'll come up." Just like that. Somehow Bobbie had struck the right button.

But the ordeal wasn't over. Jorgenson still had to climb back up and around that fence. And he had two spiked rails only a couple of feet apart to contend with.

He hung out there like a monkey for a moment. But he began to do it. Craig had always been better at acrobatics than anyone, even Bobbie. Now he deftly placed hand over hand. He hauled his body over the edge of the fence between the two railings, lay splayed out there a moment while the wind came whipping along suddenly.

Bobbie reached out a hand, bracing his feet on the small ledge. Craig took the hand and Bobbie felt his fingernail rake the palm of his own. Then Craig crouched beside him on the roof. "I could've did it," he said belligerently. "I could've took off like a big bird and flew home."

"Sure," Bobbie said. "But there are some things you don't have to prove to a buddy." He was close to sobs and was so weak, he held onto Craig more for his own benefit than the other boy's.

Jorgenson chattered incessantly as Bobbie held his wrist and literally dragged him swiftly back down the stairs. "Hey, man, I've wanted to do that ever since I saw the fence go up." His voice held a hysterical note, but Bobbie was too drained to pay much attention. He spoke, though, to keep from listening to the house. It had gone silent, the hum quieted, the stairwell sending his and Craig's sound out into empty space. The silence was more terrifying than the hum. "How come you and the other guys separated?"

" 'Count of you," Jorgenson said. He stopped a second, yanking Bobbie to a standstill, and flashed the light he'd pulled from his pack up behind them. Bobbie wondered what for but didn't ask. "What do you mean on account of me?"

"Well, shit, man, we knew you was scared. So was we but nobody showin' it. But then we got in here, and it was just a dumb old house, and I knew you'd hate yourself in the morning, and Bottoms and Hetherington, they ain't like me. Once a guys shows yellow they don't ever let him alone. I told 'em I was coming back to get you, and they said I was screwed, but I said I was goin' anyway so they said fuck off."

"So what happened?"

Bobbie started dragging Craig downward again. ("Well, well," the witch said archly. "What have we here? Two plump little darlings lost in the woods?")

"Remember that Ulysses stuff Miss Larimer read to us last week?" Craig said. "That old fence up there was like that sexy siren thing calling old Ulyss. I started out okay but then I thought, hey man, I'm alone, *alone*, in this house, and it was scary but fun, you know, and I could hear that fence callin', so up I went. I guess I forgot about you. Hey, you went in all by your lonesome," he declared suddenly. "That makes you one cool dude after all. I tried to tell 'em that. I said old Bob didn't want to come in, maybe he knows somethin' we don't know." Craig guffawed, his voice an octave too high. "Bottoms?" he shouted suddenly. "Joey?" Bobbie started violently.

They reached the bottom of the stairs, and Jorgenson jerked to a stop again and flashed his light around. "You wanna know something crazy?" he asked. "When we first come in, it felt like somethin' trying to get into my head."

Bobbie couldn't digest that. His whole being was bent on forcing a fascinated Jorgenson out of here. "Beat you to the door," he cried. Jorgenson giggled and accepted the challenge. He tore ahead of Bobbie.

It was all too easy. Something would happen there. They would find it barred to their frail strength. But it swung open easily—how *come*?—and they raced into the night air and slammed the door behind them. The wind whistled and blew around the pillars. Bobbie's relief was so great his knees buckled, and he had to lean against one.

"Funny," Jorgenson said. "I thought Mike and Joey'd be outside or they would've answered us."

"It's a big house," Bobbie said. He stared anxiously at the black window beside the door. Part of him wanted to bolt for home, but he wouldn't have had the energy anyway.

Where were they? Had it gotten *them*? Maybe the shadows could only deal with a couple of boys at once.

Then they heard a shout from the interior. And in a moment the front door flew open, and the two boys burst onto the porch. "Sheez," Bottoms said giggling. "I thought it had us there."

Joey Hetherington bounced around excitedly. "Mike wanted to look in the cellar for vampire coffins," he chattered. "The fucking door shut on us, and we couldn't get it open again."

They were nearly wild with excitement. "How'd you get out?" Craig cried. Their voices came and went like wind through Bobbie's head.

"Really weird," Mike said. "We poked around with Joey's switchblade and kicked the door a lot and nothing happened. We kept yelling for you, but I guess you must've been too far off. Then all of a sudden the knob turned and we got into the kitchen again. Guess we just didn't twist it right." He turned suddenly to Bobbie. *"He* ever go inside?" he demanded of Jorgenson.

"Inside and *alone*," Craig said pointedly. "Which is more than we can say for some people."

"Hey, all *right*," Bottoms exclaimed, and the two of them began to pummel Bobbie on the back. Craig didn't mention the fence, and Bobbie kept his mouth shut, too weak to speak if he'd wanted to.

"Well, I guess we did it all right," they said, congratulating themselves as they headed for home. Jorgenson didn't seem to remember Bobbie's cocoa offer, and Bobbie didn't mention it again. He only wanted to get home and get into his bed. He didn't even know if his feet would carry him all the way.

He felt drained and exhausted in a way he'd only felt once before — the day of Mom's small service before the furnace was to have her the way she'd always said she wanted it to be — when he wished he could just crawl into the coffin with her and fall asleep. His whole body felt dragged down, like he was hauling a couple of hundred pound weights.

He joined in the pummeling and the giggling that had changed to masterful laughs. No one mentioned his earlier reluctance to go into the house, and he knew he'd proven himself, but the victory just felt like a hollow ball in his chest. The scratch on his palm burned. Craig didn't once mention his acrobatic stunt, which seemed strange because in school Jorgenson bragged about his prowess, and if it hadn't been for the scratch, it might've all seemed a dream.

They came to a fork in the road, one section leading off to their homes, the other to Bobbie's. "We're gonna build a flatboat to take out on ASM Pond," Mike told Bobbie. "You want to help?"

"And a fort when the snow comes," Joey said.

"Yeah," Bobbie said. "I'd like that. Thanks."

"After all, you went into the house alone," Craig added. They gave him one last poke on the back, and the three of them took off down the road. The moon rode high above the woods in the distance.

Bobbie had what he wanted. He had buddies. All firmed up. Plans for next week. Plans for the winter.

He stood alone on the road for a moment, wondering what all this had cost him. He should have felt elated. He'd been *in* the house and gotten *out*. But what he felt was dread—like a mouse must feel knowing the cat can pounce when it chooses. Whatever waited in the house still waited, and tonight, he suspected, had only been a game.

He didn't look at the house as he started wearily trudging home. He tried to run for the safety of Grandpop's cottage but was unable to do more than will each foot to drag him on.

When the day of his grandfather's birthday celebration arrived a week after Halloween, Bobbie threw himself into it. For two reasons. One, he was losing Grandpop again. Halloween had been a highpoint. Moving into November, the old man had begun to go into that other world more often than before. He spoke often out of either some manufactured present or some long, distant past.

"You steal any more tacks, Herb, and you'll be wearin' a bunch in your asshole like piles." He said that once—maybe harking back to his carpet-laying days— in the middle of a normal conversation about shredding an old blanket to weatherproof windows.

The words didn't frighten Bobbie. It was the look Grandpop had fixed on him that disturbed him. It was a look that said the old man saw someone else and didn't like what he saw.

There was something else driving Bobbie, too. If Grandpop had mind shadows, so did his grandson. *It* rode with him constantly now. In school, a picture of the house got in the way of his concentration so that often Miss Larimer had to ruler-tap his knuckles to get his attention.

At night, Craig Jorgenson swung out over that balcony, wailing like a banshee, and Bobbie would wake up in a cold seat. That Jorgenson thing was a little odd, Bobbie thought a couple of times when he lay awake after the dream. The morning after Halloween, the other guys had wanted to huddle in the school yard, all sleepy-eyed though they were, and brag about their big feat. Joey Hetherington had asked for the first time what Craig and Bobbie had done the few minutes *they* were in the house.

Bobbie let Jorgenson take the lead, sure he wanted to recount the daring high-flying deed himself—which Bobbie really didn't care to relive. He didn't have to. Craig looked blank and murmured, "Jeez, I don't remember much. Must've got too excited." Bobbie eyed the blank expression, then shrugged. Jorgenson must have just realized his act had been stupid and nothing to gloat about. "We didn't do anything," Bobbie said quickly when the others turned to him. "We were just—uh—in."

Bobbie was letting Grandpop's birthday drive his mind onto something besides the house. He hadn't been able to distract himself by rowing out on Amy Semple MacPherson Pond with the other guys. On the morning they were to go out, he had gone into the kitchen to find Grandpop standing over the gas woodburning stove. He had a flaming match in his hand, and there was the smell of gas in the room.

Bobbie had halted in the doorway, mesmerized a second. The flame had burned down to his grandfather's fingers, and the old man just stood there staring at it.

"Grandpop!" Bobbie bellowed and tore across the room to smack at the match. He grabbed the old man's fingers and stared in shock at the redness there. He rushed to fill a glass with cold water. Plunging back to the old man, he remembered the stove and shut off the gas-smelling burner, then stuck the fingers into the glass. "Jeez, Grandpop," he moaned. "You could've blown us both up." The old man only stared at the glass blankly.

Bobbie hadn't given Craig and the other boys the true reason for not showing up at the pond. People already knew his grandfather was forgetful sometimes. But if they knew *how* far away he went, someone was liable to look up and notice Bobbie and think orphanage. He only said to the guys, "Grandpop isn't feeling well." They hadn't asked him anyplace else yet.

Bobbie spent more time near the old man now — except for errand time and school hours. He worried that he'd come home some afternoon to find the cottage gone and Grandpop burned up inside.

On this early November day of his grandfather's birthday, Bobbie didn't try to hide his party preparations. Grandpop was out in the back yard when he got up, poking around at some firewood Bobbie had chopped last week. Probably the pieces weren't cut right; the old man could get picky in his lucid moments. Bobbie didn't mind that. He suspected Grandpop had always been picky and this was normal.

But he didn't like the way the old man paused now and then to look off toward the house in Pellam Woods. Damn. It was bad enough when trees had been leaved and you could see only parts of the house. Now, in autumn, you could see the whole thing standing white and stark over there. White and stark and . . . Bobbie didn't permit himself to think the rest, or about how much it bothered him to have Grandpop staring at the place.

He made a cake. He'd bought a chocolate mix with a dollar skimped from the pension check grocery money. The old man never went into town anymore, and after Bobbie used his "Grandpop isn't too well sometimes" excuse, Banker Bergins had agreed to accept the monthly checks from Bobbie as long as he could coax Grandpop to put his scraggly scrawl on the back.

Bobbie had cashed one yesterday and taken out the grocery money, giving Grandpop the rest. It was a point of honor with Bobbie to wait till the old man got around to recalling his allowance. Though sometimes he did withhold utility money for payments Grandpop often forgot about.

He had icing, too, and candles. Not eighty though. Eighty would have cost too much. While the cake was baking, he blew up the balloons he'd found at the New Day Baptist Church Thrift Shop for a dime. Half of them weren't any good, but there were enough to festive up the cottage.

Grandpop wandered in while Bobbie was hanging the balloons. "We having a party, boy?" he demanded.

Bobbie grinned. Grandpop was with it this morning after all! "For you," he said.

"What for?"

"Grandpop, you're eighty today."

"Eighty?" The old man stared at him. "Eighty?" he said again. "You daft, boy? I got a year to go to make fifty." Grandpop went off to the bathroom to stand looking in the mirror. "Jesus Christ," Bobbie heard him say.

Cindy was due at one. But it was one-thirty now and no sign of her. Bobbie stood at the front window, staring up the road. The little Letkins kids played out there. One of them lifted a hand to him, and he waved back. Where was Cindy? She'd promised. She was the only one Bobbie'd invited. Cindy was safe. She was too preoccupied with the death of "the babies" to pay much attention to Grandpop if he went off in the head. Bobbie had invited her for her sake, too. Lately, Cindy had gone bleak; she needed a party. So where was she?

At three, Bobbie gave up on her. It was nearly time for Grandpop's daily nap, and who knew how he'd wake up? Sleep had a way of transferring him to that other world.

At three-fifteen, Bobbie coaxed the old man into his chair by the window. Then he went into the kitchen, fighting his disappointment that Cindy wasn't here to share.

"Happy Birthday to you," he sang, carrying the blazing cake into the living room.

"You made it all tipsided over, Vera," Grandpop said. Vera was Bobbie's grandmother.

Bobbie had to blow out the candles. Grandpop, who liked shiny things, stared at the Kennedy half dollars a while, then tucked them into a shirt pocket. He didn't say anything; he was slipping away again.

Bobbie, going a little desperate, hurried back to the kitchen to cut the cake. Three big pieces. Just in case Cindy showed after all. He put them on a tray and hurried back. Then he slowly lowered the tray onto an end table. The old man's chin had sagged. He was snoring.

Cindy found him on the front porch. The Letkins kids had been driven indoors by the cold, but he didn't notice it.

"I'm sorry I'm late," Cindy said. "I had something to do." Bobbie stared at her. Cindy was usually immaculate. Today she had smudges on her furry blue coat. She saw him regarding them and brushed quickly at herself.

"It's okay," he answered. "It wasn't much of a party."

"I can't stay," she said. "But I brought your grandfather a gift. Some chocolate cherries from Loman's.

You said he likes chocolate."

"He does." When he remembered what it was.

Cindy stood there uncertainly at his lack of response, the brightly wrapped box wavering in the dying sunlight. Bobbie reached up to take it and saw her eyes as he did. And forgot his own problems for a minute. "Cin, I'm sorry about the babies, too," he said. "But you got to quit brooding."

Tears brimmed suddenly into her eyes. "I know. But I just keep thinking maybe I could have done something."

"What?"

"I don't know. I can't talk about it now. I have to go. Mom'll be mad if it gets dark."

Bobbie rose from his step, not realizing what he was going to do. But he pulled her into his arms and patted her shoulder awkwardly, finding comfort from his attempt to give it.

She stood there a second, her hair against his cheek. Then she ran off down the road.

He stared after her. It was evening before he remembered he hadn't offered her any cake. About seven o'clock, he wrapped the whole thing in cellophane to give to the Letkins kids tomorrow.

Chapter Five

The week before Thanksgiving, electrifying news appeared in *The Daily Way*, so electrifying it appeared in an extra. Once again Lobe's office filled with questioners. Excitement spiraled up and down the street. "What is it?" "What does it mean?"

Lobe had a mock-up pinned to his wall behind the counter. "THE HOUSE IS YOURS," the headline read.

"Yours who?" Charlie Groves demanded. "Mine? Ed Kroger's? Miss Penny's? Whose?"

"I don't know yet," Lobe said. His skin glowed today. Life sparked his eyes. It had happened. By God, it had happened. He hadn't been deserted. Ms. Benedictine had come through, and he felt a rush of gratitude toward her.

It wasn't only the money, though the three hundred dollar cashier's check for the headline wasn't to be sneezed at. The house had somehow or other become the focus of Lobe's life, and even the rise in crime rate and sad events in the town of Edgar Falls hadn't preempted the importance the house held in his heart. Crime was on the upswing everywhere. Consequently, the fact that Loman's Department Store had to hire security men for the first time in its history was news. But not *news*. The house was *news*.

The Rainey boy. Lobe had given him a headline last week when he disappeared. Lobe had gotten some good pictures of the sheriff's men dragging Amy Semple MacPherson Pond and had had the good grace not to photograph the bedraggled body when the grappling hooks pulled it up. No point in upsetting the distraught parents, though there was some question as to whether they were as distraught as they appeared to be. People wondered how a retarded boy didn't always know to get himself to the toilet (although he'd made a valiant attempt once when his mother had brought him out to the house that was nearly finished. She'd let him wander off, and he'd gone in the back way and sat down on a toilet waiting to be installed. A workman found him and summoned his mother, who led him out stinking) could get up quietly in the middle of the night, dress, and wander several miles alone.

But these were only whisperings, and even though Lobe had his own suspicions, suspicions weren't news.

"I wanna know what that headline means!" Charlie said again. "Is there gonna be a contest? Some richbitch millionaire gonna donate the house to someone in town?"

"That's an interesting thought," Lobe said to the people who had set up a chorus behind Charlie. "But I don't know, folks. The note I got with the money says I'll hear something more soon."

"Why you?" That came from Miss Penny DuJong. It pained her greatly to have to come down from her sweets shop to get information from Lobe. But a desperate curiosity had overcome her reluctance.

Lobe shrugged and pushed the Ben Franklin glasses back on his nose. "No other reason than I own the paper," he said. Although it wasn't what he really felt.

He was beginning to feel chosen out — for some lofty mission he didn't yet understand.

If the week before Thanksgiving news was electrifying, the week after was stupefying. It didn't come out ahead in the paper because Lobe had no warning. On the last day of November, trucks began arriving again. The moment they were spotted, people bundled up against a possible storm and headed out to the woods.

Furniture! Miss Penny stood on a short knoll and watched with her heart in her throat. Oh, blessed Jesus, look at those loveseats. Real brocade, she'd lay her bottom dollar. Nobody made anything with that much craftmanship anymore.

"You could buy out Loman's with that mirror," she said. Stars had gotten in her soul, and they were burning right through it.

Whose was it all?

No one knew.

All they knew was that it looked like people were moving in at last. The old hope that they would be nice and not snooty floated around the crowd. But what about the headline. "THE HOUSE IS YOURS." Yours who? Yours mine?

"Look at that armoire," Miss Penny said with a groan.

Someone asked her what an armoire was, but she didn't hear. When the huge rollings she devised were tapestries went through, she broke down in tears because she couldn't watch them being hung. She was the only one in town who had a sense of how antiques should be displayed. Why, oh why, hadn't someone consulted her? What if she never got a chance to see the inside of the house when it was furnished? What if the people moving in there were so far above Edgar Fallsians you couldn't touch them with a twenty-foot ladder?

Life was cruel. Life was unfair.

On the first Tuesday in December, the mystery was solved—as much as it would ever be. In the morning, Banker/Mayor Bergins received a long distance call from St. Louis about which he said nothing until the town council convened that evening. Councilman Lobe Peters arrived early and almost dropped in shock when he saw the black Rolls parked outside the town hall. He nearly broke his neck getting inside, and sure enough, *she* sat in regal splendor in the front row. Lobe was too stunned to wonder where the faggy chauffeur had gone.

Banker Bergins was already there, and Davis Llewellyn, the council attorney, and Gorden Kristofferson, planning commissioner, all in earnest conversation with Ms. Benedictine, who wore something silver and sleek and a diamond bracelet on her arm.

Lobe sat there an indeterminate time with jealousy tearing at his heart, stood like a dog waiting to be called by his master in the form of Carl Bergins.

Ed Kroger, councilman, and Neal Blainey, the elected town clerk, came in. "Bingo!" Ed exclaimed. "What do you suppose she's up to? Says here on the agenda, first order of business."

"Agenda?" Lobe said blankly. "It's not on the one I got yesterday."

"Picked up a new one on the front desk when I saw the Rolls," Ed said. He stuck a pile of papers in front of Lobe's nose. There it was, before such important business as a complaint that Mrs. Lordstrum over on Kellogg Street was harboring stray dogs.

The Reverend Leonard Botts came in, followed by the other council member, Thaddeus Amway.

"Isn't that the colored lady connected with the

house?" Amway wanted to know. "What's she doing here?"

"Find out in a minute," Ed said. "Shut your mouth, Lobe. Somebody's gonna take you for a Venus Fly Trap, water your feet."

At seven on the dot, the council seated itself at the long table. Five townspeople had wandered in, and they too stared at Ms. Benedictine. By now, Lobe's insides churned in turmoil. Something big was about to happen; it crackled in the air.

Somehow Lobe got through the mayor's flag salute and Leonard Botts's prayer. Tonight it seemed to take Botts forever to thank the good Lord for the privilege of guiding the town. Lobe, beside him, wanted to kick him in the shins. He couldn't get his eyes off Ms. Benedictine sitting there serenely on a folding chair like some Egyptian goddess dropped among them.

Twenty thousand years later, Bergins opened the meeting. "First order of business," he said. "The house in Pellam Woods."

Afterward, Lobe could remember every word as if it had been struck in fire on his amazed brain. A museum? Ms. Benedictine explained it all in her soft, purry voice, pausing to answer questions. It was her hope, she said, that town fascination with the house would keep up with taxes. A small fee could be charged guests touring the house. But in the event that did not pull in enough money, she was turning over to Banker Bergins the moment the deed was signed fifty thousand dollars to be placed in trust for the house.

"What I am hoping to get from you tonight," she said, "is a commitment to the house. My employer, as I've told you — the donor of the house — wishes to retain the anonymity with which she (*she?* A *woman* had that kind of money?) undertook the rebuilding of the house. Therefore, all business transactions have been recorded in my name. But it is her wish, if you so will, that the house be deeded to Edgar Falls. And she insists that Lobarth Peters, your esteemed councilman and newspaper owner, be designated—shall we say curator? *If* he is willing to supervise the house tours and any maintenance work, though little should be required, I have for him a check for ten thousand dollars to cover said services. He is to be in full charge and the only set of duplicate keys is to be placed in a safety deposit box in Mr. Bergins's bank and removed only in the event something happens to the other keys or to, God forbid, Mr. Peters. Mr. Peters's integrity is known to us—and his interest in the house evidenced by the poetic words he has printed about it, all relayed to me by Mrs. Reege, our consultant here."

This time Lobe's chin made a permanent drop toward his chest. He stammered, "Jesus H. Christ, yes!" evoking a disapproving cluck from Leonard Botts.

"I don't understand this yet," Thaddeus Amway said, making Lobe want to kick him in a spot more vulnerable than a shin.

"Let me go over it again then," Ms. Benedictine said patiently. "My employer is a former resident of Edgar Falls. She feels that the town taught her everything she knows about life. She is a very wealthy woman now, thanks to the legacy of her dead husband, and she wanted to show her appreciation to the town by sending it a gift, a gift of something she has loved."

"A house that's worth a fortune?" Amway practically snorted.

"To you," she said. "In point of fact, it has hardly depleted her resources."

They all went silent a moment, even Carl Bergins trying to fathom that kind of money.

"My employer may seem to have strange whims to

you, but she wanted the town to have something fine and beautiful as a lasting memorial to her childhood years here. A museum, if you please."

"Why didn't she come to us first?" Ed Kroger demanded incredulously.

"Two reasons. One, she was afraid you would suspect her motives and deny her offer. Once the house was built, she hoped you would accept it. The mystery, the headlines, all of that is just a whimsical game she played to pique interest in her beloved offering. If the town had not been intrigued, she would not have continued her project. But your interest has quite satisfied her joy in her game. The second and most important reason is that she wanted her gift anonymous."

"So how come we can't know who she is now?" Ed exclaimed.

Ms. Benedictine turned liquid eyes on him. "The greatest gifts should only be known to God alone." To which Leonard Botts added a pious amen, and Ed Kroger had no reply.

Banker Bergins turned a saccharine smile on Ms. Benedictine. "Thank you," he said. "The subject is now open for discussion."

Everyone except Lobe burst out with something. He barely heard Ed's, "Come on now. There's a catch here somewheres. Sure Edgar Falls is a great town, but how far can gratitude go?"

Thaddeus Amway, whose small, oval-shaped face that was as smooth as a baby's above a creped neck, narrowed his eyes suspiciously and made an exclamation similar to Ed's. The Reverend Botts suggested that the money spent on the house might have fed a lot of hungry Indian or African children.

Banker Bergins let the words bounce around him for a moment. Then he said, "If I may be so bold, gentlemen. The house could hold blessings for us in these trying times. It's already helped folks throughout a bad summer. Everyone loves it. Think what it could do for town morale, knowing we own it. There isn't a house that fine for a hundred miles. And the only museum is that dinky natural history thing that weird teacher started in Gloaming."

"Shit," Ed Kroger said with a snort. "You just got no account that big in your bank. You wanta get your hands on that fifty thousand."

Bergins sat back with such an expression of aggravation the budding jowls he detested smoothed out. "Your language is out of order, Councilman Kroger," he said.

Lobe swam out of a fog into the middle of the bickering. "We've *got* to accept the house," he said.

"Got's a big word," Thaddeus Amway murmured and flinched. He wasn't used to opening his mouth much on council. "Something doesn't sit right. Nobody, but *nobody*, gives away something like that. There's a hitch."

"So be specific," Carl Bergins, still miffed, said. "Maybe it's a little unusual. And maybe rich people do these things." He remembered that to the town *he* was rich and added, "In fact, I'm sure they do these things."

Lobe wasn't certain he understood how the conversation was going. All he knew was a desperation so fierce his gut ached with it. Curator of the house. Jesus H. God. "The house is already there," he blurted. "What do you want our mysterious benefactor to do? Haul it down again? That is a beautiful piece of property out there. It's —"

"Showoff," Ed Kroger muttered. "You was that way in high school, Lobe Peters. Always got a swelled head acting as if you'd be coming to big things. You want the house because you'd be in charge. Give him that kind of power," he said to the rest of the council table, "and there won't be any living around him."

"Gentlemen," Leonard Botts broke in. "Let's remain friends, please."

"Take the house!" someone shouted suddenly from the audience. Carl Bergins banged his gavel. "The floor isn't open to public discussion, Mrs. Lordstrum." He turned to the two dissenters and Leonard Botts, who except for his starving children remark had remained noncommittal. "I don't think the motive of Ms. Benedictine's employer is really in question. Now let's look at the facts. The facts are that Ms. Benedictine arrived tonight with the deed to the house already in hand, made out to the town of Edgar Falls, and she has another paper that says we agree to let the house become a museum. Think, for God's sake — excuse me, Leonard. Ms. Benedictine has mentioned tours, but a lot more could be done with the house. Club meetings could be held there. Social events. We could charge a fee, and it would help out the city coffers." He glanced out at the audience to see if Ms. Benedictine had any objections, but she gave him a nod of encouragement. "People would come from all over to hold the events. The Moose Lodge hasn't had the money to rebuild since the fire last year. We could advertise our fine old mansion, bring in outside money — make it a show place."

He stopped a moment to light a cigarette, an act forbidden in council chambers, but nobody said anything. "Think what it could mean. Think! People come from a hundred miles away to hold an event in the house, we'll have to build a hotel. Tourists'll come, and there'll be money in everybody's pockets."

Thaddeus Amway rallied somewhat to that. Business had been falling off lately what with Ace in so much trouble. But another feeling took precedence.

"We've got by all these years without depending on outsiders," he said. "Don't need any strangers coming in now. They'll just bring trouble."

"Jesus H. Christ!" Lobe exploded. "You sure you weren't out on that road the day the cow got Cindy Newman? I think it stomped your head."

You won't get anywhere bullying, Amway wanted to say, but Lobe looked ready to attack. Instead he said, "We can't decide anything this big in one session. This needs lots of discussion. Weeks maybe."

"Gentlemen . . ." Incredible how the soft voice managed to silence them all. Lobe looked to the front row, hoping salvation had come. "Gentlemen, if I may intrude . . ."

"Please," Bergins said.

"This weekend my employer leaves for Europe. She's instructed me to say that she wants the house matter settled before then."

"I can't vote on this tonight," Kroger said stubbornly. "We need more facts. I don't like taking on something we don't know anything about. I don't see why we can't know where the house comes from for one thing."

"Is that important?" Bergins was starting to lose his temper. "If a kind lady wants to keep a little mystery about her gift, what the hell is that to us? The deed is in order. No liens, no problems. the house is clearly in the name of Jewelline Benedictine, and therefore she has the right to turn it over to us. Now for Christ sake get off the stick!"

"You piss me off, Carl," Ed Kroger shot in, "always thinking you know what's right."

"I think," Leonard Botts said in horror, "we had better adjourn to executive session." Lobe glanced at him with deep apprehension. The preacher looked on the verge of declaring that the devil had his hand in something that caused this much dissension.

"Don't need executive session," Kroger said. "I need time to think over all the angles."

"Me too," Thaddeus Amway said.

Lobe saw his dream drifting out of touch of his fingertips. Guardian of the house. His calling. Keys were power, weren't they? He wanted to cry.

Carl Bergins pulled himself together. "What *will* you do with the house if we don't accept it, Ms. Benedictine?"

"Board it up," she said sadly. "Tell my employer the minds of Edgar Falls are too small to comprehend a gift of this magnitude. It's much too large for her to live in anymore, although she did once, and she will have no use for it. It will break her heart because it was meant as a monument to her gratitude to the people of her childhood."

Mrs. Lordstrum in the audience sniffled audibly. "I wanted to see the inside," she said. Lobe turned the same look on her he had cast on Ms. Benedictine a moment ago. Maybe Mrs. Lordstrum was a crazy old lady who hauled in stray animals and kept a house that smelled like a stockyard, but surely she spoke for the town.

But Ed Kroger had settled back with his arms folded obstinately. "I won't vote tonight," he said. "I got to think, and I got to sound out a few people. There's no time to put it to election."

"To say no money," Carl Bergins put in fiercely.

"I want to hear what folks say. Take a little poll."

"It will be an inconvenience, but I could return on Friday," Ms. Benedictine said. "If your answer is no, we will board the house on Saturday. And may I add, gentlemen, that the offer will not be made again. There will be no turning back. The furniture meant for the town's pleasure will be removed and put in storage, and we will break all contact with Edgar Falls."

Lobe's heart turned over as if he had just heard a close friend had dropped over dead. But something Ed Kroger had said had taken hold. "If you will excuse me," he said to Carl Bergins, "something I ate tonight didn't agree with me. I'm going to have to get home before I puke all over everybody." He cast a pointed look at Thaddeus Amway, who scooted his chair over until he bumped into Leonard Botts.

"Suppose we meet at two tomorrow," Banker Bergins said. "In my office. We're not going to get anywhere until we've slept on this."

While they got the formalities of adjourning out of the way, Ms. Benedictine slipped quietly out of the room. When Lobe walked purposefully toward his truck, the black limousine was already gone. He looked up the street it had vanished from, feeling suddenly lost. But he didn't have time to be standing around here indulging his feelings. He had work to do. Important work. The most important work of his whole career. His whole life! The white knight was going to charge into the fray with all his banners flying. He felt as if God himself had laid a hand on his shoulder, and he went forward with holy, if somewhat self-centered, purpose.

Damn them! Listen to them in their bedroom! Wouldn't they ever shut up? They'd been at it clear since supper. It all started over bean soup. Which tasted like the rest of Bessie's food: shitty. But it wasn't just the soup. Bessie grabbed onto any old excuse to bitch. It started when Pop remarked on the brown, burned things floating in his bowl. "I thought these was white beans, Bessie," he whined.

That was all she needed. "Goddamnit, Bert," she snapped. "You gimme enough money to buy a steak, I won't burn it." Huh. If they had enough money for steak, she'd burn it all right.

"Can I help it if they're cuttin' back at Ace?" Craig had glared at his father over the table. Why the fuck couldn't his old man talk to her without whining? It *wasn't* his fault they didn't have any money. Ace *was* in trouble. Pop was just a laborer out there, but even the bench casters, the cream, had got their hours sliced down. Besides, beans was okay. If they got cooked right.

"I want some steak," Bessie said. "And I want a new dress, Bert. I ain't had a new dress in ages." Bull. She'd bought a new dress for the Fourth of July picnic, a thing that fit her like somebody had wrapped her in it. Bessie had a good figure, even at forty, and she wanted people to look at it. Craig suspected what Bessie had been before his father met her at a Gloaming tavern five years ago.

But it wasn't her body that bugged the ass off him. It was the face that went with it. Always painted up like a clown's. And bitchy-mouthed.

"Shut up, Bessie," Pop said. He didn't say it with any force. "Shut up and go to sleep."

"What d'you mean shut up and go to sleep? I ain't finished talking yet. Bert, you got to think more about movin' into the city. You could get better work there. We could get us a nice little apartment. I could have some *things*, like you promised me when you talked me into gettin' married."

"Bessie, I don't know if that's a good idea. The boy's got problems enough in school. He's not the fastest. If we move someplace else, he might get worse off."

"The boy, the boy, the boy," Bessie said with a sneer. "That's all you think about. Why the hell did you marry me anyway, Bert? Why didn't you just stay the way you was, you and the boy?" She said boy like it was a dirty word. Bessie hated him; she made that clear enough. Though not as much as he hated her. Maybe he wasn't good in school, but he was good at hating.

Why *had* Pop married her? Craig and Pop had got on good enough before she come along. They'd had their fishing trips. And even a ballgame in the city sometimes when Pop was feelin' flush. Ace had been in good shape then. They'd had some fine times. Like the Fourth picnic when they won the father and son three-legged race out by the pond and got a trophy over there on the dresser now under all the awards papers teachers give him for athletics. They'd had TV and popcorn nights, and Pop had had his Moose Lodge meetings, and Craig had the guys. The guys'd never treated him like they did Topin. Sure, Craig's mother was dead, and that made him half a orphan, which wasn't a good thing to be. But he'd been born here, and his mother was buried out in the cemetery. Wasn't like with Topin's mother who'd been burned up in a box and tossed over some hills or something. Pop'd been born here, too. It made a difference.

Now why was he thinking of Topin? Maybe because the guy had been zapping off in his head in school so much lately? "Dreamy," Miss Larimer called him.

It was a weird trick Craig sometimes wished he could copy. Like tonight with Pop and Bessie at it. Except then the other guys might sit up and take notice and start leaving him out of things.

Craig sort of liked Bobbie Topin. For some reason, he felt as if he owed the "dreamer" something, only that was silly because what could it be? Sometimes he wanted to ask Topin to do things with him—maybe take a hike now and then. Find a hill to climb maybe. Craig liked that kind of stuff, and the other guys weren't always available; they had *real* families to do things with. Craig had to rely on buddies for entertainment, and even if Topin'd gone a little weird—like

Cindy but without Cindy's foot excuse—he'd be somebody to pal around with.

Wouldn't work, though. The friendship with Bottoms and Hetherington couldn't be risked. "Topin's coo coo birds," Mike Bottoms had said the other day. "Just like his granddad. You see his eyes sometimes? Don't know what's come over him, but he looks like he's lookin' at a ghost. Gives me the creeps." Since he'd gone weird, they didn't even bother with him much in school anymore. They'd forgotten about his guts the night of the house. Though Topin didn't seem to care. Well, maybe livin' with a old man who talked to himself and didn't make much sense when he talked to *you* made you strange.

Craig shifted his thoughts. Lying in his bed, he could see the mystery house. He could see Lobe Peters's office, too. The whole place was lit up. Something was goin' on over there. Prob'ly another headline. Lobe had gone ape over that house—like a squirrel that's had a hard winter and then nuts start fallin' from the sky.

Craig's eyes went back to the house. He started thinking about the night in there, and Bessie's complaining backed off some.

What had happened in that place? He didn't know. In fact, he didn't even remember much about it. There was a time, right after, when he thought he knew what'd gone on, but he'd lost it. He remembered going in. Remembered when they all looked out the window at Topin standing there lookin' like he needed to pee.

What happened after that had got all muddy now. Seemed like he'd felt good in there. Like *good*. Maybe like he used to feel last year when Gary Purdy was still in town and sold him some of them great pills that made you go all fuzzy-head and mellow inside. Like you didn't care if Bessie was a bitch and Pop whined.

Like time disappeared.

He seemed to have some memory of air all around him, of wind whipping his clothes. But that was silly. They'd shut the door. Wind couldn't've got into the house. All he really remembered was the great, floaty feeling.

Wait a minute. There'd been another. Like somebody had tried to get inside him? Man, Miss Larimer was always yakking at him he didn't have no imagination, but what was *this*? Somebody trying to get inside you. Fuck. Craig grinned at himself in the darkness.

Well, anyway. He more or less remembered Topin heading down some stairs with him. He thought maybe Topin had seemed all excited and shook about something. But all Craig felt at that point was some kind of weird thrill he couldn't explain now and didn't care to. The rest was gone. He knew about flashbacks. Gary'd told him about them. Said sometimes you didn't even need the pills; you could flash back on them all unexpected for free. That's all that happened in the house, and it must've been great. The flashback had blacked out a couple of minutes, that's all. Because he did recollect meeting the other guys out front.

He didn't remember anything about the house itself. So he looked at it now and tried to picture what it was like inside. That gave him another kind of good feeling. Maybe it was silly, but this imagination he didn't have got hold of that house sometimes. He liked to think about how it would be to live there. Bessie would have everything she wanted, and she wouldn't bitch all the time.

Wait a minute. He didn't like putting Bessie in that place with him and Pop.

What about Mom? What if she was alive and all three of them lived in there? Wouldn't that be something?

Thanksgiving. He pictured Thanksgiving. There was a dining room in there; he'd watched them build it. And in his mind, he suddenly saw his mother, looking like the brown-colored, only snap he had of her, coming down the steps in a white gown. He always saw his mother in white. That was maybe because she was buried in that color, and he had a tiny memory of her lying in her coffin. But he'd only been three, for chrissakes, when cancer got her fast, and maybe she wore white and maybe she didn't — it wasn't a question he ever wanted to throw at Pop. But it didn't make no difference. Picturing her in her burying color didn't bother him. White was more like angels wore, and his mother was surely an angel. She'd been a good woman, Pop had said, and she'd loved them both.

The beautiful woman in white came on down the stairs, smiling. She was always smiling. "Good afternoon, Bertram," she said in her soft, sweet voice. "Happy Thanksgiving, Craig Julian." In his thoughts, his mother always called them by their whole names.

"Happy Thanksgiving, Mom," he said. Then the maid brought in a wine bottle, and they all sat down at the table that had a lot of flowers on it, and the cook carted in their turkey.

"Shit, Bert!" Damnit. Bessie's voice shattered the picture into pieces. "Things are *not* gonna get better at Ace. They're goin' down the drain, Bert. Down one of their own toilets they make. Now you get busy and start thinkin' hard about a move."

Craig didn't want to move. He wanted to live in the house.

He strained his brain hard to get back Thanksgiving again. But Bessie's voice had gone really shrill now. She sounded like the witch in *The Wizard of Oz*. And she was crying.

Oh, Jesus. Bessie crying meant only one thing.

There was only one way Pop knew to shut her up. In a few minutes, Craig could hear their grunts and groans. Even when they made out, their bodies fought each other's. He clapped his hands over his ears and blocked out everything except his misery.

At eight-thirty the morning after the council meeting, a nearly paralyzed Lobe Peters perched on the high stool behind his counter and waited. Now we would see.

It didn't take long. Miss Penny charged in first, followed by half a dozen other women. "Darn, darn," she said archly. "Scooped again, Lobe, and it's my own fault. I shouldn't have stopped coming to the meetings, but you boys are usually so boring." She gave a high-pitched giggle. "What do you want me to do?"

"Do?" His head felt ready to split off. After all, printing and delivering in the pre-dawn hours a couple thousand handbills hadn't been a snap.

"About this handbill. You said we could come in and sign petitions, but that's not enough. We are all here to personally carry these petitions to every living soul in town."

Lobe managed a smile for Miss Penny. A surge of new blood coursed through him, and he leaped off his stool to grab a sheaf of papers. "We, the undersigned," they read, "do hereby beseech the town of Edgar Falls to accept the house in Pellam Woods."

"Am I the first to sign?" Miss Penny asked.

"You're it," he exclaimed, for the first time ever feeling a spark of liking for the old harridan.

She signed with a flourish.

"You know this may bring outsiders to town," he said, hating to add the one caution he realized could kill the whole thing.

But a fire that matched his own glowed in Miss

Penny's eyes. "I know," she said. "But it will still be mi — ours."

All morning people came in to sign the petitions. "Our very own," people said. "That's so much nicer than somebody we don't know moving in. Wonder who she is?" As always, Lobe tried to conjure up a picture of this mystery person. But a lot of people had left Edgar Falls over the years, and it wasn't important anyway. A thrill ran up his spine when Jane Helen Amway came darting in to sign. "I'll take care of Thaddeus," she said ominously.

Carl Bergins stopped by at eleven. "I'm not sure this is ethical, Lobe," he said.

"Ethical, schemethical." Lobe grinned. Carl Bergins grinned back.

Oh, there were dissenters. Charlie Groves came in and said, "Nuts, you mean there won't be any rich people moving in? Somebody who could've used their influence to help us out?" Charlie's business had been suffering lately as the Ace Sanitary Plumbing closed in on itself tighter and tighter. Contracts weren't coming; some actual layoffs had begun. People who needed repairs were letting them go. Things that had been a shade bit bad a few weeks ago had approached near disaster proportions now.

"Seems to me," Lobe said, "that it wasn't so long ago you were griping about some 'rich bitches' moving in to lord it over us."

Charlie ignored that. "Ain't gonna do anybody any good to have that place out there full of untouchables either," he ranted on. "You mark my word. Way crime's picking up in this town, they won't stay *un*touchables long."

"What good's having a place around here that's like a museum," someone else said, "when you don't know its history?"

But they were in such a decided minority, Lobe's hope mushroomed. Still, it would take a majority vote to swing acceptance of the house. He wasn't sure how much weight Jane Helen carried with Thaddeus (Jane Helen had on occasion appeared in town with dark glasses and puffy cheeks, and Ed and Lobe had speculated on whether their mild little pharmacist sometimes had his own method of dealing with her tongue). Ed could be stubborn as an old donkey and, friend or not, vindictive. In high school, Lobe had once stolen a girl from Ed, and Lobe suspected it still rankled. Leonard Botts remained a complete question mark subject to get off on a "there's something wicked in all that money wasted on a museum" kick. The Lord spoke to Leonard on occasion, and who knew what the Lord might choose to say regarding the house? An antsy Lobe Peters looked forward to this afternoon's meeting. All he knew for sure was that if the house wasn't accepted, he was in for a crash ugly to contemplate. They *had* to accept it, that was all.

The crowd had dwindled off by noon. Several more petitions had been taken out with Lobe's blessings, and he debated on closing up for an hour and running out to the house. Just to feel it in his bones a minute.

Then the door opened, and Bobbie Topin came in, glancing back over his shoulder. When he turned to Lobe, Lobe perceived the dark shadows under his eyes. "You come to sign a petition, Bob?" he asked. "You're a citizen of Edgar Falls, too."

The boy looked *bad*, and Lobe's humor went right over him. "You coming down with something, Bob?" Lobe asked. "And why aren't you in school?"

"It's lunchtime, Mr. Peters." Bobbie's voice had an impatient tilt to it. "Mr. Peters, you can't open the house up to people."

Lobe blinked. "What do you mean, *can't*? And watch the tone you use with your elders, son."

Bobbie looked around the office and swallowed a couple of times. When his voice came out again, it was so low Lobe had to bend over the counter to hear him. "There's something wrong about that house. Something bad. I can't explain it. I think you should find out where it came from."

"Come on, Bob," Lobe chortled. "A house can't have anything bad about it. It's got no character, no personality. It's just a thing."

"Don't say that," Bobbie whispered.

"For God's sake," Lobe exploded. "This is silliness. Next thing you'll be telling me the place is haunted."

"Haunted?" Bobbie said.

Lobe was feeling pretty impatient to get out of here. But this kid looked downright depressed. Whatever he was trying to say, *he* believed it, silly though it all sounded. "I'm on my way someplace," Lobe said. "How 'bout I give you money to go buy a cone? Make you get over weird notions."

"No, thanks," Bobbie said. For Christ sake, why did the kid keep glancing over his shoulder? "I promised Cindy I'd get back in time to play marbles with her."

Couldn't be too serious if the kid had marbles on his brain. Lobe shrugged.

"I saw your paper this morning," Bobbie said in a rush. "If you open the house up to people, something bad will happen. I don't know why, Mr. Peters. I only know it will. That house is malevolent."

"*Malevolent?*" Lobe said incredulously.

"Yes," Bobbie said.

"Wait a minute," Lobe exclaimed. "Don't I seem to remember running into you a few times over at Amway's, especially when your mom was alive, buying spook books? I think maybe you've read one too many,

Bob."

"Please," Bobbie cried. He looked near tears suddenly. "Please listen to me. I think maybe the house can hurt people if it wants to."

Lobe's patience was gone. Why the hell was he taking time with a mixed-up kid maligning the house anyway? "I've got an errand and a meeting," he said curtly. "And you'd better get back before the bell rings. I don't know what you're talking about, Bob." He was more than sure the boy was coming down with something—maybe something serious. Probably had a fever—look at those flushed cheeks—and it affected his thinking.

Well, what had he expected? That Lobe would understand? Who would? Hardly anybody listened to what a kid had to say, especially one who must sound like he'd gone yellow bananas. It had taken all his guts to approach Lobe Peters.

Bobbie walked into the bright, early December sun. There hadn't been a storm for a week now. But despite the brightness, there was a nip in the air that suggested maybe they'd get that rarity: snow for Christmas.

He listened to himself thinking about the weather. Strange. One part of his mind functioned normally. The other had turned to shadow, and dark things lurked there.

"What am I going to do?" he asked himself. If Lobe only made fun of him, the same reaction would come from others. "What do you have to go on?" they'd ask. And his answer would always have to be, "A feeling." He couldn't reveal what had happened Halloween night without getting the other guys in trouble. Besides, anybody could make bugs out of his story about Jorgenson hanging from that balcony. Craig himself would say it had all been good fun.

Did they put kids in cuckoo nests?

Where *did* he get the idea the house could harm people? From the little bit that had happened inside that night? The house hadn't hurt him — had only tried to scare him.

Sometimes he didn't know which was worse: him maybe being crazy and imagining things, or the house being what he was afraid it was. The sane part of his mind carried him back to the school yard where Cindy needed him. All Cindy's spark had disappeared; that had been more than plain on Grandpop's birthday. It helped Bobbie to try and help her, even if he had to trust Grandpop alone sometimes after school let out. But that wasn't a problem today. For the rest of their lunch hour, Cindy shot marbles listlessly. He had to work at it to let her win his double cat's eye.

A jubilant Lobe Peters took off for *The Daily Way* at three o'clock, reveling in memory of the brief meeting in Carl Bergins's office. He actually thought fondly of Miss Penny. God bless the old war horse. The fastest tongue in Edgar Falls had rallied her petitioners to forty strong, and they were waiting outside the bank when the council members began to arrive.

When Lobe stepped out of his pickup, they cheered wildly, and someone threw a faded rose at him. "Look at this, look at this," Miss Penny crowed. "Eleven hundred signatures. And that's just for starters."

Added to the hundred and forty-four Lobe had picked up in his office this morning, a pretty strong statement was about to be made to the town council. Ed Kroger and Thaddeus Amway got booed, and people stared sullenly at Reverend Botts when he arrived in his old Datsun.

It was over fairly fast. What it all boiled down to, Lobe figured, as he changed his mind about the office and decided to drive out for a victory look at the house, was that every councilman had to be elected by the people. Not one of them wanted to give up his position of power, not even Botts, who believed he could best serve God (he had proclaimed in campaign speeches) by having a say in town politics.

Lobe stifled a cry of triumph when the vote came five to nothing. "I guess a few outsiders can't hurt too much," Thaddeus Amway muttered as he cast his ballot.

All five of them went out to the walk together for the official announcement. Banker/Mayor Bergins gave a victory signal. The crowd, which had grown considerably, erupted in a violent surge of back-pounding and tears and shouts of, "Good boys, good boys."

Lobe waited for the furor to die down. "The house will open for the first tours this coming Saturday," he shouted, and you would have thought he had just brought a rain of gold down on the people.

Lobe's only fear now was that the mysterious rich former resident of Edgar Falls would change her mind. But Carl got the call from Ms. Benedictine at eleven A.M. on Friday. At eight o'clock in the evening Lobe held a cashier's check for ten thousand dollars to cover his future services to the house (all of which he would have offered free), and, more important, a ring of keys made of solid gold. The only duplicates were in a safety deposit box that could only be opened by full vote of council. The keys to the *house*. Jesus H. Christ.

He was so undone he felt like tearing outside to kiss the faggy chauffeur who'd been so rude to him. All he remembered later was the press of Ms. Benedictine's soft hand in his as they sealed their agreement, and he went out of the council chambers finally, so choked with emotion he couldn't stay and discuss a thing.

He drove straight to the house and sat there looking

at it shining in the moonlight. He felt a little foolish sitting there crying when he hadn't even cried when Lucy left. But then Lucy hadn't meant as much to him as the house did.

For some reason as he drove back to *The Daily Way* he remembered Bobbie Topin's visit. Probably because he didn't feel too well. He was sure it had to do with all the emotion and the hope and the fear, and he hadn't caught anything at all from Bobbie. Still—better go to bed to rest up before his house duties began. Funny that kid should have the weird notion there was anything wrong with the house. If ever Lobe had seen anything pure and good, it was that house. His house.

Thirty-six people toured the house that first Saturday, although more than that showed up at nine for the first tour. Lobe Peters decided, too arbitrarily some said, how many he could handle in a group: twelve. The rest he divided up and told to come back at two-and-a-half hour intervals. The last tour would start at two-thirty; others would have to return tomorrow.

Disgruntlement rumbled through the crowd. Unmistakable snow clouds hung on the horizon, and tomorrow might be out of the question.

Lobe noted the pending weather and decided to buy mats for the front porch, maybe plastic streamers to run through. He also decided to print up some tickets. You never knew who was going to get ideas about the house. This way he could screen in or out who bought. When a couple of scroungy teenagers toured that first day, he went downright uneasy for fear they might come back to vandalize the house. Maybe he should eventually plan to spend some nights out there—take a sleeping bag and a thermos since there wouldn't be any excuse to fire up the big furnaces just for himself.

Another thing. The house needed a name. Perhaps he would start a contest. Entrants could pay a dollar to make a suggestion. The money could go for Cindy's foot since the operation still ran a thousand short; what with the economic squeeze lately, people's interest had dwindled.

The evening after the first showing, Lobe walked over to the library and checked out all Alice Poling's books on antiques. Miss Penny had been in that first group; indeed, she had been waiting on the porch at seven when Lobe arrived to let himself have the first hallowed look at the house. Miss Penny had regaled the crowd with antique tidbits at every turn, and he couldn't have her knowing more than he did.

That night, poring over the books, something else Bobbie Topin had said came back to him—about how they should know where the house came from.

Lobe thought about that. There must be ways to track its history, maybe even the person who sent it here. Although, he reminded himself, his experience with a detective had proven that kind of thing intolerably expensive. "You could spend some of the ten thou," a little voice whispered to him, and he turned on it appalled. Use *her* money to go against her wishes? Come on! Lobe had begun to think of *her* as a saint.

For every possibility that came up, Lobe found a rebuttal. But on the back of his mind he suspected the truth: He didn't really want to know these things. This way the house practically seemed like his own. He had full charge, and the feeling of power that gave him was very satisfying. He would learn about its furnishings and find a name for it, and it would be sort of his own creation, as if it had been born right here in Edgar Falls, and who cared about anything else?

One thing he knew for definite certain: There was nothing strange about the house as Bobbie Topin insisted. It had a warm friendly feeling; everybody remarked on it.

All afternoon Bobbie Topin had stood at his window, watching groups of people come and go at the house. Now, the second week in December and dusk settling over the town, Bobbie pulled his bedroom shade. He never looked out on the house after dark anymore.

The feeling of dread that had remained with him after Halloween night weighed him down now as he went to the kitchen and started supper—just hot dogs tonight since Grandpop said he wasn't hungry. Bobbie heated him some soup anyway and felt secretly relieved when the old man found he could get a cup down after all. Grandpop was all Bobbie had, and he didn't want anything to happen to him.

"You got all the shades pulled down tonight," Grandpop said as they set the kitchen table.

"Keeps the house warmer, Grandpop."

"Mebbe. But if it snows, we won't get to see the first flakes."

Bobbie suspected what would happen, and sure enough when he finished the dishes and went into the living room, Grandpop had the shades up. Bobbie glanced uneasily toward the window near Grandpop's chair. He used to prefer nighttime to day; now the dark hours unsettled him. He couldn't shake the feeling that something bad connected with the house was going to happen.

"Got an idea," Grandpop said. "You run out to the shed and bring in the Christmas lights. We'll clean 'em up tonight."

"I'll do it tomorrow, Grandpop, okay? I've got some homework."

"I want the lights in," Grandpop said petulantly.

"You get 'em, I'll clean 'em."

Bobbie stared at the old man, at the wisps of white chin whiskers, at the faded blue eyes and blue-veined hands, and knew he didn't have an answer to his grandfather's expectant look. Not when it was rare to find Grandpop in any kind of communicative mood. "So get the lights," he told himself.

Five seconds to the shed, he calculated, five back. Ten to get the key into the rusty old lock and open the door. Five more to grab up the box of lights if he lucked out and remembered for sure where it was. Ten to set down the box outside the shed and relock the door. Barely more than half a minute, he told himself. And realized that some half minutes could use up a lifetime.

He debated on facing the old man honestly. *I'm afraid*, he could say. And the old man wouldn't believe him. *Afraid of what?* he would ask. *Of the house. Of whatever is in it.* Oh, sure, yes, of course. Grandpop would buy that. Save the hassle. Spend the thirty-five seconds. "Ain't you going to take a jacket?" Grandpop asked when Bobbie started for the kitchen.

Good grief, no. He could shave maybe ten seconds off his schedule if he did it half freezing. He hurried back into the kitchen. The door opened, and he plunged into the back yard night.

No time for thought. Run. Across the yard. Reach the shed. Damn, damn the key. Hard to fit when your hands were shaking. Open the door. Don't bother to jump for the dangling bulb cord, it'd take extra seconds. Plunge over to where the box should be. Got it. Hope and pray it's the lights. Feels right. But you never knew when Grandpop might have gotten in here sometime and rearranged things.

Out the door. Box on the ground. Snap the lock back together. Straighten.

Panic!

Off to the side of their house, something seemed to scurry into the shadows. For an instant, Bobbie went numb with terror, remembering that snickering on the stairs. Oh, hell. Oh, shit. They couldn't get *out*, could they?

What they?

Adrenalin pumped again. Bobbie grabbed up the box and tore through the back door. Slammed it. Bolted it. Leaned against it, breathing heavily.

Grandpop shuffled into the kitchen in his beat-up old slippers, bringing with him a warmth of reality that made Bobbie want to throw himself into his arms. Grandpop opened up a lower cupboard door and pulled out a clean rag to wipe ornaments off with. "Hey, boy," he said. "You look like you seen a ghost."

"I hope that's all it was," Bobbie said fervently under his breath.

Grandpop stared at the box. "You got the ornaments?"

Bobbie looked down prayerfully. He had. The word was marked plainly on top of the box.

It was a good thing. If Grandpop had tried to make him go back out there, he would have had a blob of hysteria on his hands. His grandson had the awful feeling he was one day soon going to lose control of himself.

Chapter Six

Not everyone in Edgar Falls was glad to see that the promise of a white Christmas had been fulfilled. On December twenty-third, a heavy snow fell on Edgar Falls, and on Christmas Eve the town lay in unaccustomed white splendor.

Nobody sat down on a stool behind Miss Penny's counter and stared out at the bleak night. Most everyone had gone home from their shops by now. But they'd left their Christmas lights shimmering in the faint, zephyrlike breeze that sometimes comes along after a snow. *Nobody's* window came all the way down to the sidewalk nearly, and she could see little eddies of virgin snow, newly laid down this evening, sailing and swirling along the deserted street.

She hated snow. She saw *them* always on a white day, sitting in the parlor of the house where she still lived, framed by a window with Jack Frost writing on it. Oh, they'd been devious, talking about everyday things as they sipped tea, just as if that very night they didn't plan to steal off like a couple of sneaks.

"You're nobody till somebody loves you." That wasn't the music on the radio her one customer played while sitting in a corner on one of the candy-striped chairs. The radio was playing a Christmas carol. But she heard the song she always heard at Christmas. She'd been somebody once.

A fleeting thought crossed the back of her mind that maybe she shouldn't have told Albert the things she did about Lily, about how Lily slept around every chance she got. It wasn't true, but a girl couldn't be too careful when she had a sister a lot of people saw as prettier than she was. You said things to protect yourself.

Only it hadn't worked. Maybe around then he'd begun to eye Lily, intrigued by a worldliness that didn't exist. Well, nobody would ever know for sure what happened. It had turned out to be a case of now you see them, now you don't — one morning sipping tea in the parlor, the next running off to get married.

She sighed.

Might as well go home. It must be nine o'clock or better. She stared a moment at the shelves of chocolate Santa Clauses she'd ordered out from the city a few weeks ago. She'd have to have a sale next week. The candy business wasn't what it used to be, what with Loman's undercutting her prices. If it kept up, sometime soon she might have to consider closing down the shop for good.

"And do what?" she asked bitterly.

Who would she be if she couldn't be The Sweet Lady anymore? She'd stared down at her red-striped dress and apron. That's who she was, all right. This was what life had decided to dish out to her, a shop full of leering chocolate Santas and a costume fit for a clown. Maybe she could become The Clown Lady and go around and do grotesque things at little kids' parties.

"Pulie, go home," she said. "Your mother must be fretty." He probably hated the name, so she used it; it got rid of a little of her frustration.

"I wanted another hot chocolate, Miss Penny," he said. Why couldn't that boy ever look anyone in the eye? Shifty. A sneak. She hated sneaks. If she were God she would bomb them all off the face of the earth.

On the verge of telling him she wanted to close up, a sudden thought struck her. Maybe Pulie could do it.

The same desperate craving that had come over her yesterday when she thought of the idea came again. She shouldn't have mentioned it to Bobbie Topin, but he had happened into her hands, so to speak. She'd just come back from a look at the house, still a little rattled from having to drive her old black Pontiac over there. Pretty days she used to walk, but the weather'd been too bad yesterday, and she'd had to pull out the car she only used in bad weather and drive the icy streets. Not that she could have stayed away. The house drew her, more now that she'd been inside it.

Thoughts of the house sitting out there alone with no one living in it to give it loving care drove her a bit more wild each day. She had thought it would be enough just to have tours going through, but it wasn't. The house had taken on a lonely air somehow, as if it hadn't known what was going to happen to it and had hoped for a family, the kind of family it must have had once. And even though she'd whispered her love for it as she toured in Lobe's ridiculous group, that didn't seem enough. The thought of the house being alone and empty on Christmas, when there should be people swarming its halls—gentlefolk like in the old days—and a giant tree with presents underneath, pinched her heart into a knot. A house like that was almost a human being. It had feelings. Memories. "You and I, Penelope," it seemed to say on that tour. "We belong together, don't we?"

She'd been quite beside herself from the experience of that communication when she arrived to take over the shop from Mary. And Bobbie Topin had been standing there, alone, wistfully looking at a box of chocolates done up in red satin bows. She waited for Mary and Kevin to leave.

"Would you like to have that candy, Bobbie?" she'd asked slyly. "Your grandfather would sure like that."

"Not for Grandpop," Bobbie said. "I carved him a picture at school."

Miss Penny's painted brows had arched. "Ah," she said. "For a little lady friend perhaps."

Getting no answer, she pressed her goal. "I could arrange for you to get that candy free," she said. "For just a slight favor."

Bobbie turned to her, and on the back of her mind she noted the shadows under his eyes and hoped he hadn't brought anything catching into her shop. Christmas was bad enough without battling a flu bug.

"Favor?" Bobbie said.

His mind didn't seem quite on her words. She glanced up and down the street to make sure no one was about to come in. "I want the keys to the house, Bobbie."

He blinked at her. "To what house?" he said.

"You know." She winked.

Bobbie took a visible step backward. "Oh, I wouldn't keep them," she said swiftly, rushing along now that she'd plunged in. "All you'd have to do would be find a way to slip into you-know-whose office tomorrow night while he's at the Moose Club Christmas Eve dinner at Carl Bergins's where I know he's going to be. He always keeps the keys locked in that drawer under his counter. I've seen him put them in and take them out three times now." As if he couldn't keep his hands off them. Who had done this awful thing? Who had named *him* guardian of the house when there was another who would love it, cherish it, more?

"You want me to steal the keys from Lobe Peters?"

"Borrow," she said. "I just want to have the house to myself for a minute, Bobbie." She hadn't meant that to pop out, hadn't meant her voice to go all whiny with need. "Those rickety old windows in that old shop must be easy to get through, and you could put the keys back Christmas night, and he'd never know the difference." She rushed along now, the words flying out and tumbling all over each other in her desperation. "You could have the box of candy. I'll give you two boxes. One for yourself."

But the boy was backing toward the door. "No, ma'am," he said. "I wouldn't want to do anything sneaky to Mr. Peters." Sneak? He was calling her a *sneak*? When she only had a need? "He doesn't have any right to hold the keys!" Her voice came out nearly a shriek, startling even her.

Bobbie reached the door, grabbed the handle and swung it open. "You don't want to go into that house, Miss Penny," he said. "Not alone."

But she wasn't listening. The frustration had taken hold of all her senses. "Get out!" she shouted. "I wouldn't sell you that candy if you paid me a thousand dollars. Get out, get out!" The door shut behind him, and she had stood there with funny bright lights flashing around in her head. Until the door opened again and Ben Dunkle, deputy sheriff, came in to see if she had any licorice drops.

Now she eyed Pulie Gordon and thought the same thought she had with Bobbie, thought of asking him to get the keys. He was so skinny; easy enough for him to snake through a narrow window.

But this one had a slimy air about him. She'd never liked him; nobody in town did. He looked like the kind who would pick his nose when he thought nobody was looking and put it in his mouth. He looked like the

156

kind who would blackmail her for years to come, even if he did the stealing.

"Go on home, Pulie," she said again. "Go and enjoy Christmas Eve."

"I hate Christmas Eve," he said with vehemence.

For a brief instant she felt something kindred with him. But then she reverted to her other feelings; he couldn't be trusted. There was no way she could get those keys tonight and go out to the house.

On the way home, she couldn't help herself. The snow had made her bring the Pontiac today, and she had to drive out there and take a look. The plows had cleared the streets, but they were still icy, and she had to drive carefully, very carefully. Only a few cars moved about now; most everyone was holed up inside with family. Overhead, new clouds threatened to make this the whitest holiday ever. Miss Penny crept along at twenty miles per hour.

The road that led to the house hadn't been cleared, which meant she couldn't get as close as she wanted. But she parked on the last street before the road and meadows began. And stared and stared.

How beautiful it looked. The trees around it drooped with snow, bending toward the house as if paying it the homage it so richly deserved. The iron railing had a lining of snow.

But the dark windows upset her even more than she was already upset. There should be lights glowing there, candles in the windows, a holly wreath hung on the door. Carolers should be standing there on the white lawn, the way they used to stand on lawns before everything got mechanized with the church sending out a truck blaring canned carols and disgorging youth club members to beg donations.

"Good evening, Banker and Mrs. Bergins. So

charmed you could come."

"Oh, Mr. Ambassador. How marvelous that you and your wife could make it tonight. The president? Oh, my, yes, he's been here for simply hours. Hasn't been able to tear himself away."

"Champagne, Mrs. Astor?"

Somebody stood in the door of that house, dressed in shining red satin. "I don't believe you've met my husband, Mr. Ambassador. Please come with me and let me introduce you. What? Oh yes, yes indeed. It is a lovely house, isn't it? I designed it, you know. And my husband had it built for me. The tapestries once graced an English manor house."

She didn't realize that her hands had knotted into fists until she felt her nails digging into her palms. Oh, blessed Jesus but life was cruel. It was all made up of sugar plums, like in the old poem, and when you woke up they vanished and there was only the grim cold of winter. She was fifty-nine years old; she would be sixty soon. Done. Finished.

She couldn't look at the house any longer. She was too depressed.

Brandy. Long years ago she had hated the taste. But when she turned fifty, Doc Jannessey had prescribed a glass every night for her nerves. "Safer than those Valium you pop, Penny," he told her. Doc was the only one in town who called her by her name. Even her old classmates had tacked on the old-maidish "miss" years ago. She and Doc had grown up together; he might have become her beau if Annabelle hadn't moved to town. Served him right. That woman would lead a saint a merry chase with the city ways she'd never lost.

"Would you care for another?" she said to the mirror that hung in her parlor. "Thanks, don't mind if I do."

Hmm. The image in that mirror was becoming

hazy. She wondered if she'd remembered to clean it for the holidays.

The brandy plopped into its snifter. Oh, yes? Brandy wasn't supposed to plop. She slowed her movements down, tipped the glass, and let the amber liquid slide in properly. "Now, that's more ladylike."

When had the nightly glass become a bottle? Three years ago? Four? No matter. She never got drunk, and in the morning her eyes were clear.

Oh, God, God! How could she stand it? It was calling to her, she could hear it. "Pennnnnellllope. Don't leave me alone."

"There's nothing I can do," she said. No place she could get away from its calling.

Yes she could. It was only about ten-thirty. The ladies of her club would be up at least till midnight tonight to see Christmas in. At midnight, they would open the little gifts they had made: lace hankies, crocheted slippers, fancy potholders. They would draw lots. It would be the only gift she got again this year, except for the usual things like the fruitcake Loman's so smirkingly sent out to remind her they were ruining her business.

Bright lights waited for her — a hot toddy swimming with butter. And a bunch of old biddies who spent the holidays together year in and year out, dreamless old bitches who'd grown up together, gained and lost husbands some of them, and spent the moments when they weren't with each other tearing the others down. She bet they were having a field day with her right now.

How quickly the simpery little gossips would change their tune if she walked in right now. It was only three blocks away. At Alice Poling's. She could bundle up and walk.

"Why, Miss Penny," they would say. "We thought we'd lost you this year. What held you up so late?"

"My pimp is sick," she would say. "But he managed to line me up one customer. A big black buck."

She giggled. Set them back on their ears, wouldn't it?

How had the glass gotten so empty so fast? Hmm. Well, we can remedy that, can't we. Remember to tip the glass. A toast to Lily and Albert, wherever you are, and let's sing a song of "Auld Lang Syne." Bottoms up now, everybody. She wished them a gift that Albert should develop prostate.

Wait a minute. Oh, God, it was calling again. "Pennnnnellllllope. I'm alone." She filled the glass to the brim this time. "I can't help it," she cried. "Can't you see I can't help it?" And she began to sob.

The grandfather clock her father had built woke her at three A.M. Or *was* it the clock?

She still sat in the chair across from the mirror, and the face she could barely make out looked ravaged. She had slept. But she had remained aware of the aloneness. A wind had come up and sighed around the corners of her house, but it was not the wind she listened to.

The voice of the house permeated the room. Not in words. In need.

She lurched out of her chair, knocking over the empty brandy glass. It hit the rug with a thud. She had had dark moods before, but this blackness she had never dealt with. As if her soul were dying. She couldn't stand it anymore.

No one would know, would they? A couple of hours might satisfy it, and she could be back home before the town stirred. Why hadn't she thought of it before? A hairpin used to work wonders on locks when she was a youngster. If it wanted her so much, it would find a way to let her in.

She wasn't sure she was driving too well. Once or twice she thought she hit a curb. No one else moved on the streets at all now.

Why didn't the blackness in her head lift? She was doing something about it, wasn't she?

"You're being a sneak, a sneak, a sneak . . ."

"Shut up." The house had called her. It wasn't sneaking when you were invited, even if you had to break in.

What if the hairpin didn't work?

It had to work.

What if Lobe would be able to tell someone tampered with the lock?

Shouldn't be hard to put the idea of vandals in his head. Vandals were starting to run the town these days. They'd knocked out windows in several shops on White Oak Avenue in the middle of the night.

The wind whined down the street, throwing up violent eddies of snow now. Clouds scudded so low to rooftops, they looked ready to swallow up the town.

See? She was thinking quite clearly. She could see the clouds and make the swallowing observation about them.

"We're all right, old girl. Just going to see Christmas in with a needy friend."

The mood began to lift the moment the house came into sight. The ice fantasies around its windows seemed to glow with welcome. At the end of the street, she braked the car, checked very carefully to make sure she had the emergency locked. "You behave," she said, patting the wheel. "Don't let anyone see you."

A sob caught in her throat. "I'm here," she said to the house. And was sure the house said with joy, "I know."

The going wasn't easy. Two feet of snow lay along the road, and drifts a lot higher than that had lined up on the sides. She had on her galoshes, but they weren't enough. Snow got over the edges and down underneath her feet. Well, she'd thought of that. She had warm little slippies in the sack she carried that also held a fresh bottle of brandy. And she had on every sweater she owned under her heavy coat.

Besides, the beauty of being in the house would warm her. It was her soul that needed warming, and the house could take care of that. "Here I come," she called coyly. "I'm almost there."

Funny. The night seemed filled with song. Almost like it must have been on that Christmas Eve two thousand years ago. Only this was a peculiar low sound — as of male voices. No words. She couldn't hear any words. "You're probably drunker than you think," she said. And giggled.

It pleased her somehow that the house sounded male.

"Just across the meadow now," she told herself. "Up with the footsie, down with the footsie, one, two, three, four, one, two, three, four."

She reached the snow-filled yard. Stopped to catch her breath which was coming on white whiffs out of her mouth. "Mercy, we haven't had this kind of exercise in years." Her heart pounded with effort, and she stood there panting a few moments, waiting until it slowed.

Wait a minute. Had she remembered the candle? She stuck her hand in the bag. Felt around. Ah, good. Brandy had a way of playfully snitching your memory. She would light it in a corner where the flickering couldn't be seen from outside. Not that anyone could see this far, but just to be safe. She wouldn't dare risk turning on a light.

Then at dawn she would sit in one of the front windows, maybe even come out to the porch to watch. Maybe the clouds would all get blown away, and she and the house would get to see the sun come up together. She hoped it would be pink.

Ready to walk again? Good. Up, footsie, down, footsie.

She gained the porch. And stopped to stare up with awe. She had never been this close at night before. Framed against the sky, the whole place seemed to undulate with the movement of the wind-pushed clouds. Reverence filled her. She felt for a moment as if she stood centered in all of time, that the house represented everything that had ever gone before, everything that was ever to come. Tears slipped down her cheeks again, making chilled little paths. Gone the blackness. Totally. She swelled with anticipated beauty. And climbed the steps.

She had brought five hairpins just to be safe. None of them worked. One after the other she jammed them into the lock, probing delicately at first, then growing more and more frenzied. "What's the matter with you?" she demanded. "You called me out here."

But the last hairpin got wedged, and no matter how she twisted and turned it, it wouldn't budge. "Open, damn you," she cried. In a sudden fury, she began to kick at the door. Kicked again and again until her toes hurt too much to continue. She threw her weight against the door and got a pained shoulder for return.

"Let me in," she wheedled.

Nothing.

All reality, all sanity, now hinged on one thing. Miss Penny DuJong had to get inside that house. She had to have the short hours she planned to spend with it to hold against the future that seemed to swirl with darker clouds than the sky showed tonight. This was it, what every moment of her life had led to. This time of communing, of being in possession of everything she had been promised and had had snatched away from her.

"Don't do this," she said with a sob. "Help me. I need you." Where had the humming voices gone? Why was it so silent? Even the wind had stopped whining.

"You won't keep me out," she said. "You don't mean to keep me out, do you?" The last had come on a sudden and terrible suspicion. "Well, we'll see about *that*."

Miss Penny bent and picked up the heavy purse she had set on the porch beside her bag of goodies. Then slowly, deliberately, she walked to the nearest window and rared back with all her strength and whammed the purse against it.

She backed off so that the splintering glass couldn't cut her. Except the window didn't break.

"What kind of fucking game are you playing?" she screeched. "You don't invite a guest and then shut her out. I came to keep you company, damnit. Didn't you say we were meant for each other? I heard you say it. I heard you say it the first day I was inside you."

She glanced wildly about. There had to be something. No fucking house was going to issue an invitation to Penelope DuJong and back out. There! Beside the porch. Not much snow had gotten under that bush, and there was a hefty rock there.

She hardly knew what she was doing as she tore down off that porch, slipped and barely got herself righted. Oh, blessed Jesus, what was the house up to? Get her out here and make her fall and break a hip and then they'd find her in the morning frozen and think she'd been a sneak? Well, she hadn't fallen; it hadn't worked. And she *would* get in. Show it who was boss.

She grabbed up the rock with abnormal strength and made it carefully back up the porch, thwarting the house again. Then she threw the rock with all her might against the window. It fell to the porch and rolled a couple of feet. Miss Penny stared at her reflection in the black pane. She squinted her eyes. Was someone laughing? Someone better *not* be laughing.

She grabbed up the rock again and moved to another window and began to pound and pound in a frenzy. "Let me in," she screamed. "Let me in, let me in, let me in."

There *was* laughter. It filled her senses. Blotted out everything else, so that there was only the sound of the rock thudding against the window and that hideous, delighted laughter.

"We'll see, we'll see, we'll see," she said, laughing her own laugh. Reject *her*, would it? Well, there had been a time when she'd been rejected and couldn't do anything about it because the parties wisely got out of town. But she could do something about *this*. In her car, she had an old lap blanket. And she had a box full of all the year's receipts she meant to turn over to her tax man next week. A healthy box full. Make a healthy fire. "We'll see," She grabbed up her bag and went off the porch, walking carefully, smirking to herself.

"Um-hum," she told herself gleefully. "It's listening. It's not laughing anymore because it knows who's going to have the last laugh."

She began to run. Not easy in the snow. But possible. Anything was possible when black hate drove you. She neared the car, planning swiftly. The porch was hollow underneath; she knew that from all the days she'd watched the place going up. There would be crawlspaces under there. Should be easy to pull a side slat loose. All she had to do was build her little bonfire under there. She wondered how long it would take for the whole place to go.

She wouldn't be able to stay and watch, of course, only until it caught. Then she'd have to get herself on home and watch the flames from a distance. Drink a drink, she would, while she watched. Toast the house. That was funny. The house would be toasting while she toasted *it*. She laughed. And neared her car. Drove herself panting onward, forgetting to walk carefully, breathing so hard the icy air drove shafts of pain into her chest.

Near the car, it happened. She hadn't expected it to happen out here, not if it didn't at the house, and she'd gotten careless. She screamed in fury as her feet suddenly went out from under her and she fell. Her head struck the bumper, sending raging, black pain through her temples.

She came to once, lying on the ground. She couldn't feel any part of her body, only the pain in her head. She couldn't see the house; her body lay in a little gully of snow. "You called me by my real name," she moaned bewilderedly.

It had been too much to hope that the good days would last. Grandpop had broken some kind of record lately for clear-headedness, but Christmas morning did him in. He had spent the night in bed for a change, and he stayed in his room so late Bobbie got worried and finally went to check.

Grandpop lay in bed with his eyes on the frosted window. "We'll have to get the corn in soon," he said.

Bobbie looked out at the new snow that had begun to fall early this morning and was coming so thick now he couldn't see the shed. "The corn is already in, Grandpop," he said.

He went back to the kitchen feeling lost. If only the clear days had lasted through today.

Well, there wasn't any point to brooding over Grandpop's moods; it didn't change anything. No more match incidents had occurred; he was breathing easier there. He was just, today as always, grateful to have a relative to live with.

Bobbie ate a pancake, then went on in the living room to stare at their tiny Christmas tree for a while. It didn't have the class Mom's used to have. She had a way of placing a glass reindeer in just the spot where it could catch the light from a red bulb.

At ten-thirty, he put a small chicken in the oven. Grandpop didn't come out of the bedroom, so Bobbie turned on the TV.

But pretty soon the little package under the tree that had to be for him got the best of him. He might wait into next week for Grandpop to snap out of it—might as well enjoy his gift by himself, even though he knew what it would be. Last year the "mood" had come on Grandpop four days before Christmas and had lasted most of a week. Consequently, Bobbie had no Christmas except for the Bic pen he got in the school grab bag.

He got the package and ran his fingers over it. Grandpop had even wrapped it, and so what if he'd used a piece of old birthday paper. Bobbie opened the package, teasing himself about the color. But they were blue, of course; they were always blue. For years back, as far as Bobbie could remember, his grandfather had sent him blue socks for Christmas. He must have had these stashed a long time since as far as Bobbie knew his grandfather hadn't been in town for weeks.

He went to the bedroom door and said, "Thanks, Grandpop. I can sure use these neat socks."

"You're welcome, boy."

Bobbie's heart soared. Had the mood lifted already? But then Grandpop said, "Tell Gladys to turn the fire up. I want to go back to sleep, and it's cold in here." Bobbie stared at him, wondering as always who Gladys was. Vera had been the grandmother Bobbie had only seen once because his grandparents had lived in a city distant from Bobbie's and Mom's. Vera was buried in the cemetery of this town they'd chosen to move to because her lungs were bad and city smoke aggravated them. But Bobbie had no idea where the Gladys of Grandpop's mind came from.

Well, anyway, he had a gift. His own for Grandpop would have to wait until the old man could recognize it.

This seemed like a good time to take Cindy's present over to her. Grandpop was snoring again already.

"Well, for goodness sake," Mrs. Newman said. "I think we've got a walking snowman on our porch, Clyde."

"I brought Cindy a present," Bobbie said.

"Cindy's not feeling too well," Mrs. Newman said. "Maybe you can perk her up." She leaned over and confided in a softer voice, "I think she hoped to have the new foot by Christmas." There was reproach in the woman's voice, as if Bobbie might have personally had something to do with dampening the town's enthusiasm. But Bobbie knew it was more than the foot. Cindy simply had not been the same since the fire.

"Let me get her," Mrs. Newman said. Her husband had disappeared somewhere off in the house, and Bobbie stood looking at their tree. It was ceiling high and frosted—the kind that went for twenty dollars on the White Oak Avenue lots. A bunch of opened gifts lay scattered around the living room, and it briefly crossed Bobbie's mind that enough money had been spent to go a long way toward Cindy's foot. But it wasn't any of his business.

"Hi, Bob," Cindy said in a doorway.

"You children talk," Mrs. Newman said. "I have things to do in the kitchen. Oh, I'd invite you to dinner, Bobbie, but we have people coming."

"Thank you," he said. "Grandpop and I are having chicken."

"How nice."

"I'll sneak you some turkey if you want me to," Cindy said when her mother had left the room.

"Hey, no," Bobbie said. "Chicken's just as good."

He looked at the dark circles under Cindy's eyes. "How's everything going?" he asked.

"Okay," she said. "You get a lot of nice things?"

"Sure."

Damn. Sometimes with Cindy, it was like trying to get through one of Grandpop's moods.

"I brought you something," Bobbie shoved on through the non-conversation.

Cindy took the package with a show of eagerness he felt was designed for his sake. But at least she made an effort. In school lately Cindy's grades had fallen off, and sometimes when Miss Larimer spoke to her, it was like Cindy had to fight through a fog to hear.

"Oh, Bob," Cindy said. "I wanted one of these when I saw them in Miss Penny's window."

"Well, you've got one now," he said more heartily than he felt. A sudden memory he'd tried to keep back popped into his mind. He hadn't bought the Santa at Miss Penny's. She was fifty cents higher than Loman's. But he'd stopped to price them at the Sweet Lady's first. And was sorry. The joy of buying the only gift he was spending money on besides Grandpop's had been marred by the memory of Miss Penny's over-red mouth shouting at him. And the keys! Good grief, she'd wanted him to steal Lobe's keys so she could get into the house.

He didn't let himself think about why the house might have gripped her so hard. "I guess I'd better get going," he said. "I left the chicken baking, and I don't like to leave Grandpop too long."

"Did you ever think maybe *she* did it?"

Bobbie had taken off his old gloves for a moment to air sweat off his hands. Now he paused in the act of pulling them slowly back on. "Who did what?" he said.

"Bitsy. I've been thinking a lot lately. There's something I've never told anybody. A couple of times when I was down there, Bitsy laughed and said if she ever got pregnant again maybe she'd just do them all in."

"Was she pregnant?" Bobbie said.

"I don't know. There wasn't any autopsy because it was fire that killed her. If she was, she never told me."

"Cindy why do you think about them all the time? It happened. It's over. There's nothing you can do to help them now." Bobbie's voice grew exasperated. He'd been working hard since the fire to try and help bring her out of it. To make her be the old Cindy again.

"I wonder what pushed her into it," Cindy said. "Something must have."

"The fire chief said she must've fallen asleep with a cigarette in her hand. You said yourself she was careless with them." They'd been over a lot of this before. Bobbie wasn't about to have his Christmas ruined with it.

"Well, I guess she did have a chance to confess like Catholics do in movies if she wanted to," Cindy mused aloud. "Did I ever tell you I was the last one she spoke to? I think I did. She would have told me if she'd done it. Funny. She didn't even ask about the babies. She was only worried about the house. Although I never heard her call it that before. She always called her place

the McCall shack. She said it a whole bunch of times—
'the house, the house, the house. . . .' "

Bobbie was halfway home before that hit him. Then he stopped dead in his tracks. Come on now. Forget it. Nawww. Not *the* house.

Unfortunately, a reaction had been set up on the back of his brain. It was a nagging little thought: "Why not *the* house?"

The snow stopped shortly after noon. The day turned gray but clear. Grandpop and Bobbie were treated to a beautiful expanse of white lawn out back as they ate their chicken. The shed, window-deep in snow, looked like something out of a painting.

Grandpop did eat some chicken, even said it was good. But it wasn't the Grandpop of the here and now. This one rattled off in Christmas pasts. "Whoever's roasting chestnuts," he said, "will have to get the pan out of the barn." And a few other choice suggestions. Well, at least he knew it was Christmas, and he did seem to enjoy the chicken.

Grandpop went in for a nap in the afternoon, and Bobbie cleaned up, sliced the rest of the chicken and pulled off the wings for tonight, then went out back to get rid of the bones. The garbage can stood out by the shed. He didn't mind going out there so much when it was light and even managed a quick look in the direction of the house, drawn by a morbid fascination to check if it could be seen against so much white. For a second he remembered Cindy's statement about Bitsy again, but he pushed it back to where he'd stuffed it on his way home earlier. Bitsy had never shown much interest in the house as far as he knew, and he wasn't going to let his imagination get a grip on *her*.

Wait a minute! Something was going on over that

way. There were cars parked on the street. Several people moved about, and Bobbie could make out the upper half of one car in particular: a black car with a lot of snow on top.

He shrugged. Car coming from Gloaming early this morning maybe, taking the shortcut to the highway. Driver probably got caught in the storm without chains. Looked like an awful lot of people to get one car out, though. Chances were he'd hear about it tomorrow.

He let his eyes lift for a second. Standing in a woods gone white, the house was hardly visible. It just sort of blended right in with its surroundings. It looked peaceful and serene. Like part of nature.

"Don't kid yourself," he snorted in the back of his mind.

Chapter Seven

The house did it. Bobbie stood in Mike's Bottoms's front yard, nauseated. No matter how you tried to make a lie out of it, it was the house. The house had made Craig hang off that iron railing, and it had gotten Miss Penny. He didn't know how, he couldn't prove it, but it maybe got Bitsy, too, in some way he couldn't figure out. Other mothers would have died asking about their children. Not Bitsy. Bitsy had said, "The house." Over and over.

Jeez. Damn. What was happening, what could he do? He'd tried to talk to Lobe Peters; Lobe had been annoyed.

"I just want to spend a little time in the house alone, Bobbie." Wasn't that what Miss Penny had said? Bobbie felt as if he'd suddenly stumbled onto a strange planet. He stared at Jorgenson, Bottoms, and Hetherington.

He had walked into town this day after Christmas to buy a couple of items on sale at Pender's Grocery and come upon the other guys building a snowman in Bottoms's front yard. All three of them were so eager to fill him in on their gruesome tidings, they forgot he wasn't one of them. Jorgenson had spotted him first and called him over to see if Bobbie had heard the news.

"All bloody. Blood over everything. On the windows. Gooked on a rock they found on the porch," Craig said. "And there was a hairpin stuck in the lock."

Their voices came and went in Bobbie's head.

"My dad says looks as if she was trying to get in," Mike Bottoms babbled excitedly. "Says maybe her car got stuck, and she knew it was too far to walk back to town, being fat like she was, and old. Says she might've tried to break into the house to get warm."

Very logical, Bobbie thought numbly. Fascinating how logical adults could be.

WHY HADN'T IT LET HER IN?

"I don't know, Mike." Hetherington speaking? "Why would she pound till she got all bloody? And why didn't the window break?"

Because it didn't want to break, el stupido, Bobbie wanted to shout. But he didn't want them to hear his voice tremble. He let them rant on, filling him in on all the gory details, while he got control of himself. Something like black liquid seemed to be running behind his eyes. They were all in love with the word blood.

"Caved her head in a pretty good one on the car bumper," one of them said.

"That's because my pop says she was drunk and drunk people crash hard." That was Hetherington. To illustrate his point, he went limp and fell down in the snow.

"I thought we weren't supposed to say nothing about her being drunk," Mike Bottoms put in. "Mom says don't speak ill of the dead."

"Shit, everybody knows Miss Penny used to lay it away," Jorgenson said with a snort. "You ever smell her on a Saturday morning?"

"Blood on the ground was froze like the rest of her when they found her," Mike said. "Huh. Wonder what she was doing out there in the middle of the night anyway?"

Bobbie walked away from them, his head whirling. "Hey, where you going?" they called. "You ain't heard all the details."

"Uh—errands for Grandpop." He lied. He couldn't let them know if they said anymore he would be sick. He just kept seeing the craziness in Miss Penny's eyes when he said he wouldn't get the keys, and she ordered him out of her shop. She had acted as if her life depended on getting inside that house.

Oh, man. What was he going to do? It was the house; he would not, he could not, any longer deny it was the house. It was bad. Malevolent.

Something was in there. Something that could do weird things to your mind. Something that snickered under staircases and slipperied up behind you and could make you do things like hang off an iron railing and nearly kill yourself.

Something that could make a workman fall from a ladder? Or a mother burn up her children?

Maybe even make a retarded boy walk into a pond? Come on now. Let's not get *too* crazy.

Damn, *damn*. Why wouldn't it let his mind alone? Why did he have to be the one who knew? Couldn't anybody else in the world see it? Wasn't there one person in this whole town besides himself who knew what was going on? Jeez, all you had to do was look at the way the place was built. Warped.

Just because he had known things a couple of times. Like when Mom died, and he realized later that's what his fear in school that day had been about. Once as a little kid he'd dreamed of an airplane crash. It woke him up in the night. The next day the news carried it: A whole bunch of people had died. "Don't be silly, Bobbie," Mom had said. "It's just a coincidence." But he had known.

So what? He hadn't been able to keep his mother from dying. What was the good of feeling things if you couldn't do anything about them?

Where had the house come from? The thought struck him again as he hurried for the safety of his own home. There ought to be a clue there. The house didn't just arrive crazy. It had to be crazy before it reached Edgar Falls.

But who would help him find out? Lobe wouldn't listen. Who else knew anything? Nobody?

He walked swiftly and reached the place where the sidewalks ended and started down his own street. The plow had been out early, and everything was clear. He couldn't help himself; he had to look at the house. Anger born of a sudden fresh surge of fear flashed through him. "Somebody knows about you," he said. "You should have got me when you had the chance."

It was a threat. He didn't know exactly what he was threatening, but he said it with all the bluster he could manage. The house stood white and cold against the trees. Mocking him?

He began to run now, slippery road or no. Past the Letkins house. His own waited up ahead, small and cheerful and inviting despite some peeling paint. He was nearly sobbing as he rushed toward the warmth of Grandpop (even a wandering-brained grandfather was better than none at all) and the furnace and the cheerful pictures on the wall.

Bobbie screamed as the big cross dripping mud tipped toward him. Its shadow touched him first, and he began to run; he ran and ran through the countryside, the thing so close he could feel the air current moving beneath it, and he knew it was going to crush him. He turned to throw up his hands, and suddenly the cross dissolved. Bobbie stared down at what was left of it, a small pool of bubbling blood.

It happened three nights running, leaving him wide awake and staring at the ceiling of his room with burning intensity. Something else was going to happen.

He had had practically no sleep for nights now, ever since he'd learned about Miss Penny. He didn't go to the funeral, hadn't talked to anyone who had. He hadn't been back into town.

Then one day shortly before school started, a knock sounded at the door. Bobbie opened it, expecting one of the little Letkins kids to be standing there after a cup of sugar or something. But he blinked in surprise at Craig Jorgenson.

"Bottoms had to go to the dentist," Craig said by way of greeting. "And Joe's mom dragged him off to visit his grandmother. I decided to take me a hike and thought it wouldn't hurt to stop in and say hi." Bobbie obviously represented a last resort in a world bereft of kid company.

This was the first time any of the guys had ever come out here. Jorgenson had always been slightly friendlier than the other two, and Bobbie would have been thrilled if he had room in his thoughts for much besides the house. When? his mind kept hissing.

"Haven't seen you in town since day after Christmas," Jorgenson said.

"Looking after my Grandpop," Bobbie answered. It wasn't his whole reason, but it was true. Grandpop had been worse these past few days than he'd ever been. Twice this week the old man had wet himself. The odor had eventually led Bobbie to the problem, and it was no easy chore getting a bewildered old man undressed and into a shower when he didn't realize himself what he'd done. While Bobbie helped him soap himself the first time, Grandpop had stared at his withered balls hanging there like little limp sacks of water. "Oh my Jesus," he said, leaving Bobbie with a hideous sadness on top of everything else. Lately he talked to Grandpop in the sweet voice you would use with a sick child.

While Bobbie made cocoa, Craig started talking about Miss Penny again. In a minute, Bobbie, watching Craig drink his cocoa, went distant in his mind with morbid fascination. Why hadn't it done something awful to Craig, too? And Bobbie himself? The house had had two juicy young boys in its clutches and had let them go. Why? Maybe it couldn't work its stuff on children? But Jorgenson had been within a hair of dropping from that iron fence. Bobbie shook his head, trying to drag his mind back to the one-sided conversation the redhead was carrying on.

"I didn't catch that last part," he said. Then he stared at Craig in some surprise. The other boy's face had gone a fiery red, his freckles standing out like blisters.

"I said someone else is gonna die around here. Their yellin' gets worse all the time. They're gonna kill each other some night. If I don't do it for them. I hate her. Everything was okay when Mom was alive."

"How can you remember?" Bobbie asked, trying to pick up the conversation he'd missed. "Weren't you three when she died?" Bobbie knew that from Craig's stepmother's paper.

"I remember her," Craig said ominously. "She was good. This one's a damn old whore. She guzzles beer like it's goin' out of style. And our house is worse'n a pig pen. I find garbage in spots a starving rat couldn't find. And she never gets off my back."

So this was why his classmate had stopped in. He was desperate for someone — anyone to unload on. But Bobbie only gave that small thought. While Jorgenson talked on, the house went on playing itself on the back of Bobbie's mind like some warped musical instrument. Who was next?

The fourth time the dream hit, Bobbie got no more sleep that night. In the morning he made a decision to do something that had nagged him for days. There was only one more person in Edgar Falls he could talk to. It had taken a while for her to occur to him. But she held at least a part of the key; she must know where the house came from. And she was an out-of-towner. Maybe she could understand what the rest of the people couldn't.

The only problem was Bobbie hadn't been able to go outside except when necessary. He felt protected in this little house, and he dreaded having to make the long walk to school soon.

Still — he would have to go back.

And he had to see Gloriana Reege.

Someone had to understand about the house. Someone had to do something about it.

She was a pleasant-looking woman. She would probably be pretty without those glasses. But his mind wasn't on Miss Reege's appearance. He was so glad to find her alone in her office, he could have wept. This trip had cost him plenty. He had walked with his nerves so tight, his bones hurt.

"What can I do for you?" she asked in a friendly manner. "You in the market for a house?"

"I want to know how to get rid of one." Oh, man. He'd meant to work up to the subject.

"I find burning the best method," Miss Reege said. Bobbie missed the twinkle in her blue eyes. Then she said solemnly, "But of course you have a house to sell. Trouble is you're a little young to sign papers."

"You don't understand." Bobbie's voice came out desperate. "Miss Reege, I'm talking about the house in

Pellam Woods. There's something wrong with it. I know things sometimes. I always have, and there are things happening in town, things the house is doing, and something else bad is going to happen tied up with a muddy cross." He got hold of his mouth almost with physical will. Couldn't he keep his cool five seconds when it came to the house?

The door opened and a man in a red Gloaming Realty jacket came in. Bobbie ducked his head to hide tears of embarrassment and just plain weariness. "Jake, watch the office," Miss Reege said. "I'll be a little late for you."

She touched Bobbie's shoulder. He turned and followed her blindly into a storage room. "Drink coffee?" she asked.

He shook his head, keeping his eyes on the cement floor. "Well, I think you need some right now," she said firmly, and in a second he found himself holding a hot cup.

"You're trembling," she said. "Here. Give me that back before you get scalded. Look, sit on these boxes with me."

He found himself being led again. She sat him down. "Now go over that again," she said. "And don't you think I ought to know your name?"

"Robert Topin."

"I've seen you in town. Usually with Cindy Newman. But you didn't come to socialize, did you? Please. Tell me why you came to me with these feelings of yours."

"They aren't just feelings," Bobbie said. "When I was little I knew when a plane was going to crash. I knew when my mother was going to die before it happened."

"Wait a minute," she said. "Now slow down. You're telling me you're psychic, and it has something to do with the house. Do you understand what psychic means?"

"I understand," he said.

"Back up a bit. Why come to me?"

"You brought the house here," he said bluntly. "You must know where it came from. You can talk the owners into taking it back."

"Hold on again," she exclaimed. "Bobbie, that house cost a fortune to move here."

That didn't impress him. "They have to take it back!" Might as well plunge all the way now. "Miss Reege, that house is evil. I tried to talk to Lobe Peters about it, but he laughed. I tried to tell him before it got Miss Penny. And it maybe got Bitsy, too, and the workman. It's crazy, and it's going to get somebody else soon, too. I don't know who, but it has something to do with a muddy cross and blood."

He knew he was lost when Miss Reege reached out and smoothed the hair back from his damp forehead. "Bob, I know a lot of bad things have happened around here lately. They've affected us all. I wasn't particularly fond of Miss Penny, but I wouldn't have wished her the ugly death she suffered. But they were all accidents, honey. You've just let them play on your mind too much. It's happening all over town. There's a kind of morbidity. Other factors are involved, too, what with Ace getting ready to close. We're in a real economic depression around here, and these tragedies have just added to dragging people down. Do you understand what I mean?"

He looked at her intently. "You mean you don't believe me," he said.

"About your being psychic? I don't know about things like that, Bob. After all, if you were close to your mother — and I'm sure you were — you probably picked up on little signs of illness others wouldn't have noticed."

"My mother died of a brain hemorrhage," he said dismally. "Suddenly."

"Still — the signs could have been there."

"Why won't people believe what they can't understand?" he exploded. "I don't understand it either, but something's going to happen, and it'll be your fault now, too, because I've told you." The bleakness inside him took away any sense of politeness he had left. "You probably think I'm crazy, but you're going to be sorry you didn't listen to me. The whole town will be sorry. Somebody's got to get rid of that house because I think it's only just getting started." He got off the box abruptly.

Miss Reege stood as he stood. "I don't think you're crazy, Bob," she said. "I believe you're sincere. I just think maybe you suffer from an overactive imagination. But I couldn't help you anyway. I don't know any more about the woman who sent the house to Edgar Falls than anyone does — which I'm sure would surprise and delight our esteemed Mr. Peters — except that she once lived in the house. All transacting — the sale of the Pellam Woods property by a developer in Omaha who abandoned a project here in Edgar Falls — the house itself — everything was done in the name of Ms. Benedictine. She had the cash, and it was all perfectly legal. Although I did know she wasn't the real owner, I didn't know the house was intended as a gift to the town — a somewhat bizarre way to blow money, if you don't mind my saying it, but who am I to question people's whims?"

"Do you know where it came from?" he asked.

She shook her head. "If I did, I couldn't tell you. But I was kept in the dark about it." She smiled again, gently. "For the kind of money I was paid, honey, I just sold the Pellam Woods land with the biggest grin you ever saw, and when my client said no questions, I would have sewn my mouth shut if requested."

"I have to know who she is. I have to know where the house came from. Maybe she'd do something about it. Someone has to." Bobbie felt as if he had vomited the hot words.

"Oh my," she said. "Bob, I'm sorry."

"Someday," he said angrily, "you'll believe me. But then it'll be too late. The curse will be over." Bobbie found himself at a metal door leading out the back way without any memory of getting there. Miss Reege crossed silently and opened the door for him; it creaked. In a moment he found himself in the alley paralleling White Oak Avenue. He was two blocks toward home before any real consciousness came to him.

Gloriana Reege watched him go. Poor kid. What must it be like to live in a head like that, seeing ghosts or whatever he had conjured? She wished she could have told him something to chase them away.

After he left Miss Reege's, Bobbie skirted the street where his buddies lived, and then he began to run. He knew what had to be done now. They had to get away, he and Grandpop, even if he felt like a traitor deserting the town. But nobody would believe him anyway. He didn't want to be around when the next bad thing happened; it might even happen to him, although that wasn't the feeling he had. Grandpop? Could it happen to Grandpop?

He arrived home close to nervous tears. "We can't go right now," he ranted at himself. There were too many things to take care of.

Well, maybe Miss Reege could handle the cottage. He and Grandpop could get out and take whatever savings he knew Grandpop kept stashed someplace and go far away, rent a cheap room. They could send for his school records, and Miss Reege could sell the house and send them the money. They could transfer Grandpop's checks.

All the time his mind raced, he told himself how hopeless the idea was. But when he surged into the living room, his plan on his lips, it all hit him. Grandpop was sitting in his chair by the window, mumbling to himself. Bobbie ran to his side and started babbling, but Grandpop didn't even recognize his presence.

The energy drained out of his body. He stood there looking into the old man's faraway expression. Maybe Grandpop wasn't coming back at all this time.

"You can go yourself," a desperate voice cried. He was twelve. Tall for his age. Maybe he could pass for fourteen, get a job busing dishes or something.

And leave Grandpop, leave him alone to whatever might be coming?

"So what? Grandpop's gone half the time. He won't even know."

But Bobbie would know.

The year moved on out, and the new one came rushing in on a January wind. Bobbie went to school because he had to. But he hurried straight home afterward, except when he had to buy groceries or something, and it wasn't just because he thought he should be with Grandpop. The only place he felt safe at all was shut up inside their cottage.

Cindy walked partway home with him sometimes. She was better now, a little anyway, although she'd given up hope of getting her foot. "The town'll get interested again," Bobbie told her, trying to drag his mind off the shadows that moved in and out of it like clouds. "There's just been a lot happening." Ace Sanitary Plumbing had closed its doors on New Year's Eve.

Cindy hardly ever mentioned the babies anymore, although a couple of times she asked Bobbie if he wanted to go look at the ruins of Bitsy's shack. Banker/Mayor Bergins had insisted that the rubble be hauled away, but the men hadn't done a good job; there were still some burned boards according to Cindy. Bobbie declined the invitation. Once Cindy had shown him the melted remains of a silver spoon she had picked up down there. "That was mine," she told him. "I stole it out of our family trunk and gave it to baby Pammy to chew on when she started getting teeth. She loved that spoon because it was shiny."

If Bobbie thought Cindy was still a little morbid, who was he to mention it? His thoughts wouldn't take any awards for lightness.

Always he had a waiting feeling. For a time it was sort of like watching the fuse on a stick of dynamite. But the second week in January passed, and then the third, and when nothing much happened, he at least lost the feeling his head was going to be the explosion.

The wind stayed on, roaring up and down the town streets as if the sight of people walking drove it insane. Sometimes it succeeded in knocking one down. It slammed Charlie Groves into his door so hard one morning he broke two fingers on the hand he stretched out to right himself with. That necessitated calling Pulie in to work after his school hours at the high school in Gloaming. Pulie got out at noon, and he was somewhat a help, though not as good as a real employee would be. But at least it kept Grace, Charlie's sister, from whining and begging him for money. Damn her fool husband anyway, dying off and leaving her with a crummy little annuity. If he'd lived longer, maybe the kid would resemble a man; though thinking about it made Charlie wonder; his brother-in-law wouldn't have made news in that direction.

Watch and wait. That's about all Bobbie could do.

Grandpop's mind came back somewhat, so that on occasion they could talk a little, but the old man had always been taciturn, even in his good days, so there wasn't much communication there.

The first lucid day Grandpop had, Bobbie had thought about suggesting they get out of town. But by now he realized how utterly futile that idea was. Grandpop had lived in Edgar Falls for years. His wife was buried here, even though he never went to visit her grave. He had selected the town long years ago to retire in and die in. He wouldn't consider leaving now. There simply wasn't anything Bobbie could devise that sounded plausible, and the truth would have convinced his grandfather it was Bobbie who had the problem with his mind.

Watch and wait.

About once a week he had the muddy cross dream. It never changed. He didn't even wake up anymore.

But it made him think of the little gold cross that had been Mom's, and he took to wearing it around under his shirts where no one could see. He knew what he was doing. Crosses were supposed to ward off evil, at least in fiction.

He missed his mother fiercely these days, more than he ever had, and wished they hadn't had her cremated the way she'd always wanted and scattered over the Ozarks by an airplane. Even her body in a grave he could visit might do something to ease his sense of aloneness.

He didn't read horror stories anymore. He just waited.

Chapter Eight

Let 'em go suck each other's dirty old things. He wouldn't ever go home. Let 'em get on the phone to each other. Uncle Charlie could tattle till he got VD of the mouth. Shit on them.

One lousy little dollar bill.

Pulie pedaled his bicycle furiously. Shit. You worked yourself stupid for under the minimum wage, and then you got yelled at for helping yourself to a lousy dollar bill to buy some candy to get through the afternoon with.

I hate him. He thinks I don't know he laughs at me behind my back. He started the Pulie business in the first place when I was a little kid, got me to calling myself that, and I hate it. Supposed to be funny the way I said, "Pew-eee" when I smelled my dirty pants. Very funny. Make fun of a little kid doing something everybody does, only he doesn't know it; he thinks he's the only filthy thing running around anywhere.

"Why don't you *tell* me when you have to go ca ca?" His mother's voice came along on the wind that whooshed past his ears as he reached the north tip of town and began to swing east. Why had she always looked as if messing his pants was the sin next to killing

Jesus Christ?

He hated her, too. Both of them probably on the phone by now: "He stole a dollar, Grace."

"Augustine? My Augustine stole a dollar? Oh, lord, Charlie, what am I going to do with that boy?" She wouldn't even try to defend him. If dear brother Charlie said it, it must be true.

"Grace, you've gotta work with him harder. That boy is seventeen years old and outta high school soon. He's shiftless. How's he gonna make a living for you; he can't even earn two bucks an hour for me sorting nails?"

His mother would start to cry. "I just don't know what to do, Charlie. The Lord gave me a heavy burden when he left a growing boy on my hands. Augustine (or maybe *she* called him Pulie, too, when he wasn't listening) needs a man's influence."

"A man's hand, you mean, across his rear."

His mother would go afterward and have one of her enemas to console herself. Augustine (he was going to start calling himself that) had thought of hanging ornaments on her bag in the bathroom at Christmas since she could hardly ever get out of there long enough to admire the tree he'd fixed up.

Augustine stopped a minute to rest. Beyond him to his left stretched the gray, deserted buildings of the Ace Sanitary Plumbing factory. An idea struck him. Maybe he could spend the night over there — find an unlocked storage shed. Serve them right. He'd hide the bike. Let them have a night of wondering what life would be like without Augustine Gordon. Who'd Uncle Charlie get to work so cheap? And who would pick up after his mother and listen to her whining all the time? They needed a jolt. Let them think he'd been kidnaped. Maybe that'd shut them up.

But a sudden vision popped into his mind. Of

everything going on as usual. Who really cared? Nobody.

He kept on pedaling, swung past the road out of town. It wasn't helping to ride his bike. That had been his first impulse after he'd run from Uncle Charlie's store. Strange moods sometimes came on him, and riding his bike helped a little. He would pedal like a demon until he was too drained for the nasty thoughts that kept plaguing him.

They started in on him now. He saw pictures in his head, pictures of him doing bad things, of people doing bad things to him, heard his screams of pain-filled pleasure.

A shudder ran through his slim body as he tried to shake loose the images. The trouble was he didn't try to fight them so hard anymore. He found himself drifting off into them and reluctant to come out.

Wind swept hard through the town. It was the first week in March. "In like a lion," Pulie said, and that brought forth still another picture for his mind to paw with dirty fingers.

It was okay. His body hadn't gotten in on the act yet. It was when his body joined in he had real trouble.

He pedaled down the east side of town.

Little kids were coming home from school now. They skipped along in the wind, chasing papers that flew out of their hands, chasing each other. They made Pulie sick to him stomach. *He'd* never been a little kid like that. Always, as long as he could remember, there'd been his mother he had to get home to. "Mommer" was never feeling well. Mommer needed her strong little boy home all the time. He'd never skipped and played, never had anyone to skip and play with.

Mommer had caused all that. He hadn't thought of those growing up years in a long time now because when he did he had trouble handling his fury. He was about six the first time he wished she'd die; he was maybe eight when he thought of killing her himself.

"With what?" he said now, smiling mirthlessly into the wind. "Stab her to death with her douche nozzle?"

All this over a lousy dollar—all these memories he tried to keep buried churning up, just because he'd taken something that should have been his in the first place.

Instead of passing, his mood deepened.

Down toward the south side of town he rode, now, his thoughts working themselves into a frenzy. Why couldn't he just get out? What held him here?

Then suddenly Pulie braked. He dragged his foot along the ground to stop the ailing brakes. Have to fix those one of these days.

He reached the south side. Banker Bergins's house had come into view way up ahead. But that wasn't what he was looking at. Cindy Newman stood over by the spot where Bitsy McCall's shack had been; she seemed to be studying the ground.

Memory moved warmly through Pulie, of a body pressed up against him. He had seen Cindy a couple of times since the fire. She'd always looked lost in some world of her own, and he'd always had that same faintly pleasant, faintly uncomfortable feeling he had now. Sort of a shudder that started in his shoulders and hit that place between his legs rapidly. He tried to avoid making pictures out of that. Never think of real people. It was the only safe way to handle it.

Cindy wore a blue stocking cap. Her hair hung down the back of her blue coat, and he thought again she was going to be a nice-looking woman—if the town ever got around to fixing that foot. Pulie looked down at her special shoe. It gave him a sickish feeling. He didn't like any kind of deformity. "That's because you were born with one for a face," he liked to tell himself when he was in a real mood.

He started walking the bike over. "What are you looking for?" he asked.

Funny how his voice never sounded real when he'd gotten into a mood. You couldn't just snap out of it either. Once it got going, the mood held you for hours, sometimes days, and pretty soon everything got to looking flat and strange, and you went around touching things to see if they were real. He panicked sometimes when he got like that.

He felt a little panic now.

Cindy jumped. "I don't hear you coming," she said.

"What are you looking for?" he asked again.

"Oh. Things. I used to come and play with the babies. I look for things to remind me of them."

"Like what?" His voice seemed to be at the far end of a tunnel while he stood down here. On the back of his mind he had a sudden picture of Cindy with her pants pulled down. The thought shocked him. He'd never thought *that* about a real person before; he wouldn't let himself. For a second, black wind rushed so hard in his ears he thought he might faint.

"Well, I found a silver spoon once I gave baby Pammy. And a broken airplane that must have been in the yard when the fire happened. I've got a little tin box Bitsy stole — Bitsy had."

Her voice came clearer toward the end, all soft going in and out of his ears. He liked her voice. Cindy bent over and picked along through a few stubbles of burned wood. He watched her hands. She had her mittens off; cold had made her hands pink. What would it be like to have himself all swollen and ready and those pink little hands holding onto it? He looked at her mouth. Round. Pink too. Pulie touched himself, could feel what was happening down there. Oh, shit.

Not in his clothes. He didn't want anything to

happen in his clothes. He could only do the wash a couple of times a week; otherwise his mother got suspicious and wanted to know what was getting everything so dirty. He'd gotten to be a master at doing it into paper towels and then flushing them down the toilet.

"See you, Cindy," he said. She didn't look up as he got on his bike and pedaled off.

Really furious pedaling now. *Keep those legs pumping. Don't think.* Give it a chance to go down. *You've done it before. You can get rid of it.*

Horror and shame flooded through him. She was just a little kid.

But *pink.*

Get yourself back onto Uncle Charlie and Mommer. Safer. Ah. Better. *It's going away.*

Up the west side of town he pedaled, along the street where they had found Miss Penny's body. Nasty old bitch. Served her right, whatever happened. The house had been in sight most of his trip, but he hadn't paid any attention to it until now.

Now the waning sunlight glinting down on one of the spired tips on the roof fence caught his attention. Soon the sun would drop behind the woods.

Funny. Not much wind on this side of town. There was even a faint bog mist. Pretty soon their season would come in. When the weather turned warm, they came to full life, sending out the mysterious vapors that sometimes disturbed Pulie.

Pulie braked the bike again and stood there with his feet on the ground, panting from the fight to get himself under control. Most of the time it was just easier to give in and do what his body wanted. But you couldn't always. If he'd hauled it out in front of Cindy, she would have run screaming for help.

Of course *that* presented an interesting picture. Let

Uncle Charlie and Mommer deal with that. My son, my nephew, the pervert.

He *was* perverted; he knew that. Nobody else could have the kind of nasty thoughts he had.

Look out. Crazy territory. *Look at the house instead*.

Didn't do much good. He hated the house now.

Three times on Saturdays his mother had dragged him through it. "It will be a nice outing for us, Augustine," she had whined each time. "You never go anyplace with your old mother."

People made movies about people like his mother. Someone always killed them.

He saw them going through the house now, her arm linked through his. "Someday my boy is going to make a lot of money and build his mother a house like this, isn't he?" she always said. He wanted to drop through the floor because other people could hear her.

Well, he *would* get out someday. He didn't have to stay here forever and do what she wanted. He hated the house for putting ideas in his mother's head she'd never had till it came along.

"Jesus says there's no glory like a dutiful son." Sometimes his mother threw that in.

He used to love Jesus. Now he was just scared of him. Jesus always said things like "I'm here to save you" and the next verse slapped you down with what would happen to you if you didn't get with it. Pulie had gotten saved two years ago when Reverend Botts got off on a fiery kick and pitched a revival tent out here where the house stood now. But the saving only lasted until Pulie, all riled up by the yelling in tongues and going into esctasies, had gotten home to his bedroom.

Now he was in it. Now he was really *in* it. The mood had got him all the way and it would be days before it passed.

He had to do something. And it was about this time,

not quite consciously but still knowing what he was doing, he reached into his pocket and began to search around. Coins wouldn't do. She wouldn't believe that.

Ah. Yes. His fingers closed over his nail clippers.

And he rode back down to the south side, hoping she would still be there. All he wanted was to feel the warm little body next to him again. This time he'd take the resultant reaction and get home with it to the garage and take care of it there. Then maybe his head would clear a little. Sometimes it worked.

Cindy squeezed her eyelids so tightly shut the pressure against her eyeballs made them sting. If Augustine was trying to scare her, he was doing a good job, but she wouldn't give him the satisfaction of hearing her holler. He drove the bicycle so fast, he didn't seem to be pedaling. It was all a swift, almost graceful motion of leg and machine.

"I can get ahead of the wind if I want," he said. They side-wheeled around a corner. Cindy's head rolled, and the wind hit her like a scream. In spite of her determination, she gasped.

"You're not scared, are you?" Augustine asked. She could feel his stomach muscles working beneath her clutching hands as he spoke. His voice came in excited spurts, and she understood the warning: If she cried out, he was going to make them go faster. Somewhere she found some strength. "No," she hollered, and nearly choked on the air rushing down her throat. "This is fun."

They streaked on a moment. Rounded another corner.

Wait a second. They shouldn't be turning at all; her house was in a direct line north of Bitsy's.

She forced her eyes open. For an instant, everything

seemed disoriented. Lazlo Street? She nearly didn't even remember the name. And Averton Road? Bobbie's street? Pulie wasn't going toward her house.

"Where are you taking me, Pulie Gordon?" she asked. She heard that and wished she had bitten her tongue. She tried never to call him that or even think of him by that name. It was an insult, like the word cripple was to her.

"Just for a little ride," he said. "It's early. And you said this was fun, didn't you?"

"It isn't early," she said. Shadows of trees and bushes lay out across the lonely sidewalks. Someone had started a bunch of houses out here long before Cindy was born, and lots had been sectioned off and sidewalks laid before any building started. Then the company that was going to build the houses went bankrupt. Cindy knew the story because her parents had laughed about it. It was another good town joke, that outsiders had tried to come in and make money out of Edgar Falls and had been set back by fate.

Cindy eyed the shadows, and a tiny piece of alarm caught at her. She couldn't figure out why Pu—Augustine—was doing this to her. He'd promised to take her straight home, which was the only reason she'd accepted a ride with him; it was late and she could get home faster without getting yelled at. She was scared to ride double, especially now that she couldn't pedal her own bike well anymore. But it had been so late. She felt out of control now, as if Augustine had suddenly gotten a grip on her whole life. "You take me home," she said fiercely. "Right now."

And it was then it happened: Something so strange, it was a long moment of dawning horror before Cindy could react to it. Pulie Gordon let go of one of the handlebars and reached around behind her with his long arm and pressed her body closer to him.

The bike teetered one mad second and then righted itself. It had happened so fast, it might have been her imagination. Except Pulie suddenly did something else. And now the alarm turned to raging fear. He took one of her hands clutching his stomach and moved it down his body where it encountered something bulging and warm, something she had never felt before. But Bitsy had educated her well. She knew what she was touching.

She took a swift look around and realized they were heading for the mystery house. Calculated the risk. They were going fast enough for her to be killed if she followed through. But an instinct wiser than her fear caused her to throw her weight to the left.

Pulie screamed.

The bike threw them both and went careening on down the road alone, as if driven by a banshee. Cindy hit a pile of bushes, and everything went wild with stars in her head a second. But she scrambled, all but unseeing, to her feet and stood there trying to get her wind and her bearings. What had happened? It shouldn't have happened this way! Pulie had been ahead of her on the bike; he should be ahead of her on the road. But it hadn't happened that way. He lay behind her. Dead maybe? She hoped so. She was terrified, but not so terrified she couldn't feel outraged at what he had just done to her.

She eyed the side of the road quickly. It wasn't all bushes here. She didn't dare pass Pulie because maybe he wasn't dead, and he might come to any second. So she began to run as fast as her foot and a pain that shot suddenly up her left leg would let her.

He got to his feet suddenly, so swiftly she couldn't believe it. She stopped. And saw his eyes. And whirled madly, screaming, and began to run the only way she could.

No, no! her mind shrieked. *Go home, go home.*

But Pulie was between her and home. Grinning. And starting for her.

She dug wildly in her mind. "Don't you try to hurt me!" she shouted. "Bobbie Topin saw us go by on his street. I saw him. If I get hurt, he'll know it was you." Pulie's grin widened.

Frantically, she stared ahead. The house loomed there, beyond the meadow where she and Bobbie had sat so often watching it being built. And beyond that, the woods beckoned. If she could just make the woods, she could hide in there. Night would be dropping soon. That scared her, but not so much as what she thought Pulie meant to do. She didn't know all the words — Bitsy had only covered the words between people who *liked* to do those things — but it was what happened to a younger girl when she got in a car with a stranger, when her body was found in some shallow grave. Like a *woods* grave?

Cindy began to sob, and that didn't help her progress. The leg shrieked with pain now; she must have come down on it crooked.

"Wait," Pule called. "I just want to show you something. Let me show you something and I'll take you home."

He sounded so sincere. But he had sounded sincere a little while ago. She tore on toward the house. And all the time she could hear his harsh breathing, as if some huge and powerful animal were on the trail of some small supper tibdit — and excited because it hadn't eaten lately.

Across the meadow she ran. Pulie let out a holler, and she turned back without breaking her speed to see him go down on one knee.

Get to the house, the house. Put the house between you. Then he wouldn't see which part of woods she ran into.

She could hear Pullie snarling at something. Whatever had tripped him had hold of him.

That was lucky. Luck was with her. Cindy struggled to get control of her sobs because tears were blinding her. "It's going to be okay," she told herself. "It's all right."

Then her feet went out from under her, and she landed flat on her back. The grass, slick with evening dew and bog spot dampness, had betrayed her. The injured leg now raged with pain, and in total terror she raised her head and stared off toward the elusive woods. She would never reach them now. She heard Pulie's cry of triumph and knew he was free.

And then she saw sanctuary.

It couldn't be true. It was too good! She had fallen near the steps leading up to the massive porch of the house. She saw a slat a little loose there, under the steps. If she could just get there before Pulie saw. He was several hundred feet behind her.

Shrewdly, almost crazy with glee at her own shrewdness and incredible luck, she began to roll sideways. *Don't get on your feet; on your feet you're a target.*

She rolled all the way to the steps and crouched on her hands and knees as low to the ground as she could and pulled at the slat. She could only remember one prayer, "Now I lay me down to sleep," but she whispered it over and over. The slat came loose almost immediately and, forcing her sobs to quietness with almost superhuman effort, she slid behind the slat and under the steps and pulled it to.

"Thank you, Jesus," she whispered.

She heard the sound of delighted laughter in her head and knew it was her own because she had tricked him.

The darkness frightened her. But not as much as what prowled out there. She would stay here all night if she had to. At dark they'd start looking for her, and they'd find the stocking cap she'd lost in her fall. Sooner or later she would hear them calling near the house, and she would come out, and her father would wrap her up in a blanket, and Doc Jannessey would make the pain (that wasn't half so bad now that she was safe) go away, and Sheriff Hille would put Pulie where they put people like him for the rest of his life.

She rolled on her stomach and inched her way back deeper and deeper under the steps and planted little kisses on the sweet-smelling earth. To keep her fear in hand, she began to sing a song she had learned in kindergarten under her breath. "I had a little doggie, it used to sit and beg. But doggie tumbled down the stairs and broke its little leg. Oh, doggie, I will nurse you . . . " It was going to be a long night, but she knew a thousand songs.

She had sung three of them all the way through before she realized that something under here was singing with her.

"I didn't mean it, I didn't mean it." Pulie sat on the floor of his garage, hammering two large pieces of fireplace wood together. Tears rolled down his cheeks. "Jesus, keep me from all harm . . . " Singing. Where had he gotten the song? Out of his childhood? From the revival.

Jesus knew he didn't mean it. Things happened.

His head was so clear. It had never been this clear. He could hear his own voice with such clarity it nearly hurt his head. Every word like the sound of a bell. There was something terrible about the whole thing. Terrible and beautiful.

You shouldn't feel this kind of power, should you? He was sad. It was a sad thing. But this peace in his body . . . his body sang too.

Don't let the other thoughts crowd in.

But they belonged. They were part of all this peace.

He hadn't meant to take her to the house. She wasn't at Bitsy's ruins when he'd gone back, but he'd seen her small form limping up the street. Poor little thing. What a shame to be so beautiful and so maimed at the same time. Rather like his thoughts right now. He smiled through his tears. He was thinking like a poet. He'd never thought like a poet before.

He saw himself again, dropping his nail clippers into the rubble, bending to smear them a little with ash from a piece of charred wood.

"Cindy!" He got on his bike and went after her. "Hey, you missed something. I came back to look, too, and I found something you missed."

He saw her turning to him. "I've got to get home, Augustine," she said. "My mother's going to yell at me."

"Well, I would have picked it up and brought it to you. But I thought you'd like to find it so much since Bitsy's things mean a lot to you."

"What is it?"

"Come back and see."

She looked toward the house in Pellam Woods. The sun had dropped. Shadows were stretching out over the town. He could see her debating, matching her mother's yelling against some small, possible souvenir. "Tell you what," he said. "You run back and get it, and I'll ride you home on my bike. You'll get there a lot faster."

Clever. So clever.

She didn't exactly smile, but she seemed to brighten, so that the sun seemed to come back for a minute. She ran off down the street, back toward Bitsy's. He watched her go, saddened over the foot. But elated. In a few moments she would be nestled against his body. He would concentrate all his will and keep his body

200

from reacting until he got her home, then he'd let go all the feelings, rush them to his own house — correction — to the garage, and do something about them.

"Clippers?" she said a moment later. "That's funny. Bitsy had awful nails. She never even tried to take care of them."

He shrugged. "Well . . . " he said.

"She must have kept them in a drawer or something." She bent to pick them up and wiped them off carefully. "Thank you, Augustine. It's something anyway."

"You ready to go home now?"

"Oh, maybe I'd better walk. My folks might get mad seeing me ride double."

"I'll let you off a block from home." *Watch it. Don't let yourself panic. She'll do it, she's just being coy.*

Pulie hammered another nail into the thing he was making. He wished he had some good, polished wood. But these boards would have to do. "What a friend we have in Jesus . . ." Another hymn? He was full of them tonight.

"Augustine?" He started. His mother's voice came so sharply it cut right into his senses. For a second he thought she had come into the garage, and he nearly panicked. But then he realized the sound had come from the front porch. He got up and went to stick his head through the front door.

"Yes, Mommer?" he called.

Silence. Then, "Mommer?" Her voice came soft. "You haven't called me that in years, Augustine. What are you doing out there?"

"Just working on a school project," he said.

"It's late. You're home late. You shouldn't do that. I worry about you. I've got chicken in the oven." What? No mention of the dollar? Maybe his calling her Mommer had knocked it right out of her head.

"I'll be in pretty soon, Mommer. Got this thing to do

first. It's important."

"Well, I'm glad to see you're interested in school, dear."

"I am," he said. She went back into the house and shut the door.

He stood there a moment longer, at peace. Even with her.

The other end of his thoughts tried to get through and disturb him. The maimed ones.

"Where are you taking me, Pulie Gordon?"

Maybe calling him Pulie had done it.

Sitting back on the floor of the garage, he tried to remember again how it had happened. But that part of his thoughts had fogged a little, as if some bog mist had gotten inside his head.

Let me see.

It hadn't worked like he'd planned. His body got out of control.

He didn't mean to grab her bottom the way he did. Or to pull her hand against that swollen part of him. Oh, sweet Jesus. He hadn't known it could be like that. That warmth. It had been like her soft little hand burning holes into him.

"You take me home. Right now."

He hadn't consciously chosen the direction of the house in Pellam Woods when he began to veer from his intended path. Now he heard the alarm in her voice, but it somehow only served to excite him.

Did she begin to cry? He screwed up his forehead and tried to remember. He thought maybe she had begun to cry. Had he said, "Don't be scared, I won't hurt you?" Well, he'd *thought* it. He hadn't meant it to be a lie. He just had to know suddenly: *Was* everything pink?

Oh, sweet Jesus, yes. Blessed Mother Mary. Everything pink, pink and moist. And there was hair. That had surprised him. All soft and curly and sweet. All that pink to receive his burst of glory. There should have been fireworks going off.

Pulie hammered his last nail and stood up to survey the thing he had made. Rather pretty, he thought. Primitive looking. Or maybe natural was a better word.

What he had done had been a natural thing, too. She shouldn't have tried to deny him, that was all. She shouldn't have gotten on the bicycle in the first place and teased him the way she moved her little cunt against him, acting as though his speed scared her. Little tease.

He slipped off the light and started for the garage door.

Quietly, he got on the bike again. Who would have thought this old bike would become the agent of so much joy?

Were stars popping out? There should be stars tonight.

Pulie didn't turn on his headlight until he got to the street out by the house.

Then, reaching the old road beyond the meadows, something strange began to move over him. Wait a minute now. Where was all that good feeling going? He adjusted the thing he had propped on the handlebars. Wait a minute.

The tiniest point of fear began to chip away at the good feelings.

Had he done something wrong?

He looked up. Where were the stars?

He began to ride the bike again. Reached the lawn in front of the house. Stopped. Puzzled. He was losing his hold on the good feeling. Something else was creeping in. He didn't like what was creeping in.

But he started moving again. Got off the bike.

Hauled the thing he'd made down. He looked at it. Hard. A cross? Of *course* it was a cross. He'd made it, hadn't he? But for what?

Not for what. For who, stupid.

What did Cindy need a cross for?

Because she's dead.

Oh, now. *What?*

Go on and take it to her. It's a gift. That voice had control of him now. Bewilderedly, he tried to recapture one of the hymns. But he couldn't remember the name of the person they were sung to.

At the back of the house, he faltered.

What was that over there, that small pile of something. Was it blue? Blue and pink?

He ran for it.

Cindy? He called her name.

Cindy, get up and stop trying to scare me.

Hey, wait a minute. It had to be that way. She would have told.

But I didn't do it for that. It was an accident. She screamed and I stuck my hand over her face and held it there till I finished what I was doing. If she didn't want me to do it, what'd she come running out from under that porch for straight into my arms?

Then you admit you did it.

Something was making a terrible racket out here. Some ugly guy Pulie watched at a distance was hollering something awful and dragging clothes onto a rag doll. He grabbed up the doll and ran for one of the hated bog spots, pushing through mist, and threw it in. Why didn't it sink?

A rock. He needed a rock. But he didn't see any big enough.

It lay out there on the mud all stretched out on its face.

Who had thrown a perfectly good doll away?

Cindy was dead?

Cindy should have some kind of service.

He remembered the thing he'd brought. It was a cross, wasn't it? He could stand it up out here by her grave.

People get buried in the ground, dimwitto, not in a bog spot.

Well, some people did the best they could.

What was that? What was that noise way off there by the house? An animal? Whoever was fetching the cross stopped to listen, terrified. He didn't like the woods at night. He had never been in them before. Dark things might live in the woods.

No time to plant the cross. Something might be over there by the house, something waiting to grab him. He didn't have a hammer or a rock anyway to pound it in with. So he ran with it and threw it after her into the bog spot.

He ran around the house and got away from whatever there had been back there. Didn't he remember something about a chicken in the oven? But no, that was for a person named Augustine. Or maybe Pulie?

His head had begun to ache. The beauty was gone. Something terrible had happened, and he sadly feared when he found out what it was, it would have something to do with him.

Not Cindy. "What could the house want with Cindy?"

"Son?" Mr. Bottoms said.

Bobbie looked at him desperately. "I've got to see her."

"Now you don't want to do that," Mr. Bottoms said in a voice gentle for a big man. He tipped a tan mesh cap back on his head. "Wait till they fix her up. Tomorrow maybe."

"I've got to see her now." Bobbie's voice edged on hysteria.

"You don't want to see her," Mike said in the same tone as his father had used. "I thought we should run out and tell you because you liked Cindy. But you don't want to see her, Bob." Mike had gone hunting with the other townspeople when Cindy didn't come home. He'd been in that group that searched the grounds around the house.

"Wouldn't let you in anyway, son," Mr. Bottoms said. "They've got her over to Johnson's Mortuary. Coroner was off on a shooting, but he'll be over to fetch her soon and take the body to his lab in Gloaming."

Body? Bobbie shook his head trying to clear it. Maybe this was another nightmare?

Grandpop came in from the kitchen. "What's this?" he said.

"Evening, Mr. Wetterley," Mr. Bottoms said. "We came to bring bad news to Bobbie. Friend of his was killed tonight. Little Cindy Newman."

"Girl with the bad foot?" Grandpop's head had been clearer the past couple of days, if not perfect.

"*Please* take me to see her," Bobbie moaned to Mr. Bottoms. "Grandpop, I've got to see her." Outside her parents, he was afraid he was the only one in town who really cared about her; she should have a friend there.

He knew it was silly; she wouldn't know. But he would.

"You said she got killed," Grandpop said. "Car accident?"

"A lot worse than that, Mr. Wetterley." Why did people always look like they enjoyed telling bad news? Their voices took on a phony softness like Mr. Bottoms's had now. It wasn't just kindness that had brought Mike Bottoms out here to tell Bobbie. He wore the same look he'd worn the day after Miss Penny died. And a superior air, as if he had been in on something big tonight.

It's not an *event*, Bobbie wanted to scream at him. Cindy's *dead*.

Thinking the word, he reacted physically. A spasm wracked his body.

"I'm sorry, son," Mr. Bottoms said. "If I thought they'd let you in, I'd take you back. But we've all been sent on our way. Only the sheriff and his men from Gloaming and her father are with her right now. Everyone else went home to lock up doors. Poor Mrs. Newman got taken with a fit, and Doc Jannessey's seeing to her."

He signaled his son. "This is a sad night," he said. "Come on, boy. By now your Ma knows what's happened, and she's going to be pretty shook. She'll want to see I've got you safe to home. Lots of mothers going to be upset tonight."

They went out the door.

Bobbie wanted to run after them and throw himself into the car. But he stood there numbly in the cool night air, watching them pull away.

"What did they mean, worse than that?" Grandpop said. "Shut the door, boy. It's drafty."

"They mean she was murdered," Bobbie said. "They found her in a bog spot. They think Pu—Augustine—Gordon did it because Banker Bergins's wife saw them riding on his bike, and he's missing."

"That wimpy boy?" Grandpop said. "What for?"

"They think he raped her." It was Mike who had used the word when his father hesitated.

"Sorry," his grandfather said. "Sorry business. Did you see what Gladys did with newspaper?"

Oh Jesus, Grandpop, don't get off on Gladys now. Not when I need you.

Bobbie stared desperately at his grandfather. But it

was useless. The old man couldn't help him. No one could. Bobbie stared out into the night a moment longer, and then he ran for his jacket and gloves.

"Hey, where you going?" Grandpop called.

"I'll be back," Bobbie shouted. And plunged out the door.

He hadn't been out at night clear since Christmas. The darkness terrified him in a way it never had before, even when he was little. But he was doing what he had to do; he had to see for himself.

And something more. The story wasn't complete for him. It all had something to do with the house, and there had to be a clue that would prove it. He felt sure there had been clues with the others if he'd only known what to look for.

The Letkins house stood dark tonight. They couldn't be in bed — not at seven-thirty. He missed seeing their lights; the road loomed so dark before him.

He ran as fast he could, toward the town. He had no power to look at the house or to wonder if something ran with him in the night, something that smirked as if enjoying a good joke.

The funeral home was closer to his end of town than to any other. Within minutes he saw the lights of the white frame house, the Johnson Mortuary sign glowing in neon letters.

Bobbie had been inside once before. When Mom died — before the furnace got her. Before Mom died, he'd always thought the mortuary a mysterious and fascinating place. That came from reading all the horror books. But when someone you loved lay dead inside it, it became something grim.

Lights blazed in every window. A row of cars lined the curb out front. For Cindy? A momentary anger rushed over Bobbie. Mr. Bottoms had said everyone had been sent away.

Bobbie plunged through the front door and stopped, panting, startled. A big sign stood on an easel in the foyer, just as it had for Mom: Kristoff Service, 7 P.M. Tonight. People were gathered in a room up ahead. He could see the coffin: silver. Mom's had been plain wood.

For an instant memories of Mom and the news he had received tonight got all mixed up inside him, and a rush of blackness in his head threatened to cave his knees in. But he caught hold of the sign. Both of them nearly toppled.

"Can I help you, son? Why, it's Bobbie Topin." Mr. Johnson himself had come out of that room up ahead and was whispering to him.

"I've got to see Cindy Newman," Bobbie said.

"The little New—" Mr. Johnson's bland face registered shock. "You can't do that. We won't get her back until late tomorrow, and she won't be ready for viewing."

"I don't want to view her." Bobbie's loud voice startled even himself. He brought it down to match Mr. Johnson's. "Please," he begged. "I'm—I was a friend of hers."

"Quite out of the question. They're getting ready to transport her anyway. The coroner has arrived. Now you be on your way, or I'll have to remove you. You're disrupting Mrs. Kristoff's services."

Bobbie cast his eyes desperately down the hallway to his left. Was she down there? He nearly darted that way. But Mr. Johnson was not an old man. He was quite capable of making good his threat.

Something was ringing in the back of Bobbie's head anyway. Some memory. It struck! Cindy wasn't in here! She would be in that place out back, the small white cottagelike building with no windows. The ice house, the guys called it. They had discussed maybe breaking in there on Halloween night, except they knew no one had died, and there wouldn't be any bodies. Bobbie, thinking of Mom, had put the idea down the hardest.

"I'm sorry," Bobbie said.

"I understand," Mr. Johnson said, and held the door open for him. "Come back day after tomorrow. I'm sure I'll have her ready by then."

Ready? Sickness scalded Bobbie's throat. It was starting to really come through to him now. Cindy was dead. Mr. Johnson would mold her up like a clay doll, curl her hair maybe when Cindy liked to wear her pretty hair straight. Bobbie stopped a second and leaned against a wall, got his insides settled. And ran on.

He was right! The door to the ice house stood open. Men were coming out. Cindy's father was first, his head bent. He was sobbing bitterly.

"Wait a minute," Bobbie shouted. "I've got to see her."

Mr. Newman seemed not even to hear him. The man behind him, a sheriff's officer from Gloaming, stopped to stare at Bobbie, saw his intent and made a lunge, but the boy was too fast for him and darted through the doors.

The room glowed as bright as day, and he stood blinking a second. Where was she? His eyes shot around the room. There? On top of what looked to be a plastic bag?

This room reeled, too.

The sheriff's man lunged again. This time he succeeded. Arms closed around Bobbie and lifted him off the ground. But not before he had seen her. She wore her blue coat and jeans. But that was all he could make out; the rest was mud.

Of course it would be mud. Oh, Jesus.

The man carted Bobbie unceremoniously out of the building. "Cindy!" he shouted. And then, as the man started hefting him out the door and Bobbie wildly flailed out for something to grab onto to hold them back so he could see her better, his eyes lit on something else. He got only a glimpse as a second man latched onto him, and they dumped him out the door so hard he fell on his rear and jarred his teeth. "What was that?" he screamed. "What was that muddy thing I saw?"

Sheriff Hille was the second man who had grabbed him. "I don't know what this is all about, kid," he said warningly. "But don't come around here obstructing the law."

"What was it?" Bobbie hollered again. "That thing covered with mud in the corner?"

Mr. Newman stood on the sidewalk outside the ice house. He looked like a blind man waiting to be led away. "It was a cross," he said to Bobbie in slowly spaced words. "He must have made her a cross."

"You get out of here, boy," Sheriff Hille said, more ominously this time. "You get going while I'm watching you. Don't be making trouble when men are working, and you can see Clyde's grief."

A cross. A mud cross. He knew it! The clue was there, as if the house had sent it to him personally. As if it wanted to say jovially, *Hey, Bob old boy, I'm at it again, and I just wanted you to be sure who was really at the bottom of this. What do you think of that?*

Bobbie was running again. He hadn't even apologized to Mr. Newman. He ran insanely, first up the wrong block, then down another equally wrong, then stopped a moment, like an animal that has lost its scent of home, turning round and round in the wind that had died for a while and had started up again.

No thoughts at all moved in his head. He had gone beyond thinking, moving in a world of terror and rage so fierce it threatened to burn him up. Somehow he got himself going right, toward his own black patch of town.

He ran until his side had knives of fire in it, and his lungs threatened to explode. Ran and ran and ran, the way he seemed to want to run so much lately — if not in truth then in his head.

By the time he reached the street, he was near collapse, and he had no choice; he had to stop. He stood there with his hands pressed against his sides, then raised his eyes to the house. A pale moon rising outlined it clearly. The house had chosen an air of innocence tonight.

The rage rose to the boy's throat, erupting in a bellow that came out of him like no sound that had ever been heard on the streets of Edgar Falls.

Chapter Nine

"Do ye hear the willow weepin', do ye ken the night draw'n nigh? Do ye feel the rare airth movin', where my true love's bones do lie. . . ."

The old lines of a mother's made-up poem drifted through a young boy's mind. Other children had been rocked to lullabies. Robert Louis Topin had cut his teeth on *Little Orphan Annie's Come to Our House to Stay*. His mother's song had been of a highwayman riding, riding, riding, through the long and endless night; his fairy princes had been headless horsemen crying through lonely hollows. She had loved all of it with her beautiful imagination and her delicious sense that there was no thrill like the thrill of scaring yourself with words. She had loved all of it, believed none of it, but she had spawned a child who was cursed to carry it all beyond a game.

The house was eating the town.

Bobbie sat in the church staring vacantly at the wooden figure of Jesus Christ splayed out over the altar.

Listen to me, he wanted to scream. *Everybody! You've got to do something about the house. Before it gets all of us.*

He wanted to unleash the fury that had given him no

peace and no sleep for days.

He had known it all along, from that first night he sat staring at the house and felt the shadow moving inside, probably even before. But he'd tried to talk himself out of it. Something hideous had moved into the town, something that was working on the people to destroy them all. He hadn't trusted his own feelings beyond taking them to Lobe Peters and then to Gloriana Reege. Now Cindy was dead. The thought that he might somehow have saved her had driven him to the very edge of his sanity. Why hadn't he told *her*. She was closer to him than anyone. If he had, she might not have ridden off with Pulie Gordon on that bicycle. Then again, she might have thought he was crazy.

"Are you all right, Bobbie?"

Had someone spoken to him? He turned slowly, the movement throbbing his head. Gloriana Reege sat in the pew behind him. "Are you all right?" she whispered again.

He couldn't nod. He could only look full into her eyes, and what she saw in his seemed to make her shrink back against the hard wood.

"Our little Cindy is with the angels now," Reverend Botts was saying in his saccharine voice. "Running and playing with the other children in God's nest. No lame foot anymore." Bobbie threw up his hands to cover his ears at the bereaved mother screaming suddenly in agony behind the heavy curtains that screened the family.

The sound trailed off. Bobbie lowered his hands and tried to ease the contortions out of his face. He shouldn't have come today. His nerves were frayed to the snapping point. Each movement of his head made the blood pound so fiercely he felt as if it would soon have to find an outlet and pour from his ears. His eyes burned fiercely. Three nights with only snatches of sleep had left him nearly hysterical with exhaustion. But he was alert. Every emotional cough that sounded in the chapel, every sniffle, became a hot needle jabbing into his awareness. He felt as if he had been tuned to the room, his body the instrument that received every expression of grief.

Sound rushed suddenly about him—ocean waves, pounding into the room. He stared about fearfully. It was only the rustle of clothing as people began to rise. What was happening?

You remember. It's like it was with Mom. Only there were dozens of people to look now. And more outside the church who couldn't squeeze in. The whole town had turned out to say good-bye to Cindy.

Our little Cindy was dead. Our precious little girl we never got around to getting the foot for.

Bobbie glared at the figures around him. The foot money had gone to pay for her funeral; Mike had ridden out to tell him. If they'd bought her the foot, she might have been able to run from Pulie. One brief instant Bobbie thought savagely that maybe the town deserved what was happening to it.

He didn't want to see the body. But when he stood, the blood went so wild in his head it blinded him, and he got caught in the group from his row going up to the altar. They swept him along until he found himself climbing the three short steps and staring down at the Shirley Temple head, at the Mr. Johnson-created smile. Heavy flower smell nauseated him.

"What are you doing?" someone gasped. Hands grabbed at his and slapped them away.

"I want to straighten her hair," he thought he said, and was swept away under the pierced feet of Jesus and down the other set of stairs. In a moment he found himself blinking in the sun-filled, near spring day.

"You're over your flu, I hope." Miss Larimer stood

there, dabbing at one eye with the edge of a lace handkerchief. He hadn't been in school for two days. During the ten minutes he'd spent in conversation with Mike, who rode out on his bike to give Bobbie the funeral time yesterday, Bobbie'd told him he hadn't gone because he was sick.

"You missed the last midterm," Miss Larimer said. "And I was already running it late." The voice, too high for her masculine-looking form, scraped through Bobbie's dazed brain like a fingernail drawn across the blackboard.

"I'll be there tomorrow," he said.

From inside the church came the sound of the family taking one last look at Cindy. The mother made a keening sound, and it plucked at Bobbie's frayed nerves until he had to keep his mouth tightly shut to keep from making the same sound himself.

Then they came out the door, Reverend Botts supporting Mrs. Newman, who cast her eyes wildly and hopefully around the assembled crowd as if someone there might have the power to declare this all a nightmare. Clyde Newman leaned on the arms of a man someone murmured was his brother from Pittsburgh. He staggered away from his brother's grip suddenly and swung a drunken punch at the other man's stomach. "Take it easy, son," the brother said. Mr. Newman began to cry, except there were no tears.

Bobbie stood in the bright sunlight and tried to work up some emotion himself. But he had the feeling he was a black and white one-dimensional figure that had somehow blundered into a movie and couldn't remember if he had a part or not. The coffin came out the door, borne by Banker Bergins, Lobe Peters, the president of the chamber of commerce, and Ed Kroger. They moved slowly toward the curb, and Bobbie turned, drawn by the ugly blue thing glinting in the sun and the knowledge of what lay inside. How long would it be, he wondered, before the eyes fell in and the maggots got her? He shuddered, an involuntary spasm meant to throw off some of the horror. But it didn't work. He hadn't seen Mr. Johnson pull the hearse to the curb, and he watched dully now as the tall man got out wearing the same somber expression he had worn for Mom. The doors at the rear of the hearse yawned open.

"Bobbie, I want to talk to you." Gloriana Reege put her hand on his shoulder, and he jumped.

"I can't," he said. "I'm going to the cemetery."

"How?" she asked.

He could have gone with Bottoms's dad; they'd offered earlier. "I'm going to walk."

Not walk. Run. All the way. Run off some of this non-feeling.

"It's two miles," she said. "It'll be over before you get there. Come with me. I'll take you home after."

He wanted to go by himself, but he didn't have the small amount of energy required to insist on it. What difference did it make anyway? A few moments later he found himself in the front seat of her Pinto, not quite sure how he'd gotten there. They rode silently behind the other cars. Up ahead the hearse followed the straight lines of the town streets — Bobbie could see it through the other windshields. "I'm sorry for you," Miss Reege said. "I know you two were friends."

Bobbie didn't answer.

"They'll punish him when they catch him," she said. "He's nearly eighteen; he may be tried as an adult."

"It wasn't his fault," he said. "It was the house."

"Oh, Bob." It came out a sorrowful moan for his sake. He shut up and watched the line of cars turn and snake up the hill to the cemetery.

"Jesus, open thy arms to this our child, our friend, our little neighbor." Mr. Botts had gotten himself into an inspired mood, and his voice droned on the still air like a bee circling a particularly sweet blossom. Sniffles ran through a crowd which had overflowed onto several dozen graves. The greening grass under Bobbie's feet felt as if it were burning through the soles of his shoes.

And all the time, Mrs. Newman sobbed, and her husband kept shaking his head like a bull working itself into a frenzy. Bobbie was looking away from all of them. He could see the house clearly from here. It stood in sunlight, all innocence, as if it knew Bobbie's gaze was on it and was saying, "Who *me*?"

No one noticed the boy with the hollow eyes and clenched fists. Ed Kroger's wife was thinking she should have made a bigger potato salad to take to the Newman's after; people always loved her potato salad. Banker Bergins was eying Tressa Allen and thinking he'd never seen her in black before; she looked particularly fetching in black, and he must remember that. The second Mrs. Jorgenson was contemplating how she could slip away and get the cap off the bottle in her purse. She hadn't wanted to come; she hadn't known the dead kid, but her husband made her, saying Craig had known the girl. She rarely did what Bert wanted, but she was trying to be nice to him lately so he'd think harder about moving. Look at that straggly, redheaded little shit over there her husband called "son." Wouldn't he ever grow up and leave them in peace? Sass mouth. At least twice a day he needed a good one across the mouth, but he was big enough to hit her back and would.

Nola Larimer was wondering how long it would be before the excitement that had charged her classroom would settle down. Banker Bergins's wife had been looking at Alicia Newman and thinking what a sad thing to lose a child. Her own were grown now, but if she lost one, it would be hideous. And then she caught her husband's expression and looked across the casket at the woman his eyes had settled on and remembered she had something more important to brood about than a woman's losing her child.

Elizabeth Botts, bored by her husband's rhapsodizing—he was only eloquent in his official status, never where it counted—looked around at all the depressed faces and decided that maybe she wouldn't call off her next scheduled tour out of respect for death after all. Quite a few of her old-timers were here, and they needed a lift. Death was always traumatic to them, though this one not so bad as when someone their own age went. Maybe Patrice Bergins would come along and they could take an extra load.

Only Bobbie looked at the house.

Gloriana Reege parked a block from Bobbie's home. She had insisted on taking him, and he was too spent and dazed to argue, and he stared out hollow-eyed on the day. A shift in weather had begun quite abruptly. Spring couldn't make up its mind how to come in for sure, and a roll of gray clouds rolled in on the horizon and headed for Edgar Falls.

"I have to tell you what I've been doing the last couple of days," Miss Reege said.

Her voice hurt Bobbie's head. He wanted to get home. These last hours since Cindy, he hadn't been able to do much of anything except lie around. The outburst against the house the other night had drained what he had left of mental strength. Not that lying around helped much: He was going crazy with trying to dredge up enough ideas on how to get even with the house.

But Miss Reege's next words caught his fragmented attention. "I investigated the house," she said. "I found out where it came from."

For the first time in three days, energy vibrated in Bobbie Topin's body. He sat up straight, turned to her. Vindication! It was coming. Now there would be two of them, and maybe two of them could think of something.

"It wasn't so hard," she said.

She reached across him and opened the glove compartment and pulled out a pack of Salems; it took her an agonizing amount of time to light one. "I decided to pursue it because I was impressed," she said. "Your story about the muddy cross impressed me when I heard about the one that sick boy threw into the bog after Cindy, especially when I heard the bog spot was one near the house."

Bobbie winced and fought a picture of Cindy lying out there alone in that mud. "It wasn't a big cross like you said," she murmured. "But it was a cross, and it was muddy."

Bobbie leaned into her words, waiting for her to get these others out of the way and to the ones he wanted to hear. "I checked with some realty friends in the city, and they tracked it for me. I didn't do that before because it didn't seem cricket. I mean, I only accepted whatever information my client wanted to give me about her employer's plans—and I had no actual dealings with the house itself, only the property."

"Please," Bobbie said.

"It was built at the turn of the century in a small town in southern Missouri, by a man whose father made a fortune in the gold rush in California."

"Miss Reege—"

"Bob, there's nothing wrong with the house. It has no bad history. The only people who ever even died in it were an old grandmother and later her husband. The house has sold and resold many times since the original owners—too hard to keep up and people not hiring out as servants as they did in the old days. It has no reputation for evil. On the contrary, I made phone calls to people who've lived around it for years. The house has always been regarded as a sunny, happy place."

All the eagerness escaped from Bobbie. He made a wheezing noise that was like a terrible thing he had heard once on a documentary when a Nazi war criminal was shot to death by a firing squad: a sound like a dying baby's whine.

"Bob, I believe you did have some psychic intuition about Cindy, maybe because you were close to her. The muddy cross is certainly impressive. And I thought about her dying out by the house, too. But I cannot make a leap to the house itself."

She caught his look and exploded, "For God's sake, it's just wood and stone and plaster and a bunch of antique furniture. How could it *do* these things you keep accusing it of? It mustered a voice maybe and told Augustine where to find Cindy? I know they found signs she'd tried to hide under the porch. It grew a long foot and kicked Miss Penny's legs out from under her? And the fire. Now how in God's name could it start a fire at Bitsy McCall's?"

"You investigated it," he said doggedly if weakly. There it was, out in the light of a clouding day, all the things he'd told himself over and over. To no avail.

"Because I like you. Because I could see your pain and your terror the day you came to me. And because *I* needed to see if by some stretch of my most insane imagination I could hook up Cindy and the cross and the house. I can't. Give it up. It's going to drive you crazy, and then it really will have accomplished something. Only from inside *you*, Bob. Look. Look at it, for Christ's sake."

When he didn't turn his head, she grabbed his cheeks in both hands, the filter of her cigarette scraping across his right, and forced his head around. "Look at it!" she commanded. "A house!"

She couldn't see it was smirking.

Bobbie grabbed the handle and threw open the door, hurling himself out of the car. He turned back at her to scream that he didn't care what she said, *he* knew. And then he saw her eyes. They were still on the house.

He gasped and took a step backward, his hand still on the door. It was only a flash, so fast it might have been a trick of the sudden cloud that crossed the sun. Except that he knew it was no trick.

They flashed there in the space of time it took to blink. Two skulls. One in each eye. Staring knowingly at him. And grinning.

"What's the matter with you *now*?" she said fiercely, in the voice of one who had done all she could to help a maniac who refused to look on his own madness.

"It's going to get you, too," he said. And he turned blindly, forgetting to slam the door, and started running.

He burst in on the old man sitting in his chair watching the cloud bank come on. What he had seen in Gloriana Reege's eyes had thrust him into action. No more excuses. There wasn't anything he could do about the house. Multiply Miss Reege's reaction to him by the others in town — they wouldn't bother to humor him because they "liked" him.

It crossed his mind to burn the house down. But that would mean going out there again, and word from God that He would personally protect him could not have forced his feet out there.

They had to get out of town, that's all. The old man had to have some kind of bomb set under him. Maybe worry over a crazy grandson would do it.

The old man didn't turn from the window. "Spring's gonna come on hard this year," he said.

"Grandpop, we've got to move. We've got to get out of town. Right now. Today." No ceremony. No working up to it. Hysteria had supplanted all the amenities.

The old man's head came slowly around. "We *what*?"

"We've got to get out of town. Something evil's got hold of it, and people are dying, and they're going to keep on dying. Miss Reege may be next." Oh, good. Yes, sir. These were words designed to get him what he wanted, all right. Grandpop was looking at him with suddenly squinted eyes.

"You been out behind the shed with something you shouldn't be drinkin'?"

"I've been to a funeral," Bobbie shouted. "Cindy Newman's funeral. Remember? Jesus, Grandpop, you know she died."

"I know she died," he said. "Young prevert got her. Don't cuss. Gladys doesn't like foul talk."

"It was the house," Bobbie said. "The house got Pulie first." Gladys? Oh, Christ.

Grandpop blinked. Once. "What house?"

"The house out in Pellam Woods."

"The one Mizz Botts's been tryin' to get me to tour?"

"Something's wrong with the house. It's evil. I don't know how to explain it, but I know things like that sometimes, Grandpop. They call it being psychic. The house is doing things, I don't know how, but all the bad things in town, they started happening when it moved in." He didn't give a shit what Miss Reege had found out; there had to be something no one had told her. "I don't know what it does to people, but it makes them

223

do ugly things."

All the feelings he'd had for months now began to gel. The house didn't do anything itself—couldn't. Miss Reege's irony about it growing feet hadn't escaped him. But it worked on people somehow. Something malevolent inside it made people that way, too. *Maybe only people who had been inside it?* But that must be half the town by now. And why not him? He'd been inside. Bitsy—she *hadn't* been in. As far as he knew. Maybe you didn't even have to go in—only be near?

"Please, Grandpop." He hadn't felt himself cross the room or pick up the blue-veined hand lying in the scrawny old lap. But now he looked down and sat himself holding it, and he began to tug on it. "I'm not crazy. There are other people in the world who know things like I do. Just believe me. We've got to get out of this town."

And then who will know, who will help the town?

Bobbie pushed the thought aside. He was no hero, didn't have the slightest idea how to be one. He was no white light going up against evil like happened in books. This wasn't like in the books. This was a blackness that filled up your soul and let only one message filter through: Save yourself. And Grandpop if he would come.

Grandpop held back with surprising strength for one so fragile of bone. "You're telling me we have to get out of town? Because of a house?"

Bobbie could feel the draining starting again. As if all the blood were seeping out of him.

"I'll have to think on this," Grandpop said.

A small hope, winging up with half its feathers gone.

"I ain't known you to lie," Grandpop said.

"No, sir."

"You think you got some kind of power tells you this house is evil?"

"Yes, sir." Bobbie had stopped pulling the old man's hand, but he held on.

"You want to move. You're not happy here?"

Bobbie started to protest. Then he realized his grandfather was groping for his own explanation. He could almost see the wheels turning behind the eyes paled blue by age: Lonesome kid. Lost his mother. Stuck with an old man. Only one or two friends, and one of them is dead and the others never come around. Cock-and-bull storying him despite what he'd said about not being a liar. Wanted to move and knew if he'd just asked outright, it wouldn't work. Wanted to move so bad maybe he even believed this flimflam about that house. Maybe better think about this. Boy wants to move that bad should maybe get his request considered. I wanted to live out my days here, but this is my daughter's son. My daughter's son all right. But gone *looney*.

Bobbie saw that last thought come into his grandfather's face, and he knew that was it. He had failed.

"We'll talk about this some other time," Grandpop said. "Nap time." And just that abruptly, he dismissed the subject. The eyes closed, then came open a second. "You see Doc Jannessey tomorrow, boy," he said. "Flu may be comin' down on you again."

"Grandpop . . ."

The old man closed his eyes again. Bobbie stood there still holding his hand, looking out on the gray-filled day.

A matching grayness had never left him. He looked into his grandfather's face. Thin, nearly transparent lids shuttered his eyes. The hand in Bobbie's felt like a piece of soft parchment paper. He stared at the hand a long time, and then he traced its blue lines with one finger.

"I'm sorry, Grandpop," he said.

For two years now, he'd had a vision of himself taking care of the old man, on into his teens. His mother would have wanted that, and Bobbie wanted it, too. He saw that dream fade now.

Grandpop would never understand why Bobbie had left him, maybe wouldn't even care—Bobbie had never known if the old man had any feelings for him. If he did understand and care one day, it would be too late to do anything about it. One part of the boy said stay and take care of his grandfather. But there was a stronger part—one that cried out for self-preservation.

Very soon—as soon as he got up the guts to steal that part of money left from checks he knew Grandpop kept hidden somewhere in the house—he would be getting out of Edgar Falls.

He knew it sounded dumb. But other kids had gone before—were doing it all the time. Even his age. Dropping away from their homes and school. Losing themselves in cities. Working for peon wages for people who didn't ask questions about cheap labor. He was big for his age. If he got some high boots, he might go for fourteen, even fifteen. He could walk to Gloaming—catch a bus for somewhere else. Anywhere else. Maybe there'd be enough money to last till . . .

The plans whirled and whirled in his hyper brain.

The house might get Grandpop, his mind said.

He had a choice. He wouldn't listen.

Bobbie set the hand back in the frail lap and reached to smooth back a sliver of white hair that had strayed down to Grandpop's forehead. For a second, he thought he was going to cry, and the tears would have been welcome. But he didn't. In a moment he straightened. And made the decision to go into Grandpop's bedroom right now to start searching for the money Grandpop called his stash.

* * *

He dreamed a protective canvas surrounded the earth. It was a secret closely guarded by scientists so as not to frighten people; after all, canvas is a flimsy thing to stand between you and the outer darkness. The canvas was painted blue where there was sky and green where there was grass and brown where there were mountains. It changed its colors with the sun.

He had a vital job: to patrol the rim of the earth and make sure no worn places appeared in the canvas. He alone held this responsibility. People did not know who he was because he went through their cities and villages dressed in various guises, making his rounds of the canvas at night, carrying a flashlight invisible to all eyes but his (which had been specially treated). The light could flash for hundreds of miles, and he played it constantly up and down and on the ceiling of the canvas. He had never found the least problem.

Until now.

Until this moment when he stood frozen in horror, watching the tip of a gigantic knife slowly penetrate the canvas.

Frantically, he sent an SOS through the beeper at his waist. "It's your problem," the answer came back. "Why do you think we gave you the job? It's up to you to save the world."

Something snuffled around the slash the knife was creating, something slobbering and greedy and mindless. Something in the outer darkness getting ready to rip open the fabric of the earth and—and what?

He had a sword, and he ran for the knife and began to battle it, but the knife kept on coming. Then it stopped and slipped back through the ugly rip in the canvas. He heard something snicker. He did not see anything enter through the slit, but he knew when it came in.

And he threw down the light and his sword. They had not told him how to save the world because they had not really believed anything could happen. "It's in, it's in!" he screamed into the beeper.

Only one thing controlled his mind: get away and save himself. He began to run, throwing off his beggar's disguise. Then something on the distant edges of his wildly shrieking senses got through to him; it was the gentle sound of a woman's weeping.

He stopped a moment, looking behind to see if the thing had followed. He listened. "Go home," the weeping voice said. "Go home and look to my father."

"I can't," he cried. "Don't ask me that. He wouldn't believe me. He'll say the canvas is a boy's imagination."

"Go home. He needs you more."

"I can save myself. I can't save the ignorant, too."

"For me," she said.

And he answered, with a great weight settling on his soul, "Yes, Mother."

Bobbie came awake feeling listless and heavy. He lay there waiting to see if the nightmare would drag him back. But this time gloomy light showed behind his window shade.

He knew what the dream was about; he had been through this before. No matter how hard he pep-talked himself, he eventually came back to one thought: If the house tried to get Grandpop, who would protect him? Bobbie wasn't sure he could; he only had the one experience when he'd gotten Craig out of the house to back him. But there was another factor. Grandpop was old, too old to do for himself. Who would make him eat when he went off into that other world? Alone and in a long period like that, he could starve.

Hey, a voice nagged. *He had his chance. You tried to*

warn him.

Would you listen *to a warning like that?* he came back.

He had to stay. If enough things happened (not that he wanted them to, but they probably would anyway), maybe then Grandpop would listen to reason. Until then, Bobbie stood himself on a fatalistic platform. He gave up searching for the money. He couldn't leave. Not yet.

Grandpop looked a little vague when Bobbie gave him his usual poached eggs for breakfast. But he knew what day it was and that it was drizzling outside. Bobbie hated to have to go to school on mornings Grandpop started looking distant. But what could he do? He'd already missed several days, and he had no choice but to leave the old man alone. That scared him. Grandpop was within sight of the house anytime he went outside or cared to look out a back window. But maybe it only did its dirty work at night. Bobbie trudged off to school carrying a note signed in Grandpop's spidery writing, his mind swirling—part of it on the dream and the dark and gibbering thing that had gotten into the world.

He was almost glad to get back. The brick, one-story school building looked warm and comforting, as if once you walked through the iron playground gates, nothing bad could happen to you. "Don't believe it," he mumbled to himself.

A bunch of boys lounged by the gates. He eyed them, especially Craig Jorgenson. Wanting to warn them. *Don't go near the house again*, he wanted to say. But they'd laugh and ignore the warning. It might even challenge them to go back again.

Bobbie started on by. This morning huddle was a ritual a bunch of sixth grade boys went through on all but the nastiest days, and this one was only misting.

"Hey, Topin." Bobbie stopped, startled. Jorgenson was waving him over, an excited look on his face.

Oh, jeez. Something else hadn't happened already, had it? Something their ghoulish minds wanted to share?

"You hear about Banker Bergins?" Craig called, and Bobbie's heart nearly stopped.

He didn't want to hear, but he was out of control when it came to news like this; he had to know everything. "Banker Bergins?" he said, steeling himself.

"His wife shot him and Tressa Allen last night," Mike Bottoms said when he joined them. "Caught 'em in bed out at Tressa's place. Somebody called my mom and told her. I didn't get all the details 'cause I could only hear Mom's side. But I guess they been screwing a long time. Only Mrs. Bergins didn't figure it out till the funeral."

"How'd she figure out it was Tressa?" Hetherington asked eagerly.

"Didn't get that part," Bottoms said. "But she didn't do a very good job. Hit Tressa in one boob, but the bullet didn't get through there to anything vital." (Snickers all around from the seven or eight boys gathered.) "Creased him in the thigh."

"Where's the thigh?" someone asked.

Bottoms grabbed his own. "Here, stupid. What do you want to bet she was aiming at something else?" More snickers. "Anyway, they got Mrs. Bergins in custody and Tressa and Mr. Bergins had to stay overnight in the Gloaming hospital."

"Wonder if they got a coed room together?" This from Joey Hetherington, and it brought the house down. Someone in his glee—Jorgenson probably—

clapped Bobbie on the back, and he went with them as the bell rang, full of mixed feelings. One was a kind of desperate relief. It couldn't have anything to do with the house, could it, when it had been going on a long time? The other was a creeping warmth because just for a moment there, when the hand smacked on his back, he had felt a little less alone.

Chapter Ten

Shee*it*!

What *was* it? What *happened*? There wasn't anything left! Just some boards that stunk. He shuffled through rubble and picked one up. Holy Mother of Christ, man. Was it fire? This thing damp from rain stunk like *fire*?

Now wait a minute, he told himself. That didn't mean Bitsy and the kids didn't get out. They must be okay someplace. The question was where. And how to find out. It wasn't worry over his family bugging Gary Purdy, although he'd felt a little pinch in the gut there for a sec. It was money had brought him back. His usual motivation for anything. Well, maybe he had two for seeing Bitsy right now.

Things hadn't been going so hot. It was hard to find good stuff to screw when you had pockets even a rat wouldn't sniff at. Times had been hard the past few weeks. He'd come down with a lousy flu, and Jaydene wasn't into taking care of a guy couldn't get his dick up five seconds it didn't fall over on its side as sick as he was.

Now he'd got his interest *and* his dick back, she'd split before he could prove it. And he sure wasn't gonna find nothing else on the streets on short notice. Hookers even were picky over in Slopetown. They wanted to see the flash of green before they let you in between their legs or even up their rear. That was his second problem. He was out of everything, including the last dumpy little envelope of that homegrown stuff he'd nursed out by the irrigation ditch in Slopetown. Jaydene hadn't left a drawer untouched, the bitch, when she took off. When he found her, he was gonna ram himself up her so far her eyes would fall out. Not for his pleasure. To fix her so she wasn't good for some other stupid asshole to rip off when he was down sick.

Bitsy was the answer to both his problems. Temporary answer, that is. He didn't mean to hang around this pile-of-shit town any longer than to give that fat body such a going over she'd remember it forever.

Gary smiled to himself. She called it a pecker and complained every time he got near her with it they were gonna make another kid. But all he had to do was get hold of those big boobs of hers, and she fell right over on her fat back and let him go at it all he wanted.

His grin broadened. And he started going excited. He sort of missed Bitsy, even a couple of times when he and Jaydene were right in the middle of it. Jaydene was too scrawny. But Bitsy now. When you got into her, man, just the power of those huge legs wrapped around you was awesome.

The burned board went plopping back to the ground, and Purdy hurried toward the piece of junk he'd picked up in Slopetown that fondly called itself a car. But what the hell. He'd gotten it for a few lousy joints from a college kid getting ready for exams. The smartass was strung out and didn't have nothing left to sell. He was used to a lot heavier stuff than a little funweed, but he didn't have no bread, and Gary's contact—who didn't mess with small stuff—had sent him around.

"You better run, crap pile," Gary informed the car after he'd smacked the battery and got in. "Or I'm gonna run this big thing I got growing on me straight into your gas tank.

The only thing was when the mother turned over—cars listened better than women—he sat there looking out a windshield with a new mist on it (wouldn't this damn weather *ever* let up—April was supposed to bring *flowers*, he remembered from someplace) wondering where to go. There wasn't just any old body in town he could ask where Bitsy'd gone. Everybody probably had a pretty good idea who it was ripped off old man Groves's hardware back in the summer. That's why he'd come into Edgar Falls late. So he wouldn't be spotted. So he could hit Bitsy for her welfare money with a promise of getting himself some new clothes with it so he could get a real live job and haul her and the kids over to Slopetown.

Bitsy'd do it. Bitsy wanted out of this town even more than she wanted his pecker. She used to talk about it sometimes, but he'd known all along he'd split alone someday. He'd split this time, too. But when he got through showing how much he missed her by grinding her ass off enough times to keep her happy for a while, she'd trust him.

Question was where *was* she? There weren't too many places cheap enough for anybody on welfare. He knew she'd be on welfare. How else could she survive with five kids when he wasn't around to keep them going with the dealing he'd always done in Gloaming and the things he picked up now and then?

They had to be someplace. Only where? And who would tell him? He lit a cigarette and thought about it a while. He didn't like that. It hurt his brain. Everything hurt his brain lately because he wasn't clear over the fucking flu. If he was over the fucking flu, he wouldn't've had to go out in this weather and be here tonight at all. He could rip off a few places he had his eye on. But he couldn't trust himself right now. Too shaky and rattlebrained. He might do something careless. You had to have a clear head and steady hands to follow Gary Purdy's preferred profession.

And then all of a sudden it hit him! He knew who could tell him about Bitsy.

"Who the hell is *that*?"

Craig blinked a couple times before he answered. "Uh—my stepmother." He hadn't got over the surprise yet of hearing a smack on his window and finding Gary Purdy outside in a getting-ready-to-rain-again night.

"Oh, yeah," Gary said. "Bessie." He smirked, but he didn't let it show on his face. Times past he'd gotten to know Bessie Lewis—Jorgenson now—as a little something more than a stepmother. She wasn't as much fun as she'd always thought she was, though. And never worth the ten bucks. Thinking of money brought him to the subject at hand.

"Listen, kid," he said. "I got to find Bitsy, but I don't want anybody to know I'm in town. Figured I could trust you."

Craig stared at the long-haired, scroungy guy who smelled of slept-in clothes he'd let into his bedroom through the window and gasped. "You don't *know*?"

"Know what? Hey, you got anything you could find me to eat? I been sick lately, and I get kinda weak."

Craig went on staring. How could he tell him? "There's some leftover hash. But you wouldn't want that." Bessie's cooking was always left over. Sometimes it lay in the fridge for days, till it was so dead somebody—her stepson mostly—had to get rid of it.

"There's peanut butter," he said, holding off the telling.
"That'll do."

Craig went off to the kitchen, hands slapped over his ears. They were at it as usual tonight. Something again about Bessie getting sick and tired of being nice all the time and it getting her no place. That was a laugh. Bessie ever being "nice" was a real belly laugh.

In the kitchen, he had to take his hands off his ears, and his nerves shot back up to crash time. He slapped peanut butter on four pieces of bread fast. At least in his room with the door shut, it was a little better. He'd been about to get his radio and plug the plugs into his ears—a trick he'd run onto lately—when he'd heard Gary Purdy's rap.

There was half a can of beer left in the fridge, he remembered. Bessie was always accusing him of snitching her beer anyway; might as well make good this time.

Then he started back for his room. Jeez. Purdy didn't know.

"Hey, man, a brew and peanut butter. Could a king do better?" Craig had found Gary lying on his bed, damp clothes and all, when he got back. Now he was sitting up smacking his lips.

Craig waited for him to finish, shifting from foot to foot. "What a pair of lungs," Purdy muttered. "You listen to this often?"

Craig nodded.

"Well, why do you hang on here? You're a big kid. Big enough to get out on your own. What you wanna put up with that kind of shit for?"

"I don't know." Pop, he guessed. He couldn't leave his old man with this mess he'd married. Not that Pop noticed his sacrifice. Pop had gone sullen since Ace closed down. Only time he perked up was when he went to Gloaming to get his unemployment check and came home by way of The Brewery.

"Well, listen." Purdy swung his legs off the bed. "I don't wanna stay in town too long. I'd be too popular if a couple people figured I was here, if you get my drift."

Craig got his drift all right. Prob'ly have to air out the room when Purdy took his body stink away. But that ran from his mind when he saw the time was here.

"Now tell me where my wife is," Purdy said. "I got business with her, and I ain't seen my kids for months."

"Uh, Gary . . ." Craig said.

Purdy helped him out. "There was a fire, wasn't there? I been out there tonight. Jesus, ain't nothin' left but some burned boards and trash. What happened?"

"They figure Bitsy fell asleep with a cigarette." Craig coughed.

For chrissakes, why did the kid look like he had a fly up his ass? "Well, where are they?"

Craig pulled in a big breath. "They're dead, Gary."

"Aw now . . ."

"It's true. They got all burned up in the fire. Bitsy lived for a few minutes after, but . . ." Craig broke off. For crap sakes. He was seeing it for real for the first time. Five little kids. They were scrounges maybe, like their mom and pop. But just little kids. And now Cindy was dead, too. It was weird. He'd never known a dead kid.

"You're not snowing me, man?"

"I'm not snowing you, Gary."

"Well, Jesus Christ. What the hell." Purdy had gotten to his feet, and he swayed, then righted himself. "Well, I'll be damned." He hadn't really missed them while he'd been gone. Shit, he probably had a kid here and there all over the place. But he'd still been the seed that'd papa'd Bitsy's. Shit. Dead?

"You want to lie back down?" Craig asked anxiously. Purdy was taking it hard, and Craig wished he could

237

wash his mouth out for telling him.

"No, man. I guess I better get on back. I got me a little pad in Slopetown." He caught himself. "Hey, you won't tell no one that, will you?"

"I won't tell."

"Figured that. That's why I come to you in the first place. Jesus, dead?" Purdy wandered over to the window and opened it again. "Well," he said. "I guess that's that. I come back to get Bitsy and take her and the kids with me." It didn't sound like a lie right now. Maybe that was what he'd meant to do all along. In fact, he was sure it was. It all sounded kind of noble in light of the news he'd just had laid on him. He swung a leg over the windowsill.

"I'm sorry, Gary," Craig said.

"Yeah? Well, thanks, kid. I'd rather you told me than anybody. Listen, you take care, okay?"

"Okay." Craig watched him go toward his beat-up old car. And suddenly thought of something. Maybe this wasn't the right time, but he'd forgotten Bessie's shrilling for a second, and now it filled his ears again, and who knew when he'd see Gary Purdy again? "Gary?" He climbed out the window and followed the figure moving to his car in the dark. Purdy turned back to him.

"Uh—you ain't got any pills on you, have you? Like you used to sell me?"

Purdy shook his head. "Naw, man," he said. "Things been kinda tight for me. I'm sorry." His eyes went back to Craig's house.

"Okay." Craig turned back again. It was just a thought. Maybe with some of those pills he could handle this wild feeling he'd got lately.

"Hey!"

Craig spun, hopefully. Maybe Purdy's remembered he had something with him. But the other guy was all of a sudden pointing off in the darkness. "What the fuck is *that*?"

Craig looked. It was all bright tonight. Even the upstairs rooms. "The mystery house," he said. People still called it that. Lobe's naming contest hadn't worked; folks liked the name they'd already given it.

"Mystery house?"

Craig filled him in, wondering how the hell the guy who'd been shook a minute ago could be interested in the house.

"You say nobody lives in it?"

"Naw. It's a museum. And a place for meetings. Moose meet out there. Chamber of commerce. Council." Craig began to bounce around a little. The night was cool and working up to rain again; it'd been raining on and off all week. "Must be a late meeting goin' on tonight, that's why it's all lit up." He hadn't thought about the house lately — too many other things on his mind. But it did look pretty out there all shiny in the rain mist. For just a second, he thought of the picture he'd had of Thanksgiving in there. He hadn't had any kind of good feeling since then, and he wouldn't get that one back tonight. He could hear Bessie's voice even out here.

"Nobody's there overnight?" Purdy asked.

"Well, sometimes Lobe Peters, I hear. He's in charge of it, and I guess he spends some nights there."

"But not all?"

"Don't think so." Craig began to bounce more. He wanted to get back to where it was warmer and get his radio plugs into his ears. But Purdy wasn't ready to let him go, and Craig guessed he owed him something to help keep his mind off the bad news of tonight.

"You say there's antiques in there?"

"I guess that's what you call 'em." He'd gone on tour a couple of times but not to look at the furniture. He'd gone hoping to get back the good feeling he was pretty sure he remembered from there. But he hadn't.

"Well, thanks, man," Purdy said.

"What for?"

"Oh. Maybe for somethin'. Listen, you done me a favor, maybe I'll do you one someday. Things get too bad around here, you get over to Slopetown, and maybe I can get my hands on a few of them pills you like so much. Okay? You go to a place down on Third called Tamborine and ask around for me. It's a bar. I'd give you the address of my pad, but I might move from there pretty soon."

"Thanks," Craig said. "But it's thirty miles. I only been through there once."

"Well. You never know. Keep it in mind. And thanks again, kid."

For what? Craig wondered while Purdy got in and drove away. For telling him his family was dead?

Craig stood there a minute longer, shaking his head. Then he went back through his window. He changed fast out of his damp clothes and into dry pajamas. It was cold in here, but the room still smelled of Purdy, so he decided to leave the window open a few minutes. Rain wasn't likely to come on for a while. He got his radio down out of the closet and climbed onto his bed, wrapping up in a blanket. He didn't look back at the house. Didn't have any reason to.

Lord, was there ever a sight like that, Lobe wondered. It was just as pretty out here in a drizzle as any other time. Maybe even prettier since it seemed to need him more. He was looking after it, all right. Hadn't run any tours all week what with the heavy showers that came and went. No point letting people track around.

Some were starting to grumble about that, calling

him up on the phone. Said the house wasn't *only* his, and they were bored. He'd gone ahead and held the Moose meeting tonight; he had *them* all trained to be damn careful how they treated the house.

The rest of the Moose Lodge members had gone on home a half hour ago, and he'd stayed to turn off lights and clean up coffee things, lovingly soaping the china that had come with the house. He'd been leery about using it at first and had brought over the ugly tan, heavy stuff that belonged to the lodge. But the house was too classy for that. The china had an interesting effect on people meeting in there. They were politer, cussed less.

Now Lobe, like always, was having himself a few minutes to commune alone. Too bad he couldn't stay overnight again, but he'd been here two extra nights this week, seeing the house through a storm, and he did have a paper to get out. Circulation had stayed high now he had house doings to report, and since he was his only employee, he had to do everything alone, sometimes very late.

Once or twice lately he'd thought maybe he should hire some help. Then he'd be freer to roll up in his bag. He hadn't gotten as far as sleeping in one of the silk-sheeted beds yet—maybe never would. He'd even thought of Bobbie Topin. The kid had a writing bent and would probably put in a few hours a week dirt cheap.

But he'd held off, remembering that Bobbie had some problem with the house. He didn't know if the kid had gotten over that—hadn't seen him in a long time. But it was for damn sure Lobe didn't want anyone around him didn't think that house was something wonderful.

Still—Bobbie Topin had been impressed the day Lobe showed him the office, and since he was a good writer, he could even do some of the easy stuff: the obits, PTA. Maybe the kid had lost his weird notions. After all, it had been a pretty big shock to everybody, Miss Penny getting found dead out by the house. Right over there, in fact. A kid with an imagination like Bobbie's could make something out of that. But kids recovered fast.

Of course, Cindy had died out here, too, and Lobe remembered Bobbie's eyes at her funeral — the last time he saw him. Might still have a monkey on his back. Maybe he better look for another kid. Time he started thinking about grooming somebody to take over the business. He wasn't getting any younger, and the day would probably come when he wanted to retire and devote all his time to the house. By then things might need some new paint. A touch-up here and there.

"What do you think?" he said to the house.

"Bobbie's okay. He's a good boy."

Well, what did you know about that? The house was talking to him in his head now. Lobe grinned.

Bobbie Topin stirred restlessly in his sleep. It wasn't a bad dream, only relentless. And silly. A carrot floated in a huge vat of water, and Bobbie leaned over the vat and kept trying to pull the carrot out. But it always slipped away from his fingers. Over and over and over again.

Well don't tell me. That asshole Lobe Peters up there (Gary recognized the pickup) was finally leaving. Since he was parked back here in some trees off the road, Gary had thought maybe the guy would wind up spending the night the way Jorgenson said he did sometimes. Peters didn't come out of the house for a good half hour after the others left. And then when the lights went out and he finally did come outside, he'd sat in the pickup a long time. Too long. It was cold out here tonight. His clothes had got damp, and Purdy didn't need a chill. A chill might bring that damn flu back down full again.

But he'd stuck out the wait. He could come back some other night and would after what Jorgenson had said about the house. But he was already over here in Edgar Falls, and he needed some bread now. Like tomorrow. Tomorrow he'd find himself some antique dealers.

He'd have to be careful about what he took. Car space reasons. Stick to small things like lamps. Maybe there'd be some vases. He'd cram everything he could into the car and trunk. Maybe wouldn't keep him too long unless he lucked into some gold. But he'd take enough to pay the rent and get some food and get clear back on his feet again — to where his head didn't go dizzy anymore like it was doing right now.

Then he could make his contacts again and go back to dealing. Build back up till he could get himself another woman. Although he'd make damn sure this next one didn't know where he kept his cash stashed. Maybe he'd get another fat, easy woman like Bitsy. Jesus. Could you tie it? Burned up. All of them.

But he didn't have time to get off on that. What was over was over, and this was the here and now, and he had another big fat woman sort of. That house up there — waiting for him to get inside it.

Could you tie that? Damn fool supposed to be so crazy about this house, according to Jorgenson, had left the door unlocked. Gary grinned. People were such assholes. They yelled their heads off to the sheriffs when somebody put the hit on their property, but half the time that property wasn't even locked up. Even old Groves. He'd had only one old lock on his hardware store, although you could lay money now he had five. Gary Purdy pushed open the door to the mystery house.

Oh, man, it was even better than he'd expected. Just like lookin' into old King Tut's tomb. Right off, flashing his puny flashlight beam around, he'd picked up the glint of gold. Luck-out time! There were a couple of vases right here in what must be the living room. The vases had a Chinesey look to them, and he headed over that way.

And then stopped. Hold it. Why not start at the top? Take everything he could from up there and work his way down. Better hurry though. Peters might change his mind and come back. Besides, it was freezing in here. Dumb assholes. How come they hadn't heated the place up? He could feel his head plugging worse. A little more cold tonight, and he was really gonna come down sick.

Would you look at that stair railing? So polished he could see his face in it even with the dim light he carried. His face was smiling. Who'd've thought, when he came into town tonight to put the hit on Bitsy, he'd wind up with a bonanza?

Passing through the house on his way to the stairs, he'd spotted some little glass statues with gold on them. And a couple old-timey lamps with glass-decorated bowls for top and bottom shades. He'd seen one of those in a window once. With a hundred and fifty price tag on it. It was the price tag that'd caught his eye, and he'd wondered what the fuck anybody would spend hard money on something old like that for.

At the top of the stairs, he had to pause—wheezing—and hold onto the rail ending knob for a minute. His head had gone dizzy again from the climbing, and there was a crazy hum in it. Actually, the hum seemed to be coming from outside his head. But that was stupid. He waited—and finally it stopped. Gary Purdy got on to the work at hand. Grinning again.

He went into one of the bedrooms and stopped suddenly. Now that was weird. For just a second there, he'd thought he'd heard soft singing. Jesus. Was someone *in* this place? He went to the head of the stairs and eyed the pitch darkness before him. Nope. All quiet. Just imagination.

It was also his imagination that made the house feel downright friendly all of a sudden. He went back to the bedroom. Houses didn't feel friendly. They just stood there all mindless, waiting for you to rape them.

And this one was a damn good lay. "Hey," it seemed to be saying. "I don't need all this junk. Take everything you want."

"Thanks," Gary said. "I will."

The hum was back when he loaded the last stuff into the car. He had to push and shove a lot, being careful of the lamps. He didn't want no cracked glass shades. Not after all the effort it had taken to get them out here. You'd think they weighed a ton the way he'd staggered out to the car with them, rushing to beat the rain. Now he'd used up all his flu-bit energy except just enough to get him back to Slopetown.

When he got back, he'd park the car behind his pad.

Maybe even drag out his blankets and sleep in the car, flu or no flu. The blankets and the thought of the bucks he was going to rake in would keep him warm. He grinned, piling some sheets on top of everything else stacked nearly to the car ceiling. He was pretty sure these babies were pure silk, and they didn't take up much room. Maybe he'd cover himself with one of these tonight, too, just for the feel of it. Hell, maybe he'd keep one even. His next woman might like fucking on silk. No telling what it might do to her or make her do to him. His head was humming pretty bad now, but he didn't care. He was getting used to it. It'd go away when he got some sleep. He lifted the hood, banged on the battery, and got into the car. "Nighty night," he said to the house and drove away.

Gary Purdy was singing as he went through Gloaming and headed for Slopetown. It was just a silly song. He was singing to the house. After all, hadn't it sung to him? This was just a bunch of jumbled words about how he'd come in to Edgar Falls on the east side of town, by the highway in case the car broke down and he had to thumb it back home.

If he'd come in on the Gloaming road maybe everything would've turned out different. He'd've seen the house and wondered where the heck it came from, but everything else might've changed. He might've found the shack still standing and Bitsy and the kids out there, and he wouldn't have thought of ripping off the house with her welfare money in his pocket. Now he was pretty sure he had enough good stuff to keep him going a lot longer. He sang about that. And got so carried away with himself, he damn near ran off the road into the irrigation ditch that stretched from Gloaming clear the other side of Slopetown.

Oh-oh. That brought him to a little, and he shut up and tried to concentrate on driving. But it was hard with this damn hum in his head and mist on a windshield the wiper didn't work worth a shit on.

He looked out the window at the dark water below the road. Crap. It was deep. You didn't want to wind up in *that*. People had once or twice. Once a couple stupid kids who'd been out on the edge of town making it. Deputies figured the guy had his car pointed toward the ditch and got so wound up he knocked the shift into neutral and rolled. Gary looked at the water and shivered. What a way to go. The kids—the guy and his girl—had drowned. Although Gary guessed there was worse things than checking out in the middle of a good come.

He grinned again. Or thought he did. He couldn't tell. His face had gone kind of numb. And his head had begun to feel like it was going to bust wide open. Maybe after he sold the stuff tomorrow, he better find a clinic. Maybe he wasn't gonna get all the way over this flu by himself.

Careful. Another couple of minutes and he'd be heading into town. Then it was only a few blocks. And he'd get some sleep. Maybe wouldn't need medicine after some sleep, and it'd be easy street.

He looked at the pile of stuff beside him on the seat. That one little deer statue there was damn near pure gold; he was sure of it. He reached out to pat it. And his hand jumped back.

Hey. Where had it gone?

It had been there a second ago. Maybe slipped onto the stuff on the floor? Oh, crap. He didn't want that thing to break. It was maybe the best piece he'd picked up. It was the piece that'd made him think maybe he'd give up dealing and just go into ripping off antiques. He started to grope around where the statue had been on top of some sheets. And the sheets went, too. Just *went*.

What the fuck, man. The door was shut tight over there, the window rolled. They couldn't have gone out. But when he felt below the seat to see if they'd slipped down, he didn't feel anything. Not *anything*.

Whoa now. Something was going on here. And his head had started humming so he could hardly hear his own shock. What the shit. Things didn't just disappear into thin air.

He swiveled his head, and the motion set the hum up to a high-pitched squeal. Oh, Jesus. He had enough sight through the blurring in his head to see the back seat was empty. *Empty?* It had to be the flu. The flu was blocking his vision. The stuff was here, he just couldn't see it! He better stop a sec, and his head would clear. He turned back to the road. Only there wasn't any road suddenly either. Just air. Oh, God. What was *that* coming up at him?

Dumbbell. Lobe Peters stood on the porch, his heart finally calmed down. Grinning with relief at himself. (Better get some real glasses soon.) It was stupid; he'd known it was stupid all the time he was tearing back out here. Never had been much more than an impression really. And hadn't hit him at all till he'd had two cups of coffee and laid out a couple hours' work.

But all of a sudden, he'd thought he remembered something he'd seen. Like maybe a car back in some trees out on the Gloaming road. Come on now, he'd told himself. You can't think about the house *all* the time. It was probably bog mist. Bog spots were quiet during rain, but they flared up when it was just misting.

He went over an ad layout. But his heart had kept skipping beats. What *if?* those skipped beats said. And he couldn't concentrate.

Oh, hell. A few minutes of that and he threw on his slicker again and went back out. Better safe than sorry, he told himself. It was worth a few minutes drive, even in a night trying to rain, to be sure.

"You're bad as a damn mother hen," he'd muttered on the road.

But it was okay, just like he'd known it would be. Everything locked up tight. Nothing out of place, not upstairs or down.

"What makes you think," he asked himself, going off the porch, "anybody parked out here would've meant trouble for the house anyway?" Car parked out here would've just been broken down — abandoned. On the way back, he looked where his impression had been. He'd been right. Bog mist steaming up. You could make all kinds of shapes out of that.

Still — it had shaken him. Tomorrow he would definitely start looking for *Daily Way* help. Maybe sleep in the house every night from now on, too. There were still vandals around town, though not as good as Gary Purdy.

Lobe made another decision on the way home. Tomorrow morning he'd called Elizabeth Botts and tell her she could go ahead and bring her group out, rain or no rain. Old people made the best tourists. They didn't try to get their hands all over stuff like the little gold deer, which was Lobe's favorite piece; he'd just checked. Old people just sort of shuffled through the house, going "oh" and "ah." He'd make sure Elizabeth had 'em wear boots, though. They could bring spare shoes to tour in — leave their boots and slickers on the porch. Because it was for sure going to come down rain again by tomorrow.

Yes, he definitely would call Elizabeth. In light of his worry tonight, it was a good idea to keep folks going through there, weather or no weather. Put off any vandals getting funny ideas in the daytime. And on the spot, he made the decision, yes, to start spending every night in the house. He could manage that with extra help. And the idea excited him.

Hell, the prospect pleased him so much, in fact, it made him downright expansive. Maybe he'd haul out some cookies tomorrow and give all the old geezers a tea party. Wouldn't even charge 'em extra.

This was the only good part of the day in this house. When everything was quiet. Bessie's mouth not going. Pop not whining.

This morning he pulled the earplugs out of his ears. The two of them'd gone on so late, he'd slept that way. He padded out of bed. Shut the window. Shoot. It was raining some, and his sill was all wet. He started to really come awake with the cold. And stopped a second, staring out.

Seemed funny Gary Purdy'd stood out there last night. He guessed he oughtta report him, but he promised. And wouldn't turn him in anyway. Gary'd did some things around town he shouldn't. But so had he. He'd bought some pills a long time ago. Would've bought more last night. And he'd sneaked into the mystery house Halloween. He didn't bother looking at the house.

Get out of here. That was the first thing he thought every morning. Get out before they went at it again.

Craig hustled into his clothes. This wasn't a bath morning, and it was too cold anyway. Didn't look like the darn rain'd ever stop and give spring a chance. It was April for crap sakes, and the rain forced him home too much.

He got his shoes and socks on and headed for the

kitchen. Grab himself some cheese and crackers and an apple for lunch and breakfast, and he'd be on his way. He always reached the school yard long before the other guys showed up. Not that he liked school. It was just someplace to be better than here, even on rainy days when he stood around alone under an overhang. But before he got out of his room, the front door slammed.

Hey. She wasn't taking off at long last, was she? Craig shot for the living room, hopeful. In time to watch Bessie snatch open the door. "You get back in here, Bert Jorgenson," she screeched.

Pop? His *father* was leaving?

Bessie didn't notice him. She'd gone onto the porch, still shrilling away at the top of lungs that should've busted by now.

Craig ran for a window. Pop was heading up the street, hunkered into his slicker. Craig threw up the window. "Pop, where you going?" he hollered. The redheaded man moving into the gray morning didn't answer.

What was goin' on here? Pop didn't have a suitcase with him. And he wouldn't leave his son stuck with *her*, would he? But panic hit that son all the same. He didn't bother with the door. Bessie might hassle him. He climbed out the window and ran up the walk. "Where you think *you're* going?" Bessie yelled.

"Pop, Pop!" Craig cried.

His old man turned to glare at him. "Get outta here, son," he said. "Leave me alone."

"Lemme go with you. Where you going?"

"Just to The Brewery to get some breakfast."

"That's a good idea. I ain't had any either. I got plenty of time till school." Gimme this hour with you, he wanted to beg. We never got time together anymore.

But his father's eyes were flashing. "I got to have

some time for myself."

"To think about us leaving her?" Craig didn't mean that to come out. But his old man seemed to be looking that thought, and Craig just leaped on it.

"What the hell, C.J.?"

C.J.? Pop hadn't called him that in years. Craig latched onto that clue, too. "Well, ain't that what you're thinkin'? Pop, you don't have to stay around and take her crap. She don't love you. She just uses you."

He should've seen the way his father's face changed. But he didn't. He was too revved up on the sudden hope. "We could get us another place, Pop. And I'll cook the turkey for Thanksgiving." Now where the hell had *that* come from?

"What are you talking about? I'm just goin' down for an egg. What is all this crap anyway?"

He really saw his old man's eyes then. Lost everything that had hauled him out here. "I thought—uh, I thought . . ."

The eyes had narrowed. "Well, maybe you think too much, C.J. There's nothin' wrong with Bessie and me. Maybe we argue too much, but that's because she's shook right now because she's worried about money. When Ace opens up again, we'll be okay."

When Ace opened up again? Everybody knew Ace wasn't gonna open again. The property had a sale sign on it now.

"And I don't like what's comin' outta your mouth," his father said. "You have a little respect for my wife, boy. I don't know what come over you this morning, but we'll forget what you said, okay?"

Craig went on staring at him, gone dull inside.

"Okay?" Pop said again. He nudged his son's arm.

"Okay," his son said. Low.

"Okay then. And you don't tell Bessie where I'm goin', okay? Won't hurt her to know she can't boss me around all the time. Now you get your butt back in outta this rain and get you some school lunch. And look, here's a buck. I haven't give you any money lately."

Craig stared at the bill. "It's okay, Pop."

"No, come on. Things ain't so tough I can't give my kid a dollar for a treat. You go on down to Pender's Grocery after school and get yourself a treat." When Craig didn't move, Pop stuck the bill in Craig's shirt pocket. "I'm gonna forget we had this little talk," he said, and walked on.

Craig stood there a second with his hope dead on its back. Then he turned to the house. He didn't want to go back in. Bessie'd dump all her crap on him. But he had to change out of these wet clothes now.

"Where's he going?" Bessie ranted when he reached the porch again.

"Dunno." His head was still all muddied up from the signals he'd missed.

"Yeah, you do too know!" she snapped. "Now you tell me. Is he goin' off to spend some money?"

Craig had turned to watch his father. Now he whirled on her. "So what the fuck if he did?" he came back. "It's his money."

"What?" she gasped. "Bert, Bert! You come back here. You come back and tell this kid he can't talk to me—" But Pop had rounded a corner.

"You little slimeball," she hissed. "You just wait. You wait till he gets home. You wait'll he hears what you said to me. And don't try to lie about it. He'll believe *me*."

True, Craig thought, going very tired.

"Don't turn away from me," she screeched. "Don't you try to come back in this house till you apologize."

Apologize? He stared at her flushed face. "I'm not gonna apologize, Bessie."

"And don't call me Bessie neither, godamnit. When'd I give you permission to do that? I'm your stepmother, sonny, and you better get that straight. I been your stepmother five years, and you treated me like dirt the whole time. Well, it ain't gonna go on no more." He was still trying to get around her body planted with its hands on its hips. But she jumped to block his way and got right into his face. "Stepmother!" she shouted. "You say it. You call me stepmother. You say, 'I'm sorry for talking the way I did, stepmother.'"

It was the word mother on the end that did it. He might've said anything she wanted if it would shut her up for a minute. But not that.

"Stepmother, stepmother, stepmother," she shrilled.

"I had a mother," he said. So quiet all they heard for a second was the rain. "She's dead. That's the only kind of mother I ever had."

And she hit him. So hard she knocked him back against the doorjamb and his head struck wood. He went blind with stars a second.

If she'd let him alone, it might have been okay. But she didn't. She followed up with another one. A punch this time. It caught him in the stomach.

He came back with the flat of his hand. Hard. Not meaning to. It was reflex. The same way when somebody threw a ball at school he wasn't expecting. Only a ball didn't go down like a falling tree.

His eyes cleared. Enough for him to see the red streak coming out her mouth. Enough for him to know what he'd done. Oh, jeez. He hadn't killed her, had he? He'd thought about it often enough, but he'd never meant it.

He hunkered down, scared, fighting the sick her punch and what he'd done had brought on. "Bessie?" he said.

Her eyes opened. Relief nearly made him faint for

sure. He started to reach a hand out to her. She was just a woman, for crap sake. He didn't need to flatten a woman. And she screamed. She screamed and scrabbled to her feet, clutching the doorjamb, blood running down her chin.

"Don't touch me," she rasped. "Bert!" She reeled off the porch, then she screamed it again. And screamed and screamed and screamed. Up the street a door opened, and Mrs. Pender looked out. Bessie spotted her and went staggering up the walk, rain splatting her. "Bert, Bert!" she screamed. "Find Bert for me. I got to tell him what happened."

She turned once, before she reached the woman running down the walk to her. "You done it now," she screamed at Craig. "Bert's gonna whip your ass for what you done to me all because you wouldn't call me stepmother." Mrs. Pender reached her, looking at him.

Now you done it. You didn't mean it, but that don't count now. You seen what was in Pop's face. He didn't know what the heck you was talkin' about. Shoot. Pop must *like* the way he lived. And all this time dumb old C.J.'d been thinking the old man'd got himself trapped.

Craig threw stuff fast as he could into his old backpack Pop'd helped him make. Used to carry his fishing clothes in it when they spent the night at the lake hundred years ago. It was beat-up and ripped some around the straps, but it'd do.

Cut out the shaking. You're droppin' stuff. Hey, how about that three-legged trophy? Naw, he didn't want it. Let Pop keep it. Remind him he had a kid once. He skipped the Best Athlete papers, too. *Put your slicker on, booby. And don't forget that two bucks you got stashed you would've given Gary for pills.*

Hurry, up, hurry up. Wouldn't take long for somebody

to find Pop at The Brewery. Maybe even before he made it there.

It ain't fear. I ain't scared. Not about that anyway. He could square off at his old man if he had to. And he'd have to. Wasn't much doubt whose side Pop would leap into. *You don't wanna hit Pop. You just got to get away, that's all.* He'd known all along it was coming, and here it was. Only a little sudden. So sudden his heart jumped with it.

Go out the back. Don't let Mrs. Pender's big nose get a load of you leavin'.

In his doorway, he stopped and looked around. Just for a sec. A lot of years a little kid had lived in here. The little kid'd had a mother once. And some good times. Some he prob'ly didn't even remember.

What the hell. He needed that trophy more than Pop did. Pop had Bessie.

A mockingbird sat up in a tree and shook water off its wings and yipped at him as he went by. Town was just beginning to wake up. There were some early lights on here and there. Darn town looked kind of pretty getting rained on; he'd never thought of it before.

He headed for the Ace property first, plodding through puddles. Lots of buildings out by Ace, and he'd keep behind them. Not too many people lived near there. Circle out around town, that was the best bet. Work his way over to the woods, and then it'd be okay. Woods'd keep some of this rain off him and take him a long ways toward Gloaming. Have to be careful even in Gloaming before he headed on to Slopetown. Kid with an old backpack be easy to spot.

What're you laughin' at, airhead? He spit out some blood—Bessie had a punch almost as good as her mouth. He was laughing because he was so dumb, sneakin' around the outskirts of town, worrying about getting spotted in Gloaming. Pop wasn't going to send anybody out to look for him. When Bessie got through with him, he'd see it was a good idea old C.J.'d taken off. Kid was just a few months short of fourteen. Hell, he could take care of himself. Besides, he'd probably come home soon, dragging his tail between his legs.

Well, the laugh was on the old man because he wasn't coming back. Not ever. Because would it change? Shit no. It'd be worse than ever then. Bessie'd have the upper hand for sure and Pop to back her. Dumb shit. He didn't know if he meant his father or him. How come the town looked so *pretty?* And why couldn't he stop shaking?

Just one more time maybe? He'd been out there a couple afternoons, once even this week when the rain let up some. Just to sit. Doin' nothing. He didn't talk to her. He didn't know what he'd say. Maybe he thought about how proud she'd be of him if she'd've lived. She wouldn't care if he didn't make good grades. She'd just be proud of what he *could* do—like be a good athlete. Like Pop used to be proud. She wouldn't let anybody talk to him like Bessie talked to him either. He could see the cemetery hill from here. But better not go over there. Use up extra energy when he had thirty miles ahead of him. Did she know he was going—lying out there in her white dress under the spring leafs he'd picked for her?

A soppy-wet dog came out of a yard on the north side, wagging its tail. Dog followed him a good way, with big eyes. Silly old tongue hangin' out. Not many dogs in Edgar Falls. He stopped to pat it once, and it licked his hand. Maybe he should take it along?

Naw. Gary wouldn't like it. Gary was gonna be surprised enough to see a guy at his door he thought he'd said good-bye to last night. Gary'd said he owed him a favor. He just didn't expect to get it called up so fast. But he wouldn't turn Craig in.

He bent and picked up a rock and threw it, feeling bad. Hurt him almost as much as the dog. Shoot. That dumb old mutt was the first thing seemed to care about him in a long time. The dog took off.

Hey. Let's don't start feeling sorry for ourself. And let's don't cry, for crap sakes. The old man didn't care anymore, that's all. Prob'ly hadn't cared in a long time.

These were not tears he was swiping at with his slicker sleeve. Just rain. A crow cawed at him. "Shut up," he said. "I ain't after your babies." Shit. Even a dumb old crow took better care of its kids than his father did.

Oh, for crap sakes. He *was* crying. For what?

Jerkhead. Why didn't you grab that apple or something? His insides were growling. Maybe she'd knocked something crazy in there. If he wound up in a hospital, maybe his old man would see what'd happened, forgive him. Come to the hospital and even bring him a flower. Some candy. Shit. This imagination he didn't have could sure get stupid.

"Shut up," he said to another crow. Damn. Every bird in Pellam Woods was out to say he was starting through. Didn't they know enough to get in outta the rain? But a quick check of the road didn't show they had anybody to warn. Shit no. Pop and Bessie were most likely in bed by now. If that would shut her off this morning. *Craig who?* his father would say.

Hey. He forgot that and stared at the mystery house over there past those bog spots.

Nobody'd know, would they? There might be food in there. Left over from club meetings. Coffee anyway. Warm him up. He'd be careful, clean everything. Maybe even some cookies. Lobe'd taken to having afternoon tea parties, he'd heard. Tea parties meant cookies, didn't they? He'd been to a tea party once. Should't be too hard to get in. They'd got in Halloween night, hadn't they? He didn't have tools—only a pocket knife. Still—that oughtta do it.

Wouldn't hurt just for a few minutes if he went in there. Maybe the rest of his life wouldn't seem quite as lonesome as it seemed right now.

Craig stood on the porch of the mystery house, peering through lace curtains at all the pretty furniture. He looked around, really seeing it in a way he hadn't on tour. Look at those neat, old-timey lamps made outta glass. And the granddaddy clock? Everything warm and friendly. It reminded him of his mother.

But something hit him suddenly. *Wait a sec. Think this over.* They'd figure he did if he damaged the lock or if anybody like Lobe could see he'd been in. His feet were wet, for crap sakes. And even if he took off his shoes, the rest of him was dripping.

"You don't want Bessie to load any more crap on you," he muttered out loud. He jumped backward when his voice echoed from the porch roof. Jeez, it was quiet out here with only rain pattering down. Almost—well, spooky. He grinned. No spookier than Halloween.

He picked up his thoughts again. Fingered the knife in his pocket. He was hungry all right, good and hungry. But what would Pop think? Pop didn't want no thief for a son. *What d'you care what he thinks anymore?* Good question. But he couldn't help it; he did. He went down the porch steps again.

He headed for the back side of the house to start through the woods again. Eyed a couple of bog spots off over there. They didn't make clouds in the rain, but he could see the dark holes of them. Which one, he thought, did they find Cindy in?

Hey. Don't get off on that. He was a helluva lot better off than Cindy. At least he was leaving on his feet.

He'd reached the back of the house now. And looked up suddenly at the iron railing he hadn't paid any attention to out front. He stopped. Squinted. Went puzzled. How come the railing was tied up with the good feeling he'd had in the house? The feeling had something to do with flying, he just couldn't remember what, and he hadn't been able to get it again when he toured.

But he shrugged, getting no answers, and started off for the woods. He was clear to the edge before he froze in his tracks. Someone had called his name from the house! Oh, jeez. Someone had been *in* there? A woman?

He turned back slowly. "Craig Julian?" she said again.

It was pure coincidence sent Lobe past the school right after it let out. He had just magnanimously dropped off Mrs. Lordstrum, who'd toured with six other old people today. Not much of a group—cats and dogs rain kept them away. But the ones who'd gone had made a whole crowd of enthusiasm, having the place all to themselves.

Mrs. Lordstrum usually smelled of the animals she kept. But today she'd been spruced up for the tour.

Even had her hair washed and combed, a rarity. House did that to people. Lobe hadn't minded going out of his way. Rain had settled down to a drizzle for a while, and he had a soft spot in his heart for the old lady who'd spoken up the night the meeting got silly in front of Ms. Benedictine.

Bobbie Topin happened out of the school yard right when Lobe, whose car was empty, started by. And, still congratulating himself for the tea party all the old geezers had been crazy about, Lobe suddenly pulled over to the curb. What the hell. Lobe'd had occasion to note today, in the heightened awareness the house always gave him, that Bobbie Topin had good reason to think a little weird sometimes.

He leaned over the passenger seat and rolled the window down. "Bob?" he called.

The boy started. Turned. Yeah, he still looked a little skittery. But when he walked over to the car, his gaze was direct. Lobe liked that. You needed somebody direct around the office. Case anybody came in to argue over ad prices, et cetera.

"Bob, how you feeling lately?"

"Fine, Lo—Mr. Peters."

"Call me Lobe like everyone else. Listen, I got something to ask you. You got a little free time?"

"What for?"

Lobe didn't like that. But looking into the kid's eyes, he saw it wasn't meant rude.

"Well, I need some help at the paper. Thinking of interviewing a few boys."

The kid's face lit up so fast it startled Lobe. "You mean *I* might have a chance to work at *The Daily Way?*" Bobbie exclaimed.

"Now hold on. Said I was interviewing several. Tomorrow." Lobe leaped all the way in. "Noon. I'll pay only minimum."

"I'm not sure I could take time from—"

Jesus H. Christ. He didn't care to talk the kid into it. But he butted in and said, "Just weekends to start. Three, four hours a day Saturday and Sunday."

"Could I *write*?"

"Maybe some."

"Oh, gee. Oh, *gee*. I could find a way."

"Now hold it again. There'll be others." A couple had crossed his mind this morning. Billy Kroger for one.

"But I'd do it better," Bobbie said. Lobe had never seen the kid smile so big. "I'll be there tomorrow." Bobbie turned away. Gave a little hop.

"Uh, Bob?" The boy turned back, still grinning. It was tricky, what was coming up, but Lobe had to voice it. Nip the whole thing in the bud if he didn't like what he saw. "Bob, I'm getting help so I can spend more time on the mystery house. You came to me with some silly notions about the house once. And something else happened near there may have fed 'em. I need to know how you feel now."

"About the house?" The boy looked suddenly off at the woods. Then back at Lobe. The grin was gone. But he gave the right answer. "It's just a house."

"Okay then," Lobe said, satisfied. "You come on by noon tomorrow."

"Thanks, Mr. Pe—Lobe. I'll be there!"

The boy ran off, and Lobe sat there watching him bounce along a moment. Seemed okay. Lobe was pretty sure Bobbie would be his choice. He was far out ahead in brains of the others Lobe'd thought up.

Have to be watched for a while, though. If ever those weird notions reared their head again, the kid'd be out on his butt in the cold.

Then Lobe grinned. Hell. Hadn't the house itself agreed on Bobbie?

Wow. He couldn't believe it. Something good had happened. In all the darkness he wore for a mind these days, a light had come on. Just a tiny spark, but it lifted his spirits so that he hopped across puddles and gave a little skip now and then.

A job? A real job? Something besides fear and death to think about! He would be so brilliant tomorrow, Lobe Peters would be dazzled.

Bobbie leaped over two puddles in a row, glowing with excitement.

He'd almost blown it with the house question; it had startled him. But he'd seen what Lobe wanted to hear. And he sure the heck wasn't going to let that damn house get in the way of the first good thing to come along since he could remember.

It was a lie, of course. The house was never going to be just a house. But he already knew he couldn't leave town yet. And he wouldn't forget Cindy. Or let his guard down. He just had to keep hoping if (when!) the house tried something else, it'd trip itself up. Or maybe he'd get a clearer warning.

For now, he just let himself feel joy. He bounced along with it, not minding the cold and endless wet.

Tomorrow. He could hardly wait.

He could work it out. He was gone school days anyway. Few weekend hours wouldn't hurt, would they? Grandpop wasn't *always* off in his head. Like this morning—he'd been clear. There hadn't been any more match incidents or anything.

Wow. Tomorrow!

If only he had someone to share with. Craig? Not today. Jorgenson hadn't been in school. Probably a bad cold in all this rain, Miss Larimer had said. Lots of kids out with colds.

But maybe tomorrow when Bobbie'd beat out the other guys, he might just saunter by Jorgenson's.

"Guess what?" he'd say. Craig's eyes would pop. A newspaperman! Wow. That might just make all the difference in the world to a bunch of guys who'd been ignoring him unless they had something ghoulish to report.

Well, he could share with Grandpop if he'd stayed alert enough. Might even make the old man proud. Bobbie hoped so.

What the heck! Alert or not, he'd tell him anyway. Tell Gladys, too, if necessary. Bobbie tore on across town, racing the coming fresh rain.

The Letkins house had lights on against the dreary day as Bobbie rushed by. He half expected to see a light on in the cottage, too. But Grandpop had probably fallen asleep.

Bobbie reached the porch and ran under the eaves and went on inside.

A shadowless gloom met his eyes. He looked immediately toward Grandpop's chair. Darn. The old man wasn't there. "Grandpop?" he called. "I got us some news!" It was rare that Grandpop took a nap in his bed, but he wouldn't be out back in this weather. Bobbie headed for the old man's bedroom.

But the thing came at him before he got there. Making guttural noises and with a knife that came slashing down at his neck.

Chapter Eleven

He screamed and fell back against the wall. The hallway was nearly dark, but it only took a split moment to register what was happening. "Grandpop!" he screamed. "Grandpop, it's me—Bobbie."

The knife rared back and came slicing down again. This time it grazed Bobbie's cheek. The stinging pain got hold of his shock. He threw up a hand as the knife cut another arc upward and grabbed hold of the arm, but the strength there stunned him. This wasn't a frail old man; the muscles felt taut and powerful.

"Gonna get rid of him, Gladys," Grandpop rasped, and even in the gloom Bobbie saw the glint of hate in his eyes. "Never needed no new young cock in the barnyard. Too much trouble to have around." He threw off Bobbie's hand and the knife slashed down. This time it caught and carried away a bit of Bobbie's shoulder. "Gonna slit his gizzard, fry 'im up for supper. Just you and me'll eat 'im."

This wasn't the grandfather. This was a crazed *thing*.

Bobbie spun and stumbled back for the living room. It was after him, with a speed incredible. But

Bobbie was faster yet, and he made the door, threw it open, and plunged onto the porch and stood there, eyes glazed with horror and pain, one hand trying to squeeze together the bleeding area beneath his jacket and shirt. He tried one more time. "Please. Grandpop."

Onto the porch it came, mouth slack and dripping spittle. Eyes narrowed and cunning. "Gonna make us chase him, is it? Well, maybe we'll cut its little heart out first, then wring its little neck."

He knew he could get away. But he stood there one second more, a hideous sorrow mingling with the pain and fear. "Oh, Grandpop," he said.

The thing took a step forward, and Bobbie backstepped carefully off the porch. It let out a growl. And then suddenly the eyes glazed over.

A shudder like an electric shock passed through the body. Then it convulsed. The face pulled back over its bones, and the lips bared, and it went down, pitching forward, rolled once, leaving the face up. Vomit spewed violently from the lips, and there was a sound like the bursting of a water-filled balloon.

Myriad years marched into eternity while Bobbie Topin stood rooted to the spot. Rain broke again, and it drenched him. It made the stinging in his cheek increase.

He couldn't move. Pain was rolling through him, but not from his wounds.

Then he took a few steps forward, cautiously. It could rise again. Maybe it was faking. But he smelled the vile odor and knew instinctively that everything inside it had let go, as if it had tried to empty itself out.

He moved again. Up the stairs. Stood looking down. The knife lay under the fallen hand. He knew he didn't have to, but he kicked it anyway. It flew off the porch and landed with a dull clank on the sidewalk. Bobbie stared at it a moment; it was the knife he used to tenderize Grandpop's steaks.

Whatever had been in the eyes was gone. They bulged and looked like they were fixed upon something strange that needed careful scrutiny which had lodged itself on the porch eaves.

He couldn't even cry. He could only stand there staring down at his dead grandfather while the rain beat on the porch roof and on the steps and the spring grass in the yard.

Get him under the arms, it'll work better. Don't look at his eyes. Okay. Okay. Through the door. Oh, shit, the shirt's caught on something. Wait a minute. Just that sliver of molding you been meaning to hammer down. You can't throw up. Get him off the porch so nobody can see. Got to have time. Time, time, time, time.

Bobbie went in and out of blank spells. Like going through a fog that only hovered in pockets. The rest of the time his thoughts were clear—too clear. Again and again he saw the thing that Grandpop had become charging him, the knife raised. It had happened. His grandfather had gone clear into that other world, and it wasn't a world of old-time memories.

A faintness passed through him. He had to stop what he was doing and wait for a bunch of stars to shoot on by.

You're still bleeding. You better get in and take a look at that. You're not going to get far losing your blood all over the place.

In a minute, in a minute. Get him off the porch. You got to have time to look for the money.

It could take all night.

All night? Alone in the house with it?

What else are you gonna do? You got to have the money to get out of town. Otherwise, you're gonna wind up in an orpha—the faintness hit again, and he lowered his head and waited.

He swam out of it. One more good pull. There! He nearly broke into hysterical laughter when the feet dragged over the jamb. He stood, gingerly, and stepped over the body to shut the door. *Don't look at the eyes.*

Now he could see to the shoulder.

He didn't remember getting down the hallway; he came out of one of the fog spells with his shirt off, staring into the bathroom mirror.

Did flesh grow back? The knife had taken a small chunk right out of him. But not so big as it felt. He took the cup Grandpop sometimes left his teeth in at night and filled it again and again with water and poured it over his shoulder. Maybe it hurt. He didn't know. He was too dazed to feel it. His eyes kept going to the reflection of the doorway in the mirror, as if he expected to see it appear there suddenly, grinning with glee because it had him trapped in here. He grabbed a towel off the rack and pressed it hard against his shoulder. Apply pressure: It was the only thing he knew about first aid.

Come on now. Pull yourself together. You can't start crying now. If you start crying, you'll never stop, and they'll cart you off in the same basket they could've used on Grandpop.

Grandpop.

A picture of the old man sitting docilely at breakfast this morning spooning up his poached egg hit him. Oh, Jesus, what had happened to turn him into —

Something creaked. Bobbie froze in terror.

It *was* up. It was coming down the hall. He inched over to the doorway and peered out.

Nothing. Only the gloom of the hallway on a rainy day.

But it could be hiding in the living room. Behind the door? Behind the drapes?

He moved cautiously down the hall, ready to bolt at the slightest movement.

But it lay just inside the door.

Only a beam settling. Here was that wild urge to laugh like a maniac again.

You will be a maniac if you have to stay in the house very long with that.

Get moving. He went back to the bathroom and lifted the towel. It never had been bleeding heavily. Now he could see the pink, raw flesh.

Find something to make a pad with — a clean rag from the hall closet.

He got that done and somehow found himself in his bedroom pulling on a clean shirt and a sweater over that. He needed four or five sweaters; he was starting to shake.

The money. Keep your mind on the money.

It couldn't be in his own room. He knew every corner in here. That left only the living room, the hall closet, the kitchen, and Grandpop's room. But he'd gone thoroughly through Grandpop's room before.

So okay. Two rooms and the hall. And the bathroom. He decided to tackle the bathroom first. But he had to spend a few minutes doing something else, something he dreaded.

Two hours later, dark had fallen, the rain had stopped again, but a storm had raged inside the house. Furniture lay upturned; all the utensils in the kitchen had been spewed about on all the surfaces and the floor; the pantry had been emptied of canned goods. Every rug had been turned over. And Bobbie Topin stood in the middle of it all breathing in dry, desperate sobs.

Grandpop had tried to get him in life; he was going to get him for sure in death. Why hadn't the old man ever trusted him to know where he kept his savings?

He never wanted you here at all. Why should he tell you anything like that? Maybe he always hoped to get rid of you. Of all the things that had transpired earlier, one remained most clear in Bobbie's mind: the words, "Never needed no new young cock in the barnyard." That had been it; that had been why Grandpop from the suddenly ravaged brain had been out to get him. He'd wondered sometimes what his grandfather thought of getting stuck with him. The answer had nearly done him in.

Come on now. Keep your mind where it belongs. The sofa stuffing. You haven't gone after that.

Or Grandpop's bed stuffing for that matter.

Oh, I don't think it's in there.

Come on, you just don't want to go back in there. But you got to look.

He had every light in the house on.

He went down to the bedroom because he had to, because every possibility had to be investigated. The mattress had to be turned over.

He kept his eyes averted. He hadn't figured on having to come in this bedroom again. That's why he'd spent the effort to drag the body down here—so he could shut the door and wouldn't have to look at it. He'd have to hold on tight to his guts while he removed whatever money was in the pockets of the reeking pants.

He'd wanted to put *it* on the bed. Some part of him still hung onto the memory of a Grandpop who'd been good to him in spite of feeling stuck. That was the part he'd wanted to leave on the bed so that when they found him, there'd be a little bit of dignity, but his strength had given out. The shoulder was aching, and it was one thing to drag it, another to try and haul it onto the bed.

A good thing he hadn't now. After he got Grandpop's change he needed to search the matt—

The sound of the doorbell nearly brought an answering shriek.

The whole world stopped for one long, stunning moment. *Answer it*. Who could it be? Nobody ever came out here, only a couple of times.

Wait a minute. Sometimes Mrs. Letkins sent one of her kids to borrow something.

That's all it could be. Better give it to them. Then they wouldn't go home and report that all the lights were on but nobody answered. Mrs. Letkins might think something about that: old man and a boy all the lights on and no answer.

Bobbie straightened up and moved toward the hallway, shutting the door behind him. Wonder what the kid would think if he or she knew what was down here in this room? *Hey, you wanna pay a quarter see a freak show? There's a crazy old dead guy back there on the rug. No kidding.*

He got hold of that kind of thinking.

But he was in for a worse shock than he'd considered giving the Letkins kid.

Reverend Botts stood on the front porch.

Something was very wrong here. Leonard Botts knew it immediately. That odor! So offensive you wanted to cover your nose. Like a terminal cancer ward in a hospital.

And the boy. Death warmed over. That's how the boy looked peering through a crack in the doorway.

"I brought your grandfather's slicker back," he said. "He left it in Mrs. Bott's car today when she brought him back from the house tour."

"The house tour?" The boy's voice came out a squeak.

"She was surprised Mr. Wetterley went along when she stopped by to ask him," Mr. Botts said. "He hasn't toured lately. But he told her he'd heard something about the house and hadn't had a chance to get inside again to see for himself. She had to make him take the slicker, and then he forgot it."

That *was* the smell of sickness. He ought to know; he'd held enough dying hands.

He cut through all the deadwood. "What's wrong, Bob?" he asked. "Has something happened to your grandfather?"

"He's all right. He's—uh—he went to bed early."

Maybe the old boy just had a case of diarrhea? Maybe the house smelled like this all the time. Still—"I'd like to see your grandfather, Bob."

The old man could be good and sick, taken down with something this afternoon, and the boy might not even realize it.

"Come back tomorrow," Bob said. And to his great surprise and even more to the shock of his ego, Leonard Botts, for whom all doors were always open, found himself staring at a closed one.

He stood there a long moment, fighting back

unreasonable rage.

Then, when he calmed, he turned and started off the porch. And stopped a moment, arrested by something he had skirted instinctively when he came onto the porch a few minutes ago.

It had been little more than a shadow what with the living room drapes leading onto the porch closed. Now he threw the raincoat over his shoulder and bent. Studied the smear that sent nausea to curdle in his chest. It was caking vomit.

There were a couple of blood spots, too, if he wasn't mistaken. And just there—something lay in a pool of water. A knife? A good kitchen knife it looked. What was it doing out here in the wet?

Reverend Botts, greatly alarmed, headed off the porch for his car to drive to the Letkins house where he'd been going in the first place when his wife had handed him the raincoat.

"I need to use your phone," he said unceremoniously when Letkins opened the door. Deputy Ben Dunkle answered the phone at the sheriff's. "Get on out to the Wetterley house," Leonard Botts told him. "And bring Doc Jannessey."

The House! The House had gotten Grandpop. The house had made Grandpop think the way he did about the young cock in the barnyard. It had made him crazy.

The fury that roared through Bob Topin was cataclysmic. Tornado winds shrieked through his burning brain. A tidal wave churned his organs.

It was the last straw. The end. No more.

He ran for the bedroom and threw open his window. He couldn't see it in his fury. But he screamed out at it anyway: "Okay. You asked for it.

You've gone too far."

He spent precious time running wildly around the cottage looking for something suitable. For a second, he thought they had a fireplace, and he could get wood from there, and then some sense got through to his screeching brain, and he remembered that that had been the apartment in the city that had the fireplace. So okay. Think a minute. Wood.

There was wood in the shed: an old orange crate he'd dragged home from the market one time, hauling it by a rope. He'd been going to build something—his brain wouldn't remember what right now. But it didn't matter. Wood was what he needed. And newspapers.

What if it starts raining again?

Well, cover them with something. Grandpop's raincoat.

But Mr. Botts took the raincoat because you slammed the door before he could give it to you.

Plastic then. Plastic wrap in the kitchen.

He ran toward the kitchen. It looked as if a hydrogen bomb had hit it. The roll of plastic had to be here someplace.

He began to tear through the rubble he'd created earlier. Something caught his eye: a sheet of paper he must have knocked off the table when he decided to see if Grandpop had any money taped to the bottom.

Screw the money now. He had something more important to do than run away.

Wait a minute. What did that paper say? "History of the House?" he snatched at it, dropped it, snatched again. "A Reconstruction by Lobarth Peters." A brochure. The answer to what hit Grandpop had been here all along today.

The fury grew. Swelled until he felt all throbbing

head.

There! Over there. The plastic wrap. It had rolled out of its box and left a trail a quarter of the way across the kitchen. He grabbed it up.

Newspapers. This afternoon he'd tossed a million kept for wrapping garbage out of the pantry; they'd been in the house for years.

Bobbie tore a huge chunk of plastic with his teeth and scrambled to pick up the newspapers. Then he wound the plastic round and round them. Keep them good and dry.

Matches. Don't forget matches. He grabbed up a bunch and stuffed them in his pocket.

The shoulder wound had cracked open and was bleeding again. So what? No time, and it wasn't going to kill him. Something more important to do. "You've had it," he said, talking to the house. He wanted to start laughing, but if he did it would take him over, and he'd never accomplish what he had to do: his mission of mercy. He liked the sound of it. Put the house out of its misery; that's what they did with mad dogs.

A mad house. That was funny. *But don't laugh.*

The key to the shed, hanging on a nail, was about the only thing still in place in the kitchen. He tore it away, threw open the back door, and headed into the night. "I'm coming," he said to the house.

He cursed the shed key a hundred times trying to get it into the lock. But it turned finally. He knew where the crate was, and it took him only a few seconds to kick it apart. Then he grabbed up some pieces, ignoring the scratch a nail made on the back of one hand.

Into the kitchen again. Throw some wrap around the wood. Oh, shit. Someone was knocking on the front door.

"Bobbie?" Ben Dunkle's voice? Well, what had he expected? That Reverend Botts wouldn't think he was acting a little strange, slamming a door in his face?

Bobbie stared desperately at his assembled paraphernalia. He couldn't take it now. He had to get away, and it would slow him down.

Wait a sec. He didn't need it anyway. He had matches. That was all it would take. Start it with something in the house.

In?

He'd thought of setting the fire under the porch where the men had figured Cindy tried to hide.

But that wasn't such a great idea. Someone might see the fire too early, and the rain might get to it. It had to be *in* — where it could get a good start. The house may have kept Miss Penny out, but there was no way it could stand against his rage.

Bobbie was running as these thoughts seared through his brain. He grabbed a hammer off the pantry shelf. Raced out the door again, past the shed. He started in a straight line for the house in Pellam Woods. But a certain cunning took him of him.

They'd look for him. He should swerve south instead, double back.

He had plenty of time. The house wasn't going anyplace. Bobbie smiled in the dark. Not till he got there anyway. "I'm coming," he said. "I'm going to burn your fucking heart out."

It knew he was coming.

He could feel it going on guard. Feel every window alert. *Something's on its way here. I can see it out there in the fields.* It was probably squinting hard to pick up his movements. Bobbie nearly screamed out loud with laughter; that was funny—a house squinting.

But he caught himself again, short of the brink. And darted behind another bush.

It was over. They'd catch him after. But it didn't matter. Nothing mattered but his mission.

Were they close behind him back there? He couldn't tell. In his head now were only the mad, alarmed whisperings the house seemed to set up.

And he was here! He halted his holy journey a second on the edge of the road. Stared up at it one last time to let satisfaction course through him in violent, wracking waves. Rain skittered off the roof in misty little splashes. "I'm here," he said furiously.

And he did hear voices then. Not from the house. The voices were calling him from the fields.

Scratch the front, he told himself. They didn't know his intent. He'd go in from the back. Smash a window and race through. The place was huge. He could have a fire going in half the rooms before they got him.

The laughter threatened him again. It was going to be a detention home, not an orphanage, and arson the charge. Well, what the hell difference did *that* make now?

He began to move again, quickly, stealthily. Around the side of the house. Then he broke into a run for the porch.

Except his feet encountered something first. One foot came down on it. It rolled under his instep, throwing him off balance. He went down on one knee. What the hell. In the dark, he could still make out two figures. A statue? But he didn't have time for guessing games over something that had tripped him.

Maybe the house had mustered it. Meant him to fall and crack his head like Miss Penny. "It won't work." he seethed. "I'm coming in." He made his feet again. Ran.

This time he tripped over something larger. Something yielding. Went down on both knees, right on top of it. He let out another oath and leaned over to shove furiously away from the thing. And knew suddenly what his hands had sunk into. Looked at it.

He began to scream. To scream and scream, his head thrown back in agony. They found him that way, holding the other boy in his arms. Screaming on and on.

Two men carried Bobbie, wandering-brained and mewing, back to the kitchen of the cottage. While others summoned from Gloaming stayed behind to carry out another, grimmer task. What the sam hill, they asked each other, was this fool Jorgenson kid doing anyway, climbing a drainpipe like that? What'd he want to prove? Didn't have an audience.

And how the hell had he managed to get clear up to that railing without slipping and then fell off from up there?

Anybody could see what'd happened. A deputy's powerful flashlight picked up the little piece of the flimsy homemade backpack that still clung to the fence spike. Too bad, someone said, it hadn't been store bought. Might've been strong enough to hold him dangling till he got a foothold or something. Lord, who was going to tell Bert Jorgenson another kid was dead in Edgar Falls and that kid was his? Someone began to pick up the boy's things that had fallen out of the backpack when he hit. Bert might want that trophy. Wonder what the kid was doing carrying it around.

In the kitchen of the little cottage, Mrs. Letkins, shocked of face, made cocoa swiftly. They had put Bobbie on a chair, and when she got the cocoa made, she sat beside him and tried to spoon it into him. He didn't seem to realize what was going on, and most of the liquid ran out the corners of his mouth.

"Why's this place such a mess?" Deputy Coyle Mason from Gloaming wanted to know.

Nobody answered. Well, hell. Maybe the kid and the old dead guy on the floor in the bedroom had lived this way all the time. People did. Coyle'd seen worse than this. Curl your hair.

Mrs. Letkins was beginning to recover from her shock over the Jorgenson boy, and tears ran down her cheeks. "I think he should lie down," she said of Bobbie. But when she touched his hand, he slapped it suddenly away, leaped to his feet, and backed against a wall, his eyes wild and crazy, fists flailing out at empty air.

Reverend Botts was close to that wall, and he removed himself quickly, eyeing the boy warily. Grief could do a lot of things. But create this roiling monster out of a twelve-year-old? He glanced uneasily around the kitchen. It looked like the devil might have his hand in here someplace. He began to pray Jesus touch this house.

Ben Dunkle went after Bobbie to seat him again. But the boy's fist lashed out and caught the deputy a good one in the midsection. "Damn you!" Bobbie gibbered. "The house. You let me go back to the house."

"Rev, would you hold onto this kid?" Ben asked. "I got to get back out to Pellam Woods, and Coyle here needs to get over to Mizz Letkins's again and put in a call to the juvvies."

"The juvenile authorities!" Mrs. Letkins gasped. "You want to send this poor child over the brink?"

"Brink of what?" Ben snorted. "Looks like he took the plunge already."

"You can't do that to him tonight," she said fiercely, all her motherly instincts aroused. "He's lost his grandfather to a stroke it looks and his classmate tonight. He's had enough. We've got to figure something else out."

"I got my duty."

"Duty, shit," she exploded.

Ben stared at her, startled. He knew Alice Letkins, had had dinner in her home. She didn't talk that way.

"The house!" Bobbie hollered.

Leonard Botts had turned ashen at the sheriff's suggestion. *Touch* the boy? Dear Lord, demons had been known to leap from one being to another. And he didn't know if he could anyway. After all, the boy had punched a law officer.

Someone else had arrived in the kitchen: Mr. Letkins, who'd had to go fetch Doc Jannessey to look at the old man because Doc had put his car in the garage for servicing tomorrow.

"Doc's in a bad mood," he said. "Interrupted his dinner. Said if the old man was dead, why'd he have to be dragged out till he ate. He's in the bedroom now. What's the matter with *him*?" He stared at the wild eyes, at the spit drooling down Bobbie's chin.

"Fit," Ben Dunkle said.

"Shock," Alice Letkins said hotly. "George, there's something you don't know because you had to go after Doc. Bobbie didn't just lose his grandfather tonight. He ran off in his grief, and they found him over by the mystery house. But they found more than that."

Coyle Mason took over the explanation, and she began to talk to Bobbie in a soothing voice. He went on eyeing her suspiciously.

"Told you wasn't any reason to drag me out." Doc Jannessey came into the kitchen. "It was just a stroke, and he's deader'n the old doornail. What the bejeezus hit this place anyway?"

"Dunno," Ben said. "The kid here's out of his head."

"Shock," Alice Letkins insisted. "I wanted to go wild like this when I learned two of my babies were dead."

"We'll fix that," Doc said. He opened his black bag. Pulled out a hypodermic. Started for Bobbie, who growled at him like a dog at bay. While Doc held the boy's attention, Coyle Mason sneaked up on the side of him and grabbed his arms. There was only a brief struggle — kid'd lost his fight — and Doc got the shot in.

"Listen, Doc," Ben said. "Now you're here, turns out there's more than this you got dragged out for. You're needed at the mystery house."

Bobbie heard those words. Let out a scream that curdled the blood of everyone in the room. But in a second, his eyes glazed over.

And in another moment, there were no more bright lights burning holes in his head. There was only darkness. But it wasn't velvety and good. It was full of crawling, slimy things that slithered in and out of all the crevices of his body, hissing filthy things and giggling.

Chapter Twelve

The darkness was endless. You could run and run, and you couldn't get away from it because the things went with you, clinging in obscene abandon.

And when a small light appeared now and then, it was worse. Because then he could see the rip in the fabric again and what was peering through. It had mad eyes and slobbering jowls, and while he watched, helpless, two warped and twisted legs came through.

"Stop the house," he cried over and over.

After a time, everything let him be. Then there was a period when he thought he was free. Except that something else bad came, and it had only been a waiting time.

He lay, one of many, at the bottom of a pit in a pile of something soft and yielding. Warm liquid made pools on his body. Something that had been an arm rested on his neck. He could feel the bone and smell the stench of putrid flesh. "Where am I?" he screamed. There was blood in his mouth.

He looked up.

A man with a smile on his face and wearing a black uniform stood on the edge of the pit above him. He was pointing downward. At *him*. He knew what was going to happen, and he stopped screaming. He tried to fix his eyes so that he would look like the others. But the man *knew*. Another appeared, and he lifted a gun and pointed it toward Bobbie's mouth. He cowered there, the scream welling in him.

"Bobbie, Bobbie, Bobbie . . ."

It was the first time a voice had reached into his black depths. The man with the gun suddenly turned it into his own face and blew himself into a million pieces. But Bobbie couldn't hold onto the voice long enough to stop the realization of who was lying in the pit next to him. Someone the voice was too late to save. Craig Jorgenson was down here. Looking at him with glassy, sad eyes.

He began to cry, and he cried on and on and on. Why couldn't he be like Jorgenson? Why had he tried to fool the black-uniformed man? What was the point?

"Bobbie, Bobbie, Bobbie . . ." This was the worst of all. To have only the darkness and his name being called, forever and no hope of anything else because the Judgment Day you learned about long years ago in Sunday School was a joke and never coming. He hated the voice. "Bobbie, Bobbie, Bobbie. . . ."

He didn't know when the darkness first began to clear. He had been wrong about the voice calling his name being bad. It was the voice that was clearing the darkness. Some part of his senses grabbed for it, caught and held. There *was* hope.

Some angel had moved into the darkness. When it left him he was bereft. Alone.

In time there was a hand on his. Another blessing. And something warm and good sliding down his throat. His vision was the last sense to return. And when it did, he saw it was a woman. "I'm here, Bob," she said.

He still moved in and out of darkness. But sometimes through the terror that wracked him and made him tremble like a sick baby, there was a small measure of peace in him. When he slept, it was to gather strength. And there came a time when he could sit at the table in the cheerful little kitchen of Gloriana Reege's home.

"I'm glad to see you back among us," she said, and smiled gently when he held his hot chocolate cup out to her again and again. He still shook a lot, but she seemed not to notice, and she chose that morning to discuss what had happened. "We have to, Bob," she said. "You can't keep it all inside, and there are things I need to know."

Four days, she told him. The eternity had lasted only four days. "We buried your grandfather, Bobbie," she said. "We had to. Nobody knew him well, but a few of us went. Mrs. Letkins stayed with you for me. I'm sorry to mention all this, but there are facts you're going to have to know."

The only vision of his grandfather that came to him was of the old man on Halloween night, knuckling his head. He didn't say it, but he was glad the funeral was over and he hadn't had to go. Grandpop would be out in the cemetery now with Vera, but Bobbie would never go there.

"And Craig," she said. "We buried him, too."

When he started violently and threw a hand up in front of his eyes, she said, softly, "I'm sorry, Bob. But you can't hide from it. Craig Jorgenson was possibly running away from home. Nobody looked for him that day because he'd fought with his stepmother and taken off. His father was sure he'd come back after a night in the cold—" She stopped abruptly, hearing herself. Then went on. "For some reason nobody knows, he climbed a drainpipe at the mystery house. And fell from the iron fence."

"Fell?" The house had only played a waiting game with Craig. And the carrots. That stupid dream about trying to fish a carrot out of a vat: Had it been Craig? A feeble, nothing warning? He couldn't help it. He laughed bitterly.

"You think the house did it, don't you?" Miss Reege said. And shook her head sadly. "I wish it were that simple. The house could be burned down and no more sorrow."

She saw his sudden, hopeful look. "Oh, Bob," she said. "You're giving credence to a concept of evil no sane person can accept. I'm sorry," she said quickly. "I didn't mean that the way it sounded. You're as sane as anyone; you've just had more on you. Lobe told me at your grandfather's funeral the old gentleman was barely coherent on the house tour the day he died. God knows what living with a senile old man would have done to *my* mental equilibrium. It must have been a horror."

He scarcely heard the last part. He only knew that she still didn't believe. And if she, who was more intelligent and kinder to him than anyone in town, didn't believe him, no one ever would. It didn't make any difference. He couldn't fight anymore. The house had gotten Craig, probably would have killed him, too. He was worse than a fool to think he could have moved against it. Whatever else it still had to do in this town, it had lost its only adversary.

Gloriana Reege saw that in his eyes. Her sigh of relief was audible. "The only thing we don't know, Bob," she went on, "is why your house was so torn up. And exactly what happened on the porch. Why was there a good kitchen knife beside that porch?"

There was no need now to tell her or anyone all of it. "Grandpop," he said weakly, "was cutting up something in the kitchen for dinner. When I got home the door was locked, and he came to open it with the knife in his hand. When he fell, it went into the yard. I dragged him into his room because I wanted to put him on his bed."

She seemed to accept that. "And the torn-up house?" she pushed gently.

"I was looking for money Grandpop had hidden," he said truthfully. "I didn't want to go to an orphanage when he died, and I thought I had to run away."

Gloriana Reege went to a cupboard and came back with a faded envelope. "Here it is," she said. "Mrs. Letkins and the women who cleaned up your grandfather's house—your house now that will be sold and put in trust—found it pinned inside a suit jacket in his closet. They were boxing up his clothes until you could tell us if you wanted the church to have them."

Bobbie took the envelope. "Eighty-seven dollars," she said. "That wouldn't have gotten you very far."

He stared at the money. He knew instinctively that that was all there had ever been, that the women would not have stolen any. A bitter smile played on his lips. *This* was the big stash secret Grandpop had never trusted him with?

"Bob?" Miss Reege said quietly. "Your grandfather toured the mystery house that day. And you went out there at night. I won't ask why. I only hope you're not foolish enough to think that had anything to do with your grandfather's dying. He had a brain hemorrhage that had been building a long time. We are going to work very hard, you and I, on overcoming these feelings of yours about the house. We'll teach you to put a very powerful imagination to better use."

Miss Reege said something else. His head had begun to ache, and he was losing his grip on the small strength he had mustered. And the blackness was threatening again so that he had to make a tremendous physical effort to tune her in again.

"When they were trying to figure out what to do with you the other night, Mrs. Letkins, thank God, wouldn't let them call the authorities. Someone remembered I had taken you home from Cindy's funeral and thought I might be your friend. Which I am, Bob. I hope you know that."

She laid a hand on his. "Yesterday, when the authorities finally had to be contacted, they said you could stay with me until your health returns. Foster homes are hard to come by in these trying economical times. I'm going to talk them into letting me keep you."

"For good?" he managed in a small voice.

"For good."

"Thank you." Not enough. But all he could manage for now. She took his hand and led him back to bed. He was as tall as she, but he went with her as a little child would go. He didn't let himself think what staying with her would mean—that it would also mean staying in the town. He only knew he had a place to be.

* * *

Lobe Peters stared with unconcealed hostility at his visitor in *The Daily Way*. He'd smiled pleasantly enough when she came in and asked her how Bobbie was. But what she said then all but slapped the smile off his face.

"Bobbie believes the house is evil," she'd said. "You know and I know that it is not, because we're too realistic to believe in that sort of thing. But what would you say to my bringing a psychic here to go into the house?"

"A *what*?"

"Someone who can fancy he's exorcised it. Maybe that way the boy can get some peace."

Now Lobe let the fire flashing in his heart out into the room. "With whose keys, by God?" he hollered. "I got the only keys to that house, except some can only be gotten by council vote, and if you try to break in there with any goddamn idiot sees and hears things that aren't there, I'll have your asses busted so fast, you and your psychic can investigate evil from the inside of the Gloaming jail."

"Lobe, you don't have to get so upset. I just wanted to put the thought before you. You're in the house a lot, and it seems that if anything were wrong, you might feel it. Assuming such a thing could be at all."

"Goddamn right." She was placating him now, but he was still furious. "I'm in there a *lot*, and this whole town has been in there, and not one of them has ever thought any crap like that kid who's been warped by a bonkers-brained old man. And *you*." He practically spit that on her. "Now if you don't mind, I got work to do. I got a story to break took place over in Slopetown."

Gloriana Reege stood on the walk outside *The Daily Way*, remembering Lobe's fury. He'd reacted about like she'd expected him to, but she'd needed that reassurance. Lobe was about as levelheaded as anybody could get in this town, and he didn't find anything bad about the house. She sighed with relief.

Now she had to go home to a sick boy she'd left sleeping. Someday maybe she could convince him of the thing Lobe was so sure of. Poor little guy. She'd never known anybody so alone. Walking toward her car, her thoughts returned to *The Daily Way* editor. The owner of that mansion out in Pellam Woods had certainly known what she was doing when she appointed Lobe Peters as custodian. Gloriana had no doubt at all he'd be willing to kill for that house.

As it turned out, somebody else was concerned about the house. Gloriana hadn't been gone for more than a half hour when Ed Kroger came in.

"Billy hasn't come in yet, Ed," Lobe said. "School's not out." Lobe had wound up hiring Ed's teenage son to work for him. Bobbie was out of the question now. Boy had a hysterical streak.

"Didn't come to see Billy. Came to discuss something with you. Lobe, it's spooky."

"Spooky?" Lobe narrowed his eyelids behind the Ben Franklin glasses.

"Well, two kids have died out at the mystery house right close together. And Miss Penny, too."

"So?"

"So, it's spooky kind of. You don't think—well, I know this probably sounds stupid. But we never had any violent things happen to speak of in this town till—"

"Till the house came?" Lobe had actually constrained himself with Gloriana Reege; she'd only seen the tip of his rage. Now he let it all fly out at Ed Kroger. "Jesus H. Christ, Ed, you gone off your rocker? That's sick thinking. Violent things happen all the time."

Lobe waved a hand wildly. "Hell, Sheriff Hille found a guy drove into the Slopetown ditch and drowned the morning of the day the kid and the old man died. (Today the sheriff had finally been able to make identification through a college guy who'd sold the car to Gary Purdy, but Lobe wasn't telling Ed that—it was going to be tomorrow's headline.) Sheriff said the guy's fingers were raw from tryin' to claw his way out of the car. *That's* violent. Fire killed four people in a trailer in Gloaming when their heater exploded last week. Man lived on a farm between the two towns hacked his wife to death with an ax last year. Violence is everywhere all the time."

"But these deaths were near the house."

God*damn*, Kroger was stubborn. Got something in his head, it was a bone for a dog to worry.

"Listen," Lobe said, fuming. "A sicko kid killed a little girl. A drunk old lady slipped and fell. And a dumbass kid running away from home because he's got a slut for a stepmother climbed a drainpipe because he was a good athlete and probably saw too much stuntmen stuff on TV and that fence railing dared him. Didn't even have anybody to show off for; he just *did* it. Now this is all sad, and it's too bad, but it isn't *spooky*. You sound as if you think the house had something to do with all that, for christ sakes.

"Lobe—"

But Lobe wasn't to be stopped now. "That house has been the best thing ever happened to this town, and a thing that's just wood and stone which can't harm a flea is suddenly suspect because some coincidences happened, and some fucking asshole gets a bug up his behind that there's some connection between it and unfortunate doings."

It was the most impassioned speech of his life for sure, and he wasn't through. "You're jealous, Ed. I told you that before. You been jealous of me all your life because among other reasons I'm independent and you tied yourself down and never did any of the hotsy-totsy things of the crap you bragged about in high school. You're jealous *now* because I've got the keys to the house, and *you* can't get at 'em except by vote. That's why I hired that slow-witted son of yours, to make up to you because life never turned out how you wanted. Well, I'll tell you one thing. Anybody else comes to me with any of this shit, and I'll close that house up, and you won't open it because *I'll* vote against it. Then where'll the town be? That house is the only exciting thing to come along here."

He didn't know if he could legally shut it up. But by God if he had to, he'd spend every penny of that ten thou he was keeping in the bank for his retirement to find the house's owner and get *her* backing to shut it down. When he told her what was going on, she wouldn't want any suspicious people inside her beautiful gift. Maybe she'd even find a way to take it back legally and then let him keep the keys and live in there.

Ed Kroger had backed off, his big face gone red.

"You got no call to talk to me like this," he said, striving to ignore the uncalled for outburst. "I might not be the only one who feels this way."

"Feels what?" Lobe grated. "That the house is evil?"

Ed's mouth dropped open. "Evil? Say now. I was thinking more a bad-luck house."

"Evil—bad luck. What's the difference? It's all sick thinking. And as for other people thinking the way you do, nobody else has come here (well, only one, but she didn't count—she was an outsider) with this crap. So the only way for it to get around is if you start spreading it. And if you do that, I'll fire Billy. He likes this job. He's no shakes as a student, and I have to explain everything three times. The kid's not ever going to get any other chance to learn a real business. He'll wind up sweeping floors."

He went on glaring at Ed Kroger, who was thinking he didn't want his boy working here for a man just spoke to his father like Lobe had. But Lobe was right. Billy was Ed's slow one, and he *wouldn't* ever get another chance like this. "I won't say anything to anybody," he said, hating himself. But a father had to look out for a slow son, even if it meant taking abuse.

"Damn right. Because it's all stupid anyway, and they'd laugh at you. And if there *was* anybody who felt that way, he can stay away from the house. Twice as many people've been going on tour since I opened back up this week."

After Ed Kroger slunk away, dragging his tail between his legs, Lobe stood there still angry. It was all bullshit. Kroger was all bullshit. But what if a few people did feel the way he did? Lobe Peters was not going to tolerate that kind of crap. An idea took form in his head so fast it nearly blinded him. He had a way to sound out the town without saying anything.

It was a warm, end-of-April evening when the party came off. And what a party it was. Nobody in town had ever seen anything like it, much less attended an affair this big.

Lobe himself spent two days carefully working on a yard that needed mowing now even though spring was dragging its heels coming into town. He lovingly trimmed a bush here and there. Put some potted pansies all over the porches, front and back.

He spent a moment in contemplation in the back yard, about on the spot where they'd found Craig Jorgenson. If he'd only had occasion to look into the back yard that day, he would've spotted the boy himself. But he hadn't. It had been raining hard, and his concern had been to make sure the old people who toured didn't track anything up or touch anything they shouldn't. They had wanted to look out the upstairs windows, but on the front side where the whole town was laid out before them. And he'd only been in the kitchen long enough to boil up his tea and put it and some cookies on a tray.

He thought about that now, though — about how weird it was if you gave it much thought — that a kid had been lying out here dead all that time. Coroner had fixed time of death at approximately eight A.M.

Well, wouldn't have been anything he could've done anyway. Boy broke his neck. Dumbass kid, showing off to himself. Lobe went back to the task at hand, which was proving the town's loyalty to the house.

And how he did prove it.

They came by the hundreds. On a night turned so balmy, looked like the Almighty himself had a hand in the party. They ate and drank up all the eight hundred precious bucks of house money Lobe had spent on the food and wine. In fact, he had to make a hundred dollar loan from Carl Bergins, who was the only person around carried that kind of cash, and send Pender to open up his store and get more stuff.

"Let me just give you the hundred," Bergins said. "This must've set you back a fortune."

"No, I'll pay tomorrow," Lobe said. This was *his* party. Bergins shrugged and went back to his wife, who was working hard at forgiving him since he hadn't pressed any charges against her and Tressa Allen had left town.

There were a few people not here, of course: Bert Jorgenson—he was still understandably grieving. Bessie came though, in a new dress.

Gloriana Reege wasn't there. She could have come. The invitation had been issued in *The Daily Way* to the whole town. But that probably would have upset Bobbie, and Lobe hadn't expected her or wanted her. This was an insiders' party.

Ed Kroger came. He was a little sullen, but he shook Lobe's hand when he came around back to where Lobe was manning the canned music under the Japanese lanterns he'd strung. Ed Kroger looked around at all the hilarity and realized he'd been wrong anyway. It was just a house. But it would be a long time before he forgave Lobe for what he'd said about Billy. If ever.

A few incidents happened. Lobe was keeping the party outside, but he led a few tours for people who'd never toured. One of them managed to sneak a wine glass inside and spilled its contents. He didn't see who, but when he spotted it, he got down on his knees right there to clean it up, holding his temper, telling himself things like this happened at a good party.

Food got spilled everywhere in the back yard. Lobe hadn't hired anyone to clean up. He wanted to do all that personally, make sure everything looked the same after.

There was a lot of backslapping when they all left along about midnight. They left glowing and talking about the wonders of the house. Lobe wasn't able to keep a tally, but he was sure everyone in town had shown up except the obvious ones: Jorgenson and a few who were sick. Even the Newmans had come, still looking pale and not quite with it. But if *they* didn't hold anything stupid against the house, how could anyone else? Lobe was satisfied. The house could stay open.

When Bobbie read Lobe's glowing report of the party, he wept helplessly.

It was the first of May before Bobbie Topin went back to school. He still had shaking spells sometimes, though he managed to get away from Miss Reege so she wouldn't see. Tears often welled unexpectedly, but he never shed them outwardly. There were times, too, when things became unreal, and he would hover in that state until the panic that always followed struck him with clammy sweat and racing heart. Then it all would pass.

His isolation at school was now complete. Oh, they spoke to him. The first day back Bottoms had gasped, "Man you look like a skeleton," and walked away. Bottoms didn't look too good either. He and Joey Hetherington had lost their best friend, and it showed in the way they wrestled too hard in the school yard and talked too loud. Of them all, the redheaded boy had come closest to some small kinship with Bobbie. In another place they could have been best buddies.

But he was gone now.

Among his other griefs, Bobbie felt a small twinge of loss when he realized he had crossed clear over the thin line that had always separated him from the others. He guessed that somewhere deep inside, whatever else had beset him, he'd always harbored a hope that they'd all be friends. But he was as orphaned as you could get now. And more than that, he knew everyone must have heard about his actions the night Grandpop died. And they didn't want to associate with a kid who'd lost control of himself.

Well, there were worse things than loneliness.

The days went by, and May brought no light airiness to Edgar Falls. In other parts of the country flowers unfolded their buds in bursts of excitement to the warm and gentle sun.

In Edgar Falls, a few flowers bloomed and were dead before you got a chance to notice, then hung in drooping brown. The days went abruptly from cool to hot, and the bog spots sent up sultry steam and smelled of decay.

The weather lay heavy upon the mood of the town. People began to speak of the summer they knew was going to be uncommonly hot and humid as an ordeal to get through, the way they'd always regarded winter.

Pulie Gordon was found one day in a hospital in another state. No effort had been made to determine if he were a runaway since his face had gone so old he was listed as being approximately twenty-five years of age, and in these days of drug abusers and common crazies, the hospital admitted several unidentifieds every week. Pulie had been there three weeks when he finally revealed some information about himself to a psychologist. He was Joan of Arc, he said on the day he presented himself at the hospital's receiving desk, and he wanted to be burned at the stake in order to be purified of his sins. He thought perhaps they could arrange that for him. In the course of some sessions with the doctor, he finally said that his greatest sin had been the murder of someone named Augustine Gordon, who had lived in a town named Edgar Falls.

Lobe printed the story, which some people said was cruel to Charlie and his sister, but nobody protested much. At least Pulie was in a safe place where he couldn't harm any more little girls, and the story was the first thing to come along of note in *The Daily Way* since Gary Purdy.

People still toured the house, in bigger batches than before. If anything, the adverse publicity — three deaths out there — drew crowds. Maybe the new ones came out of morbid curiosity. Lobe Peters was prepared to acknowledge that. But they went away enchanted, the bad forgotten. As for the regulars, well, what else was there to do for real entertainment when the house only cost a dollar? These regulars talked fondly of what had come to be known as *the party* and hoped Lobe would have another.

Bobbie thought a lot about the house—not from choice. It would present itself to him at unlikely moments. Maybe while he sat in the tiny garden out back of Miss Reege's house. These were the only moments he really had alone. Miss Reege expected him to come straight to her realty office after school, where he did his homework in the back. The authorities had agreed to let him stay on with her; single foster parents were more and more being permitted these days, kids his age being hard to place.

The moments he thought about the house often came to him just before the unreal feeling and the panic.

He knew now what a fool he had been. He hadn't really understood, or no form of madness would have made him go for it that night to burn it down. Those days he spent in the dark pit had taught him all he needed to know. Something ghastly and unbelieveable had stalked the world since its beginning. Something as old as God Himself. And maybe as powerful.

Whatever it was wrapped itself in innocence—in such things as the white beauty of a house—and it did not have to come to people; people were all too willing to come to it. He understood now what Soul-Eater meant. It dined well, and when it spit out the bones, there was nothing left but an old man rotting in a grave or a young one cringing against hospital walls praying that the trial for heresy would be over soon and the blessed fire of deliverance set.

Bobbie did not look at the house again. And he never mentioned it to Miss Reege, nor she to him. She seemed to have given up on her promise to help him "get over his feelings." But sometimes she would come onto the back porch and stare at him sadly where he brooded among the decaying flowers.

Bobbie kept a light burning in his room at night. Miss Reege never questioned him about it or complained about the waste of electricity. She seemed to know a lot about him without asking, and he felt the bond growing between them and was grateful.

Sometimes he remembered the day he had seen the skulls behind her eyes, and then panic would hit too. But one day she mentioned she was growing tired of Edgar Falls, and he allowed a small hope to take hold of him. Maybe they would go away.

He would feel guilty about that. After all, he knew what the house was. But he couldn't do anything about it. The one chance he might have destroyed it had been lost when he stumbled over Craig Jorgenson's body that night. He needed the courage of craziness to do what should be done to save nice people like Mrs. Letkins, who had led the cleaning contingent on the cottage and helped arrange Grandpop's funeral. But Bobbie was no longer crazy. He hoped they moved before the house decided to go after someone else; he didn't trust how he would handle that. Maybe go into that black pit and never come out again.

Then one evening in June, when there were only a couple of days of school left to go, Miss Reege was waiting in her Pinto outside the gates. "I shut the office up early, Bob," she said. "Let's go to dinner in Gloaming." This was a rare treat. Miss Reege worked hard at her business and didn't have much time.

He felt his spirits lift. He still didn't have a whole lot of appetite. But just the idea of getting out of Edgar Falls a while made him happy.

Miss Reege ignored the shortcut past the house in Pellam Woods. She took the highway instead, driving out east of town to make the long circle around. She was being thoughtful, and he felt a huge and overwhelming gratitude.

Isn't this fun?" she asked.

They had done some canned goods shopping first. Then she had chosen a little Italian restaurant for dinner. Green-checked cloths lay upon the tables; candles flickered in glass bowls. Miss Reege had ordered wine and insisted he have a small glass. It made him feel lightheaded, but it was kind of a good feeling.

"Yes," he said eagerly, and ate a lot more of his lasagna than he thought he'd be able to.

Then, when they had finished the leisurely meal, she suddenly pulled the wine bottle from its straw basket and poured herself a full glass, him a half. The blue eyes sparkled behind her dark-rimmed glasses. "Bob, my boy," she said. "We're celebrating tonight. Your grandfather's house sold today. I let it go cheap so it wouldn't hang over your head. But you still have a tidy sum which will be put in trust for you till you're eighteen. Then you can have a high old time."

He smiled at her, relieved. He had never been back to the cottage.

"Wait a minute," she cried, giggling. "I'm not through. I've put my own business on the market. Advertised it in all the papers, far and wide. You and I, my boy, are getting out of Edgar Falls. Maybe we'll go all the way to the Big Apple."

He stared at her. "Do you mean it?" he gasped. "But what's the Big Apple?"

"New York, silly."

New York. Oh, jeez, that would be about as far away from the house as you could get. "Would you like that?" she exclaimed. "Oh, of course, I'd have to get permission from the authorities, but I don't think they'll balk."

"Would I *like* it?" he practically shouted. "Is this wine *red*?"

She threw back her head and laughed. "Not anymore," she cried. "You've drunk it."

She was like a little kid as they went weaving arm in arm and giggling back to the car. Some people coming into the parking lot stared at them in disgust. "Don't mind us,". Miss Reege said. "We got married tonight." Bobbie fell into peals of laughter. It was the first time in weeks there was no sign of blackness inside him. Getting out of Edgar Falls. New York. Oh, man!

"You sure you're okay to drive?" he asked.

"Oh, hey." She ruffled his hair. "I'm fine. I only had two glasses of wine. I'm just feeling good. I've never really liked Edgar Falls, and it's never liked me."

Bobbie got into the car, and they had to stop for gas. he was starting to feel a little drowsy from the wine, and he laid his head against the seat and shut his eyes.

"Too much excitement?" she said, poking him in the ribs.

He opened one eye and grinned at her. "I guess so." Too much relief more than anything; it was spinning around inside him. In a moment they were driving through the streets of Gloaming again, and he kept his eyes shut, liking the way he felt. But he opened them after a time when they hit a bump.

And sat suddenly upright. Stiff. Frightened. They weren't on the highway. This was a shortcut that would take them past the house. Oh, Christ, it had been such a good night. Now he felt the panic beginning to rise.

He forced his eyes to close again, forced his head back against the seat, not wanting her to worry about how much the house could still affect him.

The road seemed to go on forever. But the trip had to end sometime, and the house wasn't going to reach out and grab him was it?

When the car braked, it seemed a thousand years later. He opened his eyes with a relief that made them swim. And let out a cry. They weren't at home! Across a moonlit field, the house stood gleaming white.

"There's something you have to do before we leave Edgar Falls, Bobbie," Miss Reege said. "You've got to face your fear of that place head on."

"I'm not going in there." He said it bitterly, nauseated by her betrayal.

"You've got to," she cried. She grabbed for both his trembling hands. "You've got to go in there and see that it's just a house. I know you think it did something to your grandfather. You babbled a lot in your deliruum, and I don't think that's changed."

Bobbie turned fiercely on her. "He went crazy," he yelled. "He tried to kill me with that knife."

"Oh, Bob," she moaned. "I didn't understand that part of your rambling. But that was the stroke coming on, honey. He had a fire raging in his brain that was on the verge of killing him."

Bobbie stopped shaking and went very cold inside. His voice turned cold. "I thought you were my friend."

"It's because I am," she said pleadingly, "that I'm doing this. Bob, I don't think you realize what it's like when a gloom comes down over you. Those times the house is on your mind, the atmosphere around you goes black. And you're never entirely free of it, are you?" She squeezed his hands hard, but he didn't respond. "You have to understand; I can't handle it when you're that way."

"In New York—"

"It will always be with you," she insisted. "Even there. You can't escape until you've faced it. You've got to walk in there and show yourself that nothing happens."

Only Bobbie's eyes felt alive. He could feel them burning. "You've been in the house, haven't you?" he said in that same cold voice.

"Not recently."

"But you *have* been in it."

"Of course I have—long ago. I had to check on the workmen's progress for Ms. Benedictine. I always came out at dusk so the watchers would be gone. For a time I had the keys before they were turned over to Lobe Peters."

The fire burned suddenly into Bobbie's voice. "It wants me," he said. "It knows I know about it, and it's using you to get me here."

"Oh, my God," she groaned. "I only want to help you get rid of this obsession because I see what it's doing to you." She began to cry.

Bobbie watched her warily. But in a moment, he softened. Maybe the house couldn't get her. A lot of people had been in it several times, some even a lot—Lobe for instance—and nothing had happened to them. "Please don't cry," he said. "I'd go in if I could."

After a long moment, she raised her eyes and looked at him. The moonlight made glistening jewels of the tears on her cheeks. She sighed deeply. "Either you go in," she said, "and get this monkey off your back, or everything I said about keeping you with me is null and void. I can't handle a boy who keeps part of himself in shadows."

That got to him, drove his voice to a desperate pitch. "I've been in the house before. It does ugly things."

But she didn't seem to hear him. She had suddenly opened the car door and was getting out. "Where are you going?" he cried.

"Into the house. To prove to you nothing at all will happen. I want you to see it's all been your imagination."

"Don't do that," he cried. "The house can see you're with me, and it must hate me."

She had reached his side of the car and started up the walk. Now she whirled on him in savage fury. "Stop it," she snapped. "This is sick!"

She was in motion so fast, he didn't realize what was happening for a moment. Before he could react, she had flung herself back at the car, had his door open, and was yanking him out. Surprise gave her success, and he found himself standing outside the car. "You're coming with me," she grated. "We're going in there, and we're going to put an end to this sickness. Right now!"

He fought her, pulling back with all his might. But he had become frail these past weeks, and she was a sturdy woman, and her intensity lent her a strength he would never in a normal moment imagine possible of her.

She had both his wrists, and she yanked and tugged, so that nothing he could do could resist her.

He tried to sit down on the ground, and she kept on yanking so that it was impossible.

"You," she said, her voice coming in panting gasps, "are going inside that house."

The moon shone blandly down on a strange struggle that involved two people moving in erratic spurts across an open field. They reached a road. Bobbie had turned to animal, his breath pushing in terrified grunts. "If you go in there, you'll die," he shrieked out at her. "I saw it in your eyes once."

But she was beyond any attempt to talk. She was using all her strength to accomplish her goal. And she was succeeding. He fought, trying to kick her, but she seemed to anticipate his every effort. He threw his weight backward and saw stars when her ferocious yank made his head snap forward.

The steps. The steps would stop her. But when they reached them she gathered all her forces together and plunged upward, her momentum carrying him along.

The door. He would be able to get away at the door. She would have to find something to jimmy it with.

But when they reached the door, it seemed already to be unlocked. It swung open swiftly, and she pushed him hard.

"Why do you *care*? Let me go. I don't have to live with you."

But he was in the house. In blackness. He heard the door slam, so loudly it nearly burst his head. "There!" she cried. "You're in. Now where are the goblins you fear so much?"

The whole world had stopped movement. There was only darkness. And the listening.

His or the house's?

Bobbie stood like a cornered animal, all his senses alert. Something sighed through the house, like a soft, purring breath of pleasure.

It had him now. It had wanted him for a long time, was sorry it hadn't gotten him on Halloween. But it had him now. And it crooned, and sighed, and purred, and blew him kisses through the deep halls.

An it's-all-over-now feeling, if you could call it a feeling, came down over Bobbie. It had been inevitable all along. The house was too powerful for him; he should have known that. He should have offered himself up to it long ago instead of fighting and trying to fool himself it couldn't get him.

He knew when something slammed against his head, knew for one brief instant before the crashing pain and blackness claimed him, that this was the last of it—and was nearly glad. But he sobbed one wrenched sob of grief for Robert Louis Topin, who had been doomed from the beginning.

Chapter Thirteen

He knew what had him. All the time it pulled him in fitful starts and jerks along the floor through the black house, he knew. There was pain in his head. It tried to smash an escape route through his skull. But it was nothing against the knowing.

He'd been crazy to think it could have been any other way. Poor stupid little kid to take on something eating a whole town.

Despair sickened through him. Underneath it, he wished that the blow to his head had killed him. Because a time worse than death was coming. Things wild with ecstasy crooned around him in the dark and patted him with soft, eager pats.

"I love you," the house whispered. "I have loved you through eternity."

Vomit rolled from his lips; its acrid odor smelled of his death. He was lost. But before he died, he was going to learn what the house was all about. Something laughed bitterly inside him. After all, hadn't he *wanted* that knowledge?

But he already knew enough, had learned it in the brief moments—or whole eternity—right after she struck him.

It was Gloriana Reege who had tied his hands, mumbling excitedly all the while to the house, "I've got him. I brought him as I promised." There had been one brief moment of shocked denial. And then he had realized with her, too—of course. The house *had* gotten her. The skulls had come home.

He would have cried—for all the lost everything. But except for the pain, he was void of all feeling. Empty. Finished.

Suddenly the journey stopped. She released his ankles, and he lay with the house's love song in his ears. Waiting.

Light spired up, its tiny flicker hurting his eyelids. But he couldn't open them. He couldn't see her as Grandpop had been: a crazed thing. That memory jarred something not quite dead inside him. Somewhere a small tear did form, reaching his eye, his cheek.

"Oh, Bobbie," she said softly. "Don't cry. It had to be, don't you see?"

His eyes opened then. Through their own will, not his. He had no will. A candle flickered in the room—the kitchen.

She smiled at him in candle shadows, a gentle smile. She wasn't wearing her glasses now, and he stared at the same warm look she had worn that first time he emerged from another darkness and knew he had a friend. Only this time, the skulls grinned behind it.

"I wish it could have been some other way, darling," she said ruefully. "I like you. I tried to argue with the house, I really did. I said let me keep the bright young psychic as the son I never had. But it says we can't trust you. You tried to move against it once—you babbled that in your delirium. And it says you would again, when you're older, stronger."

He watched her as she cocked her head and said, "I know. You want him in the cellar. But let me tell him first."

He turned his head so that he stared into a black cavern and wondered idly what it was going to feel like to have his soul eaten. Something came eagerly to the foot of the stairs.

She bent and turned his head again, so that he looked up at her. "Why don't you kill me now?" he said. He wanted that.

And she threw back her head and laughed—in the same sweet laugh that had meant so much to him. "But that isn't *my* job, darling," she cried. "Would I deprive the house?"

For a moment her voice reeled off in the merriment. And then her face returned to the smile, and she sat down on the floor beside him and drew her knees up to her chest.

She looked as bright and innocent as a child of the sun.

"Someone has to know the story, Bobbie," she said conspiratorially. "Someone who has a right to it, even though in a little while that won't mean anything anymore."

At the foot of the stairs, it stirred. Impatient.

"My real name is Reba Munck, Bobbie," she went on. And then snapped suddenly. "Pay attention, Bob. This is Reba Munck's story, and you have to hear it." His mind had gone off into that cavern, only wanting it over. But she had jabbed him with her foot, jarring him back.

"Reba Munck spend her childhood in Edgar Falls. Oh, her family got out eventually, but not before she learned what it meant to be poor white trash in an upstanding American town. They tried to destroy that little girl, Bob my boy. Called her Munckey and made fun of her because her clothes had patches and her shoes had holes. All of them looked down on her—Miss Penny, the Amways, Lobe Peters. . . ."

Oh, Jesus, no. That wasn't a hope, was it? It had come out of nowhere—unbidden, unwanted, born of Lobe Peters's name. He couldn't stand that. The giving up was better.

But it was there. Wheeling suddenly and wildly through a brain he had thought already dead. Lobe Peters often came out here. Everyone knew he slept in the house. Maybe he would come tonight. "What's Gloriana's car doing out here?" he'd say. "And why is there a light glowing off in the kitchen?"

Bobbie fought the hope. But he had no control over it. His mind swirled with it. Keep her talking. Say something, the hope begged. Anything. Try to reach Lobe mentally while she talks, part of him babbled. He was supposed to be the great psychic, wasn't he? Maybe he had telepathy, too. "The house does things to people, doesn't it? It works on something inside them." Had that been his own voice? He went on fighting the hope, but it *would* speak.

She clapped her hands delightedly. "Blessed saints," she cried. "Facing the cellar and you can still ask questions? No wonder the house wants you so badly. No wonder it says you're the most worthy adversary it's ever had. Yes, the house works on people. But there has to be something in the person first, Bobbie. It's like the tree that falls in the forest, but there is no sound unless there are ears to receive it."

"Like with you?" He heard those unexpected words and knew that he had set off what he could see in her eyes. A moment ago he wouldn't have cared. But now the *hope* cared.

But she only grinned at him. "You think the house *got* me? Because I tricked you here tonight when it grew impatient waiting for you to come alone?" She shook her head. "I understand the house, Bob. It's my friend, my instrument. All Reba Munck's life, I prayed for revenge against this town, and I lived in this house a long time before I saw what that revenge should be: Bring it to Edgar Falls; let it play with the town."

The thing at the base of the stairs stirred again. Filled Bobbie with the horror he had not felt before. *Please hurry, Lobe. I'm here. In the kitchen.*

Sad her voice suddenly. "I came back to give the town a chance, you know, Bob. But it hadn't changed. They still treated Bitsy like dirt. I was sorry the house got her, but she was stupid, and stupidity is fair game for the house. I suspect it somehow got Gary Purdy, too."

Her smile returned. "You want to hear something funny, Bob? I went to Lobe Peters and told him I wanted to bring a psychic here. I went to sound him out on the town feeling. He almost threw me out. It's a good joke, don't you think? And now I have brought a psychic after all."

The pain still throbbed in his head, and his tongue felt engorged with blood. But the hope scrabbled frantically in the garbage of his mind fragments and spewed out another thick question. "Who is Ms. Benedictine?"

"Your curiosity is wonderful," she cried. "Ms. Benedictine was just a frustrated actress who knew only that she worked for an eccentric rich widow making a rich gift to a town she owed a debt to." Gloriana Reege chuckled softly. "She loved flashing through the town. And she loved the money I paid her to be a go-between and let me sign the house into her name. I found her though a theatrical agency, and I chose her because of her name. Clever, don't you think? Benedictine and Munck? When I came back to town, I took the name of Gloriana for glory. Reege was my very rich husband's middle name. Incidentally, the house took him eventually, but I'm too strong for it. I knew what it was from the moment I saw it and had to have it, and we understand each other."

She stopped and looked at him expectantly, as if she deserved applause. But Bobbie saw only the skulls.

"Let me go, Miss Reege. I can see what the town did to you. I won't tell anybody." *He* was talking now, not just the hope. "I'll go away."

"Munck, darling," she said gently. "Not Reege. But, Bob, it would stay with you, don't you see? Someday you would come back, and the house is impatient with interference. And you must understand that it is a natural thing. To go against it is an act against nature."

But he wasn't listening suddenly. A picture of Grandpop knuckling his head had moved behind his eyes.

She had brought the house here? *She* was the one who had turned Grandpop into a slobbering thing? Tiny beginning of reality. Tiny wisp of true recognition. He was starting to think clearly. The hope had done that.

"My grandfather was just an old man," he heard himself saying. It was crazy. He couldn't afford this sudden surge of rage now that he had chosen to go with the hope. But he had no control over the way the rage came screaming back with the same intensity as the night Grandpop had died. As if the time between then and now had only been a breath.

She understood his meaning and stood abruptly, eyelids filming the skulls. "All glory to the deserving, Bob," she said. "I'm tired of toying with you. I only wish I could be here when the tour finds you. Perhaps the great and eternal mystery of the house will be in your eyes when they find poor little Bobbie Topin. 'Whatever could he have been doing in the house?' they'll say. 'Oh, surely not stealing?' But a silver candlestick thrown into the cellar after you will give them all the answer they need. 'Not another child!' they'll say. But it won't keep them from the house. It holds them all, you see."

It was coming. He could feel the gathering of forces deep in the recesses of the house, not just in the cellar. Whatever they were—and there was more than one—they were banding to greet him.

And his rage swelled violently. Maybe the house *was* going to get him. But he was going to try and take her with him. It came rolling through him like a tidal wave. Hold it. Hold it back a minute. She had to make contact with him—with her hand or foot—to push him into the cellar. Hold it, Bob. Don't start screaming. Don't blow it now.

The rage roared and plunged. There. Now! Her foot was coming out to kick him down those cellar steps. A picture of a girl holding his hand at a picnic was all he saw as the rage spewed out of him.

He shrieked with the fury and doubled up and kicked out to hook her leg with his own unhampered legs.

She pitched forward into the cavern. The sudden movement had sent physical pain crashing back through him, and he lay there in agony while her scream tore up through the blackness. But even in the throes of the pain, he heard every thud of her body against the steps, heard the last terrible thud and reveled in the sound that was the most beautiful he had ever heard. It was the sound of a head smashing.

The pain fled almost as soon as it hit, routed by the magnitude of what he'd done. Bobbie Topin lay stunned in the kitchen of the house and knew that the sobs he heard were not his own and were slowly turning to rage. Its forces were gathering swiftly now. The game had taken an unexpected turn. And the shadows were coming to finish it.

Bobbie lay there cringing. He knew what lay in him that the house could use to get at him: the despair that had willed death.

But it had returned only a moment, then his own rage came tearing back. His eyes fell on the flickering candle. And the rage arrived in his brain again like a locomotive filling him with a strength that culminated in the same roar he had issued one night on a dark road of Edgar Falls.

The house had taken everything from him, even Miss Reege. Maybe all that with her had been a lie, but he had believed in it. Had she been crazy before the house? It didn't make any difference. All that mattered was that he survive long enough to bring it down.

Even as the thoughts slammed through him, he was in motion, forcing himself to his feet. He didn't need matches this time. He had Miss Reege's candle, and that seemed so fitting, he laughed out loud with the justice of it.

A cord bound his wrists. From one of the *house* drapes? That caused him to shudder with revulsion.

But he didn't pause to give it any real thought. Hurry, hurry. He ran for the candle, propelled by the rage and wild, maniacal glee that had begun to fill him.

It took a few precious seconds to singe the cord. He could feel the shadows swelling. In the attic recesses. In the halls. In the cellar. But the house had lost time while it rallied from shock.

The last sputtering threads of the cord snapped loose. The fire seared his wrists, but he didn't notice. He laughed again and seized the candle in both hands.

There were curtains at the two high kitchen windows. Shouting with glee, he tore for them. The first set went up with a great moaning sound that sent a thrill racing up his spine. He fired the second.

Now. He should try for the door in here. But he knew that he had to be sure. Maybe these curtains weren't enough.

The rage gave him strength to surge on into the rest of the house. Why hadn't it gotten him yet?

Then he heard it. A new sound. A blessed, beautiful sound. Was it screaming in fresh shock and confusion? He thought it was screaming, and he had to pause a moment to let a wave of nausea brought on by his triumph pass. Then he hit the curtains in this room. The flames grabbed the material eagerly and ran joyously upward. This time he waited until the fire thrust hungry fingers into the wooden frames of the windows.

On into the room with the fireplace. The drapes accepted their flames like martyrs eager to fulfill destiny. Surging with power, screaming invectives at the house, Bobbie blazed a fiery path through that room. There was no longer weariness in him, no frailty.

He had to try to get out now.

He raced for the foyer, flame shadows lighting his way.

It will never let you go.

It couldn't stop me from firing it.

But it hasn't played all its cards yet. It stopped Miss Penny from getting in; it can keep you from getting out. You'll burn with it.

He had to try.

Only something got him suddenly, wrapped him in a vise. The candle flew out of his hand. The house was dying. But it *was* going to take him with it.

"What's the matter with you? Have you gone crazy? What have you done to my house? Oh, Jesus. Oh Mother of God, I've got to save it."

As suddenly as he had been grabbed, Bobbie was released. Someone went racing away from him into the big room. Bobbie turned back, stunned. Lobe? Was that Lobe Peters tearing madly at the burning curtains—Lobe sobbing and leaping up to smack at the higher flames and crooning words like, "I'll save you?"

"Lobe, get out of here," Bobbie cried. "You don't understand. I tried to tell you before. The house is evil. It's got to die!"

He ran for the man who was doing a strange dance on the parquet floor, leaping upon burning bits of curtain, trying to stamp them out. Bobbie grabbed for his shirt. But Lobe flung his arms out and sent him spinning backward. It was an instinctive reaction; he no longer seemed aware of Bobbie.

He ran past the boy, heading for the stairway.

Bobbie ran after him. The flames were filling the stairs now, and Lobe plunged up them yelling, "Oh God, oh God, oh God." He slapped at the flames with his hands. "My poem!" he screamed.

"Lobe, please." Bobbie was crying now. "Please come back." Of all the people left in this town, he didn't want the house to get Lobe Peters. Lobe had been kind to him, and given him his only joy in long months of darkness.

But the flames took hold of Lobe's pants' legs. On up the stairs the figure plunged, a human torch, still screaming, "Oh God, oh God," until a great wall of fire went up and there was no more sight of him, no more sound except for the crackling and whooshing like a cyclone as the flames broke through the ceiling above.

Bobbie stood a moment longer. But there was nothing he could do. Lobe was only one more horror now.

He spun and ran for the door. It stood open where Lobe had come in. A few feet before he reached it, Bobbie's feet suddenly connected with something, and he tripped and went sprawling. He thought the house had done it, but he saw it was something rolled up: a sleeping bag? He threw himself to his feet. But even gibbering in pain and confusion, the house had rallied one last trick for him. The door began to swing shut.

With superhuman effort, Bobbie plunged. Made it through just as the thing crashed to. He stumbled onto the front porch. Behind him the flames roared.

His knees went weak suddenly, and he almost fell again. But he made it off the steps. And ran. Past Miss Reege's car. Past Lobe Peters's pickup. To the meadow where he had sat so many times watching

317

the house being built.

In the meadow he sank to his knees, feeling the damp earth beneath his fingers. Free. He was *free*. He knelt that way a long moment.

Then he stood slowly. Turned. There was no sound now but the flames. The house was old, the wood dry. While he watched, the fire broke through the outside walls and went screaming and whooshing up the facade. Something exploded inside there.

In the flames he saw all their faces, but mostly one old. The tears went on rolling down his cheeks.

Above the house in Pellam Woods, the night sky began to glow.

MORE EXCITING READING
IN THE ZEBRA/OMNI SERIES

THE BOOK OF COMPUTERS & ROBOTS (1276, $3.95)
Arthur C. Clarke, G. Harry Stine, Spider Robinson, and others explain one of the most exciting and misunderstood advances of our time—the computer revolution.

THE BOOK OF SPACE (1275, $3.95)
This "map of tomorrow," including contributions by James Michener and Ray Bradbury, is a guide to the research and development that will transform our lives.

THE FIRST BOOK OF SCIENCE FICTION (1319, $3.95)
Fourteen original works from some of the most acclaimed science fiction writers of our time, including: Isaac Asimov, Greg Bear, Dean Ing, and Robert Silverberg.

THE SECOND BOOK OF SCIENCE FICTION (1320, $3.95)
Glimpse the future in sixteen original works by such well-known science fiction writers as Harlan Ellison, Spider Robinson, Ray Bradbury, and Orson Scott Card.

THE BOOK OF THE PARANORMAL & (1365, $3.95)
THE MIND
Sample the mysteries of altered states, psychic phenomena and subliminal persuasion in thirty-five articles on man's most complex puzzle: his own mind.

THE BOOK OF MEDICINE (1364, $3.95)
Will you live to be 200 years old? Is pain on the verge of elimination? In twenty-four illuminating articles discover what is fast becoming reality in the world of medicine.

Available wherever paperbacks are sold, or order direct from the Publisher. Send cover price plus 50¢ per copy for mailing and handling to Zebra Books, Dept. 1656, 475 Park Avenue South, New York, N.Y. 10016. DO NOT SEND CASH.

A TERRIFYING OCCULT TRILOGY
by William W. Johnstone

THE DEVIL'S KISS (1498, $3.50)
As night falls on the small prairie town of Whitfield, red-rimmed eyes look out from tightly shut windows. An occasional snarl rips from once-human throats. Shadows play on dimly lit streets, bringing with the darkness an almost tangible aura of fear. For the time is now right in Whitfield. The beasts are hungry, and the Undead are awake . . .

THE DEVIL'S HEART (1526, $3.50)
It was the summer of 1958 that the horror surfaced in the town of Whitfield. Those who survived the terror remember it as the summer of The Digging—the time when Satan's creatures rose from the bowels of the earth and the hot wind began to blow. The town is peaceful, and the few who had fought against the Prince of Darkness before believed it could never happen again.

THE DEVIL'S TOUCH (1491, $3.50)
The evil that triumphed during the long-ago summer in Whitfield still festers in the unsuspecting town of Logandale. Only Sam and Nydia Balon, lone survivors of the ancient horror, know the signs—the putrid stench rising from the bowels of the earth, the unspeakable atrocities that mark the foul presence of the Prince of Darkness. Hollow-eyed, hungry corpses will rise from unearthly tombs to engorge themselves on living flesh and spawn a new generation of restless Undead . . . and only Sam and Nydia know what must be done.

Available wherever paperbacks are sold, or order direct from the Publisher. Send cover price plus 50¢ per copy for mailing and handling to Zebra Books, Dept. 1656, 475 Park Avenue South, New York, N.Y. 10016. DO NOT SEND CASH.